PB0r0 8|12
20-11-2012
25.01.2013
19.6 2015
27. 8. 16

PETERBOROUGH LIBRARIES

24 Hour renewal line 08458 505606

This book is to be returned on or before the latest date shown
above, but may be renewed up to three times if the book is not
in demand. Ask at your local library for details.

Please note that charges are made on overdue books

D1425441

00000 0000 72467

CROSSED WIRES

'Thornton . . . is skilled at drawing out the poignancy of ordinary life.'

The Guardian

'A super-sweet tale.'

OK!

'Heartwarming.'

Kate Long

'Crossed Wires by Rosy Thornton is a delight . . . both highly satisfying and also very engagingly written.'

Adèle Geras

'Heartwarming modern rom-com with a nice edge to it.'

Scott Pack

'Crossed Wires is about as far removed from bog-standard romantic fiction as Edith Wharton is from Barbara Cartland. It is, simply, a beautifully told love story – a modern fairy tale even – but one with a heart, a brain and both feet planted very firmly on the ground.'

Vulpes Libris

'As always with Rosy Thornton you get characters you're really going to get to know. They come off the page fully formed and it's difficult to think that they're not people you've met. Even relatively minor characters stay in your mind long after you've finished the book.'

The Bookbag

HEARTS AND MINDS

'A satisfying, plot-driven story that bubbles along entertainingly, but the power of this novel lies in the portrait of Dr Martha Pearce, the college's senior tutor. Her sense of self, her career aspirations and her role as wife and mother are all vibrantly painted and it is the passages that describe her anguish about her home life – her daughter's depression in particular and the heartbreaking efforts she makes to keep their fragile relationship intact, that really make this novel breathe.'

The Daily Telegraph

'Rosy Thornton, . . . a lecturer at Cambridge, draws on her experience . . . to fashion her second novel. Thornton's detailed descriptions of the myriad boards and committees lend a real sense of authenticity to the novel. It is the conscientious Martha who forms the real heart of the book . . . Thornton's description of her failing marriage is subtle and poignant. Martha's teenage daughter, Lucia, . . . is deeply depressed and Thornton handles this with sensitivity, movingly portraying Lucia's distress and Martha's inability to reach her. . . . it is a gentle tale of good people trying to do their best which raises many a wry smile and, in the case of Lucia, possibly a few tears.'

The Glasgow Herald

'A cleverly written and intricate novel that explores the complex relationships in the world of academia . . . a great novel.'

Peterborough Evening Telegraph

MORE THAN LOVE LETTERS

'. . . a highly original mix . . . a host of believable supporting characters . . .'

The Daily Telegraph

'Thornton's debut is charming and funny.'

Glasgow Evening Times

'Rosy Thornton has produced a real dazzler in her debut
novel 'More Than Love Letters' . . . Thornton's first offering makes for a refreshingly original and highly entertaining
read . . . A unique book that effortlessly conveys genuine
comedy, romance and tragedy, mixed with an apt social and
political commentary, 'More Than Love Letters' is a real
triumph and one you won't want to put down.'

Style magazine

'This is a refreshing twist on the romantic novel. The use of
letters, e-mails and newspaper clippings really bounces the
tangled storyline along . . . Light, frothy and delicious.'

SHE magazine

'A love story with a difference.'

Woman's Weekly

'A charming well-written book, full of sweet anecdotes and
humorous stories.'

Belfast Sunday Life

Rosy Thornton is the author of four previous novels: *More Than Love Letters* (2007), *Hearts and Minds* (2008), *Crossed Wires* (2009) and *The Tapestry of Love* (2010). In addition to writing fiction, she lectures in law at the University of Cambridge, where she is a Fellow of Emmanuel College. Married with two daughters, she lives in a village in the Cambridgeshire fens.

NINEPINS

Rosy Thornton

SANDSTONEPRESS
HIGHLAND | SCOTLAND

First published in Great Britain 2012
Sandstone Press Ltd
PO Box 5725
One High Street
Dingwall
Ross-shire
IV15 9WJ

www.sandstonepress.com

Editor: Moira Forsyth

ISBN: 978-1-905207-85-5
ISBN (e): 978-1-905207-86-2

The publisher acknowledges support from
Creative Scotland towards publication of this volume.

Cover image: David Savory www.fenland-photography.co.uk
Cover by River Design, Edinburgh
Typeset by Iolaire Typesetting, Newtonmore.
Printed and bound by TOTEM, Poland

For Mike

Chapter 1

Half past two: she was certain she'd said half past two. Oh, dear – why was there already a car in front of the house when it was only 2:17?

It was visible even as Laura slowed to turn off the main road and into Ninepins Drove: some kind of long red saloon, a smear of colour against the grubby green and grey. The driver had run it up the track on to the top of the dyke, where Ninepins stood bold and square above the risk of flooding, instead of parking down below, as English reserve led most strangers to do, in the small cindered turning space where the lane ended at her garden gate. She'd have to leave her own car there.

As she drew nearer she could see that the car was no longer new, its pillar box paintwork stained to brown round all the seams; nearer still, and it disappeared from view behind the house. She bumped off the end of the metalled road and into the soft, rutted cinders. It had rained today and she was in her office boots; she'd have to clean them in the morning.

The way up to the front door was by the track the car had taken, slanting up the grassy flank of the dyke. Shouldering her bag, she set off. As she reached the top, the water appeared: the broad, slow drag of Elswell Lode. It was then, too, that her doorstep was visible for the first time and she saw the occupants of the car. Occupants, plural, which was not what she had been expecting: a tall, blondish man of about her own age and a girl, wearing only a vest top in spite of the season, who looked hardly older than Beth.

'Hello. I'm so sorry I'm late.' She wasn't, strictly speaking, but she hated to keep people waiting. 'Have you been here long?'

Instead of answering the question, the man stepped forward and held out his hand. 'Vince. We spoke on the phone.'

'Ah, yes. Hello.' The man from the council. But why was he here? 'I'm Laura Blackwood.'

'And this is Willow, who's come to see the room.'

The girl turned curious eyes on Laura but did not speak or smile. She was no taller than Beth and slightly built: older than she looked from a distance, but surely no more than sixteen?

'Right. Good. Hello, Willow.' She was about to offer her hand, but the girl had looked away. 'Actually, it's not a room, exactly.'

The man, Vince, nodded. 'Self-contained accommodation, it said in the advert. Is that right?'

'In a manner of speaking.'

Instead of opening the front door and showing them into the house, she led the way past the end of the kitchen to the steep concrete steps which took them down the dyke on the landward side and into the garden. The Housing Aid Centre in Cambridge was one of the places she'd lodged the details; that, and the local paper on Thursday, when all the property ads went in. So she hadn't been surprised when it was someone from the council who rang to make the appointment to view. She even remembered his voice now, and the way he introduced himself – just Vince and no surname. But it didn't explain why he had come along with the girl. It seemed beyond the call of duty for a housing adviser.

'This is it. We call it the pumphouse.'

They had stopped on the path in front of it: a low, brick building, crouched close against the base of the dyke and topped at one end by a single tall chimney.

'It used to house a pumping engine, for fen drainage. Before our time, though.'

Pump and engine had been stripped away long before she

2

and Simon bought the house in 1991, sold for scrap no doubt, or broken up and turned to farm purposes. It was in use as a shed then, before Simon left and she cleared, decorated and furnished it as a bed-sit to bring in some extra income for herself and Beth. She'd had the shower and loo put in, as well as powerful electric heating to keep at bay the constantly encroaching damp.

'I'm afraid it can get a little musty in the winter,' she said, as she opened the door and sniffed the air, 'or when it's been closed up for a while.' The place was single-brick construction and low-lying. She'd had it dry-lined and damp proofed, but it hadn't seemed to work; the wet came creeping back. 'There's a dehumidifier you can keep on, and the heating's pretty effective. Electricity's included in the rent, so there's no need to stint.' Her bills were astronomical, but it seemed only fair.

Vince and the girl followed her inside.

'I put "self-contained" in the description because of it having its own entrance, though I'm never quite sure about the terminology. You can't really cook in here, you see. There's the kettle and toaster and that little microwave.' She indicated the miniature machine on the corner shelf, scarcely big enough to make a bowl of porridge. 'It's the electrical circuit. What with the heaters and everything, it tends to overload. So I can't have a cooker in here, I'm afraid, or even a full-sized microwave.'

Over by the window the girl, Willow, had been staring out at the tired October lawn, but now she turned back to face the room. 'I won't be cooking much.'

'Well, you never know, once you're settled in.' The tone of Vince's remark took Laura by surprise: briskly encouraging but with an assumption of intimacy, more friendly uncle than housing adviser. 'You could do a baked potato in that thing in just a few minutes. Bit of grated cheese on top – nothing simpler.'

'Oh, yes,' agreed Laura. 'It's certainly fine for things like that. The last girl used to swear by microwaved risotto. She made it in a cereal bowl.'

Willow regarded her without comment.

'But you'd also have use of my kitchen up at the house for cooking your meals, if you so wish. You'd have your own key for the house, as well as for here.' In fact, her lodgers had almost always ended up sharing meals round the family table – not to mention watching her television, and babysitting for Beth.

'Sounds a pretty good arrangement.' Vince was looking at Willow, who nodded and shrugged.

'I don't have a lot of rules, really. No candles is about the only thing – because of the fire risk. What's good about being separate down here is there's no need to worry about noise, and comings and goings. Though the last bus back from Cambridge is at ten pm. It stops at the end of the drove at twenty-five past.'

'Yes,' said Vince. 'We looked up the buses, didn't we, Willow? Not a bad service, considering.'

Laura laughed. 'Considering it's the butt-end of nowhere.'

'Considering all the cuts there've been to the rural bus services,' came the dignified reply. Then he cracked a grin: 'Although, yes, that as well, now you come to mention it.'

Willow had turned back to the window again. Laura moved over to stand beside her. 'It's not much to look at, is it, the garden? I don't have the time for it really.' There was just the lawn and the straggly rose hedge and the tree house that Simon had built for his new son or daughter, with all kinds of misplaced optimism, when Laura was pregnant. It was six years before Beth even mounted the ladder. 'You'd have the use of it, though, of course. It's not bad for sitting out in the summer, when the sun comes round in the afternoons.'

'Can you see the river, from up in the tree house?'

Laura glanced sideways at the girl, slightly thrown. 'I – I think so.' It must be three years since she'd crouched inside, drinking Ribena from doll-sized plastic cups. If Beth went up there at all these days, it was to be on her own. 'Though it's not a river, exactly. Just a drainage cut, built to take groundwater from the soil. Without it, we'd all be submerged.'

'I thought you'd be able to see it from the room. It looked that way in the photo.'

'Oh, yes. I'm sorry. I never thought.' When she'd been asked for pictures with the particulars she'd just sent a snap of the inside of the pumphouse – and then one of the front of the house, taken from across the lode.

Behind them, Vince cleared his throat. 'I don't think you need concern yourself too much about trade descriptions. It was just a whim Willow had.'

But the girl still frowned without turning. 'I wanted to see out over water.'

'Well, anyway,' said Laura, 'would you like to come back up to the house, if you've seen enough here? I can show you the tenancy agreement.'

'Yes, great. Thank you,' said Vince, looking hard at Willow, who finally moved away from the window and muttered, 'Thanks.'

They climbed the concrete steps in silence. Some of them were crumbling badly at the edges; one more winter's frosts and Laura would need to have them done again. On top of the dyke, they paused a moment while Vince and Willow gazed down at the thick dark water, which turned slow circles as it passed, or across to the bank opposite, of a height with the one on which Ninepins stood, and beyond, to the flat, black, hedgeless fields.

'It seems pretty full,' was Vince's comment.

She nodded. 'It's rained quite a bit this week.' After all, it was October: in most years, the level in the lode was higher than the surrounding land from September to May.

'How deep is it?' Willow wanted to know.

'Oh, goodness – I don't really know. Seven, eight feet, perhaps, at the moment.'

'So, deep enough to swim?'

5

'In theory, I suppose so, yes. But I don't really imagine anyone would want to go in there, do you?'

Even in summer, Elswell Lode was hardly an attractive spot for bathing. Or a safe one, come to that.

'Not in October they blooming well wouldn't,' said Vince. 'I'm freezing my monkeys off just standing here. It's not the most sheltered spot in the world. Didn't you say something about going inside and looking at a contract?'

'Yes, of course. Sorry. Come on in.' Laura dug the key from her bag and opened the front door, showing them into the kitchen.

'Nice.' Vince ran his eye over the Rayburn and the oak-topped units with evident appreciation. Did he cook, she found herself wondering? 'Willow, I'm going to have to buy you a recipe book.'

'Oh, you'd be welcome to borrow mine,' Laura told the girl, indicating the bookshelf. But it did seem an odd thing for him to say; perhaps he actually was a relative, as well as being from the council.

Moving over to the shelf, he scanned the row of spines. 'Thai,' he said, 'and *Flavours of Morocco*. Not sure these are quite the place to begin.'

'There's an old Marguerite Patten somewhere, too. And Nigel Slater's nice and simple.'

She had found the file, now, in the drawer.

'Here's a copy of the tenancy,' she said, taking it out and handing it to Willow. 'It's very much a standard agreement, but you'll want to take it away and have a read.'

'Thanks.' The girl gave it barely a glance before passing it to Vince.

'And then I'm sure you'd like some time to think about it. I dare say you have other places to view.'

She made to show them to the door, but Vince smiled and stood his ground. 'Perhaps we can have a bit more of a chat first?'

'Er, yes, of course. Why don't you both sit down?' They

might have more questions; Willow had scarcely asked anything yet. 'Perhaps you'd like a cup of tea?'

They both accepted this offer, with graceful thanks from Vince and a nod from Willow. As she put on the kettle and reached down the mugs she thought of what else she ought to say.

'The rent's inclusive of electricity, like I said, and water and council tax, too. There's a separate phone line to the pump-house, so you can plug in your own phone if you want, so then obviously you'd have the bills to pay for that. And there's broadband, for the internet.'

' 'S'OK,' said Willow. 'I've got a mobile. And I don't have a computer.'

It was difficult to imagine a teenager not on the Web; Beth would chat all night on Facebook if she were allowed. But – of course – how would a client of Housing Aid afford a fancy laptop? Laura felt herself colouring and was glad to be facing the worktop, squeezing teabags with a spoon.

'I've always let to students, before. Postgraduates, usually. So of course they need their laptops and internet access for work. I had someone lined up this year, in fact, coming from India to do an MPhil, but her funding fell through at the last moment and she had to drop out.' She knew she was babbling now but, having begun, she couldn't seem to stop. 'And by then the university term had started and I knew there weren't likely to be any students still looking for accommodation, not that late. They'd all be fixed up. So that's why I decided to advertise more widely.'

Turning, she placed their mugs on the table in front of them, followed by the milk and sugar. 'Help yourselves. Biscuits? I think there are some Hobnobs in the tin, if my daughter hasn't pigged them all.'

Both of them looked up at that.

'You have a daughter?' said Vince. 'How old?'

'Beth. She's eleven – twelve next month. She's just started at Elswell Village College.'

Willow smiled. She had an artless, lopsided smile: it made her suddenly less daunting.

'Now then,' said Vince, as she took a chair opposite them. 'You're aware, aren't you, that Willow is only seventeen?'

Laura glanced at the girl's thin, goosebumped arms, the pale concavities in her elbows. Even seventeen was hard to credit.

'I hope it won't be an obstacle. The rent will be paid directly by the department. We can set up a direct debit.'

'Oh?' Laura had no direct experience with benefit claimants, but it sounded a surprising arrangement.

'And there will be a small enhancement, too, an additional payment on account of Willow's age and circumstances.'

'Really? Is that usual?'

'Pretty much so, yes – with young people like Willow who are still looked after.'

'Looked after?' Her thoughts flew back first to the kindly uncle, before light began to dawn.

'In care,' he explained. 'It's the term we use for children and young people who are in local authority care.'

Local authority. Of course: he'd said Cambridgeshire on the phone. She had assumed he meant Housing Aid.

'You're from Social Services.'

'That's right. From Children's Services. I'm Willow's social worker.'

'I see.' Seventeen. In care. With a social worker.

'I'm sorry if I'm rather springing this on you. Usual practice is to consult about prospective placements in advance, but I've encountered some reluctance when I raise it on the phone. A lot of landlords look askance at kids from the care system. Won't even consider them, sometimes.' Vince caught and held Laura's gaze. 'There's a lot of prejudice about.'

Prejudice? Perhaps. But a lot of landlords didn't have Beth.

'I prefer to come and speak to people face to face. Introduce the young person.'

8

'May I ask – ?' But it was impossible, with the poor child sitting there. 'I mean, where has she – ?'

'I've been in the bin.' It was the first time Willow had spoken since they'd all sat down. Her eyes were a penetrating green. 'That's what we call it. Children's home, to you.'

Vince laid a hand on her arm. 'Willow came into care when she was thirteen. She was in various foster placements at first, and then, most recently, in a residential facility. But at seventeen we like to get young people out of institutional care and into independent accommodation, if they're ready for it. And Willow is absolutely ready.'

Independent accommodation. She still looked such a child: fragile, despite the startling eyes, which were now once more cast down and away.

'Will there be any support?' Laura asked. Would Vince be in and out, keeping an eye on his charge? Or would Laura herself be expected . . . to do what? Whatever it might be, she was certainly ill-equipped for it. *And there was Beth.*

'Oh, yes. Don't worry – we shan't be cutting Willow completely loose. There'll be regular contact for as long as it's required. But it needn't be intrusive, as far as you're concerned. I'm based in Cambridge three days a week; Willow can drop by and see me there.'

'Wouldn't a bedsit in town be more appropriate, then? In Cambridge, I mean – closer to your offices?'

It was Willow who answered. 'I saw the picture. I wanted to live by the river.' She pushed back her chair and walked over to the kitchen window. From this angle, the water would be invisible, but she stared out anyway; what Laura could see of her profile appeared entirely impassive.

'Well, I think we've seen enough.' Vince put down his mug and picked up the tenancy agreement. 'Unless you have any more questions for us?'

Laura shook her head. There were dozens of questions – but none she could ask.

'In that case, we'll be on our way. And I'll give you a ring in a day or two, if that's all right – or do ring me if there's more you'd like to know. Thank you very much for your time, Laura. And for the tea.'

On the way out through the hall, Willow dawdled behind, looking at some old, framed photographs that hung along the wall. Laura came back to see what had caught her attention: a black and white snapshot of Ninepins with the lode in spate, water swirling close to the top of the dyke.

'Is it often like this?'

Laura laughed. 'No, thank goodness. This was well before my time. It must be taken in the 'fifties, I think.' Though there was little enough to date it. The low horizon and the towering fen sky; the square-built, grey brick house; the top of the pumphouse chimney, jutting up above the dyke: the passing decades scarcely left a mark. 'They seem to control the levels much better nowadays . . .'

But Willow wasn't listening; she drifted on towards the door.

'Goodbye, then,' said Vince, extending his hand. 'We'll be in touch.'

Five minutes later, when the mugs were washed and dried and hung back on their hooks, Laura had not heard an engine start. Glancing sideways through the window she saw the red saloon still parked outside her door. In the front seats, Vince and Willow were deep in conference, their heads bent close together.

Chapter 2

Changing her work clothes for jeans and jumper always made Laura feel more at home. Not to mention warmer; the heating wasn't set to come on until five o'clock, which was the earliest time at which either of them was normally home. Half past three now: it was far too soon to think about starting the supper, and she couldn't face her study and the files in her bag.

Beth. She'd drive to school and pick her up early from homework club for once. She hooked down from the peg the black and red striped scarf and wound it round her neck. The product of a primary school knitting craze, it was Beth's first full-sized effort, bevel-edged and lumpy. Knitting was in Year 6, right after Scoobies and before the squashy juggling balls; they didn't seem to have crazes in the same way at the college.

On her way out to the car she paused, as she often did, on the top of the dyke and breathed in the open space. To her right, the lode cut straight as a furrow through the featureless fields, flanked by its twin dykes, as far as Elswell village three miles away; to her left it ran just as straight for the quarter-mile to the main road, and beyond that, through country equally unvarying, north and east to drain into the river Cam. That way, too, ran the plumb line of Ninepins Drove, hugging the foot of the dyke but itself slightly raised above the adjacent land. It was what she loved about the fens, as well as what she sometimes hated: the emptiness. But then a movement caught her eye. The drove wasn't empty, after all: it was home to a figure, familiar as her own skin, trudging towards the house. Laura raised both hands and flapped them above her head; the figure began to flap back, before stiffly lowering her arm. Laura grinned as she set off down the track to meet her daughter. Beth was funny: embarrassed to be waving to her mother though there was nobody for half a mile.

'Hello, love,' she called as they drew within hailing distance. 'What are you doing home?'

'I knew you were seeing someone for the pumphouse, so I thought I'd come early. I got the bus.'

'Well, it's a lovely surprise. But I was just going to come and fetch you. You beat me to it.'

Beth acquiesced in a brief hug, and let Laura's arm stay loosely round her shoulders as they moved homewards together.

'Thought it'd save you the journey.'

'Yes.' Don't start an argument, not straight away. 'Thanks.'

'I borrowed the bus fare off Rianna. She always has way too much lunch money, anyway. Her mum thinks she eats, and she doesn't, or hardly. Just Diet Pepsi and stuff.'

'I didn't know they sold Pepsi in the canteen.' Hadn't she had a letter about it: how they'd taken out the drinks machines in pursuit of healthy eating?

'She gets it at the newsagent on her way to school.'

'Oh, well. Remind me in the morning to give you the seventy pence to pay this Rianna back. And, you know, you really oughtn't to borrow money that's meant for someone's lunch.'

The bus conversation and the stupid crash dieting conversation could wait until later. It wasn't as if they hadn't had them both before.

'So, how was school?'

'Fine.' OK. Fine. It was always just fine. 'So, what was she like, the new person? Is she taking it?'

'I don't know yet. They're – she's going to ring back in a few days.'

'I hope she does come. Or someone else does, pretty

soon. It's boring with no one to watch TV with. Sharmila was cool.'

I watch television with you, Laura wanted to say. But when was the last time she had? 'Perhaps,' she tried, 'after homework and supper we could play a game?'

Beth shook her head. 'I need to watch *Hollyoaks*.'

'Need to?' Laura almost laughed, but prevented herself in time.

'Everybody watches it. Rianna and Caitlin and everyone. I need to know what happens. What's her name?'

'Who?'

'The person for the pumphouse.'

'Oh, yes. She's called Willow.'

'Weird name. Is she weird?'

'No, of course not. Don't be silly.' She caught her daughter's sideways glance. Had she said it a little too quickly? 'She's very nice.'

They had reached the lane end and were climbing the track towards the house.

'What's for supper?' said Beth. 'Not boring pasta again. We always have pasta.'

After Laura had tested Beth on the French words for parts of the body, and they'd decided they were both hungry early and had raced and tumbled through eight verses of *Gentille Alouette* while they chopped vegetables for a stir fry, the atmosphere was perceptibly lighter. Why, wondered Laura as she tipped in the peppers and mushrooms, did it take an hour these days for her to get her daughter back when she'd been at school? It was never like this last year.

'*Et la tête*,' she squeaked.

'*Et la tête*,' Beth growled back, turning the sizzling mound in the wok.

Fragile though she knew the détente might be, she decided to risk it.

'You know, I'm really not keen on your coming home on the bus.' Beside her, the wooden spoon froze. 'Not on your

13

own. Not yet. I come past that way, in any case, on my way home, and I can easily pick you up. I like to pick you up.'

'Not today, you weren't coming past. You were home already, seeing this Willow person.' It was all right; Beth was stirring again. 'The tree girl. Weeping Willow. Does she cry a lot, d'you reckon? Or maybe she's the Womping Willow. Does she whack you if you go near her?'

Sticking to her purpose, Laura insisted, 'I don't want you walking home from the bus stop by yourself.'

'Everyone else gets the bus. They're all allowed to. It's only me that's not.'

'Alice's mum takes her home.'

This contribution provoked exaggerated eye-rolling. 'Her mum works at the school, that's why. But everyone else goes on the bus. So I wouldn't be by myself, would I? I'd be with the others. I'd be with Rianna.'

'You'd still be walking back on your own from the bus stop.'

'*Everyone* walks back from the bus stop. How else would they get home?' Beth was bearing with infinite patience her mother's simple-mindedness.

Laura kept her voice level. 'I expect there are street lights, where the others live. Nobody lives out here where we do. The drove's unlit, and it's too far to walk from the main road in the dark.'

'It wasn't dark today.' In spite of herself, Laura found she was smiling. Arguing with Beth was like trying to negotiate a revolving door on roller skates – and besides, this time she had a point.

'Fair enough. But I was talking about in general – especially when it comes to winter. I really don't want you here on your own all that time. From three o'clock to five or five thirty – it's much too long. And it's silly, when there's homework club at school, with people to talk to.' Somewhere with warmth and light, and proper adult supervision. Ninepins was so isolated, and eleven was so young.

'Ten past three,' corrected Beth, as she flipped a stubborn piece of carrot. 'Half past, before I'd actually be home. But anyway, if it's so early, it means it won't be dark, will it, even in the winter? And none of my friends go to stupid homework club. It's for boffs.'

'It's not just homework, is it? I thought there was a pool table, and ping pong?'

'Only geeks play ping pong. And the Chinese kids.'

Laura, who wasn't entirely certain how a geek differed from a boff, reverted to her main theme.

'I don't want you being by yourself that long.'

'I can always use the phone. If anything happens, I mean. I'm not a little kid.'

The stir fry looked done. Laura reached to the back of the Rayburn for the soy sauce.

'Well, I'd much rather nothing did happen. Or that if it happens, I'm here with you when it does. Could you find the plates, please?'

Beth moved over to the dresser. 'Anyway, I won't be on my own. Willow will be here. If she's like Sharmila, stuck to her laptop all day. So she can call 999 for me, can't she, in case I can't remember the number.'

If Willow were here. But the prospect was far from re-assuring. 'We can't expect – '

'9, 9 . . . um, what was that last number, again?'

'If someone's paying rent, you can't just – '

'9, 9, 7? Was that it? No, wait a minute, 9, 9, 4 . . .'

Beth was impossible. Back at the stove, holding out the plates and grinning like a six-year-old, she was not to be resisted. Laura grinned, too.

'OK, OK. Point taken. You're not completely incapable. Just moderately.'

'Can we use chopsticks?'

'I can. You're not much good at it, I seem to recall.'

'Oh, shut up. Can we, Mum, please?'

'All right. Get them out – they should be in the end drawer, underneath the tea towels. But you're still not coming home on the bus.'

Eating slippery vegetable slivers with lacquered sticks required all their concentration, calling a temporary halt to conversation. After five minutes of struggle, Beth capitulated and fetched a fork, which meant she finished first.

'Mmm. That was totally gorgeous. Is Willow going to eat with us, d'you think?'

'I told you, love, I'm not even sure yet if she'll take the room.'

This was summarily shrugged off. 'Wonder what she'll cook for me, when you're out and she's babysitting? Sharmila did great curries and stuff. And Anna, in Year 5 – she used to make me pancakes, d'you remember, with bacon and maple syrup? She always had a big bottle of it and she used to bring it over.'

'I've no idea if Willow can cook. Or even if – '

'What's she like? You haven't told me anything.'

'Well . . .' Laura began in the same place as Vince had. 'She's quite young. Younger than Sharmila – younger than any of the lodgers we've had.'

'How old, then?'

'Seventeen.'

Beth cocked one eyebrow – a recently acquired habit – and nodded approvingly. Seventeen, the eyebrow said, was infinitely more desirable than twenty-four. It evidently qualified Willow as being on the inside of some invisible fence – rather than on the outside with her mother. 'What does she look like?'

'Small: about your height. Dark hair, green eyes. Slim.'

'What was she wearing?'

'Oh, I don't know.' A cardinal sin. 'All I noticed was, she had on a vest top and no jumper. Apart from that – jeans, I think. Maybe trainers.'

More slow, approving nodding.

'She isn't a student, like the others have been.'

16

'Oh? Is she still at school? Doing A levels or something?'

'No. At least, I don't think so.' One shouldn't assume; but Vince had said nothing about school or college.

She laid down her chopsticks and looked carefully at Beth. 'Actually, Willow's had rather a tough time, I think. She's been in care.'

'Like Tracy Beaker, you mean? Wow – cool.'

Laura, who had been fearing her daughter's reaction, couldn't help but laugh. Then she stopped herself and said, 'I don't suppose it's as much fun as it might appear on TV.'

'So, what happened to her parents? Are they dead, or drug addicts or something? Or in prison? They might be bank robbers.'

'I don't know.' Though much the same list of terrifying possibilities had run through her own mind. 'And you do know, I'm sure, that you absolutely wouldn't ask anyone that kind of question. It would be very rude, and it could be really upsetting.'

'OK.' Beth looked contrite – and more than a little disappointed.

'But, listen, I don't even know yet if she'll take the place.' If Willow would want to come – or if she was ready to have her. 'So don't get too excited about it, yet, all right? It might take a bit longer – we might end up with someone else.'

'Well, I hope she does come. I think she sounds cool.'

Laura reached for Beth's plate and placed it on top of her own. 'Why don't you go and watch your thing on TV? I'll wash up and then come and join you.' Twenty minutes of teenage soap was a small price to keep alive the mood of communication.

As it happened, though, she never made it to *Hollyoaks*. Half way through wiping the dishes, the telephone rang.

'Hello?'

'Hi, Laura. It's me.'

Simon.

'Look, I'm sorry about this, but could we possibly switch

17

Beth's weekends? You know I wouldn't ask unless it was an emergency.'

'Another one?' Simon's life of recent years seemed to be one long domestic crisis. And she'd planned to repaint Beth's bedroom this weekend.

'Yeah, I know.' She could almost hear the grin, frank and disarming but not quite apologetic enough.

'It's Alfie, this time. He's been off school with a cold but then it's turned into an ear infection and now Jack seems to have caught it, and whatever Jack gets, Roly always has next.'

A pale apple green: Beth had chosen the colour and would have loved to help, but paint brought on her asthma. It had to be done when she was sleeping elsewhere, so there was time to air the room and clear the fumes.

'You don't want Beth coming home with a cold, not with her chest. And it does seem to be an evil one. Half the nursery is off with it. Poor Jack is all crusted up and can hardly breathe, and Alfie's been mutinous with his ears. It's one hell of a job to get the drops in. There's screaming.'

When wasn't there, at Simon's house? Those three boys were the loudest children she had ever encountered, and never kept still. No wonder it was hard to get a syringe in their ears.

'Not that Beth wouldn't be a help – I'm sure she would. But it isn't really fair on her. I promised I'd take her roller skating the next time she came, and we can't do that with Alfie and Jack laid up, and maybe Roly, too. Not that they ever really do – lie up, that is.'

'I can imagine.' Beth had always been a quiet invalid, content to stay in bed and be pampered with hot water bottles and chicken soup. But her colds had always left her blue beneath the eyes, lungs tight and fighting for air. 'Look, it's OK. Don't worry – she can come the following week, we've nothing planned.'

'Thank you, Laura. Knew you'd understand – you're a star. How is she, anyway? How's school going?'

'Oh, fine, I think.' It was a struggle to know what else to say. 'She's making some new friends, I gather. And on Monday she had a merit in science – like house points, you know. She seems to like science.'

It seemed to satisfy him. 'I liked science. All kids do, when they arrive at secondary school. It's the Bunsen burners. They're irresistible. Gas and lighters and tubes of things that might explode.'

'They're doing amoeba.'

He laughed. 'Not quite the same thrill.'

'How about you; how's things? Apart from the ailing offspring, that is?'

'Not bad. At least Tessa and I haven't had the lurgy – or not so far, touch wood. And I've not been too busy, recently, so I've had time on my hands to blow noses and administer Calpol and Vick's. The article I was lining up for *Rural Living* fell through. They liked it at the initial pitch, but not when they saw the detail. A whole week's research gone to waste.'

'What a pain.'

'It happens,' he said, and she knew enough from having lived with it to be sure he was right: freelance journalism went that way. But why was he telling her about it?

'Can you send the idea anywhere else?'

'Oh, yes, probably. There are a couple of places I can try, so you never know. It might still sell. Problem is, a cheque this month is what I could really have done with.'

Laura closed her eyes in stage weariness – feeling a fair modicum of the real thing. She knew what was coming next.

'So, I wondered . . . I hate to do this to you again. But the thing is, Laura – '

'Yes, *Simon*?' She hated the way he used her name all the time, when he wanted something. He used to do it when they argued, when they were breaking up.

'Oh, bugger, sorry. You're annoyed. Are you annoyed? I think you are. Look, you know how I feel about Beth. I'd do anything for her, you know I would, give her anything.'

19

She sighed. It was true. As far as intentions went, he was a model father.

'I know I was late with her money in June and July, too, but I caught up when I did that piece in *The Observer*. And I'm not saying I can't pay anything this month, I can manage a hundred or so now, and in a couple of weeks, who knows? I wouldn't ask . . .'

Her smile was wry. 'Don't tell me – unless it was an emergency.'

'What emergency's this?' Beth, holding a cushion in one hand and the TV remote in the other, was standing in the kitchen doorway.

Laura covered the receiver. 'The boys are ill.'

'Dad! Can I talk to him?'

'Here,' Laura told Simon. 'Speak to your daughter.'

Swapping the phone for the remote, she headed for the sitting room to switch off the television before retreating to her study. Behind her, she caught the sound of Beth's laughter: a proper, leaping laugh, spontaneous and gleeful, that she hadn't heard enough lately – not nearly enough – and was struck by a shaft of pure jealousy.

'Click it down properly when you hang up,' she called back towards the kitchen. 'Or the battery will go flat.'

It was all very well for Simon to plead pennilessness. Not that he would say it if it wasn't true; a new wife and three sons must eat up money, and his work had never been lucrative or even reliably regular. But it wasn't easy for her, either, even with just the two of them. Academic researchers were not well paid. Eighteen years in the department without achieving tenure meant a hand to mouth existence, surviving on a series of precarious, soft money posts; it brought in sufficient, but only just. The outside steps needed doing, and she ought to have someone look at the roof, too; there were loose slates after last winter, and she was worried about the flashings. And now no maintenance this month, or less than she'd expected. It

20

made it imperative – she had to let the pumphouse as soon possible.

But, to Willow? Of course it was a risk, but there had been mention of an enhancement on the rent. And if not her, then how soon would she find another prospective tenant?

The space between bath and bed had always had a magical quality. When Beth was small, of course, it was literally a time of fairy tales, and the spell, for Laura at least, had never quite lost its hold.

Where once she would have been on the bathroom floor, encouraging washing operations and playing hide and seek with plastic ducks, now she liked to work with her study door open when her daughter was in the bath. That way she knew at once when she emerged, trailing warm, shampoo-scented vapour, and could follow her along the landing to her bedroom, drawn like some maternal version of the Bisto kid.

'Hiya,' said Beth as Laura came in the room, announcing her entrance with the token knock she had recently adopted in deference to her daughter's shyness when unclothed. 'How d'you think I should do my hair tomorrow?'

Laura went to the window to draw closed the curtains on the starless fen night; then she turned towards the bed. 'How about a French plait? I could put it in for you in the morning.'

'Hmm. I don't know about French plaits. Nobody really has them at the college.'

'We could frizz it? I'll do you a Hermione Granger.' This had been a favourite game since Beth was small: Laura bound her wet hair up in a dozen tiny, tight braids and in the morning it brushed out into a glorious bounce of curls.

'Uh-uh.' Beth shook her head emphatically. 'God, no. I'd get *so* laughed at. Everyone has totally straight hair. Rianna has extensions. Hers is down to here.' She indicated somewhere near the base of her spine. 'Can I have some straighteners for my birthday, d'you think? I mean, I know you're getting me the new bike, but just as an extra thing. They're not expensive. Fifteen pounds, Rianna said.'

'Well . . .'

'Or I could ask Dad.'

'We'll see. What if you used the hair dryer, for now, and combed it straight as you dried it?'

'It wouldn't stay straight, it never does. Maybe if I had some mousse – or serum. You can get this straightening serum.'

Laura sat down next to her daughter on the bed and tried not to breathe in too obviously. Even the familiar tang of tea tree and mint shampoo was overlaid with other smells she didn't recognise: smells from the expanding collection of bottles and jars on which Beth now spent her pocket money. The cleansers and toners and moisturisers – so wholly un-needed by her clear, young skin – were like a veil of teenage mystery to Laura, who used nothing but old-fashioned soap.

'Maybe we could buy you some, then.'

'Thanks, Mum. You're a legend. It comes in this little red tube and you get it in Boots. Can you get some for me tomorrow? *Please*.'

'We'll see,' said Laura again, but she was already replanning her lunch break. She knew it was pitiable, but when Beth called her a legend, she was powerless to resist.

'Could you hang my dressing gown up, please?' Beth peeled it off as she climbed under the duvet.

Rising to oblige, Laura bent over her daughter and kissed her good night. 'Light on or light off?'

'On. I'm going to read a bit.'

'Not for too long, then. It's school in the morning – light out by half past nine.'

There was no chance she'd be allowed to get away first time. It was another game, a power play of Beth's, evolved when she was a toddler afraid of the dark. Then, it had been just one more story, Mummy, one more cuddle. Now her daughter traded in the new currency: the sharing of small confidences. When Laura was at the bedroom door, hanging up her dressing gown and preparing to go downstairs, or back to her desk, that was the time Beth chose to talk.

'Break times are weird.'

Laura turned, and took two steps back towards the bed. 'Why weird?'

'Break times and lunchtimes. Nobody wants to play.'

Her stomach plunged; she sat down heavily on the edge of the duvet. 'No one will play with you, sweetheart?'

But her concern was brushed away impatiently. 'I don't mean that. It's not me especially, it's everyone. Nobody plays.'

'Oh?' By her daughter's expression, she was clearly being very dense.

'They don't *play*. They don't do anything, even the other Year 7s. They just stand about and talk.'

'Oh dear.' Now that she understood – or thought she did – Laura's relief turned to half-amused sympathy, and she leaned across to gather Beth into a hug. At primary school they'd played It and Forty-Forty or dangled from the climbing frame to gossip, even the Year 6s; how much easier than the closed circle of conversation, faced without props. Laura remembered it herself from school; girls were so political, and Beth wasn't good at that. Asthmatic or not, she'd rather run about. 'Nobody plays any games at all?'

'Well, the boys do. They're OK – they play football and stuff.'

'And you couldn't join in with them, sometimes? Don't girls ever play football?'

'Huh,' said Beth, against her chest. Not, it seemed, the girls who mattered.

'Well, then . . .' She cast about for ideas. In Year 6 they'd still skipped, or at least turned the rope for the little ones, but she knew enough not to suggest taking a skipping rope to the college. 'What about netball? There must be netball hoops,

23

aren't there? Can't you borrow a ball and shoot a few goals while you chat?'

'Hmm. S'pose so.' But she could tell she was being humoured: that Beth knew there was no point in striking against the tide, and she just had to learn to swim with it. With a sigh, Laura laced her arms more tightly about her daughter; she laid her cheek against the warm, damp hair, which was already springing into unco-operative kinks. Her eyes were closed, and she thought that Beth's were, too. 'Mum?'

'Yes, love?'

'Can I have a Power Bar in my packed lunch? Everyone has Power Bars.'

They were all on their own in the end, she reflected, as she padded back to her study five minutes later. Maybe when they were very small you could fight some battles for them but, when it came down to it, kids had to do it for themselves and all you could do was stand on the sidelines and watch and hope and ache. And Beth was more on her own than some. She had no father to hand, nor the younger brothers or sisters she might have had, to fill the house with noise and bring home germs from nursery. Not much of a family. Sitting down, she stared at the open files on her desk, but saw instead Willow's thin, bare arms, her hollow elbows. Willow, who had no family at all.

Stuck out here with only her mother: it would be good for Beth to have someone around who was nearer her own age. A teenager to talk to – it would surely be good. And didn't every kid deserve a chance?

Chapter 3

It was a Saturday when Willow moved in. Vince and his car were summoned to duty for the ferrying of possessions, making it inevitable that both he and Willow should be invited in for lunch.

Laura kept out of the way to give her new lodger space, and had instructed Beth to do the same. But it was a bright morning for the end of October, with banks of high white cloud on a canvas of gentian blue: a perfect day for an eleven-year-old to be outside in the garden, treating the dyke as a makeshift BMX ramp. When Laura glanced out of the window at half past eleven, there was her daughter turning one-eighties on the old bike that was too small for her. Ten minutes later, when she looked again, the bike lay abandoned on the lawn and Beth was in the cindered turning space, standing by the boot of the red saloon and being loaded up with cardboard boxes.

On the whole, she looked more useful as a pack-mule than Willow, who was marginally the taller of the two but by far the slighter. It was curious to watch them together: Beth, large-framed and awkward, with her size seven feet and hands to match, and Willow, who was suited to her name – though the impression of her limbs, Laura thought, was not of elasticity like the willow bough but all spike and brittleness.

The car seemed to empty remarkably quickly. Even allowing for three pairs of hands, the boxes and bags were poignantly few, since one could presume no childhood bedroom somewhere with a wardrobe of disfavoured clothes, no junk stored in a parental attic. By noon, the journeys from gate to pumphouse had ceased and all was quiet outside. At quarter past, Laura, washing lettuce at her sink, heard the thud of the front door, followed by voices in the hall. Laughter – Beth's – and Vince's light tenor, saying something about a workers' canteen.

'Hello,' she called. 'All done?'

Beth was first into the kitchen. 'We've moved all her stuff, Mum. There was heaps of it, but I helped and it all fitted in OK. Except it's still piled on the bed and all over the floor, and she says I can help her unpack later, after lunch. Can I, please?'

'Willow has a name, you know,' said Laura. 'And are you sure you won't be in the way?' She turned to Willow with a rueful smile. 'Do please just kick her out if you don't want her.'

Willow shrugged and shot a glance at Beth. ' 'S'all right.'

'Something smells good in here,' said Vince. 'A proper farmhouse kitchen smell.'

'Completely illusory, I'm afraid.' Laura smiled over her shoulder as she shook the colander of lettuce at the sink. 'That's the smell of plastic-wrapped baguettes, the kind you finish off in the oven and try to pass off as homemade. It's just going to be omelettes, if that's OK, with bread and salad.'

'Wonderful,' he said.

'Can we have Brie in the omelettes, Mum? So it goes all melty and gooey?'

'Well, I'm not sure there is any Brie. Have a look in the fridge, could you? Is an omelette all right for you, Willow? Otherwise I've got some cold chicken, or just cheese with the salad. '

'Omelette's fine.'

Upon instruction, Beth set the table with Willow's assistance, and the three of them sat down while Laura ran butter round the frying pan.

'Is it a farmhouse, in fact?' Vince asked. 'Or was it once, I mean?'

'I think so. Or a farmworker's cottage, at any rate.'

'Only,' he continued, 'Ninepins is such an unusual name.'

'I know why,' chirped Beth. 'Can I tell them?'

Laura grinned down into the pan, which had begun to smoke. 'Go on, then.' She poured in the first two beaten eggs.

'It's not after the game of ninepins, like people think. It was a bit like skittles and they used to play it in the olden days, but that's not why it's called that. It's really *Ninepence*, not Ninepins at all, only people said it wrong and it got changed over the years. Like Chinese whispers.'

'Really?' Vince's interest sounded genuine. 'Why Ninepence?'

'It's what you used to have to pay to get across the lode. There was a bridge here, you see, and that was the toll.'

Laura slid the first omelette on to Willow's plate. 'Help yourself to salad.'

'But it wasn't *9p*, it was old money – *9d* – which means it was three-quarters of a shilling, and a shilling was only 5p in our money, so it was really only about three and a bit pence.' Beth looked up at her mother for confirmation, proud of this exotic gem of knowledge.

'What happened to the bridge?' asked Vince.

'It was swept away,' said Beth with relish. 'In the Great Flood of 1947. It was 1947, wasn't it, Mum?'

'That's right.'

'Swept away?' Willow, who had been prodding at her omelette with her fork, looked up. 'Here? Really?'

'Yes, it came right up over the banks and everything. There are pictures on the internet. We Googled it, didn't we, Mum? Not of right here, but of Elswell, with water running down the High Street, and people up to their middles in it, and a man outside the Post Office in a rowing boat. And there was one of here, but later, when the water had gone down again, and you can see the end bits of the bridge, all broken off, and nothing left in between.'

Smiling, Laura moved back to the Rayburn and rebuttered the pan.

'It sounds very dramatic,' said Vince.

'I know – really cool. I did a project on it for school.' A hint of hesitation. 'Just, y'know, at primary school.'

'That's great,' he said. 'And what about the pumphouse?'

'Oh, it must have been under water, too. Just the chimney sticking out, I reckon, like a submarine with one of those periscope things. Bet it looked dead funny.'

There was a snort from Willow, and an indulgent laugh from Vince. 'I bet it did. But what I really meant was, what do you know about the place – about the pumphouse? You being the expert on local history, I thought you'd be able to tell us all about it.'

Her daughter temporarily abashed, Laura stepped in. 'Well, it housed a fen drainage engine – I think I told you? Not one of the old steam ones, the beam engines, like at Stretham or Prickwillow. They're on a much grander scale. This one was a diesel pump, which is what came in to replace steam, between the wars. Built in 1929 – there's a date on a brick above the door, but I don't suppose you'd notice.' She folded the second omelette in half and brought it to the table, where she manoeuvred it on to Vince's plate. 'It didn't have much of a working life, though, in the end. These diesel pumps were mostly disused in the 1960s. The pumping's all electric now. Much more efficient, I gather: the water here's controlled from a station up on the main road.'

Too much information. He was nodding politely while Beth and Willow were grinning at each other about something else. She clanked the frying pan back on the hob.

'I hope you won't be too bored, Willow, out here in the fens. It can get a bit lonely in the winter.' She'd misjudged the eggs. In it all went; she and Beth would have to share the last omelette. 'During the day, when I'm at work and Beth is at school, there'll be nobody.'

'I like it quiet.' Willow sounded definite, even defiant. 'I want it quiet. I just want some space to myself.'

'Well, there's no shortage of that here.' Laura cut the final omelette in two and slid it on to the plates. 'Space, that is.'

Vince looked at Willow but addressed Laura. 'Don't worry. Willow won't be sitting here by herself all the time. She's enrolled for some NVQ courses at the Regional College, so she'll be going into Cambridge a couple of days a week.'

Willow's gaze remained fixed on her side plate, where she was tugging her bread into small pieces.

'What is it?' he persisted. 'Mondays and Wednesdays?'

'Thursdays,' she said, without glancing up.

'Mondays and Thursdays, that's it. And Fridays, she's going to be seeing me, at my office. Not every Friday, but every other one, maybe.'

Beth, who had devoured her half-omelette in record time, put down her fork and said, 'Willow's a funny name. I mean, it's nice – but funny. I'm Beth 'cos it's short for Elizabeth, and 'cos Mum used to like *Little Women*. Why are you Willow?'

'My mother.' She pronounced the words tonelessly. Everyone looked at her; no one seemed to breathe. Then with sudden vehemence, she added, 'Useless bloody hippy. Waste of space.'

Beth's eyes were wide as plates. 'Your mum . . .? So, is that why you – ?'

Laura shot her daughter a silencing look, but too late.

'Arson.' The green eyes flashed with warning. 'I set fire to a heap of rubbish, up by some old empty garages. One of them caught light.'

'Wow,' said Beth.

'It was four years ago.' Vince moved in smoothly. 'There was very little damage and no charges were brought. But it did call to notice certain problems at home. That's when Willow was taken into care.'

There was an uncomfortable pause, which Laura filled

29

with the clatter of cutlery as she collected up the plates. Her hands, she found, were shaking; her head spun with questions, resolutely squashed down. 'I haven't done anything for pudding, but there's fruit, and some flapjacks left over, I think. And I can make coffee.'

'Are there really flapjacks?' Beth bounced out of her chair. 'I thought we finished them on Thursday.'

'I'm not sure how many are left. You and Willow might have to have them, if there aren't enough.'

Vince gave a conspicuous cough.

'Oh, sorry. I only thought – '

'Joking.'

By the time she had fussed about with flapjacks and plates and found the fruit bowl and boiled the kettle, the awkwardness had subsided a little. Willow was silent again, still playing with her uneaten bread, but Vince and Beth were talking about school.

'Science is good. We didn't have proper labs at the primary school, not like we do now, with poison and microscopes and everything.' *Bunsen burners*, Laura remembered and tried to smile; *things that might explode*. 'After half term we're going to dissect stuff.'

'That sounds exciting.'

'Oh, not dead bodies or anything. Not even mice – you do them in Year 11. And eyeballs – in Year 8 you get to do sheep's eyeballs, and they're full of this gruesome jelly stuff, someone said, that oozes out when you cut them open. It sounds brilliant. But Mrs Farrell said we're just doing woodlice.'

Vince nodded. 'And what else do you like, apart from pulling the legs off things?'

'Art. English, sometimes. And PE. We have way better equipment at the college. There's a gym with treadmills and rowing machines and everything, only I'm not sure when you get to go in there. It seems to be for adults: this girl Rianna, her aunty does a fitness class in there in the evenings. And the swimming pool is huge. Seriously, huge. It's bigger than Parkside – the one in Cambridge, you know. '

'You're keen on swimming, then?'

' 'S all right.'

Willow laid down her crust of baguette. 'What about here? In the river or lode or whatever you call it? Do you ever swim here?'

'Oh, we're not allowed. Mum says. It's dangerous.'

Both girls looked at Laura. 'There are sluice gates,' she explained. 'Upstream, towards Elswell, and they open them sometimes, especially after rain, so there can be sudden changes in level. The dykes are very steep, too; the sides can be slippery. It's really not safe.'

'Very wise,' said Vince. 'I'm sure you're right to be cautious. The water doesn't look too salubrious, either. It was practically black just now, when we were on the bank.'

'That'll be the rain last night. It flushes new groundwater into the lode, and the water takes the colour of the soil.'

'It is very dark round here, isn't it, the earth?' he said. 'Almost like peat.'

She nodded. 'It used to be all meres and marshland until they drained it, back in the seventeenth century. So, yes – one giant peat bog, I suppose you could say.'

'It's why it's called the Isle of Ely,' said Beth, through a mouthful of flapjack. 'It actually used to be a real island. You'd have had to go there by boat. It must have been so cool.'

'Why don't you get one?' wondered Vince, smiling at Laura. 'Just a little rowing boat, on the lode? Or would that be dangerous, too?'

'Oh, yes, Mum – can we? A boat would be awesome.'

'There used to be one here, when we first moved in – moored up below the house and all full of water. We pulled it out to have a look but it was rotted underneath. I think your dad broke it up for firewood in the end.'

'Mu-*um*.'

Why had Vince had to go and mention boats? The last thing she needed was Beth developing some hankering for *Swallows and Amazons* adventure.

'I can't swim.' Willow, swivelling her coffee mug, was frowning slightly.

'What?' Beth was incredulous. 'Not at all? How come?'

The question was shrugged off without comment. 'I want to, though. I really want to learn to swim.'

'Not here – ' began Laura, before Vince cut across her. 'You should. You should take lessons. I'm sure they have classes at Parkside pool. And it needn't be with little kids – they're bound to have sessions for adult non-swimmers. I'll look out a leaflet for you, or print it off the Web.'

Willow stared at him, still frowning, but she didn't demur. Laura had no idea why her heart should be thumping the way it was, nor why she felt a peculiar urge to pull her daughter into her arms and hold her close, as she sat there beside her ladling sugar into her mug.

'Is anyone having the last flapjack?' asked Beth.

After lunch and the gracious offer to wash up – declined with equal graciousness – Vince took his leave. The four of them went out and stood on the dyke beside the front door to say their goodbyes and thank yous; when Vince set off down the track to his car, Willow followed, while Laura held Beth back.

'Give them a minute.'

'Then can I go and talk to Willow, when he's gone? She did say I could go back and help unpack her boxes. I can, can't I?'

'As long as you don't bother her too much. If she wants you to leave, you leave. Understood?'

Beth was dismissive. ' 'Course.'

The red saloon started up with a cough, and backed slowly round on the saturated cinders. Willow bent her head to the wound-down driver's window to impart or receive some final message, before Vince drove off along the lane, his right hand raised in valedictory salute. *Come back*, Laura wanted to shout. *Don't leave me on my own with her.* Beth, at her mother's side, waved back vaguely, but she wasn't watching the departing car: her eyes were fixed on the figure remaining at the garden gate.

'See you, then,' she said, and set off at a shuffle, which tumbled into a run before she was half way down the track.

Turning away to go back into the house, Laura carried with her the image of the two girls: arms linked, laughing at something she couldn't discern as they walked towards the pumphouse.

She filled the bowl for the washing up and immersed the pile of dirty plates, watching the trapped bubbles escape and rise, and her own wrists as they gradually reddened in the heat of the water.

Arson, she thought, with a clutch of panic. *Some garages – one of them caught light.* What had she done, bringing this tinderbox into her home? Still staring at her hands, she realised she had forgotten the detergent. She reached for the bottle and squirted in a short, viscous stream. It was too late, now that the water was run, to make a proper lather; she swished her fingers round anyway, to little effect.

Money, after all, was only money. They'd have managed a little longer without a lodger, managed without Vince's 'small enhancement'. Thirty pounds per calendar month on top of the rent. Thirty pieces of silver.

What on earth had she been thinking, to bring a damaged teenager to Ninepins, exposing her daughter to who knows what unimagined dangers? Fearless, heedless Beth, who trusted everyone. Beth, who was only eleven. Oh, God – what had she done?

Chapter 4

How come she'd never learned to swim? That's what Beth asked Willow, the day she moved in, and she had no answer to give her.

There had been one time at the seaside: the only time she remembered going as a child. She had no idea where the resort was; she had been too young herself to know or care and there was nobody she could ask now who'd be able to tell her. She did recall a long train ride with lots of back gardens and washing and then cows and sheep, and her mother giving her Rice Krispies – dry from the packet, gumming the roof of her mouth – and a man with a newspaper telling her not to run up and down the carriage. She must have been four or five.

They stayed in a caravan, the two of them. It wasn't the pretty, oval-shaped kind she'd seen people tow behind their cars but plain and oblong like the back of a container lorry, and she could still feel the plunge of disappointment. It was cream on the top half and a pale salmon pink on the bottom. There were three steps up to the door with black rubber tread, which was peeling up at the corners like the underneath of a worn out wellington boot. To one side there was a single handrail of tubular metal not long enough for sliding down, but Willow spent hours dangling from it, or lying across it and lifting up her feet so that the metal dug into her tummy. By the end of the week (if a week was what it was) she could do a complete flip-over. The inside of the caravan, for some reason, was a blank in her memory.

The site was at the top of a cliff, but it can't have been a high one because there were wooden steps down to the beach and she counted them each time she went up and down. Seventeen. The beach was a mixture of sand and pebbles in stripes, and the cliff was made of sand as well, rather than rock or the white chalk that you see in picture books. It was soft and had crumbled away beneath the steps, so that in places you looked down through the gaps at empty air as if you were crossing a bridge; the sand settled on the steps, too, in a thin layer, silting up the grooves in the woodgrain and turning it as smooth and treacherous as a freshly polished floor. Clambering up was no trouble, but Willow always came down backwards, holding on tight to the step above with both hands. She counted backwards, too, starting with seventeen and ending on zero with her bare feet sunk in the fine, warm sand. There was no memory of rain, and the weather must have been hot because sometimes the sand was almost burning, so that she had to run to the line where the sea had been, where it was cooler and firmer. She didn't recollect ever wearing shoes.

One day stood out from the others. It could have been morning or afternoon but it was certainly sunny, and Willow was on the beach, on her own as usual. She had walked a little way out into the sea. The water was always cold to begin with and the first few times she'd gone in she'd hopped and splashed about to keep warm, or run straight out again. But then she found out that it stopped being cold if you stood really still. Sometimes, like this time, she went in deeper, up to her knees or even beyond, half way to the hem of her blue flannel shorts. If she stood there for long enough and then turned and walked back to the shore, something amazing happened to the sea. From being cold on the way in, the water at the edge was transformed on the way back out; it grew warmer and warmer, and the very last bit, where it lapped on the sand, was actually hot, as if you were in the bath. Willow had tried telling her mother about it but she hadn't seemed to hear. On this particular day, she was standing thigh-deep and waiting for the cold to stop when a woman in a sun-dress with big yellow roses on it called out to her from the beach. Willow turned but she didn't smile because she didn't know who she was.

To her surprise the woman hitched up her dress and waded out to where Willow stood, taking her by the hand and leading her back to the sand. She didn't like it but she didn't struggle or protest, because the woman's grip was gentle and the skin of her palm was smooth, and she had a nice smell of tangerines and sun lotion. Then she bent down to a level with Willow's fringe and asked her what her name was and where she was staying, and Willow told her and said that hers was the caravan with the cream up above and the pink down below.

They climbed the steps together, still holding hands, and then the woman went into the caravan, leaving Willow outside. She hung from the rail by the steps and watched the faint white smudges appear as the salt water dried on her legs. There was a lot of angry, quiet talking and afterwards some shouting, though none of it was at Willow.

She didn't go back to the sea again, after that.

Chapter 5

Laura scanned the homework room and experienced a moment of pure terror. It was the same physical, mind-blanking panic she had felt on occasion in the supermarket when Beth was small, or queueing for a bus, when she'd turned round to find her momentarily missing from her side. It was no different, she discovered, as her daughter grew older: the context might change but the essential fear persisted. The empty pushchair. Beth, gone.

It lasted no more than a second, of course. Reason returned and she went to check the common room next door; there was only the faintest resurgence of fear when the pool and ping pong tables, too, yielded no result. It was a fine evening, and mild: she must be outside. Perhaps she was reading a book, on the benches round by the sports hall.

The benches were empty. But as Laura was turning to retrace her steps and go to see if the school library was still open, she heard laughter. Girls laughing – not Beth, but there was an edge to it that made her follow the sound, past the corner of the building and into a narrow courtyard lined on one side with large, green plastic bins. To the other side was a windowless wall – the back wall of the gymnasium, Laura thought – and against it lolled three girls. The furthest from her was Beth.

All three looked across at her approach, and the laughter ceased abruptly. There were no smiles. The two unfamiliar faces were composed into the careful blanks presented to the world by the uncompliant young; Beth looked merely awkward.

'Hello,' Laura ventured. 'I wondered where you were hiding, Beth.'

Beth looked at her shoes. Her two companions held Laura's gaze a little longer before rolling away their eyes in studied boredom. Were they allowed to wear that eyeliner at school?

'Shall we go, then? The car's round by the front entrance, in the pull-in.' You weren't supposed to park there for more than a minute or two. 'I've bought kippers for supper.'

Her daughter shot her an agonised glance and then stared back at her feet.

One of the girls sniggered – the taller of the two, with the curtain of sheer blonde hair. 'Better go home to tea.'

The other – darker, sharp-featured – produced a perfectly manufactured smile. 'You mustn't keep Mrs Blackwood waiting.'

Eyes still cast down, Beth peeled herself off the wall and away from her companions.

Don't drag your bag on the floor: Laura carefully swallowed the words.

'See ya,' muttered Beth, without looking back.

'Later,' tossed back the blonde.

They walked to the car in silence; Laura, conscious of her unauthorised parking spot, had to slow her steps with conscious effort so as not to draw ahead of her daughter.

'Here we are.' She flicked the central locking as they came up. 'Do you want to sling your bag in the back?'

At five feet two and a secondary school pupil, Beth had recently been promoted to the front passenger seat. It had caused a subtle shift in things. In the driving mirror, she had been used to scrutinising her daughter's face as they talked; now, Beth was closer but her head was often turned away. Like tonight, for example, as she sat and looked out of her own side window, and Laura had no idea what she was thinking.

'How was school?'

' 'Kay.'

It was the maths test today – the square numbers she'd been learning. Drama, too, and the day they'd been going to do impro. But Laura knew better than to ask direct questions. She'd hear about it in the end – over supper, perhaps, or after Beth's bath.

'So, was that Rianna?' she said, remembering the hair extensions.

An affirmative grunt.

'The one with the long hair? And how about the other girl, the dark one?'

'Caitlin.'

'They weren't at the primary, were they, those two? I don't remember them.'

Silence.

'Not at Elswell, anyway. I suppose they were at a different school. Longfenton, maybe, or Wade?'

Another grunt, possibly affirmative. Then, still facing the window, Beth asked, 'Why d'you have to say that? About having kippers for supper?'

'You love kippers. I was going to do us a poached egg on the top, the way you like it.'

Beth's shoulders were hunched and tight. 'Nobody else has kippers.'

This must plainly be nonsense. No doubt plenty of Beth's classmates lived off chicken dippers and frozen pizza but there had to be some families who occasionally ate smoked fish.

'I got them in the Co-op.' The defence was oblique; if they stocked them in the village, then other people must buy them.

'Old grannies eat kippers.'

'Well, I am old.' The attempt at humour fell heavily in the car. It was too close to the truth to be funny: at forty-five she was ten years older than a lot of the mums. Her jeans were neither skintight nor voguishly labelled. Regardless, she soldiered on. 'Kipper's good for the elderly. I can chew it without putting my teeth in.'

'Shut up, Mum.' Beth wasn't laughing, but at least her shoulders softened and she turned into three-quarter profile.

'We could have ice-cream for pudding, if you like. That's also good for the aged and infirm.'

But it was too soon; she had overplayed her hand. Her daughter's jaw was again firmly set.

The best way, she had come to the conclusion in recent weeks, was to fill the difficult space with chatter, the kind requiring no response. 'Sylvia was off sick today. It was a nightmare – honestly, the whole place grinds to a halt without her. Students kept coming in demanding lecture handouts and nobody knew which ones were which. We had to put through one another's phone calls, but none of us understands how the system works. I cut myself off twice.'

They were out of the village now, and on the main road towards Ninepins. It was too dark to see anything much in the lightless spaces beyond the side window, but Beth turned that way anyway, tracing circles in the beads of condensation which lingered on the glass.

'And then, inevitably, the photocopier jammed, as it always does, and Sylvia's the only one who can un-jam it. It's a crabby old machine, and bares its fangs at anyone else. You risk losing a hand.'

Paying these banalities the heed they deserved, Beth suddenly demanded, 'Did you get three?'

'Sorry?'

'Kippers. Did you get one for Willow as well?'

'Well, no, I – We hadn't invited her for supper tonight, had we?' Arrangements were fluid. Willow came and ate with them if they happened to run into her, or if Beth was down in the pumphouse before supper and brought her back up with her. Or else she didn't.

'I really wanted her to come.'

'All right. Of course, if she wants to, she's very welcome. We can save the kippers for another night. I'll do spaghetti.'

Nothing was right, though, when her daughter was in this

mood, which seemed always to infect her after school these days. From Laura's left came a sigh of deep frustration. 'Why couldn't you have said that?'

'Said what?'

'Spaghetti. To Rianna and Caitlin. That would have been OK. But, no – you had to go and say freaking kippers.'

As soon as they were home, Beth threw her fleece and bag on the kitchen table, pausing only to extract her lunchbox and deposit it unceremoniously on the draining board. 'No homework tonight – only that geography, and it's not due in 'til Monday. Can I go to Willow's?'

Unable to think of a reason not to say yes, Laura bent to put the kippers in the fridge; as she rose again, she heard the front door clang without a goodbye. Radio voices – even the impish Eddie Mair – failed to fill the emptiness of the kitchen.

Probably she should seize the opportunity, should go upstairs and work for half an hour. Lethargy, however, exerted its pull; she'd make a cup of tea first, then think about it. There'd been no shortage of time alone just recently to spend in her study, but she felt less and less inclined to use it. Concentration, in a deserted house, should have come easily; instead, it frequently eluded her. The empty rooms held a strange oppression. After school and at weekends, Beth was spending long hours in the pumphouse. Yesterday she'd fled down there straight from the car, returning with Willow at supper-time; after a meal of silences and the exchange of surreptitious glances, the two had escaped again directly afterwards.

It was hard to say exactly why she minded so much. Willow herself had done nothing to justify alarm, but Laura had to admit to a nagging unease about her. If spoken to directly, she answered; she said please and thank you; but there was a privateness, a guardedness about her which Laura found intimidating. Nor was it as if, had Beth been here in the house, the two of them would have communicated very much

41

in the space before supper. She seldom came home talkative, particularly since September and the new school. But with Beth in the next room watching TV, or upstairs reading on her bed, the coolness was less of a threat, as if somehow the smaller physical distance made the emotional distance less. It had felt like necessary recovery time, time to recapture the closeness of home. Now every hour that her daughter stayed out of the house – stayed down there with Willow, talking about Laura knew not what – seemed only to place her further out of reach.

She filled the kettle at the tap and found herself a mug, still drying on the rack from breakfast. Beth's fleece lay sprawled across the table; Laura picked it up and smoothed it out, pulling the sleeves back right side out. From the lip of her daughter's school bag trailed a single, scarlet mitten. She opened the bag, thinking to reunite it with its mate; Beth went through five or six pairs of gloves per winter. Inside, there was no sign of the other mitten: just pencil case and exercise books and the fleecy cover of her mobile phone, with the face of Shaun the Sheep. And, tucked to the side and coiled in a knot, something mauve and chiffony and foreign. Laura pulled it out and unravelled it. It was a broad, rectangular scarf of fine, filmy cotton, the kind which is textured into permanent creases. Rianna's? Or Willow's. She raised the scarf to her face and inhaled, testing the unfamiliar smell – then chided herself for her foolish possessiveness. The mother vixen, jealous of the scent of her young.

Instead of taking her tea to the desk upstairs, she laid out her work at the kitchen table, propping a lever arch file on Beth's bag. It contained a new Forestry Commission paper on sustainable forest management that she had printed off the web that afternoon. But continuous cover silviculture failed to hold her attention; she could not absorb herself in wood energy or biomass initiatives. Her eyes kept drifting from the text – and finding their way back to her daughter's school fleece, which she had laid across the back of the adjacent chair. Really, all these unfocused anxieties were quite ground-less, she told herself; she was acting like some dreadful, clingy parent, controlling and neurotic. Beth was simply growing up. She should learn to let go.

Finally, after an hour or so, she achieved immersion, so that nothing had been done about either kippers or pasta sauce and her mind was spinning with native woodland ecosystems when the front door banged again. Just a bang – no voices.

'Hi, there,' she said, as her daughter appeared in the doorway. 'No Willow, tonight?'

'I asked her. But she said she wasn't hungry.'

Laura hid a smile in her notes as she stacked them away. Beth might well sound mystified: hunger, for her, was a given.

'Just the two of us, then.'

'Yeah.' Beth stood in the middle of the floor, arms hanging. Then she seemed to shake herself and there was the flicker of a grin. 'Bor*ing*.'

'Well, since we have no guest to impress, how about we slum it for once and eat in the other room?'

'What – in front of the TV?' It was, admittedly, a rare concession. Supper on a tray usually meant Wimbledon or the aftermath of asthma. 'Brilliant. It's *Hollyoaks*.'

It was a companionable meal. Laura needed to seek clar-ification about a number of plot points, and Beth took satisfaction in offering the necessary explanations, through mouthfuls of kipper, egg and brown bread.

As the final credits rolled, Laura drew in a breath and said, 'What about your birthday party?' They'd fixed on the date for the party weeks ago, but Beth was proving singularly evasive about finalising the details. 'It's getting close – less than a fortnight, now. We ought to be getting the invitations out.'

'Mm.' That was the reaction she'd been having every time she brought it up. *Mm*.

'Who are you thinking of inviting? I think any number up

to fifteen or sixteen should be manageable. How many did we have last year?'

No reply at all this time: just a shrug.

'Alice, for one, I assume? And Gemma and Ellie – they always come.'

'Mm.'

'What about Joanne who we used to take to Brownies? Are you still mates with her?'

'Not really.'

She took the plunge. 'And I expect you'd like your new friends to come, too? Rianna and Caitlin.'

But even this produced only another non-committal grunt.

'Come on, love, let's make a list. And then we can think about the food – whether you want party food like sausage rolls and crisps and cakes, or whether you'd rather have a proper sit-down meal, now that you're bigger.'

Beth's eyes were fixed on the television screen. Laura felt herself growing a little desperate. 'I could do you a really sophisticated birthday menu. Those chicken breasts with the creamy garlic filling, or something from the River Café. It could be like a grown-up dinner party.' Too much: she was trying too hard. 'I assume you're too old for party games, now, but what about music? Do you think your friends will want to dance?' *Did* they dance, at twelve, in the absence of boys? Should there, in fact, be boys? And why wasn't Beth saying anything?

When she did speak, it was flatly and without looking round. 'Nobody has parties.'

Just as, presumably, nobody has kippers. Perhaps ill-advisedly, Laura took the bait. 'Alice had a party in August. You went to that – and enjoyed it, I thought.'

Silence. Evidently, Alice was no argument against that 'nobody'.

'Well, what do people do instead? We don't have to have something here. It's too late to book the village hall for a disco, but you could invite a few friends and we'll go out to the cinema, or bowling, and out for a pizza. Or even to Peterborough, ice-skating. I could fit four of you in the car – you and three friends.'

Her daughter had picked up the TV remote and was fiddling with the battery cover, sliding it backwards and forwards. *Don't do that, you'll break it.*

'I just want to go into town.'

'Right. Great, then – we'll just go into Cambridge and do something there. So, what do you think – movie or bowling? Shall I see what's on at the multiplex? Or there's that new Laser Quest place – I think they'll do the meal afterwards, too, for birthday parties.'

With a theatrical moan, Beth flung herself lower on the settee.

'What?'

'Can you imagine? It'd be like having a kiddies' party in McDonald's or something. I bet they bring you balloons and the staff all sing Happy Birthday at your table. I'm not five, y'know, Mum.'

Laura felt her face heating. 'Adults go to Laser Quest. Some people from the department went in the summer, for a team-building day.'

Not the right line. Beth assumed an expression of pain.

'OK. So then, what? The cinema?'

'I just want to go round the shops. Just hang out.'

'That would be nice. We can spend your birthday money.' Simon always sent her a cheque. Fifty pounds, the same every year, and a hundred at Christmas. 'But we can do that as well, another time.' They always had a lovely afternoon of it, trying things on in Top Shop and sharing the earphones in the HMV music section.

'I thought I'd go with Rianna and Caitlin. And Willow.'

'Well, all right, if that's what you want. We can make the shopping trip your birthday treat. We'll go into town, or to the Grafton Centre, and have lunch out. And why don't we see a film as well, in the afternoon?'

45

Possibilities for the expedition began to suggest themselves. It might actually be rather fun: a girls' day out shopping. And they could all come back here for birthday cake afterwards, before she dropped them home.

'We can get the bus.' Beth was fidgeting with the remote again, turning it over and over in her hand. 'I meant just us. Shopping in town on our own, on the bus. Without you.'

Chapter 6

Willow clutched her breath tight within her chest and prepared to open her eyes. It was the next step she had promised herself to take: on the count of three she would open them.

One . . . two . . .

Maybe just a bit longer, though; she had come so far already, she deserved a little longer. The water slapped softly against her forehead so she knew she had ducked down far enough this time, that her eyes and nose and mouth were all under water. Without the motion, caused by other bathers, it would have been hard to tell; the water and the heavy, heated air were both blood-warm and equally oppressive. Her lungs burned; she imagined them shrunken, squashed flat by the water. Next time: next time she would open her eyes. But now she needed to breathe.

With a burst of released tension, she straightened her spine and broke the surface, opening her mouth to gasp in oxygen and shaking off water like a dog. Eyes still closed, she pressed her knuckles into the sockets, screwing away the wet; her nostrils felt blocked, and she dragged down a pinched finger and thumb, wringing the taste of chlorine from her nose and mouth.

Again. She reared up and filled her lungs to their fullest extent, taking in air through her mouth before closing it with a snap. This part she was good at, the holding of the breath; she had trained herself well. Then she plunged down, knees bent and neck curved forwards, immersing her head once more.

The strangest thing was what happened to sound. Above

the surface, the air was alive with the jagged shouts of children, amplified and bizarrely fractured by the moisture and the high, glass roof. But as soon as the water covered her ears, everything went dead; it was as if a switch had been flicked to cut the world off. It wasn't just that the noise was muffled or distorted or more distant than before; the sounds weren't merely different – it was as though they weren't sounds at all. Her eardrums seemed to experience them as compaction or movement rather than anything to be heard. Nor was it at all the same as putting your head under the bathwater. There was something about the pressure; she had the unnerving impression that the water was entering her head through her ears, that it was filling her skull, cutting off normal perception.

Nevertheless, she must take the next step forward: it was time to open her eyes. *One . . . two . . . three.*

At first no image registered at all but only the alien sensation of water against her eyeballs. It didn't sting, exactly, as she'd thought it might – all those chemicals and God knows what – but her eyes felt strange and invaded and sort of stretched. She wanted to blink the feeling away and couldn't: it was like having someone pull your eyelids back and not let go. But when she waited, the underwater world took shape, and it was bigger and brighter than she'd expected, wobble-edged but lit by arcs of broken light from above; she took in magnified squares of turquoise tile and snatches of legs, palely swollen, before her chest hurt and she had to come back up for air.

The pool was Saturday busy. She'd thrown away the leaflet Vince had given her: she wasn't ready for classes. All around her in the shallow end people chatted and bobbed and splashed and laughed, none of them paying her any attention. It was mainly mums with toddlers or groups of younger children of nine or ten. Anyone her own age was down the other end, ignoring the warning notices about bombing and diving, or else not in the pool at all but sitting on the edge in gaggles, preening and chatting, with their feet and ankles in the water.

Down again. This time she would open her eyes straight away and try to stay under longer, testing her lung capacity to its limit. She wanted to bob right down, but some weird reverse gravity pulled her back towards the surface. If she tucked her arms around her bended knees she might hold herself low in the water – but instead she found herself toppling forward, her feet leaving the floor so that she began to float and drift, upended and unanchored. In a flurry of panic she let go and splashed out into the air, her feet scrabbling for the tiles, arms flailing, shedding water in fat gobbets. A small boy of about eight glanced at her curiously for a moment, and then away again.

On the next immersion she lowered herself more cautiously, a few inches at a time, into a broad squat. Curiously, she examined the way the liquid made her own body foreign: the skin tinged oddly greenish, the lines of her thighs foreshortened and pulled out of shape. She could see quite well now, as her eyes adjusted to the unaccustomed medium: she saw the tiny bubbles of air still trapped in the fine hairs of her wrists, and the piping on the swimsuit she had borrowed from Beth, the logo leaping and dancing in the underwater currents. It must have been expensive – the kind you buy from a sports shop rather than the supermarket – and it wasn't her only one. Willow had chosen it in preference to the pink one when she'd brought them down to the pumphouse, as being the more businesslike. Two costumes meant Beth could have joined her, if she hadn't been going to her father's this weekend. But, on the whole, Willow was glad she hadn't had to ask her. The kid was all right, but she'd probably been swimming like a porpoise since the age of four; besides, her mother would probably have come as well, all watchful and overprotective. Vince would have been here if Willow had suggested it, even though Saturday was his day off. That might almost have been OK, except he was a man, after all, and they'd be nearly naked; she didn't want him looking at her in a swimsuit. Maybe another time she would bring Beth along. But for this – for now – she needed to be alone.

One more trip up for air and, instead of ducking down, she bent her knees and then launched herself blindly forwards with her head beneath the surface, arms outstretched like a parachutist in free fall. She wished she could have kept her eyes open for this, to witness it, to maximise the exhilaration. Some reflex shut them tight, however, so that as she surged through the water, feet lifting of their own accord to kick against nothing, the sensation of detachment was complete. For those brief moments she was nowhere; she was loosed from her earthbound self; she was free and adrift. It was terrifying and wonderful all at once.

I am swimming.

They were lucky compared with many divorced couples, reflected Laura, as she screwed the car by jerking degrees into the last available residents' parking space in Simon's street. Though perhaps it wasn't down to luck, or only partly so; they made the effort, for their daughter's sake, and what had begun as conscious endeavour seemed to have fallen at some point into amicable habit on both sides. Whatever the reasons for it, picking up Beth from a weekend at her father's house was no kind of hardship.

She leaned across to reach in the glove box for a pen and the strip of guest permits, filling in today's date in the next available box and propping it prominently inside the windscreen. Tessa helped matters, of course; outspoken, but warm and completely non-judgmental, Laura sometimes thought she would have been easier to be married to than Simon.

Climbing out and clicking the lock, she walked along the terraced row to the tall, Edwardian townhouse which Simon had bought with the equity they'd managed to release from Ninepins – something, besides Beth, to show for eight years of married life. Property in Cambridge was far from cheap, and most of Tessa's savings had been sunk into the purchase, too; the rest, she had no qualms about disclosing, was dwindling fast, being called upon at frequent intervals to bridge the gap between the mortgage and Simon's unreliable earnings. Simon, who used to be private about such things when he and Laura were together – even sharply defensive, at times – just shrugged helplessly and grinned along.

It was Simon who opened the door tonight, stepping back on to a pair of Fireman Sam wellingtons to let her into the hall. The mess was very much as usual: the coats heaped on the floor beneath the overladen hooks, the siding of plastic railtrack extending from the sitting room door. It was the silence that was a surprise.

'Are they out?'

'Thank the Lord.' He passed a hand across his brow in a gesture which, she suspected, was only partly theatrical. 'Come and have a drink, while we've got the chance.'

He took out two beers from the fridge; Laura, who would have preferred tea, took one with a sympathetic smile. At least he remembered to fetch her a glass; Tessa, she had no doubt, swigged hers straight from the bottle, as Simon now proceeded to do.

'Cheers,' he said, belatedly, as he lowered his bottle.

'Where have they gone? The park?' It was where they went at all hours and in all weathers, whenever sanity required them to vacate the house. Tessa would disappear for a moment, then burst back in with armfuls of small anoraks and scarves and mittens and bundle them all up and usher them out and along the road, swinging Roly on to her shoulders and uttering exhortations about football and fresh air.

'God knows. Probably. They took the dog.'

'They took the – ?' Laura sat down rather heavily on a kitchen chair.

'I know, I know. It was Tessa's idea – or rather it was Alfie's idea to start with, and he and Jack and Roly have been on about it every waking moment, until Tessa gave way.'

'But . . .' Laura looked round at the collected debris of the kitchen: the table strewn with colouring books and lidless felt-tip pens and half of someone's sandwich; the floor tiles sticky with nameless unwiped spillages – and, yes, she now saw, in the corner by the back door, the patch of spread newspapers and the bowl marked WOOF. Three sons under the age seven, a job which required Simon to attempt to work from home: were these not already enough?

'Dougie's very sweet.' He took another draught of beer and then eyed her entreatingly, looking so much like a puppy himself that she couldn't help but grin.

'Dougie? Was that Alfie's idea?'

'No – he brought the name with him, poor sod. He's a rescued dog, from the Blue Cross. Five years old, they said. Tessa thought it would be easier than having a puppy. With the house-training and so on.'

Her glance strayed back to the newspapers. 'And is it?'

Simon's bottle sketched a ragged arc. 'It's difficult for him. New place, new people. Doors in different places.'

'I can imagine.' The poor creature was probably deep in trauma, trying to find its feet in this chaotic household. 'What kind of dog is Dougie?'

'Hard to say, really. Small, greyish, alarmingly hairy. Some sort of terrier, I suppose.'

Well, at least he wasn't an Irish wolfhound. She wouldn't have put it past them.

'How about you?' He swept some Lego off the chair beside her and sat down. 'What have you been up to?'

'This weekend? I've been painting. Re-doing Beth's room.'

'A light green colour?'

'That's right. Apple something-or-other. Beth chose it. Did she tell you about it?'

'Actually, no. But there's a paint sample in your hair.'

When he grinned at her like that, she remembered why she'd loved him. But it was funny Beth hadn't mentioned their decorating plans.

'It's all been about this lodger of yours. Willow this and Willow that. She's talked about little else. In between Dougie, of course.'

'Oh?' Laura's stomach muscles fluttered.

'She seems really taken with her.'

He phrased it almost as a question, watching her face, so that she found herself dropping her eyes. 'Y-yes. I suppose she's younger than the grad students we've had before. Nearer Beth's age.'

'Seventeen, and twelve on Thursday?'

'They just seem to get on.' Laura tried to sound confident, casual. 'It's nice for Beth to have someone to talk to.'

'She's been in care. Is that right?'

'Yes. And?' Defiance seemed easiest: certainly easier than honesty. But he'd been married to her, after all.

'*Laura*. Are you really going to give me the big liberal lecture about prejudice and second chances? This isn't some story I'm writing for the Sunday colour supplements. We're talking about Beth.'

'Willow seems – ' she began, and then stopped. Why be defensive? Why not find out? 'What has Beth said?'

'That Willow was in a children's home. And that she set fire to a building.'

'An empty one. It was an empty garage.'

This time he didn't say anything, merely surveyed her steadily, until she sighed and relented.

'OK. What else has she said about her?'

Now it was Simon's turn to be evasive. The beer bottle rolled slowly back and forth between his palms. 'Oh, it's nothing, really. Just a silly thing.'

She leaned forwards. 'Go on.'

'They've been playing this game.'

'Who has? Beth and the boys?'

'Well, yes, she was showing them. But it's a thing she says she does with Willow. They've been holding their breath.'

53

Laura almost laughed. 'What do you mean? Just breathing in and counting?'

'More or less. Except that Beth can hold hers for a really long time. She can simply stop breathing, or so it seems. You should see her. It's a little bit alarming.'

'Right.' She frowned. 'And then she had the boys copying her, I suppose?'

'Naturally. Anything Beth does, Alfie has to do, as you know.'

'Oh, dear. I'm sorry.' Though quite why she was apologising, she wasn't sure. Beth was Simon's daughter, too.

'Tessa heard him coughing, up in his room last night after he was meant to be asleep. She went in and he'd made himself purple, trying not to breathe.'

'Oh, God.' She'd heard things about children who did this: children who held their breath in distress or stubborn resistance, until they went blue and passed out. But wasn't it usually toddlers? Alfie was six. 'And the little ones, Jack and Roly?'

'Oh, they were joining in, too, but they seemed less taken with it, thankfully.'

'Well, it sounds like . . .' What? Harmless experimentation? A normal thing for kids to try? Beth was only eleven.

'Beth says Willow has been coaching her. They've practised and practised, she says.'

Just a phase. Beth was only eleven. *But Willow was seventeen.*

'And it's what she says about why, as well – about why Willow likes to hold her breath. She told Beth that she taught herself when she was young. And she keeps insisting it's not a game, Beth says; she keeps insisting that it's important.'

Laura felt strangely conscious of her own breathing, of keeping it shallow and regular.

'She says Willow used to have to do it all the time when she was a kid. Apparently, she used to hold her breath when bad things were happening, to make them go away.' Simon pushed his beer aside and leaned towards her. 'What's she like, Laura? That's what I'm wondering. I mean, of course, I trust your judgment. I know you wouldn't let Beth hang out with someone you weren't certain was all right. But, well, she does sound rather odd.'

She groped for an answer that she could give him. 'Willow is . . . She's – '

With a crash, the front door slammed open against the hall wall, and the sound of feet and paws and high, chattering voices seized the house. First into the kitchen was Alfie, dragged on a red nylon lead by a small but determined-looking dog, which pulled him straight to its water bowl and began to slurp noisily. Then came Tessa with two-year-old Roly on her hip and finally Beth, hand in hand with an extremely muddy four-year-old.

'Jack fell over, Dad,' she said. 'In that bit by the pond where the ducks all stand and there's no grass left. He had Dougie's lead, and Dougie tried to chase the ducks, and Jack got pulled over. Tessa told him not to let go, and he didn't. He was really good not to let go, wasn't he? But now he's got mud and duck poo all over him.'

'Duck poo,' repeated Roly gleefully, as Tessa desposited him on a chair and began to prise off his wellingtons.

'Laundry room,' said Simon, with a cock of the thumb. 'Straight in there, please. Clothes off and in the machine.'

Beth obediently led away her charge while Simon rose to rescue Alfie's glove, which he had taken off and dropped and which was now in Dougie's mouth, being shaken like a rat.

'Dog towel,' said Tessa, pointing to a ragged cloth on the radiator. 'Would you mind?'

Not entirely sure whether she minded or not, Laura took it and grabbed for the terrier, rubbing rather ineffectually at his pads while he engaged in a fight to the death with the towel, growling furiously and twisting like an eel. It was a bit late, anyway: the grime of the kitchen floor was already criss-crossed with an overlay of dirty footmarks, human and canine. How could anyone live this way?

'Dougie ate my football,' announced Alfie. 'He was chasing it and he caught it and bit it and it went hiss and then it was all flat and soggy. Can I finish this sandwich, Mum?'

'No, you can't, sweetie,' said his mother, removing it from his reach and tipping it in the bin. 'I'll make you a fresh one in a minute.'

'I'll do it.' Beth had re-emerged from the laundry room, followed by a stripped but still grubby-looking Jack.

'Can I have one?' Jack climbed, still stark naked, on to the chair next to Alfie.

'Me, me,' added Roly.

'Go on, then, Beth. Thanks,' said Tessa. 'But I think the bread's still frozen.'

The boys, now flocked around the table like hungry gulls, appeared to Laura enormous. They had all inherited their father's large frame and broad jaw and brow; they all shared, already at this tender age, his tendency to jowliness. Tessa, by contrast, was five feet two and had always been slightly built; now, despite three pregnancies in quick succession, she seemed thinner than ever, as if somehow her sons were fattening parasitically at her expense.

'Can we have cheese?' asked Jack.

'Nutella,' said Alfie. 'We always have cheese. I want Nutella.'

'Why not both?' Simon swung a sliced loaf from freezer to microwave, still in its plastic bag. 'Cheese and chocolate. Might be really good.'

'Yes!' shouted all three boys at once. 'Cheese and chocolate!'

Beth laughed and went to the fridge, but not before casting an anxious eye at Laura. It would never be allowed at home. She didn't even ask if she could have one herself – though Laura would have let her, if she had.

'Don't give any to Dougie, though,' said Tessa, on her way

to the hall with the coats and boots. 'They mustn't have chocolate. Something to do with their livers.'

'Speaking of which,' said Simon, when she'd gone, 'how about another beer?'

'No, thanks. Really. I think when Beth has made the boys their sandwiches, we'd better be heading off.'

He nodded, and grinned at Beth, who pulled a face of cartoon misery. 'Oh, all *right*,' she said. 'But can Willow come for supper? Please, Mum. I need to tell her about Dougie.'

Chapter 7

Twelve was too old for strawberry milkshake mix. That's what Laura had decided when she crept into her kitchen late on Friday night, after Beth had gone to bed, to make her daughter's birthday cake. Beth had insisted on the same cake every year since she was seven or eight. A famous family recipe, hit upon at first more or less by accident but established thereafter as a fixture in the calendar for high days and holidays, it had strawberry Nesquik in the mixture and strawberry jam between the layers, topped off with butter icing made with more of the milkshake powder. But this year she knew it wouldn't do; the extravagant pink confection would have struck entirely the wrong note. For Beth's new friends, it had to be something different.

A rich chocolate torte is what she'd fixed upon, made with whole bars of real, dark chocolate, the kind with 72 per cent cocoa solids. It had whipped egg whites in it, too, and hardly any flour, and came out flat-topped and weighty-looking, the same deep colour as when it went in. She'd hidden it overnight in the back of the corner cupboard which, when she opened it just now, released the mingled, smoky scents of cardamon and roasted cacao. The cake was firm and dense and cool to the touch.

There was plenty of time to decorate it before they came back. Beth had left at eleven o'clock this morning, to call for Willow and walk to the bus-stop. Beneath her old, black duffle jacket she had put on the new birthday jumper: her extra, surprise present in addition to the new bike. Laura was pleased, because she hadn't been sure about it when Beth opened it, at breakfast on Thursday. They were in all the shops like that, with the Fair Isle pattern round the neck, but were the snowflakes too childish? And should she have gone for the one with a hood?

'It's great, Mum,' is all she'd said, and she hadn't tried it on, not straight away.

Laura had given her cash for Simon's birthday cheque, and she'd emptied her piggy bank, too – the old Eeyore one she still used to keep her pocket money in.

'I'm loaded! P'raps we'll get the train to London, and go clubbing. Back on Monday, all right?'

She was excited: sky-high and gliding. It was lovely to see her like that, even if it meant ignoring a pang. Swinging it over her shoulder as she headed for the door, Beth remembered to stop and say, 'I've borrowed your suede bag. Hope that's OK?'

Rianna and Caitlin were catching the same bus further along the route, at the corner of the road to Longfenton. The plan was for lunch out – a burger, or a jacket potato from the barrow on the corner of the market square – followed by shopping; then they were all coming back here when they were done. Four or four thirty, Beth had said, most likely. This meant there was plenty of time to whip cream and mascarpone together to pile on top of the cake, and stud it with the fresh raspberries she had bought – against all her usual principles, although it was mid-November. She had fetched the old party banner down from the loft, too: the one they'd made together for Beth's ninth and was now on its fourth outing, the cut-out cardboard letters of HAPPY BIRTHDAY beginning to curl a little, and the felt-pen colouring to fade. For once, they could use the dining room. She didn't know if the girls would stay and eat or if they'd want to be run home when they'd had a slice of cake. There were pizzas in the freezer she could rustle up quickly enough, plenty for all of them, or for just herself and Beth and Willow.

She wouldn't get the knives and forks out yet. Keep things casual, she told herself; play it by ear.

By four-fifteen she had the room arranged to her satisfaction: festive but not overdone. She switched on the small side lamps to add a final touch of cheer. Outside the window, dusk was beginning to gather. With nothing remaining to prepare, she unhooked her coat from the kitchen peg and went outside to watch the darkness fall. It was a favourite time for her, the winter twilight.

When she and Simon first came here – before the arguments, before Beth – they used to stand here side by side sometimes, neither speaking nor moving, and watch the sky slowly bleed from grey through mauve to black. There was so much sky at Ninepins. From here on top of the dyke, looking out across the lode, across the empty fields beyond, it seemed to dwarf the earth, vast and tall and toppling. On days like today, when cloud was sparse, it held a quiet luminosity which lingered even after the sun was gone; the lode and banks were lit by a soft, persistent glow which seemed to come from around and within as much as from above, outshadowing the orange smudge of Cambridge on the southern horizon.

On top of the willow tree, above the tree house roof, hunched a dark shape. A cormorant. They strayed this far sometimes, perhaps disorientated, winging in from the Wash across these tracts of land that should be water. No doubt it would roost here for the night.

Along the main road, between the sporadic flow of car headlamps, she saw by its brighter lights the approaching bus: high above the fields swayed the small oblong of illuminated windows, growing larger at each jolt and turn. It was too early, though. It didn't halt at the end of the drove but rolled on past towards Stretham and Ely. Feeling a sudden chill, Laura went back inside.

For an hour, an hour and a half, she turned her mind to forestry, and managed to make some useful notes for her article, though turning them into polished prose tonight was a demand too far. The kitchen clock crept round to six. The window, now, was a shiny blank, merely throwing back the light of the room; she rose to pull down the blind, casting her eyes as she did so in the direction of the road. The shops would have closed by five or five thirty; the girls must be here soon.

To stop herself from going outside again to wait in the cold and dark, she went to check the dining room, adjusting the clusters of balloons she had tied to either end of the curtain rail, counting again the twelve red candles which lined the perimeter of the chocolate torte. Maybe she should lay the matches out ready. It could only be in imagination that she heard the release of air, the hiss of a bus braking. Still, she found herself waiting and listening as she resumed her place at the kitchen table – five minutes, eight, ten – until it was too late for the sound of voices or the thud of the front door.

They'd been there again on Friday when she picked up Beth from school: she seemed always to be with them, now. Outside again, they were perched on the iron railings this time, in front of the main front doors, instead of inside in the warm. It was strange how different girls could look in the same school uniform. Rianna and Caitlin were slim-legged, the stretch black trousers hugging fashionable, longbow thighs; the collars of their polo shirts were turned up at exactly the desirable angle beneath their school fleeces. Even their regulation trainers ('plain black, no logo') were subtly chunkier than Beth's, the top tab undone and studiedly flicked back. Beside them Beth looked both too tidy and at the same time gawky, lumpen, aching Laura's heart; she looked like a kid.

At seven, she picked up the phone and called her daughter's mobile. Too bad, if her friends thought she was checking up on her; she was a mother and entitled to her concern. If the bus hadn't come, if it had broken down or been delayed, she could run into town in the car and pick them up. No reply;

after one ring it switched to automatic voicemail. *Where are you, love? It's getting late.* She hesitated just a second, then replaced the receiver without speaking.

For something to do, she put the kettle on; then, once she had her cup of tea she realised she was hungry, too, and cut herself a slice of bread and cheese. It was ridiculous to be anxious. Beth was with her friends; what could happen to four of them together? Her mouth, though, was dry of saliva; the bread felt lumpy in her throat. *Why was her daughter's phone switched off? She never switched it off.* But if there were a problem, she would have phoned, for sure. There were three other girls there, with three other mobiles. She took a swig of tea and swallowed.

If only Beth were with Alice, or her other old friends from the primary school – Joanne or Ellie or Gemma. People whose mums she knew; children she had known since they were four. It was doubtless perverse: they were just as un-streetwise as Beth. Rianna and Caitlin were probably far more resourceful: more use in a crisis, more aware of danger. But she couldn't help wishing for the old friends, anyway. They were such nice girls.

At twenty past seven and again at half past, she tried Beth's mobile, with the same result as before. At a quarter to eight she cleared a shelf and put the cake in the fridge. The Mascarpone was drying out and beginning to look crusty and tired. She should cover it, really, but it was difficult to see quite how, without taking the candles out again and having the cling film stick to the topping. They were with Willow, she reminded herself, and Willow was seventeen. An adult, or practically. The idea, which should have been a comfort, she found was nothing of the sort. How long ought she to wait before she rang someone? At eight, at nine, at ten? And actually, she realised with a cold clamping of the stomach, she had no idea whom to call. *Not the police. Not yet.* She had no number for Rianna's parents, nor Caitlin's – unless she could find them scribbled down somewhere among Beth's bits of paper. The plan had been to drop them home, and let them give her directions. Longfenton was all she knew – not even their addresses. Vince, was all she could think. Vince, who had left his number on the pad by the phone that first Saturday. He would know what to do.

It was just after nine thirty when the door opened. The kitchen door, that is; it was odd how, after straining her ears so long, she had not, in the end, heard the front door open and close. It was just Beth.

Where have you been? I've been worried sick.

'On your own?' she asked, rising and stepping forward, then stopping again. 'No Willow?'

'Oh, she didn't come with us, in the end. She went off. Shopping by herself, or something, she said.' Beth was casual, unconcerned.

'And the others?'

'They got off earlier, at the turning. Caitlin rang her mum to come and pick them up.' She peeled off her duffle jacket and hoisted it over a peg. Underneath, she wore just a T shirt; one sleeve of the Fair Isle jumper trailed from Laura's suede bag.

'I thought you were coming home for supper.' Her voice came out a little too high. 'I've been calling you.'

Beth turned round from the coat pegs, her face showing the first mild trace of consciousness.

'Yeah, sorry. The battery was dead. I forgot to charge it last night.'

'So, where did you go?' Again, the tight, raised note, like somebody else's voice.

'Gonzalo's. Dad's money was enough for us all to get enchiladas, and then an ice-cream. I had a hot fudge sundae.'

Stay calm; don't get upset. It would do no good to give in to the anger that was welling up now to replace her fear. Beth's stolen evening could hardly have been more innocent, after all – having an ice-cream sundae to celebrate her birthday. It was only a quarter to ten: not too late to salvage something of a celebration. The safety lecture could wait for the morning.

'Think I'll go and have a bath, Mum, if that's OK. I'm totally wrecked. Can I have some of your coconut bubbles?'

When she was gone, Laura took the cake back out of the fridge, and found two plates. Maybe the dining room was a bit much for just the pair of them, but Beth could still blow out her candles and make a birthday wish. Perhaps she'd like a mug of hot chocolate before bed, too, if she wasn't too full up of hot fudge sauce. And there might be time for Laura to see the things she'd bought: a late-night fashion parade.

After twenty minutes, she heard the gurgle in the downpipe as the bath water drained away. Ten minutes more, and she headed upstairs, calling softly on the landing, 'Beth?'

All was silent; a haze of slowly-dispersing steam hung damply around the open bathroom door. The door to her daughter's bedroom was closed and no light showed in the crack underneath. A gentle knock and she turned the handle and pushed the door wide, flooding a segment of the room with half-light from the landing. The bed lay in the portion still in darkness. Beside it in a careless arc were flung the clothes which Beth had been wearing, the jeans with legs akimbo, T shirt bunched and inside out. And, under a hillock of duvet, clutched tight at the chin and folded close round jack-knifed legs, her daughter lay fast asleep.

Laura closed the door softly and padded back downstairs. She pulled out a chair and sat down at the kitchen table. The hands of the clock showed twenty past ten. She should have a bath herself, too, and get to bed, if only she could summon the energy. Instead, she folded her arms and slid forward, elbows on the table, until her forehead rested on her wrists. The first shudder surprised her, catching her like a kick beneath the ribs; it was followed by another, and then another, until she was sobbing like a child.

Down in the pumphouse, Willow sat on the bed and closed her eyes. Except that she wasn't in the pumphouse. She wasn't at Ninepins and she wasn't seventeen.

She was eight years old, and letting herself into a silent house. It wasn't even her own house. It was somebody else's – as it always seemed to be, around that time. This one belonged to Ayodele. Willow liked Ayodele; she wore a many-stringed necklace of tiny speckled shells and smelt sweet and musty like honeycomb, and sometimes she came and met Willow from school. But not today.

Willow's mother loved Ayodele, too – just as she loved all the people whose houses they passed through, immoderately, with a promiscuous passion. She spun her round in the kitchen with extravagant vows of devotion; she threaded sticks of dry spaghetti in her springy, black hair like flowers, laughing and laughing, while on the hob the pan of water boiled over.

The house was dark and narrow, a terrace in a dark, narrow street of terraces the same. It was a side-street off a main road. She remembered that it blew with litter: not just sweet wrappers and the odd tin can but big sheets of paper which clung around your ankles in the wind, and whole broken cartons from the backs of the shops on the main road, and the stripped outer leaves of cabbages, as big as faces. If it were in Cambridge, she couldn't place, now, the main road or the shops, which smelt sour with spices; there were often fruits and vegetables she didn't recognise among the detritus. More likely, it was Peterborough or Norwich, or even London.

It must have been winter, because there were lights already on in front windows along the street, though it couldn't have been long after three o'clock. If it was cold, she didn't recall. Wet, though: it had been raining recently, filling the air with the smell of stirred drainwater. When she reached the house, there were no lights showing. Number 19, with its green front door, the paint peeling off in streaks. She had to use her key: the one Ayodele had given her, attached by a metal ring to a little wooden giraffe. The ring went through the giraffe's feet, so that it always seemed to her to be suspended upside down.

In the gloomy hallway, she stumbled over piles of shoes before she found the light switch. With the light on, the silence seemed to intensify, its edges hard and sharp, intimidating her out of calling her hello. Ignoring the deserted kitchen and living room, she mounted the stairs, slowly, one step at a time: first the left foot, then the right. Only twelve steps; far too soon she reached the bedroom door.

There she drew a deep breath and pinched her nose. *Thirteen, fourteen* . . . Let her be out. Let her have gone to the shops with Ayodele to buy food for tea. *Twenty-six, twenty-seven.* Let them come back in, laughing and banging the door, and swing heavy carrier bags on to the kitchen table. Let Mum click on the radio and sing along like she's Madonna. *Forty-nine, fifty.* Let Ayodele make one of her special curries, with fat aubergines and sweet potatoes and those skinny green chillis, the kind she gave one of to Willow once to bite on, as a joke, so that she had to stand for ten minutes with her tongue under the cold tap, hopping from foot to foot. *Seventy-one, seventy-two.* Let her mother look up, and let her eyes be shining with fun, and let her hold out her arms. *Ninety-four, ninety-five.* Don't let her be here by herself in the dark. Don't let her be in bed.

She held her breath as she turned the door handle, held it as she pushed it open. *A hundred and eight, a hundred and nine.*

The curtains were drawn shut and the room was in darkness. Stepping forward, Willow's feet met a soft obstruction: discarded clothing, perhaps, or bedding thrown to the floor. She stood still and waited for her eyes to adjust. *A hundred and twenty.* In the bed, half under the blankets, the figure was turned towards her and not to the wall. Hope rising, she took another step. *A hundred and twenty-one.* Please let her eyes be open.

They were open. But they didn't flicker, just stared at her dully, without recognition. Willow turned on her heel and fled from the room, slamming the door behind her. On the landing she stopped, closed her eyes tight and drew her arms across her chest. Let Ayodele come home; let her mother come down. Let her be back to how she was a week ago, two weeks; let her come back.

She drew back her shoulders and filled her lungs again. *One, two, three . . .*

Chapter 8

The Saturday of the birthday outing was the last fine day for a fortnight. On the Sunday morning, clouds rolled in from the north and west, stacking fold upon fold above the house, each new layer more ominous than the last, in shades of pewter grey. By noon, the individual shapes and colours had disappeared and the cloud banks had lowered and merged until the sky was one dark, uniform mass. As the air outside grew heavy with unshed moisture, so, indoors, Laura watched her daughter's breath shorten.

The Cambridgeshire fens were the worst place in the world for an asthmatic child. Beth should have lived in Italy, in air that was dry and filled with sunlight – or even just fifty miles east, on the sandy coastal heaths of Suffolk, where rainfall was low and the wind held the snap of ozone. But the research grants were not in Suffolk or Italy. Here the damp was a constant factor. It hung on the breeze like smoke; it seeped under doors and soaked through clothing; it trickled invisibly underground and gathered to run in the lodes and drains and ditches, and rose as mist from the wet, black, chocolate-fudge soil. And with the rising water in the earth, as it seemed to Laura, rose also the fluid in Beth's lungs, narrowing her airways to a needle's width and leaving her fighting to breathe.

There was no attack that Sunday night, though Beth slept only fitfully, propped close to vertical on a stack of pillows, while Laura lay sleepless in her own bed, hearing – or imagining she heard – each wheezing inhalation through two open doors and across the short stretch of landing.

She was well enough to go to school, though with a note about sitting out PE. It pained Laura to see how the short walk from the car to the double swing doors left her daughter gasping, head reared back to open her throat and snatch at the air.

It rained again every day that week, if not solidly then at least for prolonged spells. By Friday, the level in Elswell Lode was as high as it had been since the early spring; by Monday, it was higher than at any point last winter, or indeed the winter before. Beth's chest remained tight and her breathing laboured. She moved everywhere at a snail's pace, grasping at furniture and door frames like an old woman. At break times, at school, she stayed in the classroom.

'It's all right. Rianna and Caitlin stay in with me. They're allowed. Mr Burdett said.'

Laura watched each breath with a practised eye, and waited. At the moment, it was manageable. Beth's first sharp suck on her inhaler drew in through the clogged bronchea just enough salbutamol to make a difference. If she could avoid a coughing fit from the effort of pulling in the first dose, then a minute's careful breathing brought marked relief; her tube walls released their stranglehold sufficiently to increase the flow of oxygen, and hence to allow absorption of the second puff of drug.

Wednesday brought a slight alleviation. The rain held off, replaced by a soft, pervasive mist which blanketed the house and dykes and wreathed each tree and telegraph pole, filming everything it touched with fine, clear droplets. Beth's lungs seemed to relax a little. She ate a better supper, with breath to spare at last for chewing and swallowing; she was coughing less and passed an easier night. Laura breathed more easily herself. It seemed they had turned the corner.

The respite, however, proved only temporary. On Thursday the clouds piled high again and on Friday morning as they left the house, the bloated sky was releasing a steady downpour. The phone call came at lunchtime, just as Laura was peering from her office window and wondering how wet she would get on a dash to the sandwich shop. It was Mrs Warhurst, the receptionist at the village college.

'Mrs Blackwood? I've got Beth here with me.'

'What's she forgotten?' At primary school, she'd always been running back over with something: packed lunch, PE socks, recorder book. But even as she joked, Laura's pulse quickened. It was what she'd been expecting. The crisis had come.

'She's very poorly. We think she ought to go to the doctor's.'

'Right. Yes.' Phone in one hand, she was already gathering up raincoat and car keys in the other as she said, 'Tell her I'll be straight there.'

She was lucky with the traffic, which was light for the lunch hour, and in less than twenty minutes she was striding into the reception area and over to her daughter, where she sat by the wall on a solitary stacking chair.

'It's all right, now,' she told her – although it quite obviously wasn't. Gone was this morning's loose, musical wheeze. Beth's breathing, in fact, was now silent for the first time in over a week: silent and almost completely ineffectual. Her chest rose and fell jerkily, accompanied at each inhalation by an involuntary hunch of the shoulders and the appearance of alarming hollows at either side of the base of her neck, just above her collar bone. But, evidently, little air was getting through. Dark smudges flowered beneath her eyes; her lips were open, stretched and blue.

Laura stood up and looked rapidly around.

'Hi!' she called to a passing staff member whom she didn't recognise. 'Excuse me. Could you help us, please?'

With an arm apiece they half-hoisted Beth through the rain to the waiting car, where she slumped in the passenger seat like a lifeless thing.

The doctor's surgery was no distance, just along the village high street, and Laura bumped up illegally on the pavement outside. The surgery staff knew Beth well. The practice nurse was summoned and soon had her in a consulting room, face mask on and plugged into the whirring compresser. Laura stood by and filled her own lungs with draughts of calming air. As the drug began to filter through, the colour seeped back into her daughter's face. Her chest moved in and out more smoothly. The sucked-in hollows at her neck grew less pronounced with each successive breath, and her eyes, which had held that intense, strained, inward-focused look, now sought Laura's. There was no panic in them, only exhaustion.

'Back in a minute,' Laura told Beth, when the chamber of liquid was half empty. 'I've just got to move the car.' At the door she turned back and forced a grin. 'Don't run away, will you?'

After the treatment they sat for a while on the waiting room chairs, Beth leaning up against her mother's shoulder, until she could have the once over from Dr Harrington.

'Her air flow seems to have stabilised now. I think we've caught her in time. But you'll need to watch her closely for the next twenty-four hours. Use her peak flow meter. If it drops below ninety, give us a call and someone will come out with the nebuliser. I think it's Dr Taub on call tonight.'

She'd found a space in the car park not far from the back door, but the walk was still an arduous one. The rain was lashing down; Laura draped her own coat over Beth's head and shoulders as she bundled her across the tarmac. She wanted to swaddle her round and scoop her close, and never let her out of her sight.

Home. An asthma attack and an afternoon off school gave not just Beth but Laura too the dispensation for idleness. She shelved the work she should have done today in favour of children's television. Beth was too weak to do more than sniff at the soup that Laura heated for her, but she nursed the mug and inhaled the steam. Air was the only sustenance she wanted.

After that, she dozed for a while on the settee cushions and at nine Laura helped her up to bed. They took it slowly, but the struggle from her clothes and into pyjamas left her gasping, open-mouthed. Laura fetched every pillow in the house and built a padded cave round the head of the bed. Beth crawled in and lay upright, her head tilted sideways.

'Don't go.'

Laura stopped, her hand on the door handle, and turned back.

'Stay with me. I don't want to go to sleep.'

It was the first whole sentence she had spoken since Laura's arrival at the school. The effort of it took too much breath; it had her in a spasm of coughing, and Laura back at her side, stroking her hand in useless soothing.

'Of course I'll stay, sweetheart, if you want me to. I can stay all night, if you like.'

Beth gave a short nod, satisfied, and shut her eyes.

'Don't want to sleep.'

She was regulating it better now, taking a small extra breath and releasing the words in a quick, staccato burst. Laura waited.

'Dream.' Breathe. 'Don't want the dream.'

'What dream, love?'

'Always the same.' Breathe. 'Drowning.'

Oh, God. Laura squeezed her daughter's hand, where it lay limp on the bedclothes.

'Ditch. I'm in a ditch. Lying down. Head under water.' She took a longer rest and Laura wondered whether this was it, whether she should respond, or whether there was more to come.

'Can't breathe. Stupid. It's only shallow. Should sit up. Just can't.' Another pause; more spacing breaths. 'Drowning.'

A tear had formed itself at the corner of one of Beth's closed lids.

'Don't cry, love. Please don't cry.' It wasn't a mother's empty comfort; Laura had always believed in letting her daughter cry. But now, in this condition, it would be disastrous. The extra fluid in her nose and sinuses, the tightening of the throat. She really mustn't cry.

'You won't drown.' Casting around for what to say, she found as she said it that she knew the answer. 'Don't fight it. Don't try to sit up, just lie still and relax. You won't drown in the water – the water is safe. Relax, and you'll find you can breathe the water.'

Beth snorted, swallowed, then opened her eyes. They swam with liquid, but it no longer threatened to fall.

'Talk to me.'

Laura smiled. 'What shall I tell you? Or should I read you a book?'

'Dad and the tree house.' Breathe. 'Tell me that.'

It was an old family story. Beth had demanded she recite it at bedtime almost every night, those summers when she was seven, eight, and lived in the tree house from dawn to dusk. She hadn't mentioned it in years.

'It was when I was pregnant,' began Laura. 'Expecting you. I was still at work, the last week before my maternity leave was due to begin. There was one day when we had a conference on, and I was helping organise. It meant I'd left the house early, before seven, and wasn't home before nine o'clock at night. I never looked in the garden when I came in. I didn't even glance that way – why would I? I was tired, I'd been rushing round all day.'

Beth's lids had closed again, but she was nodding, eased.

'When I got inside, Dad was there to greet me in the kitchen with a cup of peppermint tea – I had a passion for it when I was pregnant – and he was acting all excited and mysterious. "Come outside," he kept saying, and I didn't know what he was on about. I just wanted to sit down with my feet up and drink my peppermint tea. But he wouldn't let me. He practically dragged me up and out again, and along the top of the dyke. It was pitch black out there. You were due very soon, so it must have been November. I thought your dad had gone crazy.' And she'd told him so, in no uncertain terms, as she recalled. 'I didn't know what it was at first: just this great, dark bulk in the tree. It looked really peculiar. But then he stood behind me, and put his chin on my shoulder, looking where I was looking and nodding at it. "It's a tree house," he said. "For our baby." '

For me, Beth used to repeat, when she was small. *He built it for me.*

'There were so many other things needing doing, in the house.' This part of the story she'd never told before. But Beth was twelve now – and more than half asleep. 'I wanted him to paint the nursery – your bedroom, I mean. And the garden gate was off its hinges. It was a struggle to get through, even without a buggy. But, no: he decided you needed a tree house.'

'A boy.'

Laura started; she had thought Beth asleep.

'Dad. D'you think he – ' breathe ' – wanted a boy?'

'He adored you. Adores you. He was so delighted when you came.' If Beth could only have seen him, seen them both; if she could remember those first few golden weeks. 'He was like a little kid on Christmas morning.'

'Alfie,' said Beth. 'Jack. Roly.' Her eyes were still shut, her breathing steady and even. 'He hasn't. Built one. For them.'

Soon afterwards, she slept. The battle to stay awake had worn her out, and she slipped back under the water. Once asleep, her breathing was easier; Laura watched it slow and grow shallower, the struggle for oxygen reduced now her body was in repose. Laura rose, but she wouldn't go back to her own bed tonight. Watch her closely, Dr Harrington had said, and she took him at his word. She went to fetch her own duvet.

In the silence which settled on the room, her daughter's slender breaths measured out a lullaby. Huddled by the radiator with the duvet tucked under her chin, she heard it sigh to a soft, insistent drumbeat: the rain on the slates of the roof. Only now, in the quiet, was she conscious of it but, as soon as it registered, she knew it had been there all along. All day and all evening: non-stop rain. The level in the lode must be dangerously high. She didn't recollect noticing it when they came in; she'd been intent on getting Beth inside. Beth's window faced the other way, out over the garden to the rear. Even in daylight she would see nothing there but the water-logged lawn. So instead of looking out she lay back on Beth's beanbag and listened. The sound was oddly soothing: the regular patter of the rain itself and the heavier, drizzling chute of run-off from the eaves. It lulled her, until she could no longer distinguish the rain, or her daughter's breathing, or her own.

Sleep claimed her, and she dreamed her daughter's dream of rising water. It was she, now, beneath the surface of the ditch; she who let herself be gathered into the arms of the flood.

Pale grey daylight wakened her, slanting across her closed lids. She had gone to sleep without drawing the curtains. The first focus of her sluggish mind was the sound of Beth's breathing. Shallow – she must be still asleep – but looser and with a throaty rattle, which was a definite good sign. The next thing she noticed was the silence beyond the room. The rain had finally stopped.

She dragged apart her eyelids, wincing at the smart of morning. It must be early yet since the light was muted and had an opalescent quality. Where it fell on the paintwork to the side of the window it shimmered and shifted and swam in a way which caused Laura a pinch of unease. Something was different; something wasn't right.

Still with the duvet drawn round over yesterday's clothes, she stood and moved to the window. Even then, realisation was not immediate. The sun was barely up so that, although the clouds had finally lifted and parted, the gleam they let in was weak and watery; the garden for the most part still lay deep in shadow. The pumphouse was a featureless bulk, only its chimney sharply outlined against the dawn sky; the lawn was a dark blank. But as her eyes adjusted she knew that something was wrong. The relationships of shape and height were all awry. The pumphouse was too low, too squat; the trees and bushes appeared foreshortened, the earth too high. As she continued to stare at the lawn, the matt black of sodden turf took on a different character: glassy, insolid. Her stomach lurched. Where she should be seeing grass, there was nothing but water.

Willow. With a glance to check Beth's breathing, and careful not to wake her, she slipped from the room and ran downstairs to the kitchen, grabbing her fleece and raincoat and wellingtons.

The water of the lode was black and angry but its swirling surface lay six inches below the top of the dyke. If it had come over the top last night, the way it had in 1947, then the levels must since have subsided with the abeyance of the rain. More likely, the electric pumps at the station on the main road had failed to cope with the quantities of water that had fallen, which had either forced its way back through the old pipework of the pumphouse, or simply risen up from saturated soil which could no longer absorb its volume.

From the top of the concrete steps she squinted down, counting those still visible above the flood. Sixteen. How many more steps there should be, she wasn't certain. Three, four? If so, that meant the water was maybe two feet deep – not too deep to negotiate on foot. The sky was lightening all the time, and she could see her way clearly, and see, too, the extent of the flooding, which stretched out beyond the hollow of her garden and across the field beyond, a silver-black parody of solid ground.

She had underestimated, but not enormously so. The water, when she edged her way down from the final submerged step, swept over the top of her boots and flooded her feet in icy liquid; it rose above her knees and up to the middle of her thighs, drenching her jeans and leaving her breathless with the shock of cold. Grey-brown and almost completely opaque, it swallowed her legs from sight. Its smell was not vegetable as she would have expected but faintly mineral, like rust. She took another step forward and almost fell. Balance was difficult even with arms outstretched. As she moved, the rubber of her wellingtons billowed against her shins, heavy with trapped water; she would have been better in trainers. Another step, feeling for the contours of the invisible turf. It would have been easier, she decided, if the water were deeper, if it were up to her waist; that way it would have held her weight, like walking in the shallow end of a swimming pool – except immeasurably colder.

It was perhaps fifteen yards to the pumphouse – little more than the width of a pool – but progress was painfully slow. Half way, she wondered whether, instead, she should have walked further along the dyke and tried to slither down to it that way. The old brick building lay in a slight depression, so that over the final few yards her footing fell away treacherously under the concealing tide. Twice, again, she almost slipped over. By the time she reached the door she was waist-deep in the flood. She tried the latch. It wouldn't budge; it must be either locked from the inside, or else jammed: swollen and distorted by the soak of water.

'Willow?' she called, pounding with her fist against the upper portion of the wood. 'Are you all right in there? Willow!'

Silence.

Turning cautiously, she edged her way round to the far side of the building, hugging the brickwork with the palm of one hand. The only window to this side was rectangular and small, no more than two feet by eighteen inches. In order to see in, she had to hoist herself half up out of the water by clinging on to the narrow ledge: a precarious operation. The catch was loose, the window resting closed by only its own weight. When she pulled herself up, she saw in clearly, or as clearly as the early morning light allowed. The inside of the pumphouse was awash, as deep in water as the garden outside. The bed was submerged. A chair lay drunkenly sideways in the wash, half grounded and half afloat. The water was thick with flotsam: clothing and magazines and shoes. But of Willow there was no sign.

Letting herself back down as slowly as she could and managing to keep her footing, Laura turned and looked about her. Up to this point she had acted without much of a conscious plan; her one thought had been to get to the pumphouse, to get to Willow. It made no sense for the place to be empty. She was suddenly quite at a loss.

Fetch help? Set up a search? Get back, first, to check on Beth, then call the emergency services. And say . . . what? That her lodger was AWOL, missing in the flood?

The door was stuck solid. Willow must have climbed out of the window to escape the rising tide. She must be somewhere safe, somewhere dry. Somewhere on higher ground. She must be, because the alternative was unthinkable. *That she was somewhere beneath the sucking blanket of wet.*

The cold was beginning to permeate now, soaking right through, it seemed, to her bones. Her hands, she saw with detachment, were shaking convulsively. Her shinbones ached dully and she wasn't certain she could feel her feet at all. And was it imagined, or was the level higher now than when she entered the flood?

Some place higher, some place out of the water.

'Willow!' Her voice surprised her with its loudness but it failed to carry, damping quickly to nothing in the heavy air.

She scanned the top of the dyke, looking for the shape that hadn't been there before, the shape she knew couldn't possibly be there now. As her eye ran along it reached a different shape, and her heart missed a beat. The tree house.

Forcing her way through the few yards of water in the shortest time, she half stumbled, half threw herself against the ladder. *Be here, be here, be here,* drummed her own voice silently in her head; but the mantra was more to soothe her numbness of body than any real anxiety of mind. Somehow, she already knew.

She mounted the ladder, freeing her legs from the pull of the water, and soon her head emerged into the interior of the tree house. There, sitting in one corner of the bare planked floor, was Willow. With hands clasped tight round upraised knees and elbows out at angles, she seemed to be all bones.

'Hi,' said Laura gently. 'You had me scared half to death. Are you OK?'

Willow raised her face, which was streaked with runnels of dirt from what could have been rain or floodwater or tears. Her eyes were blankly dark, focused inwards the way Beth's had been during the asthma attack.

'You must be freezing.' Laura pulled herself up to sit on the rim of the tree house floor; she peeled off her raincoat to pass around the girl, who sat unmoving and quite silent.

'What's that?' she asked, for now that she was closer she saw that Willow was clasping something between her chest and knees. 'You managed to rescue a few things, then?'

With a slow collapse of the shoulders, Willow let out the breath she had been holding; her grip slackened slightly on the object she held. Laura could make it out now: blue, rectangular and cardboard. It was a shoebox with a fitted lid.

'Come on,' she said. 'We need to get you indoors into a hot bath. I could do with one myself, as well.' She moved back to the ladder and stepped down a few treads, then reached to lend an arm to Willow. 'Looks like you'll be moving into the spare room.'

Chapter 9

The following Saturday, Vince came over for lunch again. This time it wasn't unpacking he was helping with but salvage operations. Apart from one further expedition into the flood on that first day to save what they could of value and importance, they had not ventured down to the pumphouse again for almost a week. The water had taken an age to subside. For a day or so, although the rain had ceased, the flood continued to rise, and even when it began at last to ebb away, it did so with inexorable slowness. And it left behind wherever it had been a fine coating of silt, filthy black and stinking of ditches.

Beth's breathing had gradually trickled back to normal. She'd spent the weekend propped up in bed, or else installed in state upon the settee with Laura in hovering attendance. Willow had come through her own adventure apparently unscathed, but it entitled her to a blanket, too, and to keep Beth company watching daytime TV. After the one treatment, Beth didn't need the nebuliser again; with just her inhaler and a high-dose course of oral steroids, she seemed to have turned the corner. By Sunday afternoon she could make the walk to the sitting room window to gaze at the flooded garden without taking more than one rest. On Monday, Laura went in to work for half a day, and left the two of them together. On Wednesday Beth went back to school.

She still wasn't fit enough for lifting and carrying, but Laura allowed her down to the pumphouse to help retrieve and sift. All afternoon, or so it seemed, Vince and Willow had been hauling furniture and bedding up to the house, and black dustbin bags full of Willow's things, with Beth under strict instructions only to watch. Up at the house, Laura was on washing duty. The washing machine and dryer had been running constantly. Even on the hottest wash and with double the usual quantity of fabric softener, the clothes came out still reeking; she put them all through twice. By four o'clock, when dusk brought down a halt upon the work, the pumphouse was declared cleared. All round the house, every rack and radiator was draped with drying clothes and sheets and pillows, or propped with books, splay-paged. An odour of cloying damp pervaded the air. It couldn't be doing Beth's asthma any good at all.

As darkness fell beyond the windows, the recovery party, after a thorough wash and scrub up, gathered round the kitchen table for a mug of tea.

'Is there much that can't be rescued?' asked Laura, as she placed their drinks before them and sat down.

'A fair bit.' It was Vince who answered, with a glance at Willow. 'We've bagged up five or six bin liners down there of stuff that's for the tip.'

'Some of it's disgusting,' said Beth, with pleasurable satisfaction. 'Just totally slimy and stinky and revolting. Seriously, you should see it. You should *smell* it.'

Laura grinned and wrinkled her nose. 'I rather think I still can.

'God, yes. Sorry about that,' said Vince, raising one sleeve to his nose. 'I think we're all going to need a good shower.'

'It's oozing out of the bottom of the bin bags,' continued Beth. 'They're all squidgy underneath when you lift them up.'

'I hope you haven't been lifting them,' said Laura quickly.

' 'Course I haven't!'

'Has she?' She looked at Vince, who smiled at Beth.

' 'Course she hasn't.'

'It's going to make a horrible mess in the car, Mum. Those slimy bags.'

'Don't worry.' Vince waved a hand. 'I'll do it. I can stick

81

it all in the boot when I go, and take it to the tip in the morning.'

'Oh, no. Really, I can easily – '

'My car's filthy already. You've seen it – old rustbucket. And the inside's even worse. A bit more mud will scarcely make a difference.'

With a nod, Laura capitulated. Then she turned to Willow. 'You must make me a list. For the insurance. A list of all the things you've lost or that are damaged and need replacing. It should be covered on the contents insurance – I've checked, and they seemed to think it was.'

Willow's nose was buried in her mug. 'None of it's worth anything.'

'What about your stereo?' said Vince gently. 'And the CDs?'

'She had *loads* of CDs, Mum. At least thirty.'

'And I thought you'd lost your mobile, too?' added Laura.

'Oh, she found that,' said Beth. 'It was in the pocket of this pair of jeans, under the bed, but they were all wrecked and the phone was wrecked, too, even after Vince wiped it clean. Totally knackered.'

'Clothes, too.' Laura was looking at Willow. 'And shoes. We can claim for all of it, if you just make me a list.'

She didn't raise her eyes. 'It was only old stuff.'

'But it still costs money to replace, doesn't it? You'll need new things.' Willow had been wearing one hoody and one pair of jeans for a week; Beth had lent her a T shirt, and goodness knows what she was doing for underwear.

'What about your box?' Beth indicated the shelf at the back of the Rayburn, where the blue cardboard shoebox had been slowly desiccating since it came down, with Willow, from the tree house. 'Is it dry now, d'you think? What's in there, anyway?'

Laura looked at Willow and hoped her curiosity didn't show too much. She'd passed the box fifty times and resisted the temptation to lift the lid.

'Oh, nothing much. Just some old photos and things.'

Beth stared at her. 'Of before, you mean – when you were little?'

The dismissive shrug did not deter her.

'Have you got pictures of your mum in there? Can I see?'

'*Beth!*'

' 'S'OK,' said Willow. 'Show you later, if you want.'

There was a short pause. Then Vince, who had been leaning back in his chair, sat forward and faced Willow. 'I wish you'd let me make you a life story book. We could do it together.'

The girl's eyes slanted away; it was clearly a discussion they'd had before.

'I'm not a child. I'm not some five-year-old you're preparing for adoption.'

'It would still be – '

'It's my life, Vince.' Her eyes rose, green and sharp. 'I've lived it, remember? I'm still bloody living it. I don't need it sticking in some book.'

In the awkward silence which followed, Laura rose to refill the kettle in case anyone wanted a top-up. *But still*, she thought, *it was the shoebox you chose to save from the flood.*

Presently, Beth headed off upstairs, announcing her intention of having a bath.

'Can you wash my jumper, please, Mum, if I stick it in the basket? It stinks like toilets, and fish, and old cabbage.'

When she'd gone, Laura found a torch and they went down into the dark garden to load the rubbish into Vince's car. As Beth had warned, foul black liquid had soaked its way to the bottoms of the bags, which left a glittering trail when moved, like some kind of monstrous slugs. Laura brought old newspapers to line the car boot, but they were quickly sodden.

'It's going to leave an interesting smell,' said Vince, as he banged the boot shut. 'When I have clients in here, they're going to think I have issues with personal hygiene.'

83

Another cup of tea, and Vince had twice said he ought to think about getting on the road, when Beth came back down. Laura had expected her dressing gown, at least over her clothes. All week, she'd been treating her convalescence as an excuse to wear it at any hour: after school, before supper. But she was fully dressed in her favourite skirt, and even wearing tights.

'Hello, love. You look nice. Good to feel clean again?'

'Mm.' Her eyes were fixed on her feet. But she always did hate compliments, especially public ones.

'Very chic,' said Vince, making it worse.

'What do you fancy for supper? Willow, I assume you're staying for supper? And Vince, are you sure we can't persuade you?'

He smiled and shook his head. 'Stop tempting me. It's much too comfortable here. At this rate it'll be me moving into your spare room next.'

'Chilli,' she suggested. 'That will warm us all up. I've got some mince I can defrost.'

'Devil,' said Vince. 'Begone with your wicked lures.'

'Why don't you help me, Beth? And Willow, too, if you like? Beth is a dab hand at chilli.'

'I'm not really hungry.'

Laura frowned. Her daughter's voice still sounded scratchy; using the inhaler frequently over a prolonged period always left her throat strafed and sore.

'Are you feeling all right, sweetheart? Maybe you ought to go and have a sit down in the sitting room, while I cook?' She hoped Beth hadn't overdone it today. Her face was pale, even after the hot water. But, oddly, it looked as if she had put on mascara. And some of her raspberry lip gloss.

'No. It's all right. I'm going out.'

She said it with perfectly rehearsed casualness; the effect was weakened only by her gaze fixing not on Laura but on the wall somewhere behind her right shoulder.

'You're doing what?' Laura, conscious of playing a part in

turn, wished her voice hadn't risen at the end on that shrill tone.

'Going out, if that's OK.'

So many objections crowded into Laura's head; she focused upon the most immediate. 'Without anything to eat?'

'There isn't time. I'm meeting Caitlin and Rianna at seven, and I've got to get the bus. There's a party at this boy's house in Longfenton. There'll probably be something there, crisps and stuff, if I'm hungry.'

So many questions, too. 'What boy?'

'Oh, just a boy in Year 9. He's called Joe, I think.'

'Joe, you *think*.' The shrill note again. 'And do you even have his address?'

'Rianna does.'

'Oh, great. So, Rianna will know where you are. But I won't.'

'I'll take my mobile. I recharged it.'

'And are you invited to this party? Does Joe's mother know you're coming?'

The eyes rolled, just a little. 'It's not that sort of party. He doesn't mind – Rianna said. Anyone can go.'

'*No.*' She didn't say it loudly, she certainly didn't shout, but all three of them looked at her: Vince, Willow and – now, finally – Beth. 'You're not well. You've been really sick, and you're still weak, still not back to normal. I don't want you going out on a cold evening, on the bus by yourself, without my even knowing where you're going or if you'll be welcome there. If you want to go out, you ask me beforehand. We arrange it. I could have driven you in – if you'd been well enough to go, that is.'

Beth's focus had dropped back to the floor and she was looking truculent. 'I didn't know beforehand. Rianna only texted me this afternoon.'

'Well, I'm sorry, but you're not going out. You'll have to text Rianna back and apologise. Tell her that you can't come.'

'It's not fair.' Beth was kicking her toe against the corner of a kitchen unit. 'You never let me do anything. Like come home on the bus, or go out, or have any fun. Just because of my stupid asthma.'

'It isn't just because – '

'You treat me like a little kid. And anyway, I've *told* them I'm going. So now they're going to think I'm a baby who's not allowed out.'

'I'm sorry, love, but my mind's made up. You can't go.'

A brief silence descended on the room. Trying to forget about Vince and Willow, Laura kept her eyes determinedly on her daughter.

Then, quietly, Beth spoke. 'You can't tell me what to do.'

It was said neither in open defiance nor for effect, exactly, in spite of the audience. It was more as if she were trying it out for sound. Experimenting.

There were a lot of answers Laura might have given. *My house, my rules. You're twelve.* But she just kept silent and held her ground.

It was Beth who turned away first. 'C'mon, Willow. Let's go to your room. You can show me your photos.' She went across to the Rayburn, reached behind and picked up the blue shoebox, then headed for the stairs.

With a glance at Vince but not at Laura, Willow rose and followed her from the room. Under the table, Laura steadied her hands by wrapping them tightly together.

'Leave her.' Vince's voice was gentle. It ought to feel good, having another adult for reinforcement, to validate her decisions. Instead, she found it unexpectedly irksome to be told what she already knew.

'Yes. She always comes round quickly enough. She's a good girl.'

'She is.' He was nodding seriously, seeking her eye. 'She's a sweet kid. Open and spontaneous, and friendly and helpful. Clever, too.'

Laura blinked at him. Of course she never tired of hearing

her daughter praised, but . . . she sensed there was a 'but'.

'Doesn't mean it isn't hard, though.'

For a moment she stared, attempting to locate her own feelings. Then she unwound a notch, unknotted her hands. 'It is. Sometimes it's bloody hard.'

'It must be. On your own.' He did this thing, this earnest thing, where he looked from one of her eyes to the other. It made her feel strangely exposed. 'Laura, I hope you don't mind if I say something?'

He paused; she frowned and waited.

'Do you think maybe, sometimes, you might let go a bit?'

She did mind. It was a damned cheek.

'Not on this one, perhaps. I'm not saying you weren't quite right, this time. But there's nothing wrong with cutting some slack – for yourself as well as her.'

Laura stared at him. Who was he, to butt in on her life? A stranger. Worse than that, a professional stranger, with a head full of social work textbooks. What right had he to assume he knew anything about her – about her and Beth?

As she continued to stare, she felt, to her horror, a dry prickling invade her eyes. She closed them, swallowed, tried to pull herself together. When she opened them again, Vince was still regarding her steadily.

Weary all at once, the abdication of responsibility was suddenly an attractive proposition. She let her chin slump into cupped palms. *Cut some slack. Let go.*

'You're probably right,' she said.

By the following weekend, friendly relations between Laura and Beth were restored. On Friday night, Beth went to Simon's straight from school, and Laura picked her up and brought her home on Sunday afternoon to tea and home-made mince pies – the first of the season.

'Seriously good pies, Mum,' said Beth through a mouthful of rich butter pastry. 'Really – they're legendary. Can I have another?'

December having begun, there was a perfect excuse for such indulgences, and then to spend the evening cutting sheets of paper from Laura's printer tray into snowflakes for the windows. Willow, who had joined them for supper, stayed to help, and her snowflakes were the best of all: meticulous confections of fine filigree. By nine, the kitchen looked as if it had witnessed the passing of a ticker tape parade.

Beth was almost off her inhaler, now, during the day, but she still wasn't sleeping well, so Laura packed her off to bath and bed while she and Willow swept the floor. All round the downstairs, she left the curtains open wide, to set off the clustering white circles against the night outside. The effect was striking; it should have been festive, but instead it set her shivering and sent her upstairs in search of her daughter's bedroom and story-time warmth.

She was already in bed, sitting up, with the duvet tucked round concertinaed knees.

'I've had pie twice today,' she announced. 'Except, the first time it wasn't, exactly.'

Laura shifted Beth's feet over a little and perched herself beside them.

'Tess was making chicken pie for lunch and she left the top on the table, all rolled out ready, and went off to the loo because Roly had got himself in a mess, and when she came back Dougie had grabbed it was eating it on the floor. She must have left it near the edge, or he climbed up on a chair. He's very clever.'

'So you had pie without the top? A sort of chicken tart?'

'Worse than that.' Beth's eyes narrowed and her top lip curled in disgust. 'Dad got it off him and picked the bits off. He said it looked OK, and he got Alfie and Jack to cut circles from the best part with a cutter, like for jam tarts. Then he sort of arranged them on the top to cover up some of the filling. He called it a gobbler or something.'

'Cobbler,' said Laura, smiling. Simon's mother used to

make blackberry and apple cobbler; she made one the very first Sunday he'd taken Laura home for lunch.

'Honestly, they're so unhygienic. I'm amazed they don't all get dysentery and diarrhoea and yellow fever.' She hunched the duvet up higher round her shoulders and closed her eyes. 'It was really nice, though. And we had sprouts with it.'

Laura went to bed herself at half past ten. It cannot have been long afterwards – it felt like mere moments – that she woke to the sound of her daughter's coughing. Dragging on her dressing gown, she padded along the landing in bare feet, stopping at the bathroom cabinet for the bottle of throat linctus. It was always this way in the weeks following an attack, the same vicious circle: the coughing which left her short of breath, the inhaler which settled her breathing but inflamed her cough.

'Here. Sit up a bit, sweetheart. Don't spill it.'

First the syrup to settle the coughing, then the inhaler to open her lungs.

'Were you asleep, Mum?'

'Not really,' she lied. 'Shall I bring you some cough sweets to suck?'

'What sort are they?'

'The green ones. Menthol and eucalyptus, I think.'

Beth grimaced. 'No, I'm fine.' She took the inhaler from Laura and had her second puff, then lay back against the pillows. 'Drama tomorrow. We're starting these sketch things and we have to be in pairs. Rianna said she'd be with me, but then Caitlin was in a horrible strop about it, so now I don't know. Do you think he'll let us go in a three?'

Laura blinked but didn't answer. Her attention had switched, and Beth's switched presently, too, to a noise from downstairs. A banging at the front door.

'What's that?' said Beth.

Laura looked at her watch: almost eleven forty-five. 'Probably just the wind,' she said, tucking the duvet closer about her daughter's legs. Beyond the paper snowflakes, the night had been frosty, clear and still. But nobody came calling at Ninepins unannounced, and certainly not at night. They had heard no vehicle.

A moment later the banging resumed, now with some urgency.

'I'd better go and look,' said Laura. 'You stay here.'

Tightening the cord of her dressing gown she descended the stairs in semi-darkness, suppressing a bubble of fear. Surely bad news came by telephone, not knocking on the door? There was no police car, no blue flashing light. And Beth was here safely with her.

She clicked on the hall light. The knocking had stopped for the moment and, in the space it left, she caught the sound of movement on the landing. Beth stood at the top of the stairs, pale and squinting.

'I told you to stay in bed,' said Laura, half-heartedly, but her daughter was already on her way down.

'I want to see who it is.'

Just as they drew near the door, it came again: three abrupt, insistent thuds. Laura pulled back the catch.

The woman who stood on the step was unknown to her. Not very old, early thirties or so, she was oddly dressed – at least for a chilly winter night – in a cotton shift dress, red, with a bold, hippy print. The sleeves of a loose-knit sweater were pushed back and emphasised the thinness of her arms, one of which was still raised, knuckles clenched, towards the doorway. Below the hem of her dress, bare shins emerged from a pair unlaced biker boots that looked several sizes too large.

'Hello?' said Laura. When the woman did not respond, she tried again. 'Can I help you?'

Slowly, the caller lowered her arm, until it hovered at waist height, still awkwardly extended. 'Ninepins.' She pronounced the word cautiously, as if she were speaking a foreign language, though her accent was neutral, south-east. Then she lapsed back into silence.

Laura smiled an encouragement she didn't feel. 'That's right. This is Ninepins. This is my house. Who were you looking for?'

Silence.

'Only, it's quite late.'

Instinctively, Laura moved closer to Beth, who was standing behind her shoulder. There was no objective reason to be fearful. It might be close to midnight, and remote out here, but there were three of them in the house. The telephone was on the hall stand, her mobile just upstairs. The woman was small, shorter than Beth, let alone Laura, and palely skinny. But there was something disconcerting about her extreme stillness, punctuated by unnatural, stiff movements; her eyes were focused slightly behind them, somewhere in the recesses of the hallway. Drugs, is what occurred to Laura, though she had little experience of the subject, and this woman's dislocated manner was nothing like the slack-limbed bonhomie of the music students she remembered on her corridor in undergraduate days, when they'd been smoking hash.

'Are you all right?' Laura asked. 'Are you lost? Has something happened?' An accident. A car. The lode. *Don't scare Beth.* 'Or maybe you've got the wrong address. Maybe you're looking for someone else, another house?'

'Ninepins,' repeated the woman, staring into the hall.

'Look,' began Laura, as calmly as she could, 'perhaps you'd be better to come back in the morning. Maybe – '

Her mistake was to shift back a little towards Beth again as she spoke, leaving a space in front of her in the doorway. Still with her eyes fixed over their shoulders, the woman stepped forward to fill the space, and before Laura could stop her she was past them and into the hall.

By the foot of the stairs she stopped and stood, rock still again, frowning down at the polished, black floor tiles.

'Ice,' she said. 'Black ice.'

'Are you cold?'

It was Beth who had spoken. It seemed to Laura a strange

91

leap to have made from the woman's words, but it was true she did look chilled; she was under-dressed and there was a tight, pinched look about her face, and the tip of her nose was redder than the rest. Perhaps she was homeless, or a traveller. But what was she doing right out here by herself? No car, no van. No bag.

'Dangerous.' The woman raised her head and stared straight at Laura so that her throat closed up. 'Ice is bad. Dangerous. Anyone could slip on it and get hurt.'

She slid the sole of one boot slowly along the shiny tiles until she stood broadly straddled, like an orator taking stance to declaim. Or more like a child, Laura decided, remembering games of Twister. And actually, she didn't seem right for a homeless person. Her hair was too clean, her skin too indoor pale.

Beth had begun to edge towards the woman, as though she were a nervous cat. Laura laid a retraining hand on her daughter's arm, and she stopped and said, 'Why us? Why've you come to see us?'

'Hurt,' repeated the woman, switching her gaze to Beth.

Laura's heart clamped shut in her chest. She strove to hold her voice steady. 'Perhaps it would be better if you went home. Can you tell us where you live? Maybe we could call you a taxi?'

Or the police. The phone was right there.

'Someone might slip. Might break their necks.' The visitor was no longer looking at Beth. She craned her head back and was staring at the ceiling – or at least her face was pointed upwards, though Laura could no longer make out whether her eyes were open or shut.

Then, so softly at first that you couldn't be sure it was really coming from her, she began to make a noise: a kind of low droning or crooning, like the rumble of a distant motorway. Laura glanced at Beth, but she was engrossed, staring at the woman. Gradually, the noise modulated, rising in pitch and volume, and beginning to stutter and fragment, until finally it was recognisable. Laughter. The woman threw her head even further back, straining her neck to an unlikely angle, and shouted aloud with laughter: great, jarring blocks of sound that shuddered her thin frame.

'Shhh. Please.' Laura wasn't sure quite why she was asking the woman to shush, and it certainly wasn't doing any good. She didn't even seem to hear her. The noise went on and on, until it hardly seemed to be laughter, hardly seemed like a human sound at all.

Upstairs, a door clanged. The woman gave no sign of registering the sound but continued with her weird, unfunny laughter. It had slowed a little now, the separate sounds diffracting themselves into a more regular pattern, each on its own gasping exhalation. It was as if she were not laughing but labouring for breath, like Beth, like an asthmatic. Or sobbing: it could almost have been sobs.

'Please,' said Laura, drawing an arm round her daughter but looking steadily at the woman. 'Please stop. You need to go home now. You need to leave, or we'll have to call the police.'

She kept her voice low, or as low as was possible while making herself heard over the woman's noise. But just as she was speaking, the laughing suddenly stopped, as abruptly as if a switch had been thrown, so that her last three words rang loud in the suddenly silent hallway.

'. . . *call the police.*'

At the same time, she became aware of movement on the stairs and someone else's presence. Willow.

The visitor, hushed now and standing very still again, looked at Willow and Willow looked at her.

'I'm sorry about this,' said Willow quietly, as she moved down into the hall. 'This is my fault.'

'Your fault?' began Laura. 'But why should – ?'

'My fault,' repeated Willow, cutting her off. She walked towards the woman and stood beside her, facing them. 'This is my mother.'

Chapter 10

They should have met in town, thought Laura, as she looked round the lounge bar. Elswell had only one pub, and the Fisherman's Arms was not a place you'd choose if there were any option. The décor was stuck somewhere between the 1950s and the 1970s, mixing the elements of each that were least worth preserving. The ceiling and walls were yellow with years of now-forbidden tobacco smoke, and hung about with lobster pots and other maritime impedimenta quite inappropriate to fishing in a lode. With Christmas now approaching, the effect had been capped by the addition of a plastic tree, some garish foil paper chains and, around each beer pump, a strand of tired-looking tinsel.

Vince, at the bar, was laughing with the barmaid while he paid for the drinks. His round; she had insisted on paying for the first one. After all, it was she who had asked him here.

'Crisps,' he said on his return, tossing the bag on the table. 'Prawn cocktail, I'm afraid. Seemed to be all they had.'

'Sorry.' Her apology took in the room: the dusty fishing nets, the carpet worn to a shine.

Vince, however, merely laughed. 'My patch covers a lot of the fen villages. I've seen worse. And the beer's still beer.' He raised his glass, as if to prove the point, and took a long pull. 'How's the clean-up going?'

Momentarily she floundered, until he added, 'In the pump-house.'

'Oh, well, I've stripped it out completely, of course. The carpet had to go, and the mattress, and most of the bedding. The furniture itself will be all right, I think. Willow's got the little desk with her in the spare room. The rest is drying out in the dining room until we're ready for it.'

'That must be a nuisance.'

'Not really. We hardly use the dining room, to be honest.'

He munched a crisp and raised an eyebrow. 'What about Christmas? Are you going to be tucking into turkey and all the trimmings, wedged in between a wardrobe and an up-ended bed?'

She shrugged. 'We'll manage.' Christmas dinner was something she wasn't thinking about; Beth was going to Simon's. 'I've had some estimates now, too, for the repair work. It's going to be pretty major. The plasterboard is ruined. It looks like a case of dry-lining the place over from scratch. The woodwork seems sound, but they can't be sure until it's fully dried out. Then there'll be that to strip and repaint, too. The insurance should cover most of the work, but I'll probably do the decorating myself.'

'How long are we looking at, then? Before Willow can move back in.'

Laura hesitated. The subject of Willow's plans had never directly been broached. 'Depends on the weather, and how long it takes to dry out. Late February or March, perhaps, before it's habitable again. But I wasn't sure . . . I mean, she may have found another place before that.'

'No.' His shake of the head was succinct and definite. 'She wants to stay.'

'Well, naturally, she's very welcome.' But in the spare room, for three more months? 'It's the least I can do in the circumstances.'

'She's had enough of moving and disruption.'

'Of course, yes.' She frowned guiltily into her gin and bitter lemon. 'Absolutely.'

More conciliatorily, he added, 'She likes it at Ninepins.'

'Yes?'

'She likes you both.'

'Beth does love having her in the house.' Then she shook herself, looked up and gave him a proper smile. 'We both do. She's a nice kid.'

More to change the subject than anything else, she asked, 'How about you? Christmas, I mean. Where do you spend it?'

'With my old mum. She's on her own – has been for four years now.'

'So sorry. Me, too. I mean, my parents both died when Beth was small.'

'That must have been bloody tough.' His fingers rested fleetingly on her knuckles. 'Any siblings?'

'One half-brother, Mark, lives in Canada now. But we were never especially close. He's twelve years older.'

'I'm an only child, so it'll be just the two of us.' A rueful grin. 'In Wisbech.'

That made her laugh. 'I bet you love it, really.'

'Home,' he said, and tilted his pint towards her. 'We're entitled to malign it, aren't we?'

'I think it's more or less compulsory.'

'Anyway, it will be mercifully short. I'm on call from the evening of the twenty-sixth.'

'What about that day?' she found herself asking. 'Boxing Day. If you've done your duty and want an excuse to get away, we'd be very glad to see you for lunch. We're thinking of having Christmas dinner on Boxing Day, because Beth's at her father's on the twenty-fifth.' The plan was forming only as she spoke, but she plunged ahead regardless. 'I'm sure Willow will join us, and it would be lovely if you could come, too. That is, if you can face roast parsnips and bread sauce and plum pudding two days in a row.'

He looked genuinely pleased. 'Any number of days. I love bread sauce. It's very kind of you, and I'd be delighted.'

The invitation and its acceptance cast a self-consciousness over Laura, so that she was pleased when he drained his glass and she had the excuse to escape to the bar. Their third drink (this time she'd better move on to grapefruit juice) and she still hadn't embarked upon the conversation she had come here to have.

Seated again at the table, she took her courage in her

hands. 'Have you heard anything more about Willow's mother?'

'Not really.' He eyed her carefully, his expression guarded. 'She's back in London, as I understand it.'

Laura nodded and lapsed back to silence. Their first call that night had been to Vince. He had come out, but not until after Willow had phoned the consultant in London, who had rung a colleague in Cambridge, who had sent round an ambulance, bumping along the drove at one thirty in the morning, with a driver and a psychiatric nurse.

She tried again. 'Is she all right?'

Such a stupid question. People weren't wrapped in a hospital blanket and led glazed and wordless to an ambulance if they were all right.

There was no answer for some little time, while Vince sat back in his chair and studied her face as if considering his options. Laura's hands strayed to the empty crisp packet, folded it in half, then in half again.

'What I mean is, was that . . . Was how she was that night how she often is? Still is?'

What's wrong with her? Is she dangerous? *Will she come back?*

Finally, Vince seemed to come to a decision. 'It's difficult,' he said. 'Marianne – Willow's mother – is not my client. And Willow is. Either way, there are problems of confidentiality.'

'Right. Yes, of course.' How naïve of her, to imagine he could just tell her the whole story, casually, over a few beers.

'But I think I can set your mind at rest to some extent at least. Marianne lives in London. She is under good care there, I believe. The night she came here, it seems she had stopped taking her medication. I understand things are very different when she takes it.'

'Right.' It was all she could think to say. 'I see.'

They paid attention to their drinks for a while in awkward silence. At least, it felt awkward on Laura's side, though

Vince appeared unperturbed. Then she said, 'What about Willow?'

She hardly knew what it was she was asking. How Willow dealt with it, she supposed, how she coped. That night, in the hall, she had been brisk and matter-of-fact. She'd made her phone calls and talked about sectioning and chlorpromazine as if they were quite ordinary and not the stuff of TV drama. To her mother she spoke scarcely a word.

'Why don't you ask her?' He regarded her steadily. He wasn't smiling, but she thought there was sympathy in the lift of his brow. 'If you want to know about Willow, then why not ask her yourself?'

'Yes.' She circled her fruit juice on the beermat. 'I should. I will.'

'So,' he said presently, 'is there anything I can bring to the feast on Boxing Day? Wine, mince pies, satsumas? Any customs of the house that I should know about? Do you wear oak green for the winter solstice, or weave herbs through your hair?'

Grateful for the switch of mood, she grinned. 'Oh, our Paganism is pretty well buried here in Elswell. Beth might wear her headband with the reindeer antlers, but that's about the limit of it.'

'And should I come prepared to play charades, or go for a long, bracing walk? I don't have you and Beth down as sofa slumpers.'

Her grin widened. 'Sharpen your pencil,' she said. 'My daughter is a demon at Pictionary.'

They talked comfortably about Christmas and Wisbech and other nothings for some minutes, before Vince asked, 'How is Beth?'

It was a strange question, on the face of it, because Laura had been talking about her fairly constantly, about her part in the school carol concert and what she wanted for Christmas. But something in the way he asked it brought her chatter to a halt.

'She has a new group of friends.' Why was she telling him

this? 'Since she started at the village college in September, she's drifted away from her old primary school friends and got in with a new set.'

He nodded. 'It happens.'

'There are two in particular.'

'The girls she was going out to meet that time? The other weekend.'

Surprised, she nodded back at him. 'Rianna and Caitlin. They're . . . well, they're different. Not like the kids she used to play with – hang out with, I should say.'

'And they frighten you.'

'Frighten me?' The word was extreme, unexpected, making her bridle; but denial evaporated before it was spoken. She saw again the three of them, after school tonight: Beth dragging away from the triangle without looking at her mother and, as they walked away, the smothered, hostile laughter and the single, ugly, trailing word, '. . . *slag* . . .'

'Yes,' she said simply. 'I suppose they do.'

'Invite them round.' Vince set down his glass and leaned towards her. 'Have them round to the house. Talk to them. Get to know them.'

'I'm not sure Beth would want – '

'Of course she would.' He was robust. 'Of course she wants her friends to see her home. If she's shy, then why don't you make it easy for her? Do the inviting. Come up with a reason, make it a date.'

'I don't know.' She thought about the birthday: the unwanted party, the uneaten cake. 'I don't want to interfere. And it's not exactly cool, is it? I can't be asking her friends round for tea and iced buns as if they're seven years old.'

Grinning, he sat back a little. 'Maybe not quite that. But is there something they would enjoy? Something that would be "cool", as you put it?'

'Such as?'

'Pity the pumphouse isn't ready to be painted. All kids love decorating.'

'Beth can't.' She chewed her lip. 'The fumes affect her asthma.'

'Laura.'

She looked at him, and saw amusement in his eyes.

'Whatever the image they like to throw out, these kids are just kids. They may act tough, but it's all defensive bluster. They're how old – twelve?'

'Caitlin's twelve. I remember a birthday being mentioned.' She smiled, a little shame-faced, though still not entirely convinced. 'I think Rianna might still be eleven.'

Vince lifted his beer glass, drained it, and replaced it firmly on the mat. 'Get to know them and you'll see. They're just children.'

No candles, because of the fire risk. That's what Laura had told her on the first day. She was talking about the pump-house, but no doubt it went for the spare room as well. It had been the same at the care home, so it didn't bother Willow that much. There, it had been nothing but rules. No candles; no drugs, cigarettes or alcohol; no Blu-Tack on the walls. Laura was much less interfering. She'd said no candles – but she hadn't said anything about incense.

Willow had found it in a little shop in Cambridge, in an alley midway between the Social Services department and the city centre. From the window display, it looked like the usual sort of Cambridge gift shop, cheap and tacky and old-fashioned, a hang-out for pensioners on coach trips. It wasn't the sort of place she'd ever go into normally, but she'd been lured by an eggcup and spoon. It was the height of naff, with a transfer of King's College chapel on the side, but Vince would laugh. They had a running joke about how she couldn't boil an egg.

Inside, the shop took on a different air. Almost literally so, with a smell quite other than what you'd expect: not lavender bags and old lady perfume, but something far more exotic, an Arabian souk or an opium den. It smelt, unexpectedly and intoxicatingly, of when Willow was small. She tracked down the scent to a table in a poorly lit corner to the rear of the shop. There were lacquered jewellery boxes, and silk batik purses on long, tasselled strings, and Indian trinkets of all kinds: brass elephants and Ali Baba lamps and wide-eyed goddesses with bare breasts and too many arms. The packets, when she found them, were of tissue paper, flimsy, with gold patterns stamped into them and Hindi lettering she couldn't understand.

'Joss sticks,' said the man whose shop it appeared to be. 'We used to sell a lot of these at one time.' His shirt was open two buttons at the front and his skin had an oiled look, all wrong for his pallid colour.

He opened the nearest packet and pulled out a few sticks, which looked like skinny sparklers. 'Sandalwood or patchouli.'

Willow bent to sniff the wares.

'This one, I think.' Yes, she was sure of it.

'Patchouli,' said the shopkeeper, also sniffing, and standing a little too close.

'Is it always in sticks like this?' she asked him as he dropped the packet in a bag, but he didn't seem to know.

On the way back to the bus station she stopped at a newsagent for matches.

The incense her mother burned had come in a cone: a tiny, solid cone of grey, like a minaret, or a miniature volcano. She never smoked that Willow could remember, not cigarettes, anyway, but she had a lighter. It was silver in colour and more diamond-shaped than square, the corners slightly rounded. One side, when Willow held it in her palm, was completely smooth. The other felt rough; when you looked closely, you could see it was engraved with a faint, twirly cipher that she used to trace with her finger. Like following the tangled lines in a puzzle book: *which one is Tommy's kite?* It might have been just a pattern, or intertwined initials she was too young to read.

She was allowed to hold the lighter, and open and close the metal lid which fitted so snugly you could hardly see the join, but never to flick the button that turned the little cogwheel and ignited the fire. Instead, she used to lie between her mother's sprawled legs and stare up in fascination. Over and over, the repeated, hypnotic action: the click of the switch, the light metallic scratch of the wheel, and the leap of flame, which gradually settled and became still, a perfect, pointed ellipse – until her mother released the catch and it died again.

Matches were not so satisfactory at all. There was only so long you could hold them, once struck, before the fire crept up to your fingers and the heat became intolerable. She worked the stem of a joss stick down into a join in the corner of the small desk, the one they'd brought up from the flood. It shed a film of greyish brown powder on the wooden surface and coated her fingers with the same dusty residue, which turned oily when she rubbed her fingertips together. But the smell was right: a smell of the past.

Sitting at the desk, she struck a match and held it vertical until the flame stilled, then applied it beneath the tip of the joss stick. After a moment, the single orange plume slipped sideways, distorting and fattening as the incense took light. She kept the match there until the last possible moment, before pulling it away and shaking it to put it out. For a while the stick continued to burn falteringly; a low, crimson flame dipped and stuttered and then died away, leaving nothing but a glowing tip of heat.

The smoke, she noticed, didn't begin all at once, but started as a trickle and then grew stronger; nor did it come from the single spot of red but spiralled up from the millimetre or so below, where the stick burned black like charcoal. Immediately above the tip it wove and twisted like a helix, made up of two of three distinct strands, but by the time it reached a level with her eyes it had merged into a single, slender column, so straight and smooth that it hardly appeared to rise at all.

For several minutes, Willow remained immobile, taking in

the aromatic scent; she sat so still and inhaled so gently that her indrawn breaths made scarcely a kink in the liquid flow of smoke.

Then she reached for the matchbox, slid it open and took out another match.

Tuesday was the best day for it, when Beth had after-school choir practice and Laura was home early, stowing Christmas presents under the bed. She knew Willow must be in. There was no sound from the spare room, but when she came along the landing there was a soft smell of perfume clinging round the door, a familiar scent she couldn't quite place, reminding her of student bathrooms when she was at university. Now would be the time to go and talk to her.

Having hidden her carrier bags and the gilded rolls of wrapping paper, she returned to the landing and stood for a moment outside the door. The silence was complete; perhaps, after all, she had been in and gone out again. Laura knocked.

'Hello.'

'Can I come in?' she asked, pushing her head round the door. Willow was lying flat on her back on the bed. No book, no magazine; nor did she give the impression of having been asleep. The floor was empty and the desktop and dressing table clear – so different from Beth's habitual, comfortable chaos. It occurred to Laura that she hadn't been inside the room since Willow moved up here. It felt different, foreign.

Willow said nothing, but pulled herself up on her pillows and looked expectantly at Laura, who moved further into the room.

'Are you warm enough in here?' she began, for something to say. 'It's been so cold out, and this radiator's sometimes temperamental.' She walked over to it, cupped both hands round the ridged metal. It was scalding.

'I'm fine,' said Willow, from the bed.

The curtains were open on to darkness, the bedroom light catching yellow flecks on the surface of the lode. Willow had her wish now: her view out over water. Laura shivered in spite of her burning fingers and resisted the urge to draw the curtains closed.

'I still think of this as my parents' room.' She wasn't sure where this had come from; she had little idea of saying it until the words were out. 'We call it the spare room, but I think of it as theirs, my mum and dad's. They always slept here when they stayed. Before they died.' Mum first, and Dad ten months later, when Beth was two. So unfair, she felt: two, three more years and Beth would have remembered them. 'It was a long time ago,' she murmured, more to herself than to Willow. Ten years.

There was a sound of shifting behind her, a half cough.

'Beth not back?'

'No.' Laura turned, took a few steps closer to the bed. 'She had another rehearsal, for the carol concert. I'm picking her up at six thirty.'

Willow nodded. Then, abruptly, she sat up, swinging her feet down to the floor. 'Can I come?'

'To pick her up?'

'To the concert.'

Laura was surprised. 'Yes, of course. She'll love to have you there. But it's only school carols, nothing exciting. Beth's duet is just one verse.'

'Still.' Her glance slid down and away.

Thank you, Laura wanted to say, but felt too foolish. Instead, she sat down on the foot of the bed.

'I didn't tell her, you know,' said Willow.

Her voice was flat and toneless, so that, despite the chime with her own thoughts, it took Laura a moment to understand what she meant.

'I didn't tell her where I live.'

'Oh?' Unable to think of any other response, she waited to see what would follow.

'No. And I'm sure no one at the care home would have said anything. They all knew. She used to turn up there sometimes,

104

and make trouble, so they all knew not to tell her anything if she came round asking.'

Her, noticed Laura. Not 'Mum', or even 'my mother', like that night; just 'her'.

'They have security there, anyway. Proper rules about not giving out people's details. And the staff all knew her. No.' She paused, staring at the carpet. 'I think it must have been Janey.'

Laura sat still and upright. 'Who's Janey?'

'Foster carer. I stayed with her when I was first in care – while they decided what to do with me. We stayed in touch a bit, so I gave her my new address.

'But surely . . . Would Janey tell your mother where you were?' A foster parent? Disclose to a woman in that state the whereabouts of her child?

Willow shook her head. 'She has teenagers. That's who she fosters. Not babies or little ones at primary school. She does older kids who need respite care, or in an emergency. They don't stay long, most of them. Like me. They come and they go.'

Laura nodded, encouraging, but she wasn't sure if Willow saw this.

'If she watched 'til Janey went out and then knocked, and one of the foster kids answered . . .' Her shrug filled in the spaces. 'There was a pinboard in the hall. Names and addresses, phone numbers. Pizza deliveries, people's social workers. Kids who'd left.'

It seemed very casual to Laura, very hit and miss. Didn't they have some kind of system to keep them safe, these children they were meant to be protecting? Not to mention those around them. *Like Beth.*

'Vince thought I ought to leave.'

'Really?' He had seemed so adamant she should stay.

'He thought I should find somewhere else, now that she knows I'm here. But I told him I wanted to stay here.'

'Yes.' You're very welcome, she ought to tell her, as she'd

told Vince in the pub. Instead, she said, 'You think she'll come back, then?'

She used to turn up and make trouble.

For a moment, Willow didn't answer, but frowned downwards, scuffing at the carpet with her stockinged feet.

' 'Course she will,' she said at length. 'She always does.'

Rising to leave, Laura moved to the head of the bed and risked, briefly, the laying of an arm along Willow's narrow shoulders. There was no flinch of recoil, as she'd half expected, which emboldened her to speak.

'It'll be OK.'

Really, what nonsense, though. What did she know about any of it, to come out with such a glib assurance?

Willow said simply, 'Thanks.'

It was as she turned towards the door that Laura noticed the matchbox lying on the desk, and next to it the pile of spent matches.

Beth had generally been located in the back row, in recent years, at primary school concerts. She hated anyone to see her feet when she was singing, and being one of the taller children in Years 5 and 6 meant that she had her wish and could hide away somewhere at the back and to the side. But now she was a Year 7 and one of the smaller ones, surely? She ought to be near the front. So why couldn't Laura see her?

The concert wasn't due to start for another five minutes. There were still choir members milling about on the stage and blocking Laura's view of the benches; others might be yet to come into the hall. Perhaps Beth had been seized by last minute nerves and nipped off to the loo. It would be typical of her.

Willow, at Laura's side, sat unconcernedly reading the photocopied programme, where Beth's name appeared in bold type among the list of soloists.

Miss Chapman, the music teacher, had appeared at the front of the hall and was persuading her choristers to sit down and stop talking.

'Where can she have got to?' whispered Laura to Willow, who folded the programme sheet in two and looked up. 'It's half past. They're going to start in a minute, and she's not here.'

A teacher Laura didn't know had been playing a Bach medley on the piano at the side of the stage as the audience found its seats, but now he stopped and looked over at Miss Chapman, who gave a significant nod. A tall, pale girl of about fifteen stepped forward to the centre of the stage and an expectant hush fell over the room. Her white shirt still held the creases from the packet. She looked, thought Laura, as if she were in the dock and about to be cross-examined.

Then she opened her mouth and a heart-stopping sound emerged, liquid and ethereal, making a cathedral of the stuffy school hall. *Once in Royal David's City . . .*

But where on earth was Beth?

'Mrs Blackwood, could I have a word?'

It was the end of the carol concert. Most of the audience had been reunited with its musical offspring and had filtered out through the double swing doors to the rear of the hall, comparing notes on the performance and exchanging season's greetings with other departing families. Laura was left sitting on her stacking chair in the middle of a row, with Willow beside her, wondering what to do next.

Miss Chapman stood at the end of the row and coughed. 'I've got Beth in the practice room. We need to have a quick chat, if you don't mind.'

'Yes, of course.' Laura rose too quickly, so that the metal chair legs shrieked painfully on the linoleum.

Miss Chapman looked at Willow and opened her mouth to speak, but Willow unfolded the concert programme and began to study it with exaggerated care.

'See you back here in a minute,' Laura told her.

Following the choir mistress out of the hall and along the emptying corridor, Laura felt her stomach liquefy. She was twelve years old herself, and being taken to the head teacher's study. *Beth, sweetheart, what have you done?* But she knew her daughter; she trusted her. It couldn't be anything so very terrible.

The room set aside for rehearsals was one of the lower school classrooms, just up the corridor from the hall. The desks had been pushed to one side to leave space for the choir to stand; chairs still stood upturned on the desks where the cleaners had left them, their legs like a winter forest. On one of the desks, at the edge of the clearing, sat Beth. Her face was a mask but her dangling feet were desolate.

'Hello, Beth,' said Miss Chapman, but mother and daughter spoke not a word to each other. Beth was refusing to meet Laura's eye.

'We need to tell your mother what happened this evening, don't we?'

Why did schoolteachers have to talk that way? That irritating 'we'. It was obvious Beth wasn't going to be telling anyone anything; she looked as though she would never speak again.

'We had a warm-up arranged for seven o'clock,' she continued, 'didn't we, Beth? The choir had eaten their sandwiches here in the rehearsal room, then changed into their concert clothes in the cloakrooms, and I'd said they could go outside to stretch their legs and get a breath of air. But they were due back at seven pm prompt.' She had apparently given up now on a response from Beth and was addressing Laura directly. 'A proper warm-up is crucial for a vocalist. It's exactly the same as for an athlete. Without warming up, you can cause serious injury to your voice.'

Laura nodded, impatient. She was no longer trying to catch Beth's eye; she gave Miss Chapman her full attention and willed the interview to be over.

'When Beth wasn't here I sent Alice Seabourn outside to look for her, but she couldn't find her. Of course we had our warm-up without her. At twenty past seven, just when we are thinking of getting ourselves into the hall and on to the stage, Beth turns up, out in the corridor with some other girls, making a frightful racket. Not yet changed, not warmed up. Naturally I had to say she couldn't take part.'

'Yes.' She glanced at Beth. 'I'm sorry. I quite understand.'

'And – ' Miss Chapman fished in her handbag ' – she had these.' With a flourish she produced a packet of cigarettes.

Laura felt slightly sick.

'It's the end of term, and nearly Christmas, so I shan't send her to the head of year for smoking. Just this once – but it must never happen again. Because you know, Mrs Blackwood, the school has a strict zero tolerance policy as far as cigarettes are concerned. It may be a rearguard action – some would say a lost cause – but we're waging it with determination, nonetheless.'

'Of course. And it really won't happen again. I can't imagine – '

'There's one thing, though,' said the music teacher, cutting through her attempted propitiation. 'I'm afraid I can't have Beth in the choir any more after this.'

With neither a word nor a glance to Beth, and with renewed apologies and thanks to Miss Chapman, Laura somehow managed to propel herself and her daughter out of the practice room and back to the hall, where they collected an unspeaking Willow before trooping out to the car. The drive home was conducted in difficult silence, broken only by occasional remarks thrown by Laura to Willow in the passenger seat, brittly cheery, about the carols they had heard. As far as commensurate with safe driving, she avoided looking in her mirror.

Once back at Ninepins, Willow fled like a rabbit for the stairs, leaving the kitchen clear for the showdown. Laura, whose wrath had been building to this moment, watched her departure and, perversely, almost lost heart. *Oh, Beth. Sweetheart.* Instead of flinging the cigarette packet on the table and demanding explanations, she sat down wearily in a chair.

'Alice had to sing on her own,' she began, her voice flat. 'The rest of the choir hummed quietly, while she sang your verse by herself.'

Still standing, Beth raised her chin. 'Bet she was delighted. Everyone looking at her – s'what she loves.'

This provoked a brief renewal of anger. 'Don't take this out on Alice. This is about you.'

Eyes narrowed, Beth glowered at the wall behind her mother.

'What have you got to say?'

' 'bout what?'

'About letting Alice down, for a start. About being thrown out of the choir.'

The chin jutted. 'Stupid choir. Like I care about that. I was going to stop going anyway, after the concert.'

'But you love singing.'

'At the primary, that was. Nobody's in the choir at the college.'

Alice is, and Gemma, she wanted to say; but self-evidently the thirty or forty kids on the stage in their clean, white shirts, the boys in ties, were all still 'nobody'. Rianna and Caitlin were not in the choir.

'So, who were these other girls you were smoking with?'

Silence. In her coat pocket, Laura's right hand closed round the cardboard packet, still smooth in its cellophane. Half the cigarettes were gone; the packet gave under the pressure of her fingers, buckling out of shape. She squeezed her fist tight.

'*How could you smoke?*'

There was a short pause, before Beth muttered, 'I wasn't smoking.'

The reply was not what Laura was expecting and for a moment she said nothing. Her daughter seemed to be mustering herself to speak.

'I wasn't. Not really. It was the others who were smoking. They're not my cigarettes, I just had them in my pocket, that's all, because Caitlin had taken them from her mum's bag, so she didn't want to be found with them on her or her mum would go mental. I'd hardly had any, not smoked one of my own at all, only had puffs of theirs, just to try. Everyone tries cigarettes. I bet you did, when you were young. Everyone does.'

'Beth.' Laura said it again, keeping her voice as even as she could, 'How could you smoke? With your asthma. Even a few puffs. You must know it's the worst possible thing.'

Beth kicked out at a chair leg, viciously, making it judder. 'Oh yes, it's always my stupid bloody asthma, isn't it? Always the reason I can't do anything, have any fun.'

'Smoking's "fun", then, is it?' But Laura knew this was a mistake: being drawn into argument, into the scoring of inconsequential points. She took a breath. 'It's not just your asthma. Of course it's not only because of that.'

'No.' Beth's voice was distorted, thick. 'It's 'cos you don't like my friends. That's what this is all about, isn't it? You don't want me having any friends.' She was visibly crying now; her eyes bloated with liquid until they released two slow, fat tears. 'You hate them, don't you? Rianna and Caitlin – you hate them. You always have to spoil everything for me.'

'I don't hate . . .'

Her daughter, however, had turned away and was stumbling for the hall and stairs, the sobs beginning only when she was out of the room. Walking over to the bin, Laura was surprised to find her legs quite steady. Nor was her hand shaking as she took out the crushed cigarette packet and dropped it in, letting the metal lid fall with the snap of finality. Beth was completely in the wrong. She'd been late for rehearsal; she'd let down her friend and the rest of the choir; she'd been caught smoking cigarettes. So why should it be Laura who was left with the aftertaste of misery and disgrace?

111

Chapter 11

Surfacing from sleep, Laura half opened her eyes. Then she remembered the date and closed them again. Christmas morning in alternate years still felt the way it should. It felt the way it had done when Beth was a baby, or when Laura was a child herself: the tingle of anticipation upon awakening. But this year, as in every year without Beth, it was just a cold December day with no need to get up for work. She pulled the duvet over her head and tried to recapture sleep.

It was no good. A lifetime of jumping out of bed on this day of all days, to look for surprises left in the night, made lying in impossible. Christmas was still Christmas, even with an empty house. And besides, it wasn't empty, was it, even if Beth's room was.

She pulled on socks, slippers and dressing gown and set off along the landing, past the unstirring spare room and down to the kitchen. It would have been too much, she'd decided, to creep in last night and leave the stocking of goodies at the foot of the spare bed. Willow had been up late, in any case, watching an old film on TV, and Laura had been in bed before her. But this morning was made for indulgences and she had no one else to indulge.

In the cupboard she had a packet of marshmallows: not the usual fat, fluffy pink and white kind but miniature plugs of chocolate and vanilla, sold to top the cappuccino of those with an expensive steamed-milk coffee machine. She'd bought them for Beth, really, for her hot chocolate in bed tomorrow morning. But there was no harm in making the same for Willow today.

Once the milk pan was on the hob to warm, she turned on the radio. The sound of congregational singing lapped into the kitchen, politely modulated and slightly nasal, unmistakably Church of England. . . . *earth stood hard as iron, water like a stone.* . . . Frowning, she smothered the thought that Beth's school choir had sung it better. But even the recollection of the carol concert couldn't damp her spirits for long this morning. She whisked up the cocoa powder and sugar in the mug with a light wrist and joined her voice softly as the invisible churchgoers reached the end of Christina Rossetti's deathless poem. *Give my heart.*

She poured in the hot milk and whisked it again before sprinkling on the marshmallows, which bobbed in the froth like tiny corks, then settled and began to blur and melt around the edges. Picking up the mug in one hand and Willow's stocking in the other, she headed back upstairs, still humming to herself.

There was no reply to her knock and Willow appeared to be asleep when she crept in. For a moment she was daunted, feeling foolish, but then Willow stirred and suddenly it was easy.

'Merry Christmas,' she said, and grinned.

'What's this?' Willow blinked and half raised herself on an elbow, and soon she was grinning, too. 'Santa Claus? And, wow – hot chocolate.'

'I've got nobody else to spoil today.'

The words, intended as apologetic, came out as grudging. But Willow's smile was undented. 'I'll help you out, then.'

After she had watched Willow unpack the contents of her stocking, and had herself opened the gift-wrapped paperback which Willow slid out from under the bed, she made them both a festive breakfast of porridge with cream and brown sugar, and oranges, and scrambled egg on toast. While Willow washed up, Laura called Simon's house and said her Happy Christmases to Simon and Tessa and Beth.

113

'It was brilliant, Mum. Dougie got under the tree, all in among the presents, and started making this growly noise and ripping the paper to bits. I think he smelled those chocolate reindeer we got for the boys. Everything got wrecked. It was hysterical – Dad couldn't stop laughing.'

Then there was the stuffing and bread sauce to make for tomorrow's deferred Christmas dinner. Willow lingered to watch and Laura suggested she might like to do the brandy butter, which was usually Beth's speciality.

'I wouldn't know how,' protested Willow.

'That's OK. I can give you instructions. It's very straight-forward.'

'No, honestly. But I can peel potatoes.'

So Willow rolled up her sleeves and prepared the potatoes and parsnips and sprouts, and giggled like a little kid when Laura unconsciously began to hum *I Saw Mummy Kissing Santa Claus*.

'Do you think I should put the stuffing inside the bird or serve it in a separate dish?' Laura asked her.

The vegetable peeler halted. 'Dunno.'

'Well, the turkey takes longer to cook with it inside. But it depends if you think it tastes better.'

The peeler resumed, gouging viciously at a parsnip. 'Don't ask me. My mother's a bloody vegetarian.'

Laura looked at her, curious at the sudden vehemence. 'So, what then, you had nut roast, I suppose?'

'Something like that,' said Willow.

Preparing all that food had failed to give either of them an appetite for lunch, so Laura suggested a walk along the lode towards Elswell. The day was bright, lifting by a few degrees the night's frost. The trodden earth of the path, though iron beneath, gave under their boots to a depth of a millimetre or so; the water of the lode might not be stone, but a lip of ice lined both banks and here and there in patches in midstream the surface had a treacherously glassy, criss-crossed look. On the north flank of the dyke, away from the sun, the tussocky

114

grass still harboured pockets of white at its roots. Below the dyke to the garden side, the empty pumphouse, still waiting to dry out before renovation work could begin, sat stoical, its brickwork sheened in pearly grey.

They walked side by side without speaking. Laura let her eye drift along the southern horizon, enjoying the uncluttered line of the land, the pale empty chill of the sky. Willow's gaze was off to the north, where perhaps she might to be doing much the same. The fields between Ninepins and Elswell village were not large by the standards of the fens. The land to either side of the lode spread out in a patchwork of squares and strips, some ploughed to frozen clods, some harrowed and showing green with winter wheat, others lumpy with white-rimed beetroot and celery and cabbages. There were no hedges between the fields, which were demarcated only by smaller drainage ditches or simply by lines of yellow grass, toughened and slanted by the wind.

Trees and shrubs were few, and grew mainly along the roads and farm tracks, where the ground was banked up above the wet. There were none of the usual stately trees that define the English countryside – no oak, beech, ash or horse chestnut – but only scrubby hawthorn and wild plum and the inevitable, ubiquitous willow.

'You've got the right name for living round here,' she said, breaking the long silence.

The girl looked at her, uncomprehending.

'Willow.' She indicated a long row of it, edging a drove which zigzagged close to them on the north side. 'There's almost nothing but, in this part of the world.'

'That's willow? The one with the red branches?'

'That's right.' That brilliant scarlet-orange of the willow rods, which was often the only spice of colour in the winter grey. 'Willows love the damp. And their roots hold the soil together.'

Willow's eyes returned to scan the horizon. 'Why are there no trees? No proper ones, I mean.'

'Like oaks, say? Like the ones in the villages south of Cambridge?' Where the land had contours, where the land was truly land. 'How long does an oak tree take to grow? Two hundred, three, four, five hundred years? This place was only reliably reclaimed more recently than that. When those trees were saplings this place was still a marsh.'

Listening, Willow nodded.

'And think how deep their roots must need to go, some of those big trees. A hundred feet or more, perhaps. Here the water table is too high.' She always imagined it there, the black water, lying just beneath the surface, waiting to take back its own – as it had on the night the pumphouse flooded. 'They'd never survive. The soil is too waterlogged. It would rot them from below.'

Laura was speaking largely to herself, doing little more than thinking aloud. Doubtless she was boring the poor kid. Though it didn't appear that way, for Willow was looking thoughtful. 'Waterlogged,' she murmured, as if she, too, were speaking to herself.

At the first of the brick cottages which marked the road and the beginnings of Elswell, they turned round by mutual consent and headed back the way they had come. On their outward course, Laura had been conscious of no breath of wind but now, turning back towards the east, she felt its sting on the bare skin of her face. Within a hundred yards, her eyes were blurred with tears and Willow's, beside her, looked the same.

'This is more like it,' said Laura with a grin. 'This is how a Christmas walk ought to be. Absolutely freezing.'

Willow nodded but she didn't smile. After a little way she said, 'Can't say I've been on one before.'

'A walk on Christmas day?'

The silence was affirmation.

'It's something we've always done. Just along the lode for some fresh air, while the turkey's in the oven.' When it was just she and Simon, before Beth was born, they used to eat

116

their Christmas dinner in the evening to give them longer out of doors. One year they walked almost to Ely. 'There's never any shortage of it here. Fresh air, that is.'

Presently, Willow said, 'Janey wasn't a big one for walking anywhere. She'd take the car to post a letter.'

'How many Christmases did you have at her house?'

'Two. It was OK, actually. Lots of people about, so plenty of laughs. And Janey could cook all right. She always did about six sorts of potatoes, so there was something everyone liked. Roast, and boiled, and mash, and chips.'

'Chips with Christmas dinner?'

Willow grinned. 'You'd be surprised. Chips are the only thing some people will eat.'

'Don't tell me. Ketchup as well as cranberry sauce?'

'You bet.'

Laura rubbed her gloved hands together, palm over knuckles, coaxing them to warmth. 'It can't have been easy, though, for some of the kids.' *For you*, is what she meant.

Willow did not respond. She was staring into the distance, where the lone grey square of Ninepins had risen into view.

Gently, Laura pushed. 'At Christmas, I mean, being away from their families.' Thinking about past Christmases. Happy memories or unhappy ones: either way, it could only be painful.

The reply, when it came, was gruff. 'Bloody glad to be there, some of them.'

And what about you? But it was too much. Of course she couldn't ask it – any more than she could reach out and hook Willow's hand under her arm, as she itched to do, and pull her nearer as they walked along.

Instead, she tried another tack. 'So you never went for walks at Christmas before that, either? With your mum?'

She wondered if she had gone too far and alienated her companion, because Willow's eyes remained fixed ahead and she didn't reply. The rasp of her breathing in the cold air had ceased. Then quite suddenly she exhaled on a short, percussive sigh, which was half way to being a laugh.

'It wasn't like that. She didn't really do Christmas.'

That evening, when Laura had taken the car to go and fetch Beth home, Willow reached under the spare bed and took out the blue shoebox. It had dried out completely now. The cardboard had rehardened, slightly out of shape and more rigid than before, with long creases set into the sides and lid. Inside, the contents were all edged in blue where the colour had run from the box. She lifted out a handful at random. Unlike the box, the paper within seemed to have softened in the water and kept its softness as it dried, like tissue or fine blotting paper. Peeling apart the individual sheets without ripping them required slow patience, teasing apart the places where they were stuck. Where there was handwriting, the ink had blurred and fuzzed. Most of it, though, could still be read.

The photographs had fared better. Their glossy surface may have repelled the moisture, their colours perhaps more securely fixed. One or two had glued themselves together, but the rest were intact.

Methodically, she worked through the small stack of prints until she found the one she was looking for. It was taken on an old Instamatic camera her mother had once had, a junk shop relic of the 1970s. The picture was of Willow at the age of five or six, holding a camping kettle and squinting at the lens. On her head was a white denim sunhat.

She recognised the room in which she stood only from the photograph. It was in Peterborough, she thought: a bedsit her mother had rented for a while. But although the background was familiar – the low, Formica-topped sideboard behind her younger self, the framed Van Gogh irises, the yellow wall – she could conjure nothing of the rest of the room. Nor could she remember the hall or stairway or the outside of the house, or any of the other tenants, but she knew there was a bus-stop at the end of the street, outside the shop with the photograph of the racehorse. A bookmakers, she now assumed. Back then it had never occurred to her to wonder what was inside the shop; she had only been entranced by the horse, which was taller than she was, almost the full height of the window, and which galloped towards her, suspended in motion with all its hooves off the ground at once.

The other clear recollection was what her mother was saying as she took the photograph. 'This is to remember us setting off. We'll take pictures of everything we do, and afterwards we'll get a scrapbook and stick them all in.' But there never was a scrapbook, nor any other photos.

It had been dark when her mother shook her awake.

'Come on, baby. Get up.' There was urgency in her voice, a suppressed excitement. 'Let's get you dressed. We're going camping.'

It was something they had never done – not then, though there was one time years later, at Glastonbury, in a van belonging to a man called Snake. Camping had made her think of story books. She had an old picture book with a torn cover that she'd found in a room they once slept in, about Orlando the marmalade cat who went on a camping holiday, with a little green tent like a wigwam, and a fire made of twigs, and a kettle hanging between two forked sticks.

'Like Orlando?' she remembered asking.

Her mother went round pulling all sorts of things out of drawers and cupboards and piling them on the carpet. Clothes for herself and clothes for Willow, T shirts and shorts and jumpers; knives and forks and spoons and the plastic bowls, one red and one yellow, that she'd had when she was a baby and might break the proper ones; blankets and sheets and a thermos and the tin-opener; the frying pan from its hook, and the little tin camping kettle. Willow had never seen the kettle before. At least, it wasn't something they ever used or that she'd noticed packed in the boxes when they'd moved house. She liked its round shape, the high curved handle, the stubby spout. It was exactly like Orlando's kettle in her book. She recalled picking it up and stroking it – or was that something her mind had constructed later, because she was holding the kettle in the photograph?

'Are we going to the seaside?' Willow had wanted to know.

But Mum told her they were going to the countryside. She said they'd find a place near the woods where they would gather wood for a campfire, and there'd be a stream nearby where they'd draw their water for cooking and washing, and where Willow could clean her teeth.

'We'll find wild garlic and pick nettles for soup, and maybe there'll be mushrooms in the wood that we can fry for our breakfast. If it's fine weather, we'll sleep out under the sky. I'll show you the houses of the zodiac and tell you the meanings of the constellations, and you can count the stars until you fall asleep.'

She had no recollection of packing the things or what they carried them in, or whether there was even a tent. Her only memory was of being at the bus stop and gazing at the suspended racehorse. She was fascinated by the pieces of soil thrown up by its feet, which hung in the air, so still that you could see the grass stuck to them. She loved its narrow nose, which looked so velvet soft she could have stretched out her hand and stroked it, if she could have reached. And if it hadn't been split by those two terrible nostrils, which she didn't let herself look at properly in case she could see right inside its head.

The bus didn't come.

On the backs of all the photographs, as nearly as she knew them, Willow had written the dates. Vince, who had the files, had sat down and helped her; he'd seemed to think it served a purpose. For this one, she wasn't sure of a year. It must have been 1999, she supposed, or maybe 1998. But for once she could be certain about the date. *December 25.*

*

120

'We saw a heron, Mum.'

Beth burst into the kitchen ahead of Vince and Willow. Laura hadn't joined them for the Boxing Day walk, but had sent them the other way along the lode, towards the main road and beyond in the direction of Wicken and Ely, while she stayed behind to keep an eye on the turkey.

'It was in some bushes on that lower path – you know, where the fishermen are, sometimes – and it didn't see us 'til we were almost up to it, and then it flapped up right in front of us. It was huge.'

Her cheeks were flushed but she was scarcely wheezing at all. This cold, clear weather was what she needed. 'Seriously, it was massive. It didn't half make us jump. Willow shrieked.'

Vince grinned; his face also had more colour than usual. 'I'm not sure it was a shriek, exactly. But a definite squeak, shall we say?'

Willow looked conscious but not displeased. 'It was a pretty big beast,' she said. 'You don't expect a bird to make that much noise.'

'It's true.' Vince sat on a chair to unlace his boots. 'You expect a bird to be elegant, don't you? This one was heavy and clumsy, all flopping wings and trailing legs.'

'Willow'd never seen a heron before, Mum. I had to tell her what it was.'

'Looked more like a vulture,' said Willow.

Laura picked up Beth's scarf from the floor and looped it over a peg. 'They're not exactly elegant when they're taking off, I agree. But once they're in flight . . . Well, maybe not elegant, but they're certainly imposing. Beautiful, I'd say.'

Vince looked across at her and smiled, but Beth was unimpressed. 'I think their legs look weird when they fly. Like a daddy-long-legs. Like they're too long and might snap off.'

'How far did you walk?' Laura asked her.

'As far as the second sluice, just this side of Wicken. Then there were cows on the dyke, all standing round the stile on the far side, and we didn't fancy it. Willow doesn't like cows. It's that blowy noise they make, she says.'

'Quite right,' said Vince. 'Stary-eyed, slobbery creatures. And their feet had churned up all the grass and turned it into an absolute mudbath.'

Beth nodded relishingly. 'Mud and poo.'

'Dinner isn't quite ready yet, anyway. Another twenty minutes. Maybe you girls could set the table? I thought we'd eat in here, since the dining room is still full of furniture. If that's OK?'

This last question was directed mainly at Beth, who was a stickler for Christmas tradition, but it was Vince who answered, with a mock-solemn bow of the head. 'We'll be honoured. The kitchen is perfect.'

'As long as we can still have candles and crackers and everything. We have got crackers, haven't we?'

Laura grinned at her daughter. 'In the corner cupboard. Top shelf.'

While Beth and Willow began to count out knives and forks, Vince approached the Rayburn and lifted a pan lid. 'Smells good. I can see this is going to make up more than amply for yesterday.'

'Yesterday?'

'At Mum's. She's not very good with her hands these days. Rheumatoid arthritis – she's got it bad in her fingers. So it was me doing the cooking, but acting under instruction. And I'm no good at doing anything when I'm being watched, least of all by my mother. A recipe for disaster and recrimination, all round.'

'Oh, I bet you managed all right.' She remembered his interest in her cookbooks, the day he and Willow first looked round.

'Put it this way,' he said grimly, 'roast parsnips are not supposed to come in handy at the end of the meal for cracking walnuts.'

Laura bent to open the oven and lift out the turkey, to

suitable expressions of appreciation; Vince closed the oven door for her and then watched as she slid the bird on to a serving plate.

'It's a good big 'un.'

'Twelve and a half pounds,' she said. 'I don't think we'll starve.'

She shuffled saucepans about to make room on the hob for the roasting tin. 'Please could you pass that bottle of wine from on the work surface there, over by the kettle? And pour one for yourself. The glasses are just next to it. Er, and Willow, too, of course, if you'd like one.'

Did Willow drink? She really had no idea. But she was seventeen and virtually an adult, so it must surely be right to offer – especially at Christmas.

'What about me?' Beth demanded.

'I bought some of that apple juice with elderflower, the one you like. It's in the fridge.'

For the moment – for this year, at least – this answer satisfied her. 'Great. Cheers, Mum.'

Laura poured a generous splash of red wine into the roasting tin and began to work at it with a wooden spoon.

'The real McCoy.' Vince peered over her shoulder, and waved his wine glass approvingly at the tin. 'Yesterday I was only permitted to use hot water from the kettle. Not the same thing at all.'

Willow and Beth, who had finished laying the table, also hovered close with their drinks. 'Mum makes the best gravy ever,' announced Beth. 'Her Christmas dinners are seriously brilliant.' She took a sip of apple juice, then frowned at Willow. 'Sorry, though. I shouldn't go on about it, should I? Not when your mum is so hopeless and you never had proper Christmas and stuff.'

'Beth – ' Laura spun round, spilling turkey juices from her spoon to the floor. But it was too late.

Willow said nothing at first, but only glared from Vince to Laura to Beth. Her cheeks were white; the outdoor colour had fled in an instant, leaving only strange smudges of angry red at her temples.

'You.' When at last she spoke, she was looking straight at Laura. 'You told her what I said.'

'I only thought – ' she began, then stopped, abashed. There was really no excuse for repeating what Willow had said to her. Yes, it had been well-intentioned; she had wanted to prime Beth, to give her some awareness of Willow's past, some sensitivity to her feelings about Christmas. But it was still wrong; she had no business betraying Willow's flimsy confidences.

'I'm sorry,' she said.

'You talked about me, the two of you. Poor Willow. Better be nice to her – poor fucking deprived Willow.'

'Willow.' Vince placed a hand on her arm, but she shook herself free.

'It's only bloody gravy, anyway. What's wrong with crap out of packets, like the rest of the world eats? And you.' The green eyes were on Beth now, and narrowed to slits, like a cat's. 'You, with your cosy bloody life. Spoiled little princess Beth. What do you know about my mother? Nothing, that's what. You know nothing. You don't know you're born.'

She was out of the room almost as soon as the words were spoken, and running for the stairs. Vince took two steps as if to go after her, then seemed to change his mind. But Laura's eyes were on her daughter, who stood stiffly, still clutching her apple juice; her shoulders were fixed at an odd angle, slightly hunched, as if she had received a physical blow and was waiting for the pain to register. Then her face contorted. She thrust the glass down on the table and stumbled towards the hall. Laura followed almost immediately. She didn't wait to say a word to Vince, but as she reached the landing, she heard his feet on the stairs behind her, and halted for a moment.

'In there,' she said, with a thumb at the spare room, before she turned and knocked at Beth's bedroom door.

124

There was no reply, nor any sound at all from within, not even audible crying. She pushed open the door and stepped inside.

'Beth?'

Nothing. The figure on the bed neither moved nor acknowledged her presence. She was bent forward from a kneeling position, head down so that her face was pressed into the pillow, and arms clasped tight around her knees. If there were tears they were silent ones; no sobs stirred her back and shoulders.

'Sweetheart?' Laura crept closer to the bed, unsure quite why she was cushioning her tread, as if to avoid disturbing a sleeping Beth. 'Are you OK?'

Such a stupid question, even though it was what everyone always asked. Better just to sit down on the bed and say nothing. *I'm here. I love you, and I'm here.* After a short time, she stretched out a hand and smoothed it over her daughter's back. She could feel the rigid tension in every knot of her spine. She lifted her hand and repeated the motion, stroking slowly downwards over the vertebrae, coaxing them to unlock.

Finally, after a minute or two, she sensed beneath her fingers the faintest of loosenings. Perhaps a minute more and Beth spoke. 'I was trying to be nice.'

The licence to speak brought a wash of relief. 'Of course you were. I know that. Willow knows that, too, really. You meant to be sympathetic, of course you did. It's just, well, it isn't always nice to feel people's sympathy.'

Maybe she'd said too much, because Beth's back had stiffened again; but then she felt a tremor which broadened into a heave, and her daughter was crying. The sobs were ugly: wet and clogged and gulping, and out through them came a single, strangled word. 'S-s-sorry.'

'No, love – don't be silly.' Laura leaned forward and wrapped her arms round her daughter's back. 'It really wasn't your fault. There's nothing to be sorry for. You meant no harm. As you say – you were trying to be nice.'

Beth continued to cry for some time without saying any more, and at length the sobs subsided and her breathing calmed. She remained crouched in that awkward posture, making no attempt to rise or turn; she accepted her mother's embrace but did not return it. From her own semi-recumbent position, Laura glimpsed a movement. She saw the doorway, and framed in it, silently, Vince. He caught her eye and raised one questioning brow.

He must have left Willow and come along the landing to see how Beth was feeling. It was kind of him – and wrong of her to feel it as an intrusion. She resisted the impulse to sit up, to let go of Beth. Without speaking, Vince advanced a step into the room.

Beth, apparently unaware of his presence, began to speak. 'She said it herself. She said herself about her being useless. You remember, that time, Mum, when I asked about her name? "A waste of space", that's what she said. "Useless bloody hippy".'

'Beth – '

'Well, she did. It's what she said. I only said the same thing she did, that's all, and without the swearing.' She snorted noisily, and swallowed. 'It's not fair.'

Laura was considering her answer to this when Vince took another step forward.

'Maybe we shouldn't look for logic.' His voice was gentle, but beneath her Laura felt Beth's spine brace, her muscles clench. 'Maybe we're none of us entirely logical,' he continued, 'when it comes to family.'

''S'not fair.' The assertion, however, carried rather less conviction than before.

He was standing over the bed now. Laura half wondered whether he would sit down, perhaps even put his arm round the two of them. She couldn't have said whether she wanted him to or not. She lay still and closed her eyes.

'Willow may say all kinds of things about her mother. Hurtful things. She may even mean some of them – although

126

also she may not.' He didn't sit. He just stood where he was, but his voice was very soft. 'Willow may say things. But it doesn't mean she likes it when other people do.'

Laura felt Beth shift and twist; she sat up, allowing Beth, too, to straighten to a kneeling position and turn to face them both. Her eyes were red and swollen. Laura put an arm back loosely about her shoulder and was about to tell her again that it wasn't her fault when something caught at the back of her throat.

Smoke. Scrambling off the bed, she ran to the bedroom door and sniffed. The bloody gravy. She must have left the roasting tin on the hottest part of the Rayburn.

'Damn it.'

Acrid fumes already filled the stairs and hall as she raced down; in the kitchen it was black and choking. She grabbed a cloth and lifted the roasting tin off the hob. The outside of it was red hot and hissed angrily where she laid it on the damp draining board; the inside was blackened to a sticky, charred mess. The gravy was ruined, the tin wrecked.

'Damn. Bloody hell fire and blast.'

She knew that Beth was in the doorway with Vince, and she shouldn't be standing here swearing like this. She knew it was stupid to be so upset, stupid to cry about something as banal as gravy. And maybe it was just the smoke, after all, that was stinging her eyes and making them swim with tears. But her throat felt peculiarly tight, and Vince's hand on her shoulder was only making matters worse. She must get a grip before she made an utter fool of herself.

'So stupid of me,' she managed to say. 'Leaving it on the heat like that and going away. I just wasn't thinking.'

'I was the last one out,' said Vince quietly. 'And anyway, who needs gravy?'

'Right. We're fine, Mum. We've got cranberry, haven't we?'

'You're very sweet. But still, I can't believe I did anything so idiotically thoughtless.'

127

She'd caught no hint of Willow standing by the hall door, until she heard her speak. 'Dangerous, too.'

They all swung round to look at her. Her face was pale but her voice was matter-of-fact. 'You could have burned the house down.'

Chapter 12

The end of the Christmas holidays marked a loss for Laura. The awareness didn't strike her at once; it crept over her only after Beth had been back at school for a week or so, and withdrawn back into her term-time self. It was only then that Laura appreciated the comfortable, open, unself-conscious child that had been hers during their fortnight at home together – and mourned her passing.

It was not too distant for her to recall the experience in her own case. She remembered how, at primary school, your worlds could still be all of a piece, with no real separation between school and home. How you could tell your mother everything that had happened, and feel she knew and understood every corner and cranny of your life, how it was imperative, indeed, to feel she did so. And Laura had felt the same way with Beth, too, until this year. The name of every classmate, the detail of every friendship, could be relayed and absorbed. But of course it had to end. She must adjust to the acceptance that Beth had now, as she herself had had, two selves. There was the home self, who had laughed and chattered her way through the holidays, or even when upset had shared her woes. Then there was the school self, who now sat sullen at the breakfast table on weekday mornings and hardly raised her eyes from her cereal. She would not mind so much – or if she minded, she could at least accept it as a necessary change – if only she could be sure that this school Beth was not as unhappy as she often seemed.

At breakfast today she had uttered scarcely a word beyond the necessary minimum for passing milk and marmalade.

Even the winter's first fine covering of snow, which last year would have seen her galloping through her Weetabix and toast to get to her wellingtons and the glistening outside world, had raised no more than a flat 'uh-huh'.

'Aren't you taking your wellies?' Laura had asked when they were getting their things together. 'In case you want to go outside in it at break?' *Play* outside, she'd almost said.

A grunt indicated the negative.

'Don't people make snowmen any more?'

Grunt.

'We even made them at university,' she persisted, even while knowing she should let it drop.

Beth stuck her hands in her pockets. 'Nobody has wellies.'

On the way to the car, she had not so much as run a glove along a windowsill to gather together a snowball.

At nine the skies over Ninepins were a clear ice blue, but in Cambridge at ten Laura's desk fell into shadow and she found herself peering from her office window at cloud the colour of wet sand. The first flakes showed at a quarter past and by twenty past the window was a swirling mass; the sky had paled again so that the falling snow appeared in negative, black on white.

With a wary eye to the roads, and in common with most of her colleagues, Laura set off early for home. The pavements in town were white over and pedestrians were stepping with care as afternoon brought down the freeze; the roads were clear, but nevertheless the traffic stood stationary for long spells before edging forward at a snail's pace. She'd hoped to arrive at the school by ten past three and surprise Beth, who was still in protest about homework club. In fact, the gridlocked roads meant it was after half past four when she finally swung into the drive which led down to Elswell Village College.

As soon as she turned the corner she knew that things weren't right. The school buildings, usually ablaze with light at this time of day, lay in semi-darkness, with just an isolated light over the entrance and one or two others off in offices or

130

upstairs classrooms. The car park was almost empty. She didn't bother to turn into it but pulled slowly along in front of the main doors. A whiteboard had been wheeled to just inside the double glass doors, blocking any entrance or exit. On it was printed in red dry marker three emphatic words. SCHOOL CLOSED 2PM.

It was immediately evident that Beth was not here. The glass-fronted reception area where Mrs Warhurst normally sat was shuttered fast; the windows of the homework room were unlit. It was unthinkable that Beth could have remained in the deserted school for the best part of three hours. There was only one answer. She must have gone home.

Two pm, thought Laura as she pulled back out into the drive: when the school rang the office, she'd already have been on her way to the car. At least it would have been daylight when Beth left. The journey would have been safe enough. There would have been none of the patches of metallic black that now glittered threateningly in the melted snow by the kerbsides, obliging her to keep her wheels carefully in the tramlines swept dry by earlier vehicles. The bus would have been full of other children; Ninepins Drove would have been an easy walk. She just hoped Beth would have had the sense to switch on the central heating, which they'd left on the timer, and to stay indoors in the warm.

Beyond the village boundary, the snow lay thicker. At the margin of her headlamp beams the verges loomed lumpily, the dried heads of hogweed and thistle distended out of recognition; her tyres made a different noise here, slushing through a layer of wet snow. From out of the blackness above, fresh flakes began to fall, speckling the windscreen. She hunched lower in her seat and switched on the wipers.

The snow was settling fast on the sides of the road. Laura slowed almost to a halt to take the turn towards Ninepins, feeling beneath her tyres the change from slick tarmac to a creaking coat of white. But the grip seemed sound, so with caution she accelerated to a steady crawl.

Prudence dictated that she leave her car by the gate and mount the dyke on foot. The silence was blanketing; the slow, soundless snow fell about her like a curtain from the world. There was almost no light – except from the snow, which seemed to give out a luminosity of its own, so that colour and orientation were distorted, and the earth was paler than the sky. The square bulk of the house appeared larger than usual, and very black; a curtained square of yellow showed at the sitting room window.

'Hello, love,' she called, as she let herself in the front door.

There was no reply. The hall and kitchen were in darkness. But at least it was warm; Beth had remembered the heating.

'I went round by the school,' she called from the hallway, picking up a scatter of bills and circulars. 'I saw the notice. Why didn't you call me?' Illogical, perhaps, as there was nothing she could have done, stuck in snowbound traffic. 'It would have been nice to know – '

She broke off as she entered the sitting room and saw them. Beth lay stretched along the settee, her feet up on a pile of cushions at one end. Sprawled alongside her head-to-toe, with her feet on a matching pile at the other end was the girl: the tall, skinny one with the artificial, straight blonde hair. Rianna.

'Oh. Er, hello there.'

Neither of them replied at once. Rianna looked up from under heavy lash extensions, the slide of the eyes just too slow for spontaneity. Beth started and made to struggle up, as if caught with her hand in the biscuit tin or (Laura banished the uncomfortable image) with a boy; then she subsided, resuming her attitude of uncharacteristic langour. 'Hi,' she said finally, addressing the cushions.

'I really think you might have rung.' Laura tried to sound brisk and keep out the complaining note. 'Just to say you were OK.'

There was silence. The fake eyelashes narrowed disdainfully; Beth continued to scrutinise the cushions.

'Well. Never mind. You're nice and warm in here, anyway. It's snowing again, outside. Coming down quite thick, and freezing, too, so it's going to settle, for sure. There's already a couple of inches. I shouldn't be surprised if school is closed again in the morning.' She winced to hear herself, the way the words tumbled out, the edge of desperation. 'Did they say anything about it?' she continued. 'About tomorrow?'

The direct question at least produced a shrug from Beth and a mumbled 'Not really'.

'I suppose they don't know yet, do they? I mean, it will depend on the weather overnight.'

With an effort, she gathered her wits. What was it Vince had told her? *Have them round. Get to know them.*

'So, Rianna, are you staying for supper? You're very welcome, if you'd like to. I can run you home afterwards. I shouldn't like to think of you waiting for a bus in all this – besides, they might be late, or not running at all. But do stay and have something to eat with us first, won't you? There are lamb chops in the fridge.'

At least it wasn't kippers, she thought, and almost raised a smile. But Beth had sat up and was chewing her lip; Rianna, still horizontal, was smirking.

'Actually, we had them earlier, Mum.'

'Earlier?' It was barely five o'clock.

'We were starving. And Caitlin was here.'

'Caitlin . . . ?'

'She went home. She was meeting someone.'

Laura swallowed. Of course Beth was welcome to the food, she chided herself. It was cold, and kids got hungry in the cold. And she wanted Beth to feel she could bring her friends home, didn't she?

'What about Willow? Did she eat with you?'

'She went off, soon as we got here. In the sitting room while we were in the kitchen, I think, then off upstairs.'

'Oh, well, I'll do some pasta later for Willow and me. Would you like a cup of tea, Rianna?'

Whether or not in response to this invitation, finally, unhurriedly, Rianna sat up.

'I'll get going, I think.'

'But I'll give you a lift? It's perishing out there.'

The girl unfolded herself from the settee, flicked back the stair-rod hair and fished in a pocket for her mobile.

'S'all right. I'll text my brother. He's got the van.'

'Well, if you're sure . . .' But Rianna was already thumbing buttons, holding the phone hip-high, barely glancing at the display. *They're just children;* that's what Vince had said. Absently, she retrieved the TV remote from the floor and began to right the disordered cushions. As she returned one to the armchair, her eye fell on a handful of blackened matchsticks lying on the side table. No cigarette butts, though, which was something. She swept the matches into her hand and closed her fingers.

'Where's Willow now?' she asked Beth.

'Dunno. In her room, I s'pose.'

Laura nodded, frowning. 'Could you go up and ask her if she's hungry, please?'

Beth turned to Rianna, but she gave a swift shake of the head. 'Liam's coming straight over. I'll go out and meet him.'

'Then let Beth walk with you, at least,' said Laura. 'And do take a torch. You can give it back to Beth at school. Have you got a hat? I'm sure we could lend – '

Rianna, though, was heading for the hallway, with Beth following close behind. Laura let them go.

Alone in the kitchen, she dropped the matches in the bin. She hung up her daughter's school fleece, extracting from one pocket the wet gloves, unballing them to lay out flat on the back of the Rayburn. She picked up the school bag which lay upside down on the floor, and opened it. On the top lay Beth's uneaten packed lunch.

Willow lay on her bed and stared at her toes. She let her feet grow leaden and then her legs, heavy as stones, as heavy as if there were rocks piled on top of them, or cold, wet sand. Then she let the heaviness spread to her hips and back and the rest of her body, sinking deep into the duvet until, slowly, the weight in her stomach merged with the weight of her limbs. Then she could relax.

It was still difficult to distinguish between the two feelings: being full and being empty. Between this feeling now of the bulk of Laura's pasta inside her and the other one, the aching heaviness of hunger. The stretch of one and the tug of the other – they were so hard to tell apart.

This was the way to make it go away, the emptiness: she had learned that when she was very small. Turn yourself into wood or stone and let the weight spread and take you over until the hunger drains away.

Not that she had to do it so very often – or not all the time. Sometimes not for months on end. There were times when her belly was the other way, crammed to bursting, when she could look down along the angular lines of herself and see it mounded there, tightening her T shirt. Her belly was full of amazing things, sometimes, like Ayodele's curries, or something outlandish her mother had cooked, sweet and syrupy or stinging with spice. There were whole packs of trifle sponges, crusted with sugar, and cold cling peaches eaten from the tin. They ate silver balls meant for cake topping, swallowed by the handful; they shared peanut butter straight from the jar, taking turns with the spoon.

In foster homes you were fed, at least, with no stinting and at regular meal-times. It might be chips and junk, but it was never not there. But Ninepins was different. Here at Ninepins food seemed to have an extra, hidden meaning, some moral substance that was completely foreign to Willow. Laura acted as if fresh vegetables and proper home-cooked meals could solve every problem, could make things whole again when they were broken. But they couldn't. Nothing could.

She wriggled her toes, releasing them from their weight of stone. She loosened her legs and arms and let her body feel again its own life and lightness. And there in her middle the solidity stayed: that solid, spreading warmth which meant being full.

Laura was wrong, though, just the same. Food was just food, and had no special magic. All it did was take away hunger. Feeding someone and loving them were not the same thing.

There were many telephone calls which Laura, in moments of private torment, had imagined receiving. This, however, wasn't one of them. It came not from the hospital nor the police but from the school, and at ten past nine in the morning. She had scarcely had time to take off her coat and scarf and boot up her computer, and her mind was full of last night's e-mails. It was a voice she did not recognise at first. Mrs Leighton, the deputy head.

'Dr Blackwell.' Nobody at the school, to her recollection, had ever used her proper title before. 'We'd be grateful if you could come in, please.' No apology, no noises of reassurance. A simple summons. Laura's screen leapt out of focus; her stomach crawled.

Of course, she tried to say.

'I have Mr Burdett here, with Beth. And Sergeant Peverill from the Cambridgeshire police.'

Police. Flashing blue lights filled her vision. But Beth was there with Mr Burdett. Beth was all right; it must be all right.

'So, if you could make arrangements to come into school as soon as possible, Dr Blackwell . . .'

During the drive to Elswell she kept her mind carefully closed. She filled its surface with radio phone-in chatter and allowed in no other thought. Such journeys were supposed to be unending, but it seemed no time at all before she was checking in with Mrs Warhurst – whose face betrayed nothing – and walking the short distance to Mrs Leighton's office.

'Come in,' she called promptly at Laura's first knock.

The office was a small one and crowded by an oversized desk. Behind it, Mrs Leighton did not rise. In front of it, four upright, upholstered chairs were grouped, so close together that the knees of the three occupants were almost touching. Beth sat very still beside her form teacher, Mr Burdett, and didn't look up. The police sergeant was a woman, and the only one of the four who smiled.

'Dr Blackwood,' began the deputy head. 'Thank you for coming. Mr Critchley is not in school today, or he should have been dealing with this himself. In his absence, I hope you will understand, it has fallen to me. Do please take a seat.'

Dumbly, Laura sat down on the fourth chair. There was a smell of perspiration.

'This is Sergeant Peverill, as I mentioned on the phone.'

Laura glanced at the police officer, who was no longer smiling.

'I shall leave it to her to explain why we are here.'

As the sergeant began to speak, Laura looked not at her but at Beth. She appeared small and shrunken sitting next to Mr Burdett. There was mud on her shoes.

'. . . received a call at around twenty to nine this morning from Mr French who runs the newsagent in the High Street here in Elswell . . .'

Must they have the heating on so high? How did Mrs Leighton work in this oppressive heat? Or maybe it was all the bodies in the room.

'. . . shop has a policy of notifying the police of every instance of shoplifting.'

The immediate feeling was of detachment, almost of dislocation. It was as if she could both be here and yet at the same time also miles from here, when all this was in the past; it was as if she had absorbed and understood it all in a moment, and already put it behind her. *I know*, she could almost have said. *I know it all; I've known all along.* But then she saw Beth, the top of her bowed head, and the present rushed back up at her, putting her in a fury to deny the

137

charge. She wanted to pull her daughter close and shout at them that they were wrong. *Not Beth.* She couldn't, she wouldn't; it's not her, not my Beth.

'. . . items of relatively low value,' the policewoman was saying. She picked up a padded envelope and tipped its contents on to Mrs Leighton's desk. Two KitKat Chunkies, a Dairy Milk and a small box of matches.

Not my Beth. Not unless . . . unless they . . .

'Beth has admitted to taking the things. She told the truth straight away, and apologised to Mr French, and that has helped matters immensely. Her frankness and co-operation in this respect is greatly in her favour. Mrs Leighton tells me that Beth has never been in any trouble at school for taking other people's things, or for dishonesty.'

'No.' Laura's throat was so constricted that speaking pained her physically. But she had to; she had to speak, for Beth. 'She's never been in any trouble, not here, and not at primary school either. Believe me, this is completely out of character for her. She has always been completely trustworthy.'

Beth still wouldn't look up at her, so she turned her eyes to Mr Burdett for support. He looked uncomfortable, but at least he was able to meet her gaze.

'Yes. Er, quite. It's true, I've never known Beth to be dishonest. In fact – ' he cleared his throat ' – she is normally a very responsible girl, and a valued member of the class.'

'Indeed,' said Mrs Leighton. 'There have been no problems at all. Until now.'

Laura thought of the choir and the cigarettes and offered silent thanks to Miss Chapman.

'In these circumstances,' said Sergeant Peverill, 'with a first offence, and in view of Beth's young age and her previous good record of behaviour, we shall be taking the incident no further.'

At this, for the first time, Beth's head came up; Laura glimpsed her face, flushed scarlet, for just a moment before it was buried again.

'This is not, therefore, an official police caution. Nothing will be formally recorded on any file. However, I hope that you understand the seriousness of what you have done, Beth, and that you can give us your assurance now that it won't happen again.'

Beneath the crown of the bent head, Laura saw her daughter's throat working, saw what it cost her to produce the words. 'Y-yes. I mean, no. I promise.'

Their formal parts played out, there was relief but at the same time more awkwardness. Sergeant Peverill went back to smiling; she couldn't be more than twenty-two or -three. Mrs Leighton smuggled a glance at her wall clock. Mr Burdett was the first to rise, just a little too eagerly.

'Come on, then, Beth. Back to lessons. It will still be double science – let's get you to Mrs Farrell in the biology lab.'

Mother and daughter exchanged no word but they moved close together as they passed through the door; Beth slipped her hand briefly into Laura's, and Laura gave it a squeeze.

When she reached the end of the school drive, Laura did something normally unthinkable. Instead of swinging the car left towards Cambridge and her office, she turned right and headed home.

She needed space, and there was plenty of it at Ninepins. She needed to get out and walk. In her bedroom, she swapped her work shoes for outdoor boots and pulled on a fleece over her blouse. Changing her clothes would take too long; she burned with impatience to be out of doors.

Work had begun on the pumphouse, but she was relieved to see that the builders' van was not in evidence today; she couldn't have faced a conversation about studwork and draught sealing. For once she walked in neither direction along the lode but took a third footpath, which struck off at an angle from near the garden gate, across the fields to the north-west. Most winters, this path would have been prohibitively muddy, but not this year, or at least not in the past few weeks. The snow that came in January had not stayed long, dispatched by a day of wintry rain. But the thaw had been brief and although no new snow had fallen, they'd had night after night of hard, penetrating frost, day after day when temperatures stuttered barely above zero. The soil was churned to clods but Laura's boots made scarcely an indentation on the ridged and rutted surface. In all the small drains and ditches, water stood solid.

For more than two hours she strode along without caring where she went, eventually finding herself on a farm track which took her to the edge of Elswell village, and thence back home along the lode. But if she'd thought by walking to clear her mind and bring some measure of calm to her spirit before she had to face her daughter, the plan was not a success. Stooping to unlace her boots by the back door, she felt her blood pumping from the exertion, and with it the same hammering, half-formed thoughts that had chased round her head all morning.

After a sandwich – most of which she threw away uneaten – she went upstairs and tried to do some reading. She turned the pages; she moved her eyes assiduously over the words, but the ideas refused to take hold. By three o'clock, when it was time to collect Beth, she was strung to a worse pitch than if she'd been at work.

Beth's whispered 'I'm sorry, Mum' as she fumbled with her seatbelt eased things slightly, but the car was still tight with tension all the way home. In the kitchen, Laura played for more time, putting on the kettle, finding mugs. But then it could be put off no longer. She took one chair and pulled out another for Beth.

'Tell me,' she said.

Any hopes that it might be easy dissolved at once. The answer came quickly. Too quickly. 'Tell you what?'

Quietly, she insisted. 'Tell me what happened.'

'I took the stuff. Like I told them – like I told you. I took it.'

If she'd been less adamant, if she hadn't inflected that final pronoun, Laura might have remained in doubt. But she knew her daughter. She knew Beth. *She knew.*

'Who made you do it?'

'What d'you mean? Nobody did. I just took the stuff. It was me.'

'Three chocolate bars? Was it all for you? Or were you going to give it to somebody?'

'I – I dunno. Might have given some to people. Everyone shares round their sweets.'

Three chocolate bars. Three. Very gently, she asked, 'And Rianna and Caitlin? Have they given you a lot of sweets?'

She waited for the outburst, the defensive assault. The wounded loyalty: leave my friends alone. When it didn't come, Laura's certainty wavered. But she plugged on anyway.

'Did you feel you owed them, maybe? If they're always giving you things and you have nothing to give back? Because you know, I could always let you have chocolate to take in and share.'

Beth was fiddling with the ends of her scarf, which she hadn't taken off. Nor her fleece, either; she looked bunched, lumpy, miserable. She said nothing.

'Was it their idea? Did they tell you what to take?'

Still there was no angry reaction, no vehement denial.

'Were they there with you, in the shop?'

Then, quite suddenly, her mind spun off at a lurching tangent. The matches.

'Or was it Willow? Did Willow ask you to steal the things?'

Finally, to this there was a response. Beth looked up at her, aghast. 'No!'

'All right.' Laura drew a breath and held it. 'So, then,' she said gently, 'tell me.'

Head down again, mouth half muffled in her scarf, Beth began to talk. 'The matches were for Caitlin. She wanted cigarettes, she said. But they were behind the counter and I didn't dare.'

Closing her eyes, Laura breathed out slowly.

'Mr French was over by the newspapers. They said they'd keep a lookout. The cigarettes were too hard but the matches were on the corner, near the sweets. I just put them in my pocket.'

There was a pause. Laura kept very still, waiting.

'I'm sorry,' whispered Beth, and the end of the word was lost in the first sob.

It all became simpler, then. Laura pulled her chair up close to her daughter's and put an arm around her, shielding her, letting her cry.

'Baby,' she murmured, hardly knowing what words she chose. 'Sweet love. My baby girl.'

And after that, after the weeping had stopped, it was easy to ask the rest of her questions.

'What about the chocolate bars?'

Beth gulped wetly. 'They said it'd be no problem.' Laura wondered if there were more tears to come, but Beth swallowed again and her voice came out steady, if flat. 'The sweets are just there on the counter. They said it's easy, they do it all the time. Rianna went along the row of magazines and sort of messed them up, opening them and not putting them back properly, you know, so Mr French had to go and straighten them. Rianna went out of the shop when she'd done the magazines, but Caitlin stayed inside to signal when.'

Laura nodded, but Beth was gathered to her chest and couldn't see.

'I got them in my pocket OK. He hadn't seen, I know he hadn't, he was still looking down at the magazines. Caitlin ran for it but he came over and, oh, I don't know, maybe 'cos I had my hand in my pocket, or he saw there weren't as many KitKats left or something, but he looked at me and just said "Empty your pockets, please" and it was horrible.'

'And they just left you there.'

Beth grunted her assent. Then her shoulders jerked and she was sobbing again, forcing out words between the gulps. 'But they . . . didn't mean . . . not their fault . . .'

Say nothing else, Laura warned herself. Say nothing for now, at least. She tugged Beth closer against her and crushed her hard, contenting herself with that. But of one thing she was now absolutely certain. If Rianna or Caitlin crossed her path any time soon, so help her, she would kill them with her bare hands.

'I don't suppose it's the start of a life of crime.' Vince took a sip of beer and sat back comfortably in his chair.

Laura looked at him with some ambivalence. On the one hand, this was exactly what she wanted to be told, and actually the reason she had asked him to join her for this second evening in the pub. Vince, in his professional capacity, must have seen it all before, and ten times worse besides. She needed his broader and calmer perspective. On the other hand, he might have shown just a little more concern.

'Half the kids I knew at school tried shoplifting.'

He sounded like Beth. *Everyone tries cigarettes.*

'Charlie Leadbetter used to nick chewing gum – and he's in the police force now. Gareth Fraine: he runs a road haulage firm in Slough. Ed Howell's a geography teacher.'

This was meant to mean something. He was being kind.

'Really, with Beth I don't think you need to worry. She'll have had her warning, I'm sure. She's much too sensible not to heed it.'

'Hmm.' She raised her gin and lemon, wet her lips abstractedly and put it down again.

He was studying her more seriously now. 'You're not convinced?'

'Oh, I don't know. Maybe. You're right about Beth, I suppose. She's a good girl.'

'But?'

She tried, but failed, to muster a smile. 'As you say – but.'

Vince was waiting, placid, unhurried. She could see how he'd be good at his job.

'It's the others,' she said eventually. 'These girls she's got

143

herself in with, Rianna and Caitlin, the ones who put her up to it. I suppose I'm scared they'll do it again. Put pressure on her to shoplift, or other things – worse things.'

'You don't think Beth can stand up to them?'

She hesitated. 'I'm not sure. They're . . . well, they're pretty intimidating.' This time she managed the smile. 'They certainly intimidate me.'

He smiled back and sat passive for a while, allowing her thoughts to settle. Then, quietly, he said, 'Don't underestimate your daughter.'

The words were spoken without any note of reproof, but she felt their cut nonetheless.

'It's easy to underestimate the people closest to us. We want to protect them, we're afraid for them, it's only natural. So we see their vulnerabilities and not their strengths.'

She examined his face and willed herself to believe him. It was so beguiling: to believe in her daughter's toughness and resilience. But dare she trust to it? Beth still seemed to her so unprepared to deal with a world of Riannas and Caitlins.

An oblique idea occurred to her. 'Did he get caught? Your friend the policeman. And the other two, the teacher and the haulier. Did they ever get caught?'

Vince narrowed his eyes, temporising. 'We all knew.'

'But none of them was actually caught by the authorities, right?' Because that was the difference, wasn't it? That was Beth's true vulnerability. It was the same with the cigarettes, the night of the carol concert: it might not have been her smoking, but she was the one left holding the goods. Her sweetness, her honesty, her naïveté, this was where it was going to land her: being the one who took the rap.

She picked up her gin, which she had barely touched, and swallowed a large mouthful, wincing as the burn hit her chest.

'Look at it this way, Laura.' Across the table, Vince leaned forward in his chair. 'Yes, she was found out, when lots of kids aren't. But that just makes it doubly certain she won't be doing it again. Now drink that one up, and let me fetch you another.'

This time it was his car they'd come in, so she could have said yes, but the warm candlelit bar felt claustrophobic all of a sudden.

'No, thanks. Look, do you mind if we go outside? I'd really like some air.'

The inappropriateness of her proposal struck her, along with the icy air, as soon as they stepped beyond the airlock of the pub's porch. A fen night in early February, in the middle of a cold snap, was hardly the time or place for a social stroll. Nor could they harbour in the shelter of Elswell High Street. For tonight's rendezvous they had rejected the dubious comforts of the Fisherman's Arms for a smarter pub slightly further afield, with scrubbed pine tables and an adventurous menu designed to attract diners out from Cambridge. In summer it traded on its 'riverside' billing, although an eight foot bank divided the outdoor dining terrace from a view of the water. In winter, it was a bleak and cheerless spot.

'Along the river?' Vince suggested economically, from behind a swathe of scarf. The air furred at his escaping breath.

They mounted the bank together at the trot required to give them the impetus to climb its sharp sides. 'River', in fact, might be deemed a misnomer, even though one title attached to this waterway was the Bedford New River. Its other name, the Hundred Foot Drain, was a more honest description. One hundred feet was its width from the top of one embankment to the other; the drain was a man-made cut-off of the river Great Ouse.

'Goodness.' On reaching the path which topped the bank, Laura stood rooted. 'Is that ice?'

They both peered down through the darkness at the surface of the drain. Even without adjustment of her vision to the night, she could make out the too-black glitter. She kept her head very still until she could be sure of it: there was no movement at all. The whorls and craters that she saw were frozen solid.

'It's funny,' she said. 'You expect ice to be smooth and flat, don't you? Not textured like that.' It was almost lumpy; as if the water had set fast in the middle of swirling motion.

Vince nodded, chin still buried in his scarf. 'You'd wonder how it could freeze at all. So much of it, I mean – such a big body of water. And with a current, presumably.'

'Yes. It runs up to Denver Sluice. It's even tidal, I think, further up. Not here, though, I don't suppose.' She shifted her feet, raising her toes away from the ground, which seemed to transmit cold even through the soles of her boots. 'The lode at home has been frozen for the best part of a week. But that's much smaller, and has much less flow. I don't remember ever seeing the Hundred Foot iced over before.'

'That's global warming for you.'

They both grinned, though there was nothing funny about it. Then they turned and began to walk along the embankment, away from the pub and the road and into the denser darkness beyond.

'Shit.' Vince stumbled sideways, then stopped and flexed his foot, catching hold of her wrist for balance. 'Ouch. Lump of wood or something. Should have brought a torch.'

'My fault, sorry. You hardly expected to be dragged out for a moonlit ramble.'

'No bloody moon, or it might be all right. Hey – your hands are as frozen as the river. Don't you have gloves?'

'Forgot them. Stupid.'

'Here.' He took off his own gloves as they walked along and she put them on without argument. They were square and leather, cotton-lined, warm from his blood.

'There's something else you shouldn't forget,' he said, 'about Beth. She cares a great deal for your feelings. She'll have seen how this has hurt you, her being in trouble. She won't want to be the cause of that again.'

They had reached a place where a fence rose to cross the

146

bank, surmounted by a small stile. Laura stopped and stared out across the expanse of eerie, motionless water.

'Thank you,' she said.

'Come on.' He turned round. 'Bollocks to this, if you'll excuse my French. It's like Siberia out here. Let's get back to the car. Unless you fancy that other drink?'

The heating in Vince's old, red saloon could best be described as temperamental. By the time they reached Ninepins they were both chilled to the core, so he came in for a coffee and a warm-up by the Rayburn.

'I should get one of these,' he said, leaning back against it with his hands behind his haunches. 'Except it would fill the entire kitchen in my flat. Might be room in the bedroom, though. That would be an idea.'

She laughed as she filled the kettle. 'Handy for breakfast in bed.'

There was another thing, though, that she needed to talk to him about, a thing she'd put off until now. Pressing down the plunger on the cafetière, she took the plunge herself.

'Vince, do you mind if I ask you something? It's about Willow.'

He looked across at her, hands now flat on the top of the Rayburn behind him. He didn't speak or nod, but his face was open, attentive.

'It's probably nothing. Probably just me being foolish. And none of my business, either.'

His gaze was steady. 'Go on.'

'Well . . . does Willow smoke?'

'Not as far as I'm aware, no. In fact, I'm pretty sure she doesn't.'

'Right. I thought not.'

Now it came to the point, she felt how ridiculous it was going to sound.

'The thing is, I sometimes find matches. Just piles of used matches, in her room and around the place. I expect you think

147

it's odd – an odd thing to worry about, I mean. But, I don't know, I just can't help wondering – '

There she broke off. Willow was standing in the hall doorway, and with her, in pyjamas and dressing gown, was Beth.

'Mum, your mobile was switched off.'

'Oh. Was it?' She collected her thoughts. 'I'm sorry, love, I didn't realise. Why – did you need me? Is everything all right?'

'Fine.' Beth grinned at Willow. 'We've been playing Ludo. But it's Dad. He was trying to reach you. Says could you call him tonight and to tell you it's urgent.'

Chapter 13

Urgency was an everyday feature of her ex-husband's domestic life, so she saw Vince off before she lifted the phone, and then not with any great sense of apprehension.

'Oh, Laura – fantastic. Thanks so much for calling back. Where were you? I couldn't reach your mobile.'

'I must have had it switched off by mistake.'

'Well, I've got you now, thank the Lord. Laura, you are my life-saver. My rescuing angel. What would I do without you?'

It was impossible not to smile. 'And?'

'I need to ask a desperate favour. It's quite beyond the call of duty – beyond all reasonable expectation. But you know I wouldn't ask if it wasn't an emergency.' How many times, she wondered, had he used those words to her? 'I wouldn't ask it of anyone but you.'

'Go on.'

'Thing is, I'm at the hospital.'

Her smile disappeared on the instant. Her heart tripped a beat.

'Simon. What's happened? Is everyone – ?'

'We're all right. Don't panic. Nobody died. It's really not too serious. It's Alfie.'

'Alfie? Has he had an accident?' Alfie was always falling off things and crashing into things.

'No, nothing like that. But they've got him under observation and it looks like he's going to need an operation. He's been having abdominal pain, and today it was a lot worse, suddenly. We came in this morning – been here all day.

They've done dozens of tests. They've decided it's a problem with his kidneys.'

'Oh, God. That doesn't sound good. Poor Alfie. How's he coping with it? Is he in a lot of distress?'

'Well, they've been very good here. Marvellous, in fact. Everyone who's seen him has been great about explaining things, talking him through it. Even making him laugh. And they've got him on painkillers, on a drip, so at least that's under control. He's mainly just drowsy, now.'

'Poor Alfie,' she said again. 'So, what is it I can do for you? Is it Jack and Roly? I'd be happy to take them if you and Tessa need to stay with Alfie overnight.'

Happy was hardly the word. The boisterous four- and two-year-old, exhausting enough at the best of times, and then displaced, upset and missing their parents and brother: it would be, to be honest, a nightmare. But Beth loved the little boys; she would help. And she could scarcely do less for Simon.

'No, that's OK. They're here with us. Tessa picked them up from nursery at three. We all want to be here with Alfie. Be together, you know.'

'There in the ward?' She pictured the chaos: the bored, rampaging toddlers, the beleaguered nurses.

'They've moved him to a little side room by himself now, so it's no problem. We've brought in a folding camp bed for the night, so Jack and Roly can share that. They do have some family rooms, actually, for parents staying over, but they're way over the other side of the site, and have no space for kids. We all want to be near Alfie. Tessa and I can sleep on the floor.'

'And they're OK about it?'

'Seem to be. With a little persuasion.'

Simon, no doubt giving the nurses his wounded puppy act.

'So then, what's this favour? Do you need some things bringing over?'

'Actually, Laura, I need someone to have Dougie.'

Dougie? For a second, her mind was a blank. Then she remembered. 'The dog?'

'I know. I wouldn't ask. But he's been on his own since this morning – except when Tessa dashed in and fed him after nursery when she picked up the overnight stuff for us and the boys. I really can't think who else could take him. And they said absolutely not, we're not allowed to have him here.'

Laura actually found herself wincing. 'Simon. You didn't seriously ask if you could have a dog in the hospital?'

'Worth a try.' She could almost see him grinning.

'Well, yes. Of course I'll have him. But you know I know nothing about dogs. Is there food for him? And how much, and when? And where will I find it, and his lead and dog bowls and whatever it is he sleeps in? I shall need some instructions.'

'Come here to the hospital. Children's surgical, G3. I can give you the house key and tell you what you need to know.'

'OK.' She glanced at her watch. 'I'll be straight over.'

'And bring Beth. Dougie loves Beth.'

'Right.'

'Oh, and Laura?'

'Yes?'

'Thank you.'

It was late to be taking Beth out on a school night, urging her out of her pyjamas and into jeans and a jumper and coat. Not that she needed much persuasion. The excitement of the excursion and the hospital was allure enough – even without the dog.

'Dougie! We're actually going to have Dougie here living with us.'

'I don't know about living, exactly. It's only for a little while, until Alfie is better and can go home.'

'How long? A week? Can we have him a whole week?'

'I've no idea. Now, get your gloves and scarf on. It's freezing out there.'

As they were putting on their shoes, Willow appeared, also coated and gloved. 'Can I come?'

'Why not?' She might be grateful for any help on offer.

It was an odd sort of mercy dash, driving with slow circumspection on the icy lanes, and worrying about the mysteries of canine care when she should have been thinking about Alfie and his operation.

'Does he have that dry food?' she asked, scanning her daughter's face in the mirror.

'Oh, he'll eat anything. Vegetable lasagne's his favourite. And he just sleeps on people's beds.'

Oh, God. Simon had never been much of a one for boundaries.

'Can he sleep with me, Mum? Pleeease.'

'What about your asthma? I'm not sure pet hair is – '

' 'S'OK, Dougie's no problem. He always sleeps on my bed at Dad's.'

It was eleven thirty by the time they arrived at the hospital, after midnight before they reached Simon's house. All the other residents were already home and in bed or watching TV, and finding a parking spot was a struggle. Eventually, they squeezed into a half-space two streets away.

'Right, then. Let's go and find the hound.'

It never seemed quite so cold in Cambridge as out in the fens, but her fingers still tingled when she took off her gloves to fit the Yale in the lock. No excited barking greeted the sound of their entry, as it had on recent occasions when she had picked up Beth; no small flurry of hair and tongue launched itself at their ankles. The hall was silent and apparently deserted. Beth switched on the light – though not before Laura and Willow had both tangled painfully with a metal tricycle.

'Dou-gie,' Beth called out. 'It's only us. Where are you, Doug?'

They tried the sitting room, where Beth said he favoured the corner armchair, and the playroom at the back, where there were Duplo bricks to chew, both without success. That left the kitchen.

'Dou-gie,' sang Laura, without much conviction. 'Here, boy.'

The room bore evidence of Tessa having flung in and out again in a hurry with Jack and Roly on her way back to the hospital – though it was equally possible that the clutter on the table and floor was no more than the usual state of things. Laura picked up a carton of milk and put it back in the fridge. If it hadn't been late, and school in the morning, she might have done some washing up.

'Can't see him anywhere,' she said. 'Might he be upstairs?'

At least she could see the bag of dog food, and the two tin bowls, as Simon had described. And on the window ledge – she shuddered – the 'poop scoop' and bags. At Ninepins he'd be out in the fields and they wouldn't have to bother with that.

Beth had run upstairs, followed by Willow; she could be heard moving from room to room, banging doors, calling Dougie's name. Presently, she clattered back down.

'We can't find him. Oh, Mum, you don't think he's run away or something, do you?'

Laura's heart sank. What if he really wasn't here? What if Tessa, in her hurry, had accidentally let him slip out of the door? Her mind conjured visions of a small hours neighbourhood search, of the police and the RSPCA. Not to mention the phone call to Simon.

Just when she was steeling herself for the worst, she heard a sound from down by her feet. Disturbingly human: a soft, plaintive whimper. She squatted down on her haunches and peered beneath a deep-set shelving unit stacked with basins and saucepans – and into a pair of inscrutable amber eyes.

'Hello there, lad,' she said, in her best jollying tones. 'We're not going to hurt you. We've come to take you for walkies.'

Dougie stared back at her, unblinking. He did not move.

Kneeling down beside her, Beth began to croon. 'Dou-gie. Come on out, boy. Waaa-lkies.'

But there was no movement. Very cautiously, Laura began to extend a hand towards the darkness beneath the shelves – and quickly retracted it, as the yellow eyes narrowed and an ominous, low grumbling noise arose.

Beth clambered to her feet. 'Food. He always comes for food. Let's see what there is.' She opened the fridge door. 'What d'you think? Cheese? But it's that sliced kind in the plastic, like in MacDonald's. Or, hang on, here's some sausages left over, on a plate. Ugh – they're all white and furry at one end. Would they poison him, d'you reckon?'

'I expect he's had worse.' There was Alfie's football, for a start.

'Here, Dougie. What's this?' Beth was back on all fours, dangling a cold sausage towards the void.

Suddenly there was a scrabble of claws and a rush of hair and teeth and Dougie rocketed out and across the kitchen, emitting a siren wail. Leaving them rooted, he shot through the door and out into the hall and freedom.

'Little devil,' said Laura. 'How on earth are we going to get hold of him?'

'Don't be horrible. Poor Dougie – he's scared.' But Beth, Laura could tell, was also enjoying herself royally. She pointed her sausage towards the hallway. 'Come on.'

More quietly this time, in order to avoid setting their quarry to flight again, they retraced their earlier steps through the downstairs rooms. It was a laborious operation, since it involved crawling on hands and knees among the questionable dust and debris of Simon and Tessa's floors and peering under bookcases and behind settees.

'Not here,' decreed Laura eventually. 'Better try the bedrooms again, I suppose.' She sat back on her heels. 'Where's Willow?'

Beth shrugged. Their eyes met.

'Upstairs.'

They mounted them together, side by side. When they reached the top, there was Willow at the end of the landing, sitting cross-legged in the far corner. She didn't even glance up at their approach, but remained completely motionless, head bowed low so that only her fringe and the tip of her nose were visible. And on her lap, curled as serenely as if he had been asleep there all evening, was Dougie.

In a spirit of rapprochement following the shoplifting incident, Laura allowed Beth to come home by herself on the bus twice a week. It might seem paradoxical, but instinctively Laura judged it to be the right move, an extension of trust to inspire the deserving of it.

On Wednesday afternoon, therefore, as she drew near home, she was met by Beth and Dougie, walking towards her along the drove. She was earlier than usual, and the clear, frost-bright skies which had been with them all week served to emphasise the lengthening of the days. Almost five o'clock, and she could make them out clearly against the pale ribbon of the road. They approached in a drunken zigzag, the small terrier scurrying to one side and then the other at the limit of his lead, nose to the ground and tail aloft, dragging Beth behind. Laura slowed the car and wound down her window, letting in a shock of icy air.

'Dougie's sniffing for rabbits,' Beth called out as soon as they were within hailing distance. 'I'm sure he is. He doesn't do this at Dad's.'

Rats, more likely, thought Laura, along here by the dyke. 'Have you brought a torch?' she asked, when Beth came up. 'It'll be dark soon.'

'Oh, we're not going far. He already had a walk when I first got in. Me and Willow took him over the fields. This is just an extra.'

Meeting me? Laura smiled. 'Hang on, then. I'll just go and park the car and then I'll walk back along and join you.'

The thermometer was falling with the dusk. Laura's legs

felt naked in the tights she'd worn for work; the cold air sliced straight through them. It really would be a short one: catch up with Beth and then straight back home.

They seemed to have stopped, though. In the lowering light, she could make out her daughter's stationary figure, hunched in her coat with collar up and hands in pockets. The grey dog merged to invisibility with the grass of the verge.

'Come on, Beth,' she muttered to herself as she walked towards them. 'Get a move on, and let's get inside.'

'I think he's found one!' Beth's shout was still from a distance, but Laura could see her face, turned towards her and glowing. 'He's found a rabbit.'

Coming closer, she saw that Dougie's head was indeed hidden in the earth, plunged deep in some hole or burrow; only his rear end was above ground, and wagging furiously.

'Oh dear, but you don't think he'll actually catch it, do you, Mum? He might kill it. Oh, he won't kill the rabbit, will he?'

Quite possibly, thought Laura. He had terrier in him, after all. 'I hope not. Let's try to get him away from the hole.'

Taking hold of the lead, her hand round Beth's, she began to tug hopefully. 'Come along, silly dog. Come away from there.'

Dougie pulled back, harder, and began to growl under his breath in the determined manner of one not to be deflected.

'Dougie,' pleaded Beth, as she lent her weight to the tussle, 'please stop that. Leave the poor bunny alone.'

It was surprising that so small an animal should be so strong. The two of them hauled on his lead, leaning hard to the task, but they couldn't budge him. Until suddenly, like something straight out of Laurel and Hardy, the resistance ceased and they staggered backwards across the tarmac, clutching each other for support. Dougie went sharply into reverse and then swung round towards them, triumphant, with something dangling between his teeth.

'Nooo,' wailed Beth, burying her face in Laura's shoulder. 'He's killed the rabbit!'

Laura advanced towards the dog, not at all sure she wanted to look, either. But she should; she must, in case by some miracle the rabbit was still alive.

'Drop it,' she commanded, and to her amazement he did.

The rabbit lay where it fell. Even in the gathering darkness, she could see the stained fur, and an eye, glassy and staring. There was no movement at all. But maybe it was only stunned? She took another step forward and peered down at the lifeless form – and then she laughed out loud. No wonder Dougie was gazing up at her, tail beating, with the expression of a magician who has just produced his best trick. Not, in this case, a rabbit, but a child's teddy bear.

'How could it have got there?' Beth wanted to know as they set off for home.

Laura had only guesses. 'Dropped from a car, perhaps, on the main road? And then maybe an animal picked it up – a fox? Or it was washed there by the flood?'

Dougie was trotting ahead of them, in a straight line now, with his trophy in his mouth.

'Clever boy,' said Beth. Then, after a moment, 'By the way, Dad rang.'

'Oh, yes?'

'He's home now.'

'Alfie's out of hospital?'

'No, Dad. He's gone home with Jack and Roly, but Tessa's still at the hospital with Alfie. They're keeping him in a few more days, Dad says.'

'Right.' She must call Simon. She knew the operation had gone well and Alfie was recovering nicely, but she should ring for another bulletin.

'Anyway, Dad's still going backwards and forwards a lot, he says. So he says, could we keep Dougie another week? Can we, Mum, please?'

Laura looked ahead at the dog with his bear, then across at her daughter, and smiled. 'I don't see why not.'

Beth drew closer and squeezed her hand beneath her mother's arm. 'Brilliant.'

It seemed like an opportunity to ask, 'Was Rianna on the bus today?' *Do you still hang out with them – with her and Caitlin?*

The hand stayed put but Laura sensed a withdrawal, nonetheless. Hostility? Or merely awkwardness?

'Mm.'

Don't pick at it; that's what she would have told Beth. Leave well alone. But something impelled Laura to talk about it, confront it. Tensions unvoiced were always worse, spreading beneath the surface like a bruise.

'Did you sit with her, as far as Longfenton?'

A shake of the head.

'No?'

'She was with some Year 8s.'

Laura nodded. For a minute they walked on without speaking, while she considered her next approach.

'And how are things, at school? OK?'

'Fine.'

Of course it was a dead end. The wrong moment, the wrong questions: she always got it wrong. Better to put back the lid, to close the box back up.

'So, what do you think he's planning to do with it? Dougie, I mean, and his teddy? Take it to bed with him?'

'Eat it, more likely,' said Beth, her voice eager with relief. 'He eats everything. At Dad's once, he ate nearly the whole of a papier mâché snowman that Jack had made at nursery. Tessa said he pooed solid newspaper the next morning when she took him for his walk. She said you could still read bits, but I think she was messing about.'

Just as they were coming near the front door, though, in the midst of her chatter about the dog, she casually said, 'I might have Alice over. On Friday after school, if that's OK? We want to practice this thing we're doing for drama, and walk Dougie, and then she could stay for supper.'

Laura didn't react, beyond a brief nod; she kept her satisfaction to herself.

'And can we have macaroni cheese?'

The Sunday outing was Vince's idea. His original suggestion had taken Laura by surprise, because she had come to think of him as a townie.

'Let's go skating. There's a place where everyone goes, up near Downham Market, on Salter's Lode.'

'But we don't have skates.'

'I do. And I could borrow some for the rest of you easily enough.'

She had forgotten he was raised in Wisbech, making him really more of a fensperson than she was herself.

'We used to go when I was a kid. Never Mum, but me and Dad and my uncle and cousins.'

'At Downham?'

'No. Not on the lodes at all – it wasn't cold enough, most years. You need at least a week's good, solid freeze to make them safe enough. But there were some fields near us which always flooded in the winter, along the side of the Nene. The water was shallow, only a foot or so, so it was always safe to skate.'

It was the first time she'd heard him so enthused.

'The whole town used to turn out. All the boys from school would be there, staging races. Seemed like everybody had skates, and if they didn't they came anyway and just slithered about. Some brought toboggans. There'd be dogs pulling people along, and little kids sliding in just in their wellies.'

She tried to picture it: Vince as a small boy, scarved and hatted, ruddy-faced.

In the end, though, the skating expedition had to be shelved. On the Friday, clouds rolled over and a westerly wind blew in, bearing a scatter of rain; the temperature rose above zero and stayed that way all day and even through the night. By Saturday afternoon, walking across the fields with

159

Beth and Dougie, the sound of trickling could be heard where all had been silence.

Vince rang that night. 'It won't be safe, after this thaw. No one will be skating.'

'We can't go?'

Across the room, Beth looked stricken, and Laura was surprised at the depth of her own disappointment.

'Maybe we could do something else instead? Go somewhere. I don't know – a walk? Take Dougie out.'

'Let's. And then a pub lunch.'

They fixed on Wicken Fen. Vince drove, insisting that if there were to be muddy paws on a car seat, that car seat should be his. The fen itself was a nature reserve, and the National Trust took an unsurprisingly dim view of dogs disturbing the flora and fauna, but all around the perimeter ran paths and tracks accessible to the public, both human and canine. On this side of the boundary, Dougie could run and bark and scramble the moorhens with impunity.

'Can I let him off, Mum? Please.'

The terrier's inclination to come when called was unreliable at best. At Simon's, Beth assured them, he wore his lead on the pavements but ran loose in the park at the end of the road. Laura was more circumspect, feeling you couldn't take risks with someone else's dog. At Ninepins, therefore, the lead had so far remained firmly attached. But out here at the fen, so far from any roads, with the sun breaking through cloud and four of them here to look out for him, she felt an upswell of confidence.

'All right then.'

Beth crouched to release the clip from his collar. 'Go on, boy.'

For a moment, Dougie appeared to be unaware of his freedom; he stood planted in front of Beth, tail slowly waving, squinting up at her face. Then he was off.

'Blimey,' said Vince. 'He can't half move for a littl'un. Will he come back OK?'

'I hope so.' Laura spoke bravely, but it didn't look good. There was an unwavering sort of determination about the way he was streaking away along the path before them, head low and tail out horizontal. Tales filled her head, of animals who ran for home from distances of more than this. But up ahead at a turn of the path he swerved abruptly to one side, spun round and halted; after sniffing the air for a second, his head came down again and he charged back towards them at full tilt.

'Oh, good boy,' cried Beth at his approach, clapping her hands so that he launched himself at her across the final yard, blotching the front of her jeans with mud and almost knocking her flat.

Vince hooted with laughter and Beth and Willow joined in. Laura was smiling too, even while she said, 'I hope that's going to wash off.'

After that, Dougie didn't stray as far. He still trotted ahead of the party, and sometimes sprinted off at tangents after some scent, real or imagined, but his attention was never entirely elsewhere. Every now and then he threw a glance back at them over his shoulder, slantwise, just to check.

Soon they came to a junction of tracks and turned right, crossing a wooden footbridge and then swinging left along the bank of Wicken Lode. The path was elevated here, commanding to one side, across the ice of the lode, a view of the nature reserve, and to the other an expanse of frozen reedbeds. Now and then, above their own breaths and the panting of the terrier, the croak or whistle of some waterfowl split the silence.

'What a great place,' said Willow, stopping to gaze out over the marsh. 'Weird, but beautiful.'

'Most of the fens must have looked like this once,' said Laura, 'before it was all drained.'

Vince drew alongside them and followed their gaze. 'Like looking back in time.'

'Yes.' Laura glanced at him in surprise. 'Yes, I suppose you're right.'

At the next bend of the lode, two boats stood moored, bound fast to the bank by ice as much as by their slack ropes. One was a traditional narrowboat, the once gaily-painted woodwork peeling to naked grey beneath the blues and reds, the chimney-pipe leaning at a drunken angle. The other was shorter and taller, more of a broads cruiser shape, metal-hulled and rusting. It was not only the ice which lent them an air of permanence here, of immobility, of being a part of the landscape. The ropes were decayed, the windows filthy and filmed with green.

Beth tried to peer in through the algae. 'D'you think anyone ever lived in them? All the way out here?'

'Someone must surely have used them once,' said Laura. 'Nobody buys a boat and doesn't use it.'

'Wouldn't it be so cool, to live on a boat?'

'Well – ' Laura smiled at her daughter ' – these might not have been lived in, as such. They might have been used for holidays.'

'Not in a good long while.' Vince had joined Beth in squinting through a window of the narrowboat. 'And not here, I'd guess. I think this might be the place where house-boats come to die.'

'A boat graveyard?' Beth gave a theatrical shudder. 'Spooky.'

Willow had stopped, too, but without coming near. She stood back a few paces in the centre of the path. 'Careful,' she said.

They all turned.

She nodded at the frosty grass which edged the sloping bank beneath their feet. 'Looks slippery.'

Laura looked down into the space between the narrowboat and the land, where ice and icemelt merged in blackness, and experienced a moment of vertigo. She stepped back hastily, drawing Beth with her.

162

They moved to set off again, but Willow still lingered, staring at the boats.

'I remember . . .' She tailed off, her brow set in a puzzled frown.

'What is it?' They had all come back, and Vince laid an arm round her shoulder.

She shook her head, as if trying to shift an irritant. 'Nothing, really. It's just, I think I stayed on a houseboat once.'

'Tell me,' he said.

Another shake of the head, slower this time. 'I can't remember anything much. But I think it was a boat.'

They all waited, feeling the stillness.

'It must have belonged to one of her friends.' She looked hard at Vince. 'Mum was there, but she wasn't, if you know what I mean. And I can't remember the friend, either, really, except that I think she knew we couldn't swim. I think I told her we couldn't swim. She kept me inside, in this little wooden room with bunk beds in, and we played Snap. The window was high up so you couldn't see the water, but there were blue checked curtains and I'm sure there was one of those orange rings, outside on a post. A lifebuoy. So it must have been a boat, mustn't it?'

He nodded, eyes on her face. 'How old do you think you were?'

Willow shrugged, still frowning. 'Four? Three?'

Just then, Dougie, bored by the extended halt, came back and began sniffing impatiently at ankles, huffing under his breath. Willow bent and ruffled his head, in the process ducking out from under Vince's arm. But after a moment she looked up, her hand still buried in the terrier's grey hair, and they saw that she was smiling.

'I do remember I was rubbish at Snap.'

They had an excellent lunch. It wasn't a pub any of them knew. Laura had found it in a pub guide still on the shelf from

163

Simon's day, back before Beth, when they used to head out regularly at weekends to find new places to eat. The pub must have changed hands three or four times since the book was published, but by good luck the current proprietors understood the virtues of traditional steak and kidney pie, and of local winter vegetables, properly cooked. Beth managed all of hers, along with the last of Willow's roast potatoes. She even had room for the apple crumble, and Vince gallantly kept her company. Under the table, Dougie, despairing of scraps, lay flat and dreamed of moorhens.

It was half past three by the time they arrived home. They'd had coffee in the pub, so it seemed redundant to ask Vince in for tea, but Laura did anyway, since he had done the driving. It was the last hour of a beautiful winter's afternoon and house and dyke were basking in watery sunshine, the air milder than it had felt for weeks. On the grass, as they stepped from the car, the frost was turning greasy underfoot.

'I won't stay long,' Vince was saying. 'I've got some case notes I need to write up before the morning. Why do I always leave doing any work until Sunday evening?'

There he broke off, and Laura followed his gaze down along the lode. At first glance, just for a moment, she thought it was the heron, though it was rare to see it this close to the house, and why would it be standing there so still in the middle of the ice? Then her eyes focussed and she saw that it had been a trick of distance and perspective. The shape was further away – perhaps a hundred yards in the direction of Elswell – and much larger. A chill doused her stomach. The shape was human.

'Who on earth . . . ?' she murmured, then took two strides forward, calling out, 'Hey! What are you doing?'

The figure on the ice neither moved nor reacted, but continued to stand hunched and immobile, facing away from them along the frozen water. Her mind panned for sensible solutions but none of them fitted. A fisherman, when the lode was ice-bound? It made no sense. Certainly no fisherman would venture on to the ice in this thaw.

'Hi there!' she shouted again. 'Come off the lode. It's not safe.'

Willow began to run. She was running along the top of the dyke in the direction of the figure, with Vince close behind. Beth ran after them, Dougie barking and tugging at his lead. Laura's legs felt unconnected to her: they started to move of their own accord, and soon she was running too. Her eyes were locked on the dark-coated shape. It was the unnatural stillness that triggered recognition, even from the back. She was suddenly certain. It was her – the same woman as before. Marianne. Willow's mother.

Level with her, they stopped and all stood looking at her, unsure quite what to do next. The water had been at mid-height when it froze, and the lower path, visible here sometimes at low ebb, was covered over. There was nothing but twenty feet of slippery, rimed grass, pitching down at an angle of maybe fifty degrees towards the treacherous ice.

'Mum.' Willow didn't shout; she spoke in her normal voice, conversational. 'Mum, you need to come off there, OK?'

'Marianne,' said Vince. 'It's all right. We're here – you're all right now. Just come over to the bank.'

There was no answer, no acknowledging movement. *Mum was there, but she wasn't, if you know what I mean.* Laura wondered if she knew where she was at all. The ice beneath her boots – the same biker boots – was no longer a uniform white, nor really white at all, but a dull putty grey, only veneered in silver. Darker greys bubbled and pooled beneath the surface. And at the margins where the ice met the bank, especially at the near side which lay most in sunlight, there glinted black snatches of water.

'It's all right,' said Vince again, coaxing. 'Come to us.'

The woman moved a step forward, away from them and further out of reach. Under her feet the ice creaked audibly. Beth slipped a hand into Laura's.

'Mum,' said Willow, voice still level. Then, with only the slightest rising note, 'Please.'

On the ice, still without turning, her mother took another step. There was a sound like a whipcrack, not loud but eerily resonant, ricocheting off the embankments and magnifying through the surface of the ice. From a point beneath her left boot a dark, jagged line appeared, tracing a path with meandering slowness towards the near bank. It was followed by another, shorter but broader. Water was clearly visible now, creeping above the ice.

'Mum!'

Dougie gave one sharp, high bark. It was never clear to Laura, afterwards, what was in his mind: whether he thought to see off danger or to make some valiant, crazed attempt at rescue. For a second, Beth succeeded in holding on to the end of his lead as he flung himself over the rim of the dyke; she was jerked forward, to the very edge herself, before Vince grabbed her by the shoulders and drew her back. With a cry, she let go of the lead.

Down on the lode, Willow's mother dropped to her knees as the terrier half ran, half tumbled down the slope towards her. Then she was crawling off the sinking ice and on to the safety of the far bank. Behind her, at the shift of weight, the fractured surface parted, leaving clefts of gaping black.

'Dougie – no!' screamed Beth, and seized hold of Laura, twisting round away from the lode, hiding her face in her neck. Laura closed her eyes, too, and clung tightly to her daughter, seeing nothing, thinking nothing, hearing nothing, beyond Beth's disbelieving wail.

Chapter 14

Laura had no idea what she would have done without Vince. It was he who shouted at them to stay put while he slithered down the steep embankment towards the surface of the lode and beyond until he was shin deep in ice and water, in a vain attempt to save the terrier. It was he who, still perching at the base of the near bank, talked Willow's mother quietly into calm, he who persuaded her to turn round, there on the far bank, and look at him, and to promise him to remain exactly where she was. And it was Vince who hiked up to the main road along Ninepins Drove and back along the opposite dyke until he reached her and coaxed her home, while Willow phoned the consultant to arrange an ambulance. Laura was left with nothing to do but deal as best she might with a pale and shaken Beth, who couldn't even look at her mother, nor listen to assurances that it was nobody's fault and particularly not her own, nor speak herself, except to repeat the same words over and over. *I let go of his lead. I let go. I let go.*

She was even more grateful later, when it was Vince, who – having escorted Willow and her mother to the psychiatric hospital and Willow home again once they had seen her settled – walked back along the lode in the darkness by himself with an old corduroy jacket from the boot of his car and a long-handled rake from the shed, returning after half an hour or so with a sorrowful bundle in his arms. Beth, thank heaven, had been persuaded to go upstairs and have a bath. Laura met Vince at the door and when she saw what he was holding, her fingers trembled on the latch.

'Is he in there?' The jacket hardly bulged at all. 'I mean, it

167

looks so small.' She swallowed, twice, but her throat still filled with salt liquid.

'I can take him home with me, if you want.'

'No.' If only it could be that easy. Carefully, she looked anywhere but at the jacket. 'No, Simon might want to . . . have him back.' *Bury him.* It was too hard to say.

Vince's boots, at which she had been staring, shifted into focus. Mud coated the leather and clogged the eyeholes. Duckweed clung to his trousers, which were darker almost to the knee. How could it have taken so long to dawn on her that his feet were soaking? That they'd been drenched in freezing water for three or four hours?

'What am I thinking of? You're going to catch five kinds of pneumonia. Come on in and I'll see if Beth is out of the bath yet so that you can have one.'

'Pneumonia, perhaps.' He laid his burden down gently on the step, then straightened up and gave her a grin. 'Frostbite in the toes, certainly. And maybe just an outside chance of leptospirosis.'

His trousers were thick canvas, and even the Rayburn's side oven could not dry out the legs in an hour. The only thing she could provide was an old pair of Simon's jeans that she used for decorating and that had stayed when he left. They were spattered with paint but at least they were dry. His coat was damp and smeared with mud, but her big blue walking fleece seemed to fit him all right, as did a pair of her outdoor socks.

'Have you rung and told him?' he asked, over the cocoa she made him, topped up with a dash of rum.

'No. No, I haven't. I can't tell him over the phone, not a thing like this. I'll have to go round. I owe him that, at least.'

He nodded his approval.

'But not yet. It'll be better when the boys are asleep. Supper first. Will you stay and have some?'

It was a subdued meal, functional and with little attempt on anybody's part at conversation. Willow wasn't hungry; she toyed with half a slice of bread and escaped back up to her room almost at once. Beth ate wordlessly and mechanically, rarely raising her eyes from her plate.

By the time the plates were washed and dried and Vince had left, with final words of sympathy and encouragement, the time was close to nine.

'I'm going to Dad's,' she announced, on her return to the kitchen. 'You'll be all right here, won't you, for an hour or so? Willow's upstairs.'

'You're going to tell him?' Beth was finally looking straight at Laura, and with eyes that seemed twice their usual size. She had to force herself to meet them.

'Yes. I've got to.'

Beth pushed back her chair and stood up. 'I'm coming, too.'

'Well . . .' It was late, would be later still after this was over. And there was Vince's bundled jacket on the doorstep. 'There's really no need – '

'It was me that let go of him.'

'Sweetheart, you know it wasn't your fault. You couldn't hold on to him – nobody could have. You really mustn't think you were the least bit to blame.'

But Beth wasn't listening; her balled fists were pulled up into the cuffs of her jumper. 'I want to come with you.'

Too tired to argue, Laura told her, 'Get your coat on, then.' After all, Beth knew Dougie first. He was much more her dog than Laura's, and she'd loved him.

In the car, though, she sat unspeaking in the corner of the passenger seat. Her shoulders grew tense and bowed forwards, as if shielding her chest from a blow; her neck stiffened, jaw slightly raised. Laura knew that attitude. She sensed it even without turning to see.

'Are you OK? Can you breathe?'

This was always how it began, with these rapid-onset attacks. Human bronchea could narrow a good deal before breathing was visibly impaired; with Beth it was the body language that changed first.

'Fine.' The tightly clipped monosyllable told her all she needed to know.

'Have you got your inhaler?'

Beth fumbled in her coat pocket and pulled it out, shook it, took a puff. For a few seconds her upper body remained frozen, strained, as the drug leached its way to her lungs. Then came a relaxation. Laura, at the wheel, felt her own tension ebb in sympathy.

'Better?'

'Bit.'

The second puff brought further relief, but quarter of an hour later as they pulled into Simon's street, the silence had returned, and with it the taut, bunched shoulders.

'Can I – ' with a gasp ' – stay here?'

So Laura, with Vince's jacket in her arms, walked to the door to face the task alone. Tessa was upstairs at Alfie's bedside, so it was just the two of them, and she told him right there, standing in the hall. She had said some things to hurt him when they were breaking up, but this was worse, far worse. Then, she had been angry – they'd both been angry – but now she was cold and composed and he had a sick child upstairs. He was kind and offered her sympathy, which was all wrong-ended and made her feel a charlatan as well as a murderer. And all the way through the painful interview she couldn't even give him her full attention because half her mind was outside with Beth, struggling for breath in the car.

This one thing, nagged a voice in her head on the drive home. He asked you to do this one thing.

The upside of Beth's occasional sharp, unheralded asthma attacks was that they usually fled as quickly as they had come. Something to do with stress, Laura supposed – though in this case she couldn't imagine that the source had gone away. By the time they reached the house, Beth's posture was more natural and her chest rose and fell evenly. She made it upstairs to clean her teeth with only one pause for breath.

170

'Where's your inhaler? Shall I bring it up for you, in case you need it later?' But it was merely precautionary; they both knew it was over.

As Laura was doing some final tidying up in the kitchen, the telephone rang.

'Hi. How did it go?'

Vince.

'Oh, you know.' What was there to say?

'Right.' A pause. 'How's Willow?'

'OK, I think. Gone to bed.'

'And Beth?'

'All right, now.'

Another short pause. 'And how about you, Laura?'

'All right.' She would be. 'Yes, thank you. We're going to be all right.'

On her way to Beth's room ten minutes later, she looked in on Willow. She'd hardly touched anything at supper so maybe she could be persuaded to come down for a hot drink and a biscuit. They might both appreciate the company. The spare room door was ajar, but when Laura tapped on it and stuck her head round, all was darkness. Willow was in bed and apparently asleep.

Along the landing, Beth's door was closed. Quietly, she pushed it open and stepped inside, standing in the middle of the room while she waited for her eyes to adjust to the dim light.

'Beth?'

Asleep, too, by the sound of it. The slow, nasal snuffle of her daughter's breathing was a double blessing: no asthma and no anxious, guilty wakefulness. The curtains, she saw, were still open, so she moved to the window and drew them shut, before returning to stand near the bed. She could make Beth out clearly now: the disordered pillows, the left arm crooked behind her head, the hair she'd forgotten to brush. Her face, in repose, bore no trace of the day's distress and grief. But her right arm was curled into the place which, for

171

the past ten days, had been Dougie's, and in her fingers she clutched the ear of the foundling teddy bear.

Laura walked back down to the kitchen alone.

On the Thursday of the following week, Laura came home at lunchtime. It was not a scheduled return. She had realised as soon as she reached the office that morning that the box file she needed still lay on the kitchen table where she had put it out the night before to bring with her. There were other, minor tasks she could be getting on with for a few hours, but by twelve o'clock she had reached a full-stop and really needed the file. The best thing seemed to be to collect up her papers from this end and decamp to Ninepins for the remainder of the day.

She had, in fact, spread out her notes and been working in the kitchen for over an hour when she was startled by the bang of a door upstairs. Footsteps, and another door – the bathroom. Not a burglar, then, but only Willow. It was strange, though: Thursday was one of her days at the Regional College. She waited for the flush of the toilet, the sound of running taps, the renewed bang of doors. After a polite interval, she put down her pen and went out into the hall.

'Hi! Willow, is that you?'

An answering hello sounded faintly from the depth of the spare room.

'Would you like a coffee?'

There was no reply this time, and Laura was re-immersed in her notes when she heard a door again, and a tread on the stairs.

'Sorry,' she said, as Willow emerged from the hall. 'I hope I didn't make you jump.'

Willow shook her head. 'I heard the car.'

'I know I'm not normally home in the afternoons, that's all. I hope you hadn't been asleep or something, and then woke up and didn't expect anyone to be here.'

Why was she apologising for being in her own house, as if she were the one skipping class?

'I thought Thursday was one of your college days?' Was it the college half term, perhaps? 'Didn't you have any classes?'

'Not today.' Willow was gazing idly at the papers on the table. 'Anything interesting?'

'Not really. Or probably not to you, but it is to me. Finding ways of managing woodland to mitigate the effect of climate change. I have a report to write on it by the end of the month.'

'Funny,' said Willow.

Laura looked up at her inquiringly.

'You doing stuff about woods, I mean. When there are no trees round here.'

'I suppose so.' She smiled. 'I've never thought of it that way before.'

As Laura rose to fill the kettle, Willow slid into a seat at the table. 'So you like it, then, your job?'

'Yes.' She plugged in the kettle and switched it on; it emitted a series of ticks, and she cupped her hands round the metal as the warmth began to spread. 'There were times,' she said, 'when Beth was little, that I hated the mornings. I hated having to go in to work and take her to the nursery, missing all that time with her. Not that she was one to cling, particularly, or make a fuss. She was pretty good. But it was still a wrench, sometimes.' Her hands were tingling; she pulled them away. 'Apart from that, yes, I guess I'm lucky. I enjoy what I do.'

She wasn't sure Willow would care about these small private revelations, but she was looking across at Laura and nodding slowly. She fingered the corner of a file. 'Vince likes his job, too. Says he loves it.'

Laura smiled. The fact did not surprise her, although she couldn't, personally, have done his job for the world. She simply could not imagine. . . . But it was hardly a thing she could say to Willow. The kettle clicked off and she poured the steaming water into the mugs.

There was silence for a while when she sat down, as both of them blew on their hot coffee. Then Willow said, 'I'm looking for another place.'

'Sorry?' Though she'd heard quite well what she'd said.

'Another room. I've got the paper upstairs, with all the ads in.'

Remembering last time, Laura asked, 'Does Vince know?'

Willow stared into her mug, her brows gathered and set. 'Not yet.'

'What do you think he'll say?'

A shrug.

Stay. Go. Both, in their own way, Laura realised, were equally unimaginable.

'It's the best thing,' said Willow, still frowning down at her coffee. 'I've brought you all this trouble, you and Beth. All this – Dougie – it's all my fault. It's really best that I leave.'

There was something about the way she said it – a mulishness, or an angle of the chin – which reminded Laura painfully of her daughter. Whether it was that, or the unfairness of it, she didn't stop to question: she only knew that the doubt had cleared. Her mind was made up.

'Don't go.' She said it plainly, neither prescribing nor pleading. 'We want you here. What would Beth do if you left?'

Beth already blamed herself for Dougie. If Willow left now, it would be one more scourge with which to lash herself. 'It's nobody's fault. Nobody's to blame for what happened to Dougie: not Beth, not you. It was just one of those things.'

Willow's eyes flickered up from her mug and Laura made bold to trap her glance and hold it.

'You're not responsible for your mother.'

For a moment it seemed that Willow might almost be able to believe her. But then she went back to the contemplation of her cooling coffee, twisting the mug to and fro on the table top.

At length, she said, 'They're keeping her here.'

'Here?'

'In Cambridge, at the hospital here. They're not moving her back to London this time. At least, it seems not. The consultant here is going to take her on – the one who admitted her.'

Cambridge. Panicked, Laura's mind leapt into estimates of time and distance. It meant she was barely ten miles from Ninepins. Alarmingly near. And yet, be sensible, she told herself; the seventy miles between here and London had failed twice over to keep her away.

'I suppose . . .' She hesitated, uncertain. 'I suppose it means you can visit her more easily. If you want to, I mean.'

Willow's face tilted up, at that. The green eyes looked straight at Laura. Oh God, she thought, was that the wrong thing to say? But then, slowly, the stare softened. Willow shrugged again.

'Mm.'

Even this non-committal response was some kind of concession; a chink of light, an opening. Or Laura, at any rate, chose to take it as such.

'Is she – ? That is, when she's herself, when she's a bit better . . . What's she like?'

The question was so unfocussed, so unspecific, that she had little idea what form of answer she hoped to provoke. She only knew that she wanted something, some fragment of information, or at least a reaction. She needed to know what Willow would say.

'Herself,' is what she said, picking at the word. 'Not sure I know what that is.'

'Well, when she's on the medication, then? Vince said – '

'Vince?' Willow's glance was sharp.

'Yes. But he didn't tell me anything – not really, nothing he shouldn't. He only mentioned that she's better when she takes her medication.'

Apparently satisfied, Willow lowered her chin and began to play with her mug again, until Laura wondered whether the conversation was at an end.

175

'Flatter,' she said finally. 'With the drugs. She's sort of flatter. Like she's been emptied out and left hollow.'

There was nothing Laura could think to say in response to this, no consolation which didn't sound utterly trite. If she'd been braver, or more demonstrative, she'd have reached out and held Willow's hand. It was doubtless what Vince would have done.

Instead, she took a deep breath and asked, 'What is it she has wrong with her, exactly?'

'Their diagnosis, you mean?' She spat the word like a profanity.

'Yes. But, of course, don't say anything if you'd rather not. I don't want to be intrusive.'

Willow regarded her impassively. 'Oh, they have words they use, things they fill in on forms. Bipolar spectrum. Auditory hallucinations. They never make up their minds. But it's all crap – doesn't mean anything. Just stupid, useless words.'

After that, there really did appear to be nothing more to be said, so Laura rose and picked up the mugs. Neither was empty and both were cold. 'Shall I boil the kettle again?'

As she swilled their undrunk coffee down the sink and made some fresh, she filled the space with trivialities: the forgotten box file, the recent thaw.

'I suppose I should be thinking about picking up Beth. I could fetch her early today, perhaps. I don't know about you, but I'm starving. I was so busy coming home, I forgot about lunch.'

Psychiatric hospitals reminded Willow in many ways of children's homes. They shared a particular kind of forced informality, a disorder which meant that it was hard to tell residents from visitors or staff. Of course, the chaos was only surface deep; neither place could ever quite shed the odour of the institution. Here, beneath the sunshine and floor polish, lurked the sour tang of vomit.

At least in the bin you could tell the kids – or, anyway, the younger ones – because they were kids. And most of them washed themselves, sometimes compulsively, even the boys. Cheap supermarket aftershave, on the whole, she decided, was a better smell than armpit stains.

The ward which housed her mother was hardly a ward in the usual sense at all, but a low, single storey building set apart from the main complex. It was quite a walk from where the bus dropped her, past chess squares of car park and lawn, where skinny trees were lashed to stakes with bands of orange plastic. Willow had imagined rows of metal-framed beds, or at least shared rooms and a hospital feeling, as there'd been on the acute admission ward where she and Vince had left her mother on Sunday afternoon. But inside Stanforth House, opening off the central television lounge, were corridors of single rooms behind unnumbered doors.

'Marianne Tyler?' A woman who might or might not work there had checked a chart on the wall. 'She's in room 8. Down the end, turn right, second door on the left.'

Maybe the numbers were removed in some hopeless attempt to create a family atmosphere – or perhaps to confound the enemy, in paranoid delusion. The most it was likely to do, in reality, was further disorientate the already confused. At the bin, they'd all had numbers.

In room 8 her mother was asleep. She was fully clothed, including boots, and a dressing gown over her jeans and jumper in spite of the overheated room. The bed was pushed up against the wall and she was curled on her side, knees tucked and face to the pale yellow paintwork, where scuffs and scrapes suggested the moving of furniture, making Willow think vaguely of barricades. There was almost no furniture in the room now: just the bed and a tiny chest of drawers. On the back of the door hung a red dress that Willow thought she might remember. Everything else was strange.

She looked completely out of it. Willow wondered if the

177

drugs always made her tired in the daytime, or whether they might have changed her medication since Sunday's jaunt, or upped her dosages. The doctors might tell her, she supposed, if she could find one to ask – even though she wasn't eighteen yet, nor living with the patient. She didn't really know; she didn't want to know.

There was no chair, so she sat down on the scratchy carpet and crossed her legs. That was how Mum used to sit sometimes when she was all right, cross-legged by Willow's bed with the story book on her lap like any ordinary mother. It was always the same book, at least in Willow's memory: the *Bumper Book of Fairy Tales*, bound in stiff board, with a grinning green dragon on the front. The stories Willow remembered were anything but ordinary. They twined and tangled round her bed like real, live witchcraft, thick with fantastical creatures, and transformations, and shifting, formless terrors. Willow was too young to read, then. It was only later that she came to know that the angels and demons her mother had summoned, the smoke and fire and ice and flood, lay nowhere in the pages of the book.

It was later, too, much later, that she saw how her mother was not like other children's. She was extraordinary. Often she was wonderful, magical, intoxicating. But there was one thing she never was, there was one thing that Willow had never felt with her, not once. She'd never just felt safe.

Chapter 15

Beth remained subdued and uncommunicative all that week and the next, spurning suggested half term outings and sticking largely to her room, or Willow's. Quite unprecedentedly, she even ducked out of her scheduled visit to Simon's house at the weekend, pleading stomach cramps which Laura was convinced were psychosomatic, if not entirely fabricated. She might have bounced her into going, but decided to take pity on the child. Give her more time, she told herself. Vince stayed away, too; he neither rang nor dropped round to the house. No doubt he was giving them all some time and space – though Willow saw him as usual, on Friday at his office. Laura was surprised how much she missed having him to talk to.

Given her daughter's fragile state, Laura didn't like to raise the question of inviting Alice for supper again. But on the Tuesday after half term, the issue was swung for them by Mrs Farrell, the science teacher, who decreed that the class should prepare PowerPoint presentations on the life cycle of the woodlouse for their homework, and that for this purpose they should work in pairs.

'Alice says, can we do it at ours, please? Her brother always hogs the computer at their house, stuck in the World of Warcraft.'

They were there already when Laura arrived home on Wednesday, having taken the bus together. The old desktop PC that was kept for Beth's use lived on a side table in the sitting room; she heard the giggling from that direction as soon as she entered the hall.

'Hello, love. Hello, Alice. Sounds as if you're having fun with those woodlice.'

'Hello, Mrs Blackwood.' Alice was always polite.

'Look at them when they've just hatched, Mum. We got this off Google images. Isn't it *gruesome*?'

Something almost transparent, with an orange head and fragile spindly legs, stared out at Laura from the screen, like a cross between a maggot and an uncooked prawn. Underneath, one of the young biologists had typed the helpful words: BABY WOODLOUSE.

'Not "hatched",' said Alice, the literalist. 'It's just come out of its mother's pouch. Like a kangaroo. And they grow by shedding their skins.'

'Yeah. Like snakes.' Beth was examining the screen again, with prurient pleasure. 'They're disgusting. Look, you can actually see their insides.'

Laura ruffled her daughter's hair. 'Shrimps for supper, then. Hope that's all right with you girls?' She left the room to the sound of two very gratifying squeals.

In fact, they had spaghetti Bolognese. They called Willow, who emerged from upstairs with her nose in a paperback and spoke scarcely two words during supper. Afterwards she disappeared again with her book, while the kids headed back to the computer, and Facebook. It was a mystery to Laura, who had grown up with strict limits on midweek telephoning and no other communication medium to hand, how girls who spent all day at school talking to their friends, could yet feel the need to chat to them again all evening online.

Laura made a coffee for herself using the small Italian percolator that she rarely had out. At the back of the cupboard she found a bar of chocolate-coated marzipan left over from Christmas, which she unwrapped and cut into slices. With the marzipan in one hand and her coffee cup in the other, she returned to the sitting room.

The PC was still switched on, but the screen had reverted to an energy-saving blank. Social networking abandoned, Beth and Alice had also reverted: in their case to the age of six, by all appearances. They lay side by side on their stomachs on the carpet, emitting strange, snuffling, snorting noises, interspersed with volleys of laughter.

'What on earth . . .?'

'We're baby woodlice.' Beth wriggled her feet gleefully in the air behind her.

Alice was humping and writhing like a dyspeptic sea lion. 'I'm shedding my skin. Only it's got stuck.'

'I'll help!' cried Beth, and flung herself upon her friend and began to tickle her, and soon they were rolling in a helpless, giggling heap.

Laura stood over them, smiling. 'Do woodlice like marzipan?'

They drove Alice home soon afterwards, through Elswell village and out the other side to the cluster of whitewashed buildings on the Longfenton road where Mr Seabourn farmed.

'Thank you for having me,' said Alice, then, over her shoulder, 'Bye, Beth,' and she ran towards the door, where her mother raised a hand from the step.

All the way back in the car, Laura listened with satisfied half-attention to her daughter's jabber, about Mrs Farrell and school and marsupial bugs and tomorrow's packed lunch. It gave her quiet pleasure to hear her talk that way, without self-consciousness – and laugh again, as she'd been laughing with Alice on the sitting room floor – for the first time in more than a fortnight.

It was nearly nine when they reached the house. Laura mentioned the bath, but didn't press the point in the face of Beth's protestations.

'I just want to go back on Facebook a minute. Please, Mum – I won't be long, I promise. I only want to say g'night to Alice. And I thought of something I forgot to say to her.'

So Laura subsided into the settee and flicked on the TV news. A car bomb attack in Karachi flooded the surface of her mind. The unimpassioned voice of a translator only half masked the hand-wringing wail of a headscarfed woman: her sister and two nephews, missing in the mêlée. But presently, in another layer of consciousness, Laura registered a silence behind her. The tapping at the keyboard had ceased. She glanced round, saw Beth's rigid back, and knew instantly that something was amiss.

'What is it?' she asked, rising to move across the room. There was no reply. But as she neared the computer, Laura caught a glimpse of the screen before her daughter hit 'delete'. Next to the box containing the short, illegible message was the photograph of the sender. With the hard shell of make-up and the glamour model pout, she would pass for twenty-five, but the steely blonde hair was unmistakable. Rianna.

'Beth, what was that? What was she saying to you?'

'Nothing.'

'But then why did you delete it, love? Why not let me see?'

'Honestly, it's nothing. Just a stupid wall post. No big deal.'

Laura strove to master her fury against Rianna, and her own impatient curiosity. She spoke gently, one hand on her daughter's shoulder. 'Was she saying something nasty to you – or about you? You know you can tell me, sweetheart.'

Beth shot her an agonised, sidelong glance. 'Mum, please don't. I told you, it's stupid, it doesn't matter.'

'Of course it matters. It matters to me. If anyone is picking on you, or being mean, then – '

'Shut up!' Shrugging the hand from her shoulder, Beth stood up, the movement so violent that her chair toppled and fell backwards on to the carpet, bashing Laura's shin on the way down. 'Stop it, Mum, for God's sake. Just leave it alone, OK? You always have to bloody interfere. Why can't you ever just leave things alone?'

She kept her face averted, so that Laura couldn't see if there were tears, but there was something blind about her progress as she stumbled from the room.

Righting the chair, Laura sat down at the monitor and stared at it for a long moment, her mind as empty as the blank, grey screen. Then she pressed the space bar to kick it back to life. Up came the screensaver: an oceanscape, the glistening wall of water topped with leaping dolphins, chosen by Beth last summer during a craze for marine mammals. Laura clicked the Safari icon, and selected 'history'.

Home-made pizza was the solution that Laura hit upon. Beth had never been able to resist the allure of the floury work surface, pounding two-fisted at the squidgy dough, then stretching it out into rounds in the air, as she used to love to watch them do behind the counter in Pizza Express. She was persuaded to brave the overdue visit to her father's house at the weekend by the promise of pizza-making for Sunday supper on her return. They would make a party of it; they could all do with some cheering up. Alice was invited but had to turn them down, having a great-aunt's seventieth to attend over near Bury St Edmunds. Then Ellie was going to come, until her mother rang on Sunday morning to say she was down with a nasty cold, and shouldn't be spreading it about. Laura swore as she replaced the phone; Beth would be disappointed when she got home, if it was just the three of them after all. There was nothing for it but to call Vince; Beth was always pleased to see Vince.

Laura made the dough in the afternoon. She made a big batch of tomato sauce, and assembled all the toppings. Simon ran Beth home, for once, although his motives may not have been entirely altruistic, since it was just at the boys' bath- and bed-time. They were slightly later than he'd said – not unusual for Simon – and Vince had arrived before them. He had left his car behind for once and come by bus, bearing wine and declaring the intention of taking a taxi home. He and Willow were already aproned and scrubbed to the elbows when Simon and Beth came in. Laura was laughing and clattering pastry boards and heard neither the car nor

Beth's key in the front door; she caught sight of Beth in the kitchen doorway, with Simon at her shoulder, just as Vince, in retaliatory action, was lunging at Willow with floured hands and dabbing her on the nose.

'Hello, there. Are we interrupting something?' said Simon, with brows raised infuriatingly at Laura, who, vexed at herself for being flustered, effected the introduction.

'Simon – Vince.' She wished she hadn't felt the need to add, 'Vince is Willow's social worker.'

She felt uncomfortable, too, when he looked round her kitchen that way – the kitchen that used to be his, too. So she said, 'How's Alfie?'

'Absolutely back to normal now. You know how it is with kids. They're ill, but it leaves you more knackered than it does them.'

Beth circled the table, casting off coat and scarf and staring at the row of whitened boards on the worktop. 'You started without me. Why did you start without me?'

'Oh dear, I'm sorry, love. But we hadn't really got going, we were just getting things ready.'

'Hmph.' She didn't sound ready to be mollified so easily, until Vince dabbed her nose, too, and said, 'Here, we were just going to divide up the dough. Why don't you take a lump and show me what to do?'

His ability to get round her was galling, sometimes, even while it was handy. 'Wash your hands first, then,' she said.

Simon could not be persuaded to stay for a cup of tea, pleading the requirement of his presence at home for good-night tuckings-in; but she was irked by his grin as he told her at the door, 'I'd only be in the way here.'

They each armed themselves with a quarter of the dough and began to knock it into shape. The mixture seemed to Laura too sticky; hers came up in strings when she tried to knead it and adhered to the board in spite of the liberal application of flour. Then, when she began to pull it out flat, it stretched unevenly and tore to holes. The others all seemed

184

to be managing all right, so it must just be her. What was wrong with her tonight?

Once it was on the oiled baking tray, she pressed closed the rents with her fingers, disguising her botched handiwork with tomato and mushrooms. Vince opened his wine: an Italian name she didn't recognise, red, full-bodied and good. She emptied her glass more quickly than was sensible, and found it refilled.

By the time the kitchen warmed to the aroma of oregano and melting cheese, she was starting to relax. Beth was having fun, which was, after all, the object of the exercise. If the shadow of Dougie had haunted her weekend at Simon's, she showed no sign of it now as she shouted suggestions for novel pizza toppings.

'Pepperoni, pea and prune,' she squealed, wrinkling her nose. Beth abhorred prunes.

'The Lancastriana,' countered Vince. 'Black pudding and fried egg.'

'Anchovy and custard. That would be so gross.'

'Or how about eel? The *Feneziana*. For every pizza sold, 25p will be donated to the Elswell in Peril fund, for improvements in land drainage.'

Willow, Laura noticed, wasn't joining in, though she watched the two of them closely. And when the pizzas were decreed to be done and the trays lifted steaming from the oven and on to the table, three were dismembered and three-quarters dispatched before hers missed more than a slice. And as soon as Beth sat back in her chair and declared herself 'totally stuffed', Willow took hold of her arm.

'C'mon, let's go upstairs.'

To her credit, Beth looked doubtfully at her mother, though any sense of obligation was apparently limited to practicalities. 'What about the washing up?' she asked.

Beth had spent increasing hours in the spare bedroom over the past two weeks. But Laura resolved to say nothing; what was there she could say?

185

'Don't worry about the dishes. You two go.' It was only twenty to nine.

Vince replenished her glass with a roll of the eyes. 'Kids.'

'Perhaps I'll make a start . . .'

But as she began to shuffle the remains of pizza on to a single baking tray, he trapped her hand and held it still. 'Later. Just sit. Drink.'

She did as she was told, and presently the warmth of the food and the glow of the wine seeped up to flood her with lassitude and she lost all thought of clearing up. For some time, she allowed Vince to talk, and for once he seemed very willing to do so, though not about his work – never about that. He related some story about a social worker friend of his up at King's Lynn who kept a fishing boat there. It had been his father's, and he still went out in it at weekends. He'd had to let go of the family fish shed when his father died and no longer had an outlet for his catch, so had developed the habit of pressing his clients to gifts of mackerel, bass and pollack.

'We had a lad in the office this week who'd turned up at Social Services in Lynn. A runaway. One of ours, so they sent him back down to us. I knew it must have been Sam who'd seen him there. The lad was giving off a stink of fish. When someone finally asked about it, he produced a pair of dabs from his pocket, wrapped in greaseproof paper.'

Laura laughed, and more than merely dutifully, though her mind was running on other tracks.

'Next time I come I'll bring supper, shall I? I can get Sam to look out four nice fat sea bream.'

'That would be nice. Beth likes fish. Anything, as long it doesn't have tentacles.' Then she took a slug of wine and said, 'Vince, I'm worried about her again.'

What is it this time? If he was thinking it, he gave no outward indication. But, poor man, he must be fed up of her bending his ear about Beth.

'I think there are some girls at school giving her a hard

time.' *Bullying*, she almost said, but the word seemed too portentous.

He surveyed her across the table and said nothing.

'It's these girls that she was friends with, and now they've fallen out and I think they're being nasty to her about it.'

His eyes narrowed. 'The shoplifters?'

She nodded. 'The girls who put her up to it, yes.'

'And what kind of thing are they doing?'

'I'm not exactly sure. About what's going on at school, I mean. Beth never says anything. Not to me. I've tried, but asking makes it worse. She just clams up.'

There she lapsed into silence, so that he had to prompt her. 'So, then . . .?'

'Well, I saw something on the computer. Or rather, I didn't actually see it, not to read, but I knew it was there, and I'm sure it won't have been the first or only time, not by Beth's reaction.'

'On the computer?'

'Yes. She was on Facebook, and there was a message there. A "wall post" is what she called it, which I gather means it's public, and all her friends could see it as well.'

He didn't need to nod; his frown was confirmation. 'But you don't know what was said – what's being said?'

Miserably, she shook her head. 'I only know she was really upset.'

'Poor old Beth,' he said, and she felt a moment of anger, or at least of disappointment. Was that all he had to offer?

'The thing is, I wonder if I should say something – do something.'

'Complain to the moderators, you mean?' She must have looked blank, because he added, 'Networking sites, chat rooms, they all have rules against posting abuse.'

Impatient, she shrugged. 'Beth deleted it.'

'But if these girls are going to post more messages – '

'It's not that. It's not Facebook, not really – or not only that. I mean, it won't be just the computer, will it? I'm

187

worried they're being spiteful to her in other ways, in other places. At school, for instance.' In school or outside school, spreading their poison; talking or texting, to her or about her; jeering, telling hurtful lies. 'I suppose I was wondering if I should tell her form teacher.'

After a pause, he said quietly, 'What does Beth think?'

She looked at him, with a feeling of slipping, of the ground falling away. 'She wants me to leave it alone, to keep out of it. At least that's what she says. But I can't just do nothing, can I?'

That's what she'd done last time, over the stolen chocolate bars. She hadn't gone marching into school with her denunciations; she'd kept Beth's confidence and not named names. And precious good it had done. Weren't you supposed to stand up to bullies?

But Vince was unmoved. He reached for the wine bottle and measured out the final inch between their two glasses.

'In the end,' he said, 'it's down to Beth. You can't fight her battles for her.'

There was some truth in it, Laura supposed as she gazed at him helplessly, yet there was surely an irony in his saying it. Wasn't that what he did all the time at work, fight kids' battles for them? It was practically his job description.

Letting her thoughts drift into absence, she broke off an edge of pizza, encrusted with cheese and a final olive. She took a bite but it was dry as polystyrene.

'Shall I open another bottle?' She rose, collecting up, now, the baking trays and plates. 'There's some red in the corner cupboard, though I'm sure it's not as nice as yours. Just cheap supermarket plonk.'

He made polite, demurring noises and tossed back the remnant in his glass. When she'd recovered the corkscrew from the washing up bowl, given it a wipe and uncorked the Côtes du Rhône, she poured them both a generous helping. She was about to sit down again when he stood up.

'Let's go outside.'

'Outdoors?' It had been close to freezing all day.

'Do you mind? Just for a breath of air.' He laughed. 'Stupid habit of mine. I used to smoke, and I miss it. At work I go and stand out the back by the bins every day for five minutes in the rain.'

This, she assumed, could not be true, but he seemed to be serious. He was already half way down the hall, taking his wine glass with him. She took hers and followed.

It wasn't as cold as she'd supposed, not as cold as when she'd made him walk by the Hundred Foot Drain. After nightfall, cloud had crept across, blotting out the stars and drawing the temperature up by a few degrees. There was certainly no frost: the chill had a damper, blunt-edged feel. It was hard to make out anything beyond the semicircle of electric light cast by the open front door. She wrapped her arms around her body and wished her wine were cocoa.

Vince had taken a few steps along the top of the dyke. The darkness, which had seemed as dense as bitumen, thinned to show her his silhouette. She moved forward and stood beside him, squinting the way he was looking, across the lode and into nothing.

He didn't move or speak, and presently she found herself asking, 'How's Marianne?'

He turned a fraction. 'All right, I think. Back on her pills.'

There was nothing more she could think to say – not about the mother, not directly. But there were things she wanted to know.

'Vince, do you mind if I ask you about bipolar disorder? I talked to Willow, and she mentioned that might be the issue, with Marianne.' It was manic depression – she knew that much, of course, and she'd looked it up to find out more. But she hadn't found an answer to the doubt that dogged her. 'Is it hereditary? Might Willow . . .?' She let her question drift, thinking of the silences, which might be troubled, unhappy or merely self-absorbed; the long days in the spare bedroom, alone.

Vince replied from the textbook. 'It's not that simple. The

medics talk in terms of percentage risks of developing a given condition. Of increased percentage risks.'

Frustrated, she jabbed her glass at him in the air. 'But what do you think?'

There was a brief pause, and then he said quietly, 'Listen.'

'To what?' Was this another diversion? She could hear nothing: no trace of voices from the spare room window, no slur from the sluggish lode, no breath of wind, no lone night bird.

'Just listen.'

'I can't hear anything.'

'Exactly.' Through the dark, she could see his half smile. 'The fens,' he said. 'You live here in this silence. Just look at it – listen to it. You live here and you ask me, is it nature or nurture? Depression, madness, are they in-bred or a factor of the environment?'

Laura gazed at him, a little helpless.

'More than a little of both, out here, I'd think. Wouldn't you?' He laughed, and she heard it as at a distance, strange and jarring. Perhaps it was the wine making her dull, but she could see no cause for humour in it. 'Come on. Let's go back inside.'

In the kitchen, they sat down again at the table on opposite sides of the litter of crumbs. It was still early, so why did she feel so tired?

'What about Marianne, then?' She knew she should drop it. She knew she was getting nowhere, only banging her head against a closed door. She knew the answer already. Bloody confidentiality.

'What about her?' he said, and sipped his wine.

'What's the prognosis? Will she ever – ' it sounded so trite ' – get better?'

Vince shrugged. 'I'm not a psychiatrist.'

'But,' she persisted, 'you'll have seen her medical files, or at least spoken to her doctors. You must liaise.'

'Naturally.'

'And? Is she ever likely to improve? Or will she always be that way?'

He eyed her levelly. 'I'm really not in a position to say.'

So there it was. The same stone wall, the same professional cold shoulder he'd shown her in the Fisherman's Arms, that first time they went for a drink, back before Christmas. Still keeping her at the same stupid, superior distance.

Something of her irritation must have shown in her face, because he unbent a degree or two, conceding, 'She hasn't always been so acute. She had spells, I gather, when Willow was younger, when things were at least less volatile. More manageable. And she manages now, too, when she takes her medication.'

Flatter, remembered Laura. *Emptied out*. 'So she's safe where she is now?'

'And by "safe" you mean secure, I assume. Not liable to go walkabout again.' He was smiling; he could be infuriating with his judgments about her – all the more so when, as this time, he struck close to the truth. 'Look, don't worry. I'm sure when they moved her to Cambridge, they were well aware that Willow is in a placement nearby.'

'*Placement?*' The word came out dangerously high; she struggled to contain a tide of anger. 'So that's what we are, is it, Beth and I? A placement.'

She saw something cross his face, some flicker of self-consciousness – Vince, who was never known to doubt. But her blood was up; she pressed on furiously.

'I'm not some foster carer you're liaising with, Vince. This isn't a placement. This is our home you're talking about, Beth's and mine. This is our lives.'

If she expected capitulation or apology, she had misjudged him. 'Of course. I know that. But Willow is still my client, and as such she has to come first. My duty to her – '

'Your duty, always your bloody duty. What about Beth and me? Where do we fit in? What's your professional duty there?'

'Laura.' He reached for her hand but she snatched it away.

'Just part of Willow's placement, is that what we are? Some case notes in a file? I suppose you fill us in on your time-sheets. I thought we were friends, but it turns out we're just part of your caseload.'

'We are friends – I hope. But I'm also Willow's social worker. You knew that from the start. My first responsibility – '

'Oh, yes. Your responsibility.' She heard the bitterness in her own voice; she felt the heat in her face too, but there was no help for it. Her anger had seized its own momentum. 'You always hide behind your jargon, don't you? Your duty, your responsibility. Your confidentiality and your increased percentage risks. Your damned stupid bloody placement.'

'Don't be silly. You know I – '

'Don't be silly? Don't be *silly*!' What was she, now – one of his problem fifteen-year-olds? She took a deep breath. 'I think it's best you just leave.'

'Listen, Laura – '

'I want you to leave now, Vince.'

He rose and came round the table.

'Laura, please.' His hand was on her shoulder. He was looking down at her searchingly, with eyes as brown as Willow's were green.

Determinedly, she closed her own. 'Just go.'

Laura wasn't sure how long, after the front door banged, she sat there among the pizza crumbs with her head on her arms. It was some time before she was even aware that she'd been crying. Her watch face, when she managed to bring it into focus through the blur, told her it was only a quarter past ten, but her limbs were leaden and a tightness behind her eyes told her a headache was on its way. The washing up could wait for the morning. She wanted to be in bed with her mind blanked shut.

No noise from upstairs had made itself heard at all, not

since Beth and Willow disappeared after supper. Maybe they had gone their separate ways to read or sleep. But as she made her way along the landing, heading for the bathroom and her toothbrush, she heard the murmur of voices. Outside the spare room door, she halted, hand raised to knock. They might want a drink, and she should at least say goodnight before turning in. Besides, it was school in the morning. But there her hand stayed, suspended. Red-eyed and tear-streaked, she was in no fit state to face her daughter.

As she stood there, trapped in uncertainty, a word caught her attention through the closed door.

'. . . Vince . . .'

She leaned closer, torn between curiosity and guilt. She heard Beth's voice.

'. . . didn't even come up and say goodbye to you before he went.'

Willow, laughing dryly. 'It's not me he comes here to see.'

It was impossible, then, to make herself walk away.

Beth said, 'What do you mean?'

Willow's laugh again, rasping, mirthless. 'We meet on Fridays at his office, for my sessions. He doesn't need to come out here to see me.'

'So, what then?' demanded Beth.

Laura's blood pounded and the tension behind her eyes resolved itself into the colour of pain.

'Obvious, isn't it?' came Willow's voice. 'He comes to see your mum.'

There was a silence. Laura held her breath.

'Has she had any boyfriends, since your dad?'

'No.' Beth's voice sounded tight, resentful. That rhythmic thudding would be her kicking something: the bed, the wall? Then, quietly, 'I don't believe you. You're wrong. She doesn't even like him much. I'm sure she doesn't. Else why would she be shouting at him, earlier?'

Oh shit, thought Laura. Had she really raised her voice? She hadn't been aware of shouting.

She imagined Willow's shrug. 'Because. I bet she's down there right now, crying.'

Laura's throat was flooded with saliva, but she feared to swallow; in her madness, she was convinced it would be audible through the door.

'That's how it is,' said Willow. 'I was always crying when I was going out with Carl, last year in the bin. I was bloody miserable the whole time.'

Distracted, Beth snorted. And then both girls were laughing: choking, helpless, a little wild.

'What happened to him?' asked Beth, when she could summon the breath.

'Youth custody.'

'What – you mean, prison?'

''S'OK. He was a loser anyway.'

That set them off again, and nothing more was said for a minute or two. I should get away from here, Laura told herself; I shouldn't be listening. Now was the moment, while they weren't talking; she should clean her teeth and go to bed. But her feet remained stubbornly rooted.

At length came Willow's voice again. 'It would be perfect, though, her and him. Just perfect, don't you think? I mean, we've neither of us got a dad – '

'I've got a dad.' The words were sharp, the note rising; the rhythmic kicking had begun again.

A grunt from Willow. 'He's not here, is he?'

Then Beth again, more doggedly than before. 'I've already got a dad. Where d'you think I was all weekend?'

'OK, I was just saying. Thinking what it'd be like, that's all. Like being a proper family.' She sounded, suddenly, younger than Beth.

Laura felt a wave of pain as physical as nausea. Even with her eyes screwed shut, the headache dazzled to a piercing point of light.

'You're wrong,' came Beth's voice, finally, flat and sullen. 'We heard her shouting, remember.'

'All right – whatever. Forget it, OK?'

Laura had heard enough; far more than she wished she'd heard. Stomach pitching, she lurched away along the landing towards the open bathroom door.

Chapter 16

They were all sick during the night. All three of them in the house, that is – Laura didn't know about Vince. The Mozzarella seemed the most likely culprit. Willow's tin of tuna was freshly opened; Beth's sausage was reheated but only she'd had any; but the cheese was the buffalo kind, wet and unpasteurised. It had to be that.

Laura succumbed first, almost as soon as she reached the bathroom. The spasms were violent, racking her guts, burning her chest and exploding her vision into blinding scarlet stars. After the first wave came another, more painful now that her stomach was empty, leaving her sore and spent. As it subsided she heard Beth's voice behind her in the doorway.

'Mum. Are you OK?'

'Mm,' she mumbled, 'don't worry, just sick,' and rose to flush the loo.

Beth had never coped well with vomit, her own or other people's. Once, at Brownies, she'd gone to the aid of a younger child who'd been sick in the toilets and ended by vomiting herself. Yet now she stepped forward.

'Sure you're all right? D'you want a cup of tea or something?'

Laura's stomach turned another somersault at the very idea, albeit kindly meant. 'No thanks, love. I'll be fine. I'll just get to bed.'

She rinsed her mouth at the basin while Beth hovered uncertainly; out on the landing Willow stood with watchful eyes.

'Honestly, it's nothing,' Laura insisted. 'I'll be fine now.'

The optimistic prognosis proved premature. Twice more over the next two hours the heave of weakened muscles sent her stumbling along the landing. It was on her third visit, kneeling on the cold tiles, that she remembered Vince hadn't come by car. She had sent him away without calling a taxi home. He'd have his mobile, of course, but he might still have walked twenty minutes through the unlit night before the cab had arrived to meet him. She would have felt some compunction on his account, had she the strength to spare from her own wretchedness – and if she hadn't still been angry with him. Why didn't he say something? It was typical of him not to say anything – his smug, stupid pride.

Back in bed, she dozed uncomfortably and had little idea of the time when she awoke to sounds of distress from the bathroom. Beth. She wrapped her dressing gown around her and set off blindly, as she had done fifty, a hundred, two hundred times, for early feeds and wet beds and asthma and nightmares, over the past twelve years. But when she got there it wasn't Beth; it was Willow.

Bent over the bowl in just her T shirt and knickers, she looked about eleven. Knobs of vertebrae studded the worn cotton; her arms were white but the soles of her feet were a blotchy pink, like Beth's after a bath. Too exhausted herself for diffidence, Laura approached and took hold of the girl's shoulders.

'You, too? Poor sweetheart.' Automatically, she fretted the skin of Willow's upper arms. It was goosebumped, clammy to the touch. 'You're freezing. Here.' She reached for a bath towel from the rail and passed it around her.

A spatter of vomit had missed the bowl and raked the upraised seat. Laura pulled a handful of tissue from the roll and wiped it clean. She dropped the soiled wad into the toilet and flushed, then crossed to the basin and washed her hands. Willow's flannel was there so she ran it briefly under the cold tap, then wrung it out. Willow's face was grey, her forehead dewed with sweat. Still on instinct, Laura bent and smoothed the cool flannel over her brow.

There was a recoil, and for a second Laura was afraid of what she'd done: the intrusion on privacy, unasked for, unwanted. But after the first flinch, Willow didn't move away. Instead, she closed her eyes and groaned.

'I'm never sick,' she said.

Laura laughed softly. 'Me neither. I'm really sorry. I think it must have been the Mozzarella. But I don't think I shall ever want to eat mushrooms again. Or olives.'

There was a grunt. 'I'm never eating anything again.'

Laura swilled out the tooth mug and half filled it with water. 'Rinse your mouth,' she said. 'Get rid of the taste.'

Willow did as she was bidden, still in her kneeling position, and spat in the toilet bowl.

'Are you done with being sick, do you think? Shall we get you back to bed?'

It must have been nearly dawn when she heard Beth. This time Laura had fallen into a sounder sleep and awareness took longer to reach her consciousness. When she got to the bathroom, Beth was not alone. Willow stooped beside her at the toilet; while Beth retched, she held back her tumbling curls of hair.

Willow but not Beth looked up at Laura's appearance; Beth's eyes were clamped tight shut.

'This is what I learnt from the bulimic girls in the bin,' Willow remarked. 'Always hold your hair up out of the way, they said.'

Beth's eyes opened then, and she shook herself free of Willow's grasp with a small, protesting moan.

'What's wrong?' said Willow, straightening up.

'Get off.' Beth scowled, her face a mask of misery. 'Don't want touching.'

With that she pitched abruptly forward, shoulders braced as if for the onslaught of asthma, and let forth a stream of thin bile. She gasped twice, spat in the bowl, then turned, wet-mouthed, to Laura.

'I want Mum.'

Wakening again at nine, Laura dragged herself downstairs to call the school absence line. Beth, when she had glanced in, was fast asleep, her face pale and washed out on the pillow. Having informed the automatic machine that Beth Blackwell of 7JB would not be in today, Laura's energies were exhausted and she crawled back up to bed.

At ten she rose once more and took a shower. Washing was beyond her but she stood with her eyes closed under the gush of warm water and hoped it might do her good. When standing became too much, she stepped out, and dried herself sitting down on the mat. She determined to dress, which took another effort of will and necessitated a short rest on the edge of the bed before she made her way back down to the kitchen. Putting the kettle on was a reflex, but she didn't make a drink. She sat and stared at yesterday's *Observer*, but the attempt to read made her eyes blur and her head pound. It was dehydration, she told herself, and filled a glass with water. She stood at the sink and drank – but too quickly, her sore stomach jolting as the cold liquid struck – then took it to the table and confined herself to slow sips.

She was still sitting there when Willow came down twenty minutes later.

'Hi,' said Laura. 'How are you feeling?'

'Ugh. You?'

'Ugh,' she agreed.

Rousing herself, she clicked back on the cooling kettle and made them both some weak, black tea. The thought of sugar turned her stomach, but she offered it to Willow, who stirred some in. Dry toast, she thought, might help a bit. She made two rounds and laid them on the table. Willow didn't touch hers; Laura took one bite before pushing her own away.

Dimly, it occurred to Laura that she hadn't yet called work.

She rose and dialled; Sylvia answered at the first ring, sounding horribly bright and healthy.

'Department of Land Economy.'

'Oh, hello. It's Laura. Just to say I'm sick, and I'm staying at home today.'

'Okey dokey. Shall we expect you in tomorrow?'

'Um, I guess so.' Although right now, she could imagine no end to this queasy torpor.

'Great, so we'll see you then. Look after yourself, won't you?' And Sylvia rang off.

Still holding the receiver, Laura glanced over at Willow. 'Shall I phone in for you as well?'

The green eyes registered nothing: a simple blank.

'What I mean is, don't they expect you to let them know, when you can't make classes? Or doesn't it work that way?'

Again, no reaction.

'It is Monday today, isn't it?' Monday and Thursday: Willow's college days.

Willow's eventual reply was so brief as to be cryptic. 'It's OK.'

'OK for me to ring them for you, or OK you don't need to let them know?'

'It's OK, there weren't any classes I was going to today.'

There was something about this – the way it was phrased perhaps, or a tone of the voice, a dip of the eyes – that convinced Laura it was evasion. It made her remember that other day, the recent Thursday, when she'd come home at lunchtime to find Willow here and not at college. The direct question would quite evidently be disastrous, but she was too weak and tired for artifice.

She sat back down at the table. 'Is everything all right at college?'

It was hardly subtle. But Willow was weary as well, of course: too weary, it seemed, to dissemble. She said nothing – an immediate admission of guilt.

200

'Only, I notice you've been missing a few classes, and I wondered if there was a problem.'

Willow prodded her mug of cold tea, pushing it away. 'I've stopped going.'

Unsure quite what to say, Laura played for time. 'You've stopped . . .?'

'College, yes. I've dropped out.'

'Since when?'

A shrug. 'Since Christmas. Or a bit before that.'

The parent in Laura, and the university researcher, wanted to seize on all the irrefutable arguments. The need for qualifications; the expansion of personal horizons along with job opportunities. But she was too tired and she knew it would do no good.

'Why?' was all she said.

Instead of bridling, Willow gave the question thought.

'I do want to learn things,' she replied, after a moment. 'There's such a lot to learn. I'm learning to swim. I can nearly do a width.'

This seemed to call for comment, so Laura said, 'That's great.'

'But I didn't want to learn there. Not at college, sitting in rows in classrooms like school. Not now, not at the moment. Not yet.'

It gets harder when you're older, Laura thought of saying. It was what people always claimed. But was it true? What could be harder than being seventeen?

'I only just got out of school, last year. And then out of the bin, too. I've had enough of those places. I just want to be here.'

Freedom, Laura supposed; independence. And you couldn't really blame her. But there was a fine line between independence and isolation. Or was it something else she meant? *Like being a proper family.*

'You are here,' she said. 'You've got this. So why not college as well? It's only two days a week.'

But Willow's eyes were flint; and besides, it wasn't Laura's responsibility to persuade her, even if she knew how. It was someone else's job; which led to the question, 'What does Vince say?'

There was no answer; Willow's lids dropped.

'He doesn't know?'

The eyes came up again, half pleading, half warning. 'Don't tell him.'

'Well, I . . .' But she was hardly about to tell Vince anything, was she, or even speak to him in a hurry. And why should he be the only one with secrets? 'All right, I won't.'

'Thing is . . .' Willow traced circles on the table, which was still not wiped clear of last night's pizza crumbs. 'Vince always wants me to talk to him, tell him things. And I do talk to him, I like talking to him.' Then she looked up, and straight across at Laura. 'But I don't tell him everything.'

The following week, work was completed on the pumphouse. The new plasterboard was up inside, and the damp course replaced. The door and window frames had been checked over and renewed where necessary, and were ready to paint.

'All yours, then,' said Alan Cowling of Cowling and Son, builders, as he drained his final mug of tea. Laura had not, in the event, ferried down that many mugs to him over the four weeks or so, on and off, that he'd been working on her property. She had generally been at work while he was here and refreshment had been dispensed mostly from his own thermos. Today, before they exchanged brown envelopes (her cheque for his final invoice), she had brought him digestives on a china plate by way of partial recompense.

'So, all the plaster is dry, is it, and the chemicals from the damp-proofing and timber treatment? It's all right to go in there and start on the decorating?'

The builder narrowed his eyes. 'Should be fine by the weekend, if you open all the windows.'

That, of course, ruled Beth out – had she not been ruled out already – from helping with the interior paintwork. But Saturday dawned bright and fresh with a stiff, easterly breeze, apt for quick drying and the efficient dispersal of fumes. Laura had said that Beth might join her and Willow in priming and undercoating the exterior woodwork, with the proviso that she stand down immediately should she feel the slightest tightening of the chest.

It was more than a week since the last frost and the lawn was squelchy underfoot, especially where it dipped down towards the pumphouse. Any indentation deeper than a bootprint back-filled rapidly with peaty liquid. The wind was biting so they all wore ancient sweaters of Laura's, and she found them each a pair of old gardening gloves to paint in. But March had brought new growth stealing in everywhere to places Laura hadn't noticed. The grass itself was higher than she remembered its being last week, and would need the mower putting over it as soon as the water table subsided enough to allow it. Every limb of every shrub seemed to be longer by a tender half-inch, and fat buds tipped the branches of willow and hazel, splitting already in places to reveal the emergent catkins. Across the far side of the lawn, where the soil was better drained, a rash of crocuses had erupted, livid in purple and gold against the muddy green. A couple more weeks and there'd be daffodils.

'Why is primer always pink?' Beth wanted to know as she dipped her brush in the pot. 'We're doing it white, aren't we?'

'Maybe so you can see where you've been,' Laura hazarded. 'Now, make sure you cover all the places where there's bare wood.'

Beside them Willow worked in silent concentration, her tongue tip trapped between her teeth. She wetted only a careful triangle of brush at each dip, pausing for a second above the pot each time before transferring her hand to the window frame; Beth's brush, by contrast, was already thickly clogged, with runnels of pink streaking the handle as far as her gloved fingers.

It was fast work with three. In less than an hour, the last sections of exposed wood had disappeared, and Beth was dispatched to the kitchen to make tea while Laura fetched a jam jar of turpentine from the shed.

'Leave your gloves here,' said Laura. 'And don't lean against anything with those painty sleeves.'

By the time the tea was drunk, the first parts they had primed were dry and ready for undercoating. This was slower work, especially round the edges of the glass. Several times, Beth smudged the parts she had done by leaning against them with her other hand; then, climbing the stepladder to paint the top of the window, she contrived to dash the pane with a long trail of white paint. Laura, armed with a rag and the turpentine, followed behind righting the mishaps and resisting the temptation to dismiss her daughter summarily from the project.

'I think you're getting rather too much paint on your brush,' she observed mildly. 'Try dipping it less far into the pot, and then really work it on the wood until all the paint is gone before you dip again.'

'I am. But it's hard. It all gets up the end near the handle and then it squishes out and drips down.'

'Not if you get less paint on your brush. Look at Willow.' Below Beth's ladder she was making a meticulous job of outlining the sill; the roots of her bristles glistened clean and black. 'She isn't dripping everywhere.'

'Isn't she the clever one?' muttered Beth beneath her breath.

As the areas of window frame left to undercoat diminished, so it grew tighter for three people to work, and presently Laura moved round to start on the door. This side of the pumphouse was sheltered from the wind, and the sun, which had seemed to have no power in it, began to warm the back of her neck. Her muscles were heated now, too; her right arm felt the pull as she plastered to and fro. She was just contemplating the removal of a jumper when a sudden shriek sent her back round the corner to Beth and Willow.

204

'Sorry,' mumbled Beth, standing pink-faced and unrepentant at the top of the stepladder.

Willow, underneath, was feeling in her hair for the blob of paint.

'Here, let me.' Laura found a clean rag and, bending Willow's head towards her, rubbed at the smear, wiping it away as best she could. 'Beth, what were you doing? You really need to be more careful. Look down here.' She indicated the grass beneath the window, which was spotted and splashed in white. 'What's all this?'

Beth looked belligerent. 'It's only the lawn. What's it matter?'

'It looks a mess, that's what. And it won't do the grass any good.'

'Dad wouldn't mind. He never minds a bit of mess. He's fun.'

'Dad?' Suspicion formed in Laura's mind. 'You've never done any painting at Dad's, have you?'

Beth's eyes slanted away. 'Not really.'

'What do you mean, "not really"?' Simon knew about her asthma; he knew she shouldn't be breathing paint fumes.

Her daughter, apparently, could read her mind; or else, poor child, she'd heard it all too often before. 'S'OK, it was outdoors. It was nothing – just putting some browny-black stuff on the garden fence. Ages ago. Last summer.' She sat down on the top step of the ladder with her brush across her lap, transferring an oblong of white to her jeans. 'Honestly, Mum, I knew you'd go ballistic about it. That's why I told him not to tell you.'

'Was it creosote? Or Sadolin?' She wasn't sure which was worse. Inhaling coal tar couldn't be good, but those liquid woodstains no doubt contained all kinds of evil fungicides.

Beth stared blankly at her mother. 'How should I know?'

Willow, meanwhile, had reached across to the bucket of soapy water which still stood, now grey and cold, where Laura had left it after washing down the woodwork before they began. She drew a cupped handful of water and suds and flung it up at Beth, catching her across the midriff. Beth gasped, and sent Willow a look of pure venom, so that Laura thought she might either cry or launch a murderous assault. But then she was down the ladder in one bound and over to the bucket and the two of them were at it like warring washerwomen, flicking each other with filthy water and cackling fit to burst.

When order was restored, along with Beth's fair humour, Laura sent her up to the house to fetch dry jumpers for herself and Willow, and to put the kettle on again. 'You'll both catch your deaths out here, else, in this cold wind.'

The window frame completed, Willow came to join Laura in painting the door. For a while they worked together side by side in companionable silence. When Laura paused to flex her stiffening wrist, she took the moment to examine Willow's handiwork. It was tidy; very tidy indeed.

'Nice,' she said. 'You seem to have quite a knack for this. Have you done any decorating before?'

Willow worked her brush slowly up and down the wood. 'We never lived anywhere like this. Anywhere with an outside.' Then, catching Laura's puzzled expression, she laughed and said, 'Well, of course there must have been outsides. But you know what I mean – bedsits, people's spare rooms. It was always someone else's job.'

It made sense. One year at university, Laura had lived in a high-rise student residence and it had taken her until Christmas to work out, from down below, which one was her window.

'What about the insides, though? Didn't you ever help to paint your bedroom?'

Willow's brush halted for a moment; liquid paint gathered at the tip to form a welling bubble, which distorted, broke and began to roll. Then she shrugged, neatly trapped the escaping drip, and the slow, even strokes resumed. 'No. We were never anywhere long enough, I guess.'

'Tea break,' called Beth, approaching across the lawn with a tray. 'Hope it's OK, Mum, I've brought down that packet of digestives. I'm totally starving.'

Willow sat cross-legged on the floor in the room which had belonged to Laura's parents, and stared at the wallpaper. It was vinyl coated, a green lattice pattern on a white background with tiny sprigged roses in lemon yellow. As she stared, the pattern performed a slow dance, twisting and merging into itself and away, like moving scenery behind a play.

She held her breath. *One, two* . . .

When it resolved itself it was a different wallpaper in a different room. She didn't know where the room was, or how old she was in it, but she saw the paper with a keen clarity: vertical stripes of gold on cream, narrow then wide, and, round above the skirting at the height where her blue tractor bumped, a horizontal frieze of cream on gold. This was a wall she had looked at for a long time, with her mother in the big double bed behind her, that they shared at night and never got made. *Eleven, twelve.*

There was a room with pale yellow paint, but that one swam out of reach in her memory; when she tried to grasp for it, it transformed itself into the paint of her mother's hospital room in Cambridge, scuff-marked and stripped of furniture. The original, she thought, had been the small back bedroom in a house in London, belonging to a man; the landing had been dark, with just a hanging wire and no bulb, but she couldn't call the room itself to mind at all. Except that the bed was narrow and small; she hadn't shared the room with her mother. Now, even with her eyes closed, she could neither picture the man nor remember his name. *Twenty-eight, twenty-nine.* She wondered whether Mum could.

Another wall. This one was painted, too, no plain canvas this time, but a wild panorama of colour. It was a mural, executed in a naïve hand. She recalled it exact in every detail, from the purple mountains at the top to the thick forest undergrowth at the front, tangled with a gnarl of roots and branches. The image was endlessly seductive and Willow sat lost in it for hours. The place must have been a squat. Sometimes there was no water in the taps and they told her not to flush the toilet when she'd been, and there always seemed to be someone different minding her.

Next she saw dark blue tiles, a double row of them at the back of an electric cooker, and above the tiles a wall which had once been white, now stained and splashed with grease. *Fifty-two, fifty-three.* She was nine or ten, and cooking scrambled eggs in a saucepan she'd found. But the ring was too hot and she didn't stir fast enough and the bottom part went dry and brown and smelt of burnt car tyres. She scraped off the top part on to a plate to take up to her mother, but the rubber smell went all the way through. *Fifty-nine, sixty.* She threw it away later, when Mum was asleep.

Finally, she remembered a wall in a toilet, a public one with an electric hand dryer. *Place hands under nozzle. Rub hands gently in warm air flow. Air stops automatically.* She read the instructions over and over so she didn't have to look in the mirror, which stared from the wall to her left in metallic accusation. Behind the dryer, the wall was painted an institutional cream, the same cream as in the corridor outside, where the WPC was standing waiting for her. The same cream as in the interview room, three doors along, where there was a desk with a tape-recorder in the middle. *Seventy-six, seventy-seven.* On one side of a desk the police sergeant was sitting, next to an empty chair which was the WPC's; on the other side were three chairs. *Eighty, eighty-one, eighty-two.* A social worker occupied one of the chairs. Not Vince, not then: this must have been the duty social worker, a name from a telephone list. She was greying and weary, with a voice that dragged like boots on gravel. The second chair was Willow's. *Eighty-eight, eighty-nine.* While she held her breath and counted, she could stay here in the toilet; she didn't need to go back in. Not yet, *ninety-one*, not yet, *ninety-two*. The lighter was in there with them. It lay on the desk beside the tape-recorder and the sergeant's notebook, not her mum's silver one, but a cheap disposable thing from Forbuoys. *Ninety-nine, a hundred*. While she held her breath, she didn't have to go back in there and see her mother in the third chair, and face the look in her eyes.

A hundred and one, a hundred and two, a hundred and three . . .

Chapter 17

When Vince finally called it was with a peace offering of lobster.

'It's my friend Sam, with the boat. He's got some beauties. And nobody can eat lobster alone. It wouldn't be decent.'

There was nothing sheepish in his voice, no indication that he even remembered the terms on which they'd parted. But if he'd been awkward it would have made her awkward, too – and he wouldn't have been Vince.

'He landed them at the weekend, and he's got me down for two nice big ones. I know you said Beth didn't eat things with tentacles, but you never mentioned pincers.'

'At the weekend?' It was Thursday already. How long did lobster keep? Then a nasty thought struck her. 'Are they . . . still alive?'

He laughed. 'Naturally. But don't worry, I shan't ask you to do the deed. I was going to suggest you all come over to my flat, and I'll be the one with blood on my hands.'

Prospective murderer or not, this softened her towards him at once. An invitation to his private space must surely represent a gesture of compromise, a lowering of professional walls.

'That would be lovely,' she said, and hoped he heard her mean it. 'Though not for the lobsters. Is it true about them screaming, when you drop them in the pot?'

Another laugh. 'Utter nonsense, I gather. Pure urban myth. Sam says they don't have vocal cords, or any means of vocalisation. There's a bit of a hiss sometimes, but he reckons it's air escaping from their stomachs through their mouths when they hit the boiling water.'

'Oh. I see.' This information didn't make her feel much better about the barbarity to which she was to be party. But she was very fond of lobster.

'Anyway,' said Vince, 'I have a colleague who claims the same thing about carrots.'

'What about them?' Laura was confused.

'That scientists have recorded a cry of pain when they're uprooted. But she's a fruitarian, this colleague, and completely bonkers. Works in family liaison.'

When, over supper, Laura told Beth about the invitation – omitting specifics as to the provenance of the lunch – she was not enthusiastic.

'I wanted to have Alice round on Saturday.'

'Well, you still can. Why doesn't she come over in the morning before we go, or else later on, for supper?'

'S'pose so.'

Laura looked at her in exasperation. She would have hoped for curiosity, at the very least, about seeing where he lived. Beth had always been so keen on Vince. Until just recently.

'What's lobster like, anyway? Sounds disgusting.'

'It's a bit like crab. You love crab.' Beth used to demand crab paste in her sandwiches every day at one time, in about Year 4. 'Or king prawns. Except it's even nicer.'

Cambridge was not a city known for its purpose-built flats, but Vince lived in one of them. It was in a compact two-storey development, perhaps fifteen or twenty years old at most, tucked down a cul-de-sac off the Milton Road and set back behind plantings of firethorn and cotoneaster. There was a small car park round to one side, and nowhere was it indicated that it was for residents only. Laura pulled into the last free space. The flats had intercoms; when she rang Vince's bell and said, 'It's us,' he didn't speak, just buzzed them in. His flat was upstairs, past a small landing where a bedraggled pot plant stretched thirstily towards a high window, and along a carpeted corridor.

'Welcome,' he said with deadpan formality as he pulled

back the door. Then he grinned. 'Better come in quick, I've left the pan on.'

Laura tried not to picture the bubbling cauldron of death as they followed him in and through a door at the end of the tiny hallway. In fact it was a frying pan that he whisked off the gas, smelling smokily of garlic and butter.

'Sam's mother's recipe,' he explained, as he caught Laura's glance. 'Brown butter with garlic and parsley. Sam insists it's the only thing to serve with lobster.'

'It sounds very nice,' she said, polite and a little awkward.

Willow, meanwhile, had found the fridge where she helped herself to a Diet Coke. 'Want one, Beth?'

'Uh-huh.' Beth installed herself on a stool at the breakfast bar and looked at nobody. *Yes, please*, Laura thought but didn't say.

The room was untidy, she was surprised to note. Not in the way that Simon was untidy, that wanton disorder that hit you as soon as you entered the house, but still, a mild slovenliness in corners which wasn't what she'd have associated with Vince. The imperfection gave her covert pleasure.

'How about you?' He waved a glass in her direction. 'Coke as well, or orange juice, or will you join me in a glass of wine?'

'Oh, sorry, yes. I brought some. It's in my bag. It's sparkling actually, if that's OK?' She felt foolish now, especially at a lunchtime, wishing she'd stuck with chardonnay. 'Not the real stuff, I don't mean, just some Italian fizz. But I thought, you know, with lobster . . .'

'Perfect. Like Guinness and oysters. Or vodka and caviar. Shall I open it, or will you?'

'Or fish and chips in the paper,' she said, smiling as she unscrewed the wire, 'and a glass of real, old-fashioned lemonade.'

There were only two bar stools, but Willow had hopped on to the worktop and Vince was back at his pan, stirring, so Laura climbed up next to her daughter. She filled the two glasses he had placed before her, watching the bubbles rise and then subside. The girls were both drinking straight from the can.

'Anyway,' said Vince, without turning round, 'are you ready for the main attraction?'

Laura hoped he didn't mean what she thought he meant. 'What's that, then?'

'The lobsters, of course. I assumed you'd want to watch.'

Oh, God. 'Well, I don't know. I mean, I know you said there's nothing to it and they don't really scream, but I'm not sure I really want to see them go in.'

Willow surveyed Vince from her perch on the worktop. 'Are they alive?'

'Of course they're alive. You have to cook lobsters from live, it's the whole point about them.'

'Where are they now?'

'Bucket in the bathroom. I'll get them in a minute. Come on, Laura. I'll stick the water on to boil, and then I can show you how it's done.'

The skin of her arms felt hot and cold at the same time. 'Honestly, Vince, I really don't – '

'*Shut up.*' It was Beth; they all turned to look at her. 'It's cruel and horrible. She doesn't want to look and I don't blame her. Why don't you leave her alone?'

'Sweetheart – ' began Laura, but Vince cut across her calmly. 'It's OK, Beth. Don't worry.' In fact, he almost seemed amused. 'They're already cooked and dressed and in the fridge. I sorted it all out this morning. I was just teasing your mother.'

He tried to lay a hand on Beth's shoulder, but she ducked away. 'Well, don't,' she muttered.

It took a second Coke and half a tube of Pringles – which Vince set down at the table in the living room and announced as 'the starter' – before Beth recovered anything like her usual countenance, and even then Laura sensed she was out of sorts. She spoke little, and when her half-lobster appeared, surrounded by salad and dressed with the steaming garlic butter, she prodded it with theatrical suspicion. It was, however, undeniably delicious. They all set about it with a will, and the assortment of forks and skewers and nutcrackers yielded by Vince's kitchen drawers. By the time Laura had leisure to sit back, take stock and lick her fingers, the shell on her daughter's plate was more than half empty.

'I don't care if they died in agony,' Laura declared. 'They're absolutely glorious.'

'Mm-*mm*,' agreed Willow through a mouthful of claw.

After lunch was over and the debris scooped into the kitchen bin, Vince hauled them away from their offers of washing up and back into the living room. 'I'll make some coffee in a minute. Or there's more of that bubbly.'

'Coffee would be lovely,' said Laura. 'Would you like me to – ?'

'Sit!'

Willow, however, disobeyed; instead, she hovered. 'I thought I might go into town.' She looked at Beth. 'Just round the shops, you know. D'you want to come?'

Beth bounced up at once, all too obviously anxious to be out of there; then she remembered herself and turned to Laura. 'S'that OK?'

'Fine. How long will you be, do you think?'

'Back by four,' said Willow.

'Take a twenty from my purse, sweetheart. It can be an advance on your pocket money.'

When the flat door banged, Vince poured himself some more of the *spumante* and Laura subsided into her armchair, uncertain whether to feel more relaxed or less.

'So,' she said, 'was this supposed to be revenge? For last time.' Immediately, she wished it unsaid; the reminder of that previous encounter set her cheeks uncomfortably aglow. She rushed on. 'The lobsters, I mean. Was it revenge for the pizzas? Were they booby-trapped?'

He wasn't helping at all; his face was a blank.

'After we poisoned you with the Mozzarella. Weren't you sick?' Coffee would have helped; she wished he'd let her make it.

'Sick?' A smile twitched his mouth. 'Oh dear.'

'We were all three sick as dogs the whole night afterwards. I assumed Willow would have told you. You mean to say you escaped?'

'Not a twinge. I came home and slept like a baby, before rising to breakfast, as I recall, on sausage and eggs. They were excellent pizzas, I thought.'

'Excellent pizzas that gave us all food poisoning.'

'Well, I'm very sorry to hear it. Willow didn't say. Poor you.' He sipped his wine with what looked suspiciously like satisfaction.

I'm sorry, she knew she ought to say. For the row; for sending him out in the dark with no taxi. But it was difficult to know quite how to begin, and then he was speaking again and it was too late.

'Beth didn't seem herself today.'

'No.'

'Look, I'm sorry about the thing with the lobsters. I shouldn't have joked about it. I didn't mean to upset her. Animal cruelty – at that age, it's no laughing matter. Or at any age, come to that.'

'Oh, I don't think it was that, not really. It's like you say, she's not herself, hasn't been all day. I don't know what's got into her.' Though she might, perhaps, have some inkling. *You're wrong. I've got a dad.*

'How is she, otherwise?'

'Oh, all better now,' said Laura, still distracted. 'It was just a twenty-four hour thing.'

He grinned. 'I didn't mean the vomiting. I meant at school. Those girls who were giving her a hard time.'

'It's eased off, I think. At least, she hasn't said anything recently.' But then, she never said anything before, did she? 'She seems happier about school, anyway. She's been seeing a

215

lot of one of her old friends from primary school. Alice – a lovely girl.'

Nodding, he took another swallow of wine. 'What about on Facebook?'

'No more trouble that I know of. She's always on there, chatting in the evenings and she never seems upset.' Maybe she should have another half-glass of *spumante* herself, but Vince's wine glasses were large and she was driving. 'Are you on there?' she asked him. 'Do you have a Facebook page, I mean?'

He showed an apologetic palm. 'Guilty as charged. I have some ex-clients on there, like to use it to stay in touch. Funny thing, really. Bit of a far cry from Ivy League alumni tracking their frat house chums.'

'True. And the same goes for twelve-year-old schoolgirls, swapping gossip out of class. Actually, the reason I was asking is that I've got a page now, too.'

'You have? There, you see, it gets us all in the end.'

'It was this post-grad student we had in the Department, doing her PhD. An Indian girl, Punita, working on water management. Anyway, she's finished and had her viva, and she's leaving to take up a teaching post at the university back home in Delhi. Getting married later in the spring, too. She persuaded us all to sign up so we can look at the wedding photos.'

'And what did Beth have to say, about her mum being on Facebook?'

'Oh, she thought it was hilarious. She's convinced it's only for people under twenty. But she made me a Friend. She said otherwise I'd have no mates and look like a loser.'

'Ah – sweet, innocent child.'

Laura looked at him. 'Why?'

'I see she isn't the only one who's sweet and innocent. Because Friends have access to everything on one's Facebook page. You'll be able to see all her embarrassing ramblings, her seditious slanders, her debauched photographs.'

216

Debauched? 'Vince, she's twelve.'

'And twelve-year-olds don't have anything they wouldn't want their mother to see?'

No doubt she was frowning, because he said, 'Don't worry. I can't imagine Beth with any terrible, dark secrets. I expect it's all about question 12 in the maths homework and how big the art teacher's bum is. At the very worst, it'll be which boy they're all fancying this week.'

'I suppose so.'

'There is one thing, though.' He rose from his chair. 'It's like listening at keyholes. Not everything you discover may be to your advantage.'

With a guilty lurch she thought of the spare room door.

'Come on,' he said, 'let's go and put on that coffee.'

Installed at the breakfast bar, and with a cup to occupy her hands, things became easier again. While she speculated about the girls, and what magpie pickings they would come back with from town, he pulled the other stool round opposite her, elbow to elbow across the laminate. His coffee was good, strong and smoky.

When smalltalk lulled, Vince laid down his cup and said, 'Marianne was undiagnosed.' He was looking unwaveringly at Laura, who held her breath and said nothing. Was this the apology? The concession to friendship? 'When Willow was living with her, she wasn't known to the mental health services. Her condition hadn't come to light.'

He stopped there, so she edged her way gingerly to a question. 'Does that mean she wasn't so ill then, perhaps? When Willow was little, she may have been all right?'

But he shook his head. 'Unlikely, as I understand it. Not with her symptoms the way they are now. They're likely to have been with her always – probably since she was a teenager herself. There are blanks there unexplained by bipolar disorder, suggesting long-term damage. Drug use, perhaps, when she was young.'

'Well, then, how – ?' She hesitated, but his face signalled

encouragement, so she said, 'It's hard to imagine how she'd have managed, that's all, with a child, and her illness. With no support, no medication. How she'd cope.'

He smiled faintly. 'It's surprising how people do manage.'

'But also,' she persevered, 'it's so strange that nobody noticed how things were. I don't know . . . the school, the GP?'

'They moved around a lot. Willow may not have been in schools for long at a time – or sometimes not at all. And I don't think Marianne ever went to the doctor. Willow was seen, for the usual childhood things – earaches, rashes, minor ailments. Marianne took her to the surgery or other people did. Friends. She seems to have had a lot of friends, and stayed with them. Maybe they helped her with Willow, even took her off her hands for spells. But Marianne never saw a doctor herself.'

'But that's awful. Someone as sick as she is, I mean, slipping through all the nets like that.'

'It happens,' he said simply. 'Marianne and her friends were mobile, probably suspicious of authority, a lot of them. Hard to pin down. An alternative lifestyle will cover a multitude of sins.' Then he grinned. 'Bloody hippies.'

But Laura wasn't ready to laugh. 'What about the child? What about Willow? With children, there should be tabs kept, surely? The health visitor, for a start, when she was a baby.'

'I think . . .' He was frowning now, no longer making that training-manual eye contact of his, but staring down at her hands where they circled her coffee cup. She wondered if, as she did, he saw the newspaper photographs, the litany of names: Victoria Climbié, Baby P. 'I think,' he resumed at length, 'you can never underestimate the resource of a mother in shielding her child. It's amazing what even the most apparently dysfunctional parents can do, if think their child may be taken away. Perhaps when there were visits from the health visitor or the practice nurse, or headteachers to talk to,

Marianne managed to get her act together. For all we know, in fact, she may have done a pretty good job of looking after Willow, even while she was neglecting herself.'

'Is that what Willow says?'

He didn't reply at first, and she was afraid she had pushed too hard. But then he looked up at her, and his answer had the ring of candour. 'She doesn't say much. She's very loyal.'

'I bet she is,' she said, surprised by an upsurge of anger. 'So basically, Marianne hid from the doctors who could have helped her, and Willow was left to run wild and play truant.' Reminded of the abandoned courses at the Regional College, she felt a twinge of guilt towards Vince, but rapidly suppressed it. 'To play truant,' she repeated, 'and worse than that, in the end.'

But something of the old, guarded manner had come back over Vince; he became again his professional self. 'It's hard to judge these things from the outside,' was all he said; then, signalling an end to further confidences, 'More coffee?'

As he was pouring it, the entryphone buzzed and he put down the percolator to go to the door. Hellos in the hallway, Vince's and Willow's, and then they were in the kitchen. Beth swept past Vince to deposit a carrier bag in front of Laura on the breakfast bar.

'Willow got a T shirt,' she announced. 'A black one, with long sleeves and a hood and it was only ten pounds. Show her, Willow. It's really cool. And I got some sparkly bangles from Accessorize. They came in a set, six of them for eight pounds.' She pulled them out, still joined by the plastic tag, and slid them up her wrist, jingling them in evident satisfaction.

'And look.' She rummaged in the bag and drew out a flat parcel of white tissue paper, folded to a square and sealed with Sellotape. 'This is just the best. Willow bought it for me with her own money. She really wanted to – that is OK, isn't it, Mum? It was on this stall in the Grafton Centre, next to that African one that's always there, where I got my wooden elephant.' As she spoke, she was carefully unfolding the tissue paper, layer by layer. 'It was mostly a bit New Agey for me – crystals, you know, and CDs of whales moaning and stuff. Though they did have some nice dolphin earrings. But then Willow spotted this, and said I had to have it, and she was right. It's perfect.'

'This' was revealed to a necklace; or rather, it was a pendant on a fine string of plaited red cotton. The pendant itself was small, about the size of a ten pence piece, and resembled a blazing sun.

'It wards off evil spirits, apparently, the lady said. That's what the mirror's for. She had loads of things with little mirrors on – bags and purses, as well as jewellery – and all of it's for getting rid of spirits. It reflects back the evil, she said.' Beth twisted the pendant round so it caught the light, like ice in car headlamps. 'Isn't it gorgeous?'

Around the perimeter of the mirror were tiny tongues of wire-framed glass in orange and red and gold. As Laura watched, they trapped the light and seemed to come alive, curling and licking outwards like so many dancing flames.

Chapter 18

'Mum, can I bike to school tomorrow?'

Laura, who had half her mind on the benefits of sustainable woodland management for the local economy and the other on the pan of water coming up to the boil behind her, adopted the parental default position of equivocation. 'Why?'

'Because I've hardly used my new bike since I got it because it was winter, but now it's spring, and it'll be fun and *everyone* cycles.'

Putting down her pen, Laura looked up properly at her daughter and smiled. 'Not many reasons at all, then?'

It was true that since a couple of weekend try-outs soon after Beth's birthday, the much-coveted bicycle had scarcely been out of the shed. And the weather had been fine this week, the few clouds mobile and high-riding, sharp-edged as in a child's drawing, white against a sky of brilliant blue.

'I thought I'd ride along the lode. It's much shorter than by road.'

'Really? Won't it be filthy? Everything's still so wet out there – the garden's a bog. You don't want to arrive at school all covered in mud, do you? Or the bike either, for that matter, when it's so new.'

'I meant the path on the top of the dyke. It's not too muddy up there.'

'Well, I don't know.' The pan was boiling now; Laura rose from the table and picked up the packet of spaghetti, sliding out a fat handful. She slipped it into the rolling water, pushing down on the ends until it disappeared beneath the foam. 'It's pretty slippery,' she said, 'and the banks are steep.'

'Mum, I'm not eight. I'm not going to wobble off my bike and fall in the lode.'

Laura, who had been picturing more or less exactly that, shot Beth a grin through the cloud of starchy steam. 'All right. But it's pretty lonely along there, too. Suppose you had an asthma attack?'

It wasn't a fanciful fear; Beth had sometimes had attacks triggered by exercise or exertion. In a public place, on the road, there would always be someone who'd stop and help, someone with a car.

'I'll have my inhaler with me, won't I? And my mobile.'

'What good is a mobile, along that footpath? The ambulance couldn't – '

'*Ambulance*? Mum – seriously. You make it sound like I'm some kind of old lady or cripple or something. I'm sure I can manage to bike three miles to Elswell without having to be carted off on a freaking stretcher. It'll only take, like, fifteen minutes.'

The spaghetti, revolving slowly under Laura's wooden spoon, was starting to yield and soften. 'Go and give Willow a shout, could you, please, love?' she said.

They were back before she'd drained the pasta.

'What's in the sauce?' asked Beth, lifting saucepan lids.

'Bacon and mushrooms. And I've done some runner beans. Now wash your hands – and could you get the knives and forks, please?'

'Willow'll do that. I'll grate the Parmesan.'

When they were all seated and served, a brief silence reigned. But Beth seldom let go of a bone for long once her teeth were in it.

'It doesn't get dark now 'til six o'clock. I'd be home ages before that. I could stay at school 'til half past four or something, be home a bit before you, and it would still be daylight.'

Laura nodded. The longer evenings certainly made things easier.

'And biking's good for you. They're always on at school about kids not getting enough exercise because they're guzzling snacks in front of the computer.'

'Doubly bad,' said Laura, choosing the side alley. 'Crisp crumbs in the keyboard – fatal.'

Beth refused to be diverted. 'And that asthma doctor, at the hospital last summer, said exercise was good, didn't she? "Regular gentle exercise" is what she said. So if I bike every day, there and back, that's regular. And along the lode I'm not exactly going to be zooming along, am I? It's too lumpy.'

There was nothing here Laura could easily disagree with, so she focussed on wrapping spaghetti round her fork.

'Might be good for my flabby thighs, too.'

'What nonsense,' she said. 'Your thighs are just fine.'

She'd seen Beth through the open bathroom door, sitting on the linen basket with her legs pressed flat, prodding censoriously at the pale, splayed flesh. But somehow her daughter, now shovelling spaghetti and sauce like a brickie's mate, did not seem a high risk for anorexia nervosa.

'Is your old bike still in the shed?' They were the first words Willow had uttered since she came down. Laura and Beth, battle lines momentarily abandoned, both turned their eyes to her.

'Think so,' said Beth. 'Unless Mum's chucked it.'

'No, it's still there. I keep thinking we should find some younger child who'd like to have it, and then not getting round to doing anything about it. Why?'

'Thought I might have a go on it sometime, that's all. If you don't mind?'

'Of course not, but it's very small. Beth had outgrown it.'

'It's teeny weeny. I had it when it was about seven or something.'

'Well, nine, maybe. Nine or ten.' Beth had been riding it around quite happily in the early autumn, and now she made it sound like a relic of infancy. 'But it is small.'

Willow shrugged. 'I'm not very big.' And indeed, sitting

223

across the table in her skinny black T shirt, there looked to be nothing of her. The half-inch spurt that Beth had put on since the end of the old year might, in fact, have taken her past Willow, though they were still very much of a height.

'Try it, then, by all means. The saddle and handlebars will already be up at their highest.' She refrained from asking Willow whether she had a helmet.

'Thanks. So, Beth, d'you mind if I come along the lode with you in the morning? Just for the ride?'

'Yeah – that'd be great.'

Thus it was settled between them, and Laura knew herself outmanoeuvred. Gracious defeat seemed the only option. She arranged her face in a genial smile. 'Would anyone like more Parmesan?'

Willow was twelve years old when she learned to ride a bicycle.

It wasn't her first. There had been an earlier bike – actually a tricycle with pink plastic wheels and white tyres that smelt like rubber bands. Her mother had brought it home one day, tied all over with big pink ribbons and shiny foil streamers. It might have been a birthday or it might not; nothing was said. She sat on the moulded pink saddle, and her mother pushed her down some long, uncarpeted hallway; the pedals turned so fast that it was all she could do for her legs to keep up, and now and then her feet spun off and the pedals clattered her shins. They left that house with people after them and no time to pack. Willow never knew if the chasing demons were real or only in her mother's head, but either way, the trike was left behind.

The bike she learned to ride on wasn't hers at all. She had found it in a brick lean-to at the back of the house which was still black inside from when it had been a coal shed. They were living in a council house on an estate on the edge of Cambridge. The tenant had gone away to Ireland for the summer and left Mum with the rent book and a bunch of keys. According to the officious neighbour, Mrs Pauling, the council would be down on them like thunder if they knew, since subletting wasn't allowed. So Willow hauled the bike to the end of the garden, away from Mrs Pauling's windows and out of view of the road. It was old and heavy and too big for her, as black as the coal shed and stiff with rust. The three-speed was jammed in place and wouldn't have shifted, even if she'd known what gears were for. The chain was brittly dry and creaked as it turned.

She taught herself because there was nobody else to teach her. It was four pedal turns from one side of the garden to the other, with the gears stuck on '3'; four long, slow, wobbly pushes with her right leg and four with her left, while her hands on the handlebars kept up a constant frantic fight, adjusting and readjusting to keep her weight above the wheels. The turf was threadbare and dry, each lump and bump set hard as concrete in the August sun. When she overbalanced and fell – which at the start was often – it came up to meet her with a breath-depriving slam and the dry grass burned her skin. The bike was too heavy to turn in the short space, so at each end, uncertain of the brakes, she jumped down to stop, learning to land on her feet before the bike toppled over and took her with it.

It was impossible to say, now, how long she'd spent riding the bike to and fro across the narrow, yellowed lawn. It could have been every day for a fortnight, or just a couple of afternoons. She remembered the sun on her shoulders, which were turning pink and she knew she ought to go indoors or they would burn, but was too caught up to stop. She remembered the slight rise of ground by the left-hand fence, which meant the bike was liable to tip the other way as you stopped, unless you leant into the slope for the last half-turn of the pedals before you jumped off. She remembered the worst fall, close to the other end, when she tugged the handlebar too suddenly and caught the mudguard on the toe of her trainer, sending herself sprawling flat to the side with the bike on top of her. She remembered the broad graze which stretched down her thigh as far as the knee, streaky white at first and blotching slowly to purple, and the blobs of blood which appeared only later, welling from a series of tiny parallel nicks; but she couldn't recall any pain.

What if I fell? she remembered thinking. What if I really fell and hurt myself, like kids sometimes did, and broke their arms or ankles or cracked their heads and had to be in hospital? What would happen then? In hospital, there were meals, weren't there, normal meals that an adult had cooked, and someone to make sure you had clean pyjamas. It could happen so easily. Maybe out on the road, on the tarmac, where she'd be going faster. It wouldn't take much. One sharper turn, a heavier fall, the negligent snap of bone. What if . . . what if . . .?

It was close to the Easter holidays when Laura found the hair straighteners. Sunday morning, after breakfast, was when she always changed the sheets. She'd stripped Beth's bed and thrown across the fresh sheet, smoothing it over with the heel of her palm to work out the wrinkles. She pulled it tight and tucked it in along the front edge, then dragged the bed away from the wall by six inches or so to tuck it in behind. The straighteners were underneath the bed, right at the back by the wall. Either they must have fallen there, slipping down between bed and wall – or else they'd been hidden.

There had been no mention for months of Beth's desire for straightening tongs. Laura had not bought them for birthday or Christmas, and Simon's cheques had gone on other things. She reached down and picked them up. They were square-edged in cream plastic, the metal jaws closed tight and wrapped neatly around with the black flex. There was no brand logo, but they didn't look cheap.

At the spare room door she paused and knocked before entering. Willow sat cross-legged with her back to the door, facing the bed on which Beth lay prone, head to the foot and feet on the pillow. She was sure there had been laughter, but they were silent as she came in. It was too late, however, to dissemble or delay her purpose, to begin with something else, since the straighteners were in her hand and Beth had seen them.

'These were under your bed,' she said. 'Where did they come from?'

Beth raised herself on one elbow and looked at Willow, but there was no help from that quarter; her hair was short, choppy and unkempt as always.

'They're mine.'

'I see.' Laura waited. They both knew it wasn't what she'd asked.

Beth's voice rose a defensive notch. 'Someone gave them to me.'

'Lent them to you, do you mean, or actually gave?'

'Gave.'

Simon, perhaps. He'd always watched her battles with her hair in sympathetic amusement; the stubborn kinks had come from him. 'Were they Tessa's?'

But she knew she was clutching at straws; Beth looked down and said nothing. Laura tried another tack.

'What were they doing at the back there, under the bed?'

Again, nothing. Instead it was Willow who spoke. 'Bad idea.'

'What is?' Beth blinked at her, surprised from her silence.

'Putting them under the bed. You could cause a fire that way.'

'They weren't hot.' But she spoke rather too quickly, and Laura's nostrils twitched with the smell of scorched carpet and smouldering bedlinen.

Collecting herself, she said, 'Beth, love, would you mind coming and helping me with your bed? You can put the duvet in its cover for me.'

Back in Beth's room, she finished tucking in the sheet while her daughter obediently started on the duvet. It made it easier to be doing something.

'Were they from Willow? The straighteners, I mean.'

227

'No.'

This came as a relief, though Laura wasn't sure quite why, and it was, in any case, shortlived. 'Then who? Sweetheart, please tell me where they came from.'

'I said. Someone gave them to me.'

Shoplifting. Her mind, which had been resolutely shutting out the word, suddenly shouted it loud. The hiding place; the evasive answers. Shoplifting – again.

'Who did, Beth?' she asked quietly. 'Who gave them to you?'

No shop in Elswell sold electrical goods. It must have been in Cambridge. But how, and when?

'Rianna.'

Laura's thoughts were so busy forging their own track that the answer threw her for a moment. 'I'm sorry?'

'It was Rianna that gave me them.'

Her head spun. 'When?'

'Last week, week before.'

'But I thought . . .' What had she thought, exactly? 'I didn't know you two were friends any more.'

'We weren't, for a bit. But she kept on at me, being really nice and everything. And the thing is she's fallen out with Caitlin so she'd got no one to hang out with.'

Poor little Rianna, thought Laura bitterly. The friendless loner act, and Beth was fool enough to fall for it. Except it was also just like her daughter: staunch and kind.

'I thought you were mainly in with Alice now, and her friends. Ellie and Gemma.'

'I did try. I said to them, let's include Rianna, but Gemma hates her. They all do. Gemma said some really spiteful things about her, and about her family, too.'

'Well, of course, that isn't nice. It's really not right of Gemma, to say mean things . . .' Laura could feel her ground begin to crumble. She dug in her feet. 'What about Facebook? Those things Rianna said about you. She really upset you. And now you're friends again?'

'What things?' Beth's face fought between anguish and denial, before resolving itself into accusation. 'How do you know?'

'I saw on the screen, that day – or guessed. I'm sorry.' But this was not the point; she was losing her way again. 'Look,' she said, 'I'm not sure you should be accepting a gift like that.' Though this, as well, glanced off from the central issue. 'Sweets, perhaps, all right, but not big things, things like these hair tongs. It's not as if it was your birthday or anything.'

'You didn't mind when it was Willow. She gave me the mirror necklace, and that wasn't my birthday, either. You never said anything then.'

'That's different.'

'Why?'

Why was it different? *Because I know Willow; because she's family.* Laura took two corners of duvet and cover from her daughter and together they shook it into shape. Instead she said, 'They must have been expensive.'

'No.' Beth shook her head, eager to reassure. 'No, she said Liam got them. Her brother, you know. He had loads. He has a van and does deliveries for people, and sometimes they give him stuff. I think they were free, or at least really cheap.'

Oh, God. Perhaps not so far off, then, when she'd thought the straighteners stolen.

Between the two of them, they lifted the duvet on to the bed and tugged it smooth. Beth tossed her pillows, freshly cased, towards the headboard, where they lodged at rakish angles.

Laura straightened her back. 'You know, you don't have to be friends with someone just because she gives you things.'

'I do know that, Mum. I'm not a total div.'

'Beth, you know I don't like your using – '

'Anyway, it wasn't like that. You make it sound like she was bribing me, or paying me to like her or something, but that's not how it was at all. She just had these spare straighteners lying around in a box at home, and she knew I'd been wanting some for ages, so she was being nice, and I don't see how there can be anything wrong with being nice to someone.'

She spoke in a rush and with an intensity that brooked no contradiction; a year or two ago, she'd have finished, 'So there.' The set of her lips was suddenly so precisely the same as when she was seven years old that Laura couldn't help but smile.

'Come here,' she said, and stepped forward to pull Beth into a clumsy hug, their feet tangling in the discarded heap of dirty sheet and duvet cover and pillow cases. *I love you, I am afraid for you, I don't want you to get hurt.*

Rather than voice these impossible things, she pushed Beth gently away to arm's length, and held her eye. 'All right. But you use them only on the dressing table, in a nice, clear space. And afterwards you leave them out to cool properly, and never, ever put them away hot.'

Chapter 19

It was sheer chance that Laura noticed the swallows. On the first Monday of the Easter holidays she was working at home; at ten o'clock she went out to her car, which was parked on top of the dyke as usual, to fetch a file she'd left on the back seat. With the folder in one hand and the car keys in the other, she turned for a moment to look out across the empty fields before going back inside the house. It was a habit with her, almost a superstition, like touching a charm. She drank in the fens as she'd draw in cool water, to reassure herself of their existence, or take a slice of them back indoors with her to sustain her at her desk. More often than not she hardly looked, or saw, at all; the long habit had become a reflex.

It was a movement, now, that caught her attention: a sudden streak, low over the winter wheat, that was gone before she truly saw it. It was no more than a tick, a dash. Could movement have a colour? If so, she sensed that its shade was dark – though the field itself was dark, too, black soil between green shoots, so there was nothing to differentiate what she saw but the simple fact of motion. She knew at once what she had seen. That dizzy speed, that plunging arc, had been missing from the landscape since last summer's end. It was the swallows, back again; it was the spring.

As every year, she found their absence registered consciously only on their return. In August and September, when they ceased their skimming and swooping and congregated on the wires that, in places along the road, were the only architecture of those unbroken levels, she'd felt a sympathetic, gathering sadness; yet when they were gone she'd given

231

them no thought again until just now. The place had been lifeless without them – how was it she had not missed them?

'Beth,' she called towards the stairs, as she stepped back inside the house. 'Come quick, and see the swallows.'

There was no immediate reply, and Laura mounted the stairs, calling again as she went. 'Beth?'

'Hmm?' Her daughter appeared in the doorway of her bedroom, looking decidedly rumpled. She had been tidy and wide awake at breakfast, but that was two hours ago; the dishevelled curls and blurred features suggested that sleep had since re-exerted its pull. 'What?'

'Oh, nothing.' Laura's urgency melted. 'Never mind.' It was the first day of the holidays, after all, and what were holidays for? The swallows would still be there later.

'I was just reading on my bed,' said Beth.

Yeah, right, as she herself would say. Laura grinned. 'Go back to sleep.'

She was on her way along the landing towards her desk when Willow's head showed round the spare room door. 'What is it?'

'Nothing, really.' But actually . . . 'It's only that there was a swallow, out over the fields just now, when I was outside. It's the first one I've seen this year, that's all.'

Willow blinked at her, expressionless. 'Show me.'

There was a sharp morning breeze, and Laura pulled on a fleece this time before they headed out, though Willow did not follow suit. It was a mystery to Laura how one so skinny should not appear to feel the cold. She was young, of course, but so was Beth, and she was always freezing. The sky was ragged with wind-whipped cloud, so that the light brightened and dimmed by turns as if by an electric switch. On the top of the dyke they stood together and stared down over the wheatfield. Laura's eyes, narrowed against the wind, scanned the ground for any sign of movement, straining until they stung. Nothing.

'It was here before. I know it was.'

Willow turned towards the lode at their backs. As Laura swung round too, she saw them: not just one this time, but two or three, or six, tracing low zigzags across the furrowed surface of the water. They must be feeding on some kind of insect, invisible to the human eye, freshly hatched, perhaps, in the patchy sunshine.

'So those are swallows, then?' Willow stood transfixed, gazing at the darting birds.

Laura nodded. 'They always arrive back about this time – late March or early April. This year they're a bit later. It's maybe been cooler, or the spring a little later after all that ice.'

After a pause, Willow said, 'They look like stars. The shape, I mean – like stars, or starfish.'

'I suppose so.' Laura had never seen them that way before. 'The wings, and that forked tail.'

'Shooting stars. Except their shape keeps changing as they turn.'

She spun on her heel and set off along the dyke, away from the house and the drove, leaving Laura to follow, still watching the swallows as she went.

'They're all the way along,' called Willow from up ahead. 'There must be dozens of them. Hundreds, even. Funny, that they all arrive at once.'

She was right: the lode was alive with movement as far as the eye could see, perhaps all the way to Elswell. How odd that she should not have noticed this before, the sudden mass appearance of the birds after their long months' absence.

'I know.' In front of her, Willow had stopped abruptly. 'The tree house.' At once, she was scrambling down the side of the dyke on the garden side and heading for the ladder. Laura, in shoes she hadn't planned on walking in, went back to the concrete steps to make her way down; the lawn was drier than a month ago but still fat with moisture below the springing surface.

'Like those huts they have for birdwatching,' Willow said, as Laura joined her on the planked floor.

'A hide.' The word, and the image, pleased her. She sat down cross-legged and leant close to Willow to peer out through the rectangle of window that Simon had meant to glaze but never got round to. Only a strip of water along the far bank of the lode was visible from here with the flow at its current depth, but it was enough for them to glimpse the swallows when they swerved that way.

They watched in silence for some time, before Willow asked, 'How do you know about them? About the swallows?'

'My brother taught me. He knew the names of all the birds.'

'A brother?'

'Yes. One brother, Mark. But he was much older than me – twelve years older. He left when I was seven. And even when he was there, it wasn't much like having a brother, most of the time, with such a big gap. It was more like being an only child.'

'Like Beth.'

'Like Beth,' agreed Laura, wondering what defensive impulse led her to add, 'Simon left when she was just a baby.' There had been no time even to talk about whether they'd have more. How would life have been different, if they had? Would another child have made things harder for her, out here on her own? Or would it in fact have made things easier, by diluting their relationship, hers and Beth's? A boy, perhaps, like Tessa's boys, to kick a ball and wrestle with and not always to be tiptoeing and negotiating and worrying and being judged.

Willow was staring down at the water. 'He showed you the birds, though. Your brother – he taught you about the birds.'

'What about you? Any brothers and sisters?' It must have been the intimacy of the tree house, and the sharing of the swallows, that made her ask the question, reaching out beyond safe ground.

'It was just us,' said Willow. 'Me and Mum.'

Laura waited, and watched the turn of dark wings in the wind, the rare flash of a white belly.

'She told me lots of things.' It was Willow's turn to sound defensive. 'Wild plants and herbs and their properties. The ones to make you sleep or dream, or stay awake, or fall in love. About the stars, and all that stuff, you know – the zodiac and seeing the future. The earth, and its buried lines and forces. And stories, sometimes: she told amazing stories. But she never showed me a swallow, or a willow tree.'

'Mum?' They hadn't heard Beth's approach across the soft grass, and so were startled by her voice, sudden and loud at the foot of the ladder. 'Are you up there?'

Laura felt a stab of guilt, as if somehow she'd betrayed Beth. 'Oh, hello, love. Come on up.'

Her daughter's face appeared, and then her shoulders and hips, as she hauled herself up. The space was tight for three, of whom none was exactly a child any more.

'What are you up to in here?'

'The swallows are back, that's all, and it seemed a good place for watching them.'

Heavily, Beth sat down on her heels, her back to the window, barring their view. 'Oh, yes?'

'They're down there, flying over the lode. Catching insects, I think.' Laura knew she sounded rather too cheery, and very slightly desperate.

Beth stared at her mother. 'It's my tree house.'

'Sweetheart, please don't – '

'It's mine.' She turned her gaze on Willow. 'It's mine because my dad built it, when Mum was pregnant and I was going to be born. He built it for me.'

'Beth, I don't think – '

'*Shut up!*'

The words bounced off the roof and walls like bullets; there was no ducking them in that small space. For a few seconds, Laura was unspeaking, summoning her resources to remonstrate and make peace. Before she could do so, Willow had swung her thin denim legs through the hatch to the ladder, and was gone without a backwards glance.

Laura applied the handbrake, cut the ignition and wondered why she was here. On the passenger seat beside her was a carrier bag from Tesco Express on the main road. She had pulled in on impulse and then stood for long minutes in front of the fresh produce, gazing helplessly at grapes and bright, cellophane-wrapped flowers. Those were the things you brought with you when you visited a person in hospital; those, or chocolates, or a bottle of Lucozade. *Get well soon*, they said, but it was hardly appropriate in the circumstances. Magazines might do, if she had any notion of which ones. Something ordinary, she reasoned, that's what I'd want – something normal I could buy if I were in the shop myself. So now here she was, sitting in the car park with a bottle of hand cream and four bananas in a Tesco bag and wondering what on earth she was doing.

She hadn't told Willow she was coming here, nor Vince, though they would have to know; she'd have to tell them before they heard. Nor had she said anything to Beth, at breakfast, or afterwards as she gathered her things together for her first day back at school. Maybe she hadn't told anyone for exactly this reason: in case she wanted to change her mind. To chicken out, said a voice in her head. Would that be what it was, though, if she drove away now? Because another voice was whispering that she had no business to be here. She didn't know this woman and had no real desire to connect with her; she wasn't even certain that empathy was in her power. What was this need she felt to come and talk to Marianne? More than shameless curiosity, she very much hoped, or worse, some voyeuristic urge, like a Victorian thrill-seeker on a visit to Bedlam. In the end, defensible or not, she knew it came down to this: that if she was afraid of some-thing, she had to look it squarely in the face.

Stanforth House. That was the name she'd heard Willow

say, and there it was on the signboard, over to the left of where she was parked: just the name, with no explanatory designation underneath. At ordinary hospitals, all the wards had labels: *General Surgical, Orthopaedic, Children's*. Was there no need here, or was it thought not quite polite? Were the sub-categories of mental illness so much more shocking to the sensibilities than genito-urinary medicine, for instance – or oncology?

However, she couldn't sit here prevaricating in the car all morning. There was a stack of work to do, back in the department. In the end it was that which pushed her into movement: the thought that otherwise she'd wasted her time. She picked up the carrier bag and climbed out of the car.

There was no reply when she tapped on the door she was told was Marianne Tyler's. Her first instinct was to flee for the car in relief. She had come, she had tried, it wasn't to be. But that would be cheating, dodging a decision by the fall of the dice. Now that she was here, she needed to pursue this thing to its proper end. Marianne might not be asleep, or ignoring the knock. She might be elsewhere in the building.

First she tried the main television lounge, which formed a kind of central atrium to Stanforth House: a focal point to the ward, with the big, flat-screen television serving in turn as the focal point of the room. She scanned the blank faces, but none of them was Marianne's. Off the corridor through which she had first entered, she'd noticed a door which had been open on to a sort of kitchen, so she tried that.

'Hello?' she called uncertainly from outside the doorway. There was no reply, but she could hear someone moving about inside, the clink of cutlery and the spurt of running water. No sign instructed her to keep out, or warned her that the room was for staff only – though that apparently meant little, since there were few signs anywhere in this strangely inward, self-sufficient world.

Stepping inside, she saw that this was not a kitchen where meals would be prepared, but just a coffee room. A stainless steel counter ran round three of the walls, empty but for two jug kettles the size of buckets and a sprawl of dirty mugs. The fourth wall housed an enormous battered fridge, at which stood the young man whose movements she had heard. He was overweight, pale and puffy, squeezed into a blue nylon football shirt that looked as though it belonged to a much slighter man, and he held in each hand a carton of semi-skimmed milk. Without acknowledging Laura's presence, he opened the cartons one at a time and sniffed their contents. Then, 'What d'you think?' he asked her, thrusting them her way.

Resisting the recoil, she sniffed. Both smelt to her faintly of paraffin. 'That one,' she said, pointing at random.

His eyes slid up to focus on her. 'You new?'

'Er, no. Actually, I'm looking for someone. Marianne Tyler.'

He nodded, incurious, so that she was not obliged to add her prepared lie: I'm a friend.

He shuffled back to the steel counter and sloshed milk into a mug. 'Might be outside. The smokers all sit outside.'

'Ah. And Marianne smokes, does she?'

Before answering, he stirred his drink methodically, three times one way and three times the other. 'Don't think so, no.'

Laura forced a smile and strove for patience.

'Can't say I've seen her with a cig,' he went on. 'God knows what she might have smoked when she was outside, of course. But there's no need in here. They give you enough of their stuff.'

She cleared her throat. 'Perhaps you could tell me, where do people sit when they go outside?'

'Patio. Through the double doors from the lounge.'

Across his ample nylon chest was stretched the name Marcus Evans in bold white letters. 'Thank you, Marcus,' she said. 'For your help.'

He stared at her indifferently. 'I'm Dave.'

The patio consisted of square concrete slabs paving the

strip of land immediately beyond the double doors. It was furnished with three wooden benches, planted in a line along the wall of the building, so that the three women who were occupying them gave the impression of spectating, or waiting for something to happen. Two sat together, with a coffee mug between them in service as an ashtray. The third woman sat alone, on the bench furthest from the doors, not smoking. Her face was turned the other way, but for Laura there was no mistaking her.

'Marianne.'

It felt intrusive to be addressing her with familiarity, but at least it made her turn her head. Besides, it was a bit late now to be worrying about intrusion. The woman stared at her, and Laura noticed that her eyes were the same cool green as her daughter's; more dull and clouded, perhaps, but that could be the drugs. She saw in them no flicker of recognition, and for a moment resolution faltered. How had she not thought to plan what she should say?

'Marianne, I hope you don't mind my coming here. I'm – '

'Yes. I know who you are.'

The words were calm: perhaps a little flat, but certainly with none of the high, hysteric edge she remembered from their first encounter, nor the mumbling half-silences of the last.

'I – I've brought you some things.' She proffered the Tesco bag, feeling its fatuity. 'I'm afraid it's nothing much.'

There were no thanks. Marianne took hold of the bag, where Laura had laid it next to her on the bench, and pulled it closer without looking inside. As she stretched out her arm, the sleeve of her jacket pulled back a little way and Laura glimpsed, on the underside of the wrist, a series of marks where the skin was puckered, deep pink and oddly shiny; the healing scars from old cuts, perhaps, or fresher burns. She looked away quickly but if Marianne had seen her notice, she gave no sign of it.

Willow's mother. It was odd how something already

239

known with the mind could still startle you with a realisation that was wholly new for being physical. *Her mother's arms.* What must it be like for Willow to look at them and see the damaged flesh?

Because she must say something, she said, 'It seems quiet here.' Banal, perhaps, but there was truth in it, she thought: the unregimented feel of the place, the sense of drift. 'Do you find it quiet? After London?'

'Quiet,' repeated Marianne, and it was neither a confirmation nor a question, but meditative, as if she were assessing the word for weight and dimension. It was a habit of Willow's, too, a verbal tic they apparently shared.

Uninvited, Laura nevertheless sat down; it must surely be easier than standing up. 'It's rather out of the way, though. For getting anywhere, I mean. To the shops, or just out for a coffee.' She hesitated, aware that she had no idea whether Marianne was allowed off the premises, then blundered on, 'I suppose there are buses, at least. That's how Willow gets here, isn't it, when she comes to see you.'

Her eyes dropped to the expanse of bench between them, to the Tesco bag, and Marianne's fingers, which were playing over and over something she held in the palm of her hand. Something metallic, flat and slightly lozenge-shaped, with rounded corners. The movement was rhythmic, perhaps self-soothing, almost mesmeric; Marianne's eyes had closed. 'When she comes,' she repeated. 'When Willow comes.'

Of course, thought Laura. *The drugs.* What an idiot she was, to come here and expect . . . whatever it was she'd been expecting. Explanations, reassurance, to discover anything at all? Of course it was all impossible with Marianne doused and dampened down with medication. There could be no reaching her, even had she wanted to be reached.

Gently, though without much hope, she tried again. 'Willow, yes. She comes to see you quite often, I believe?'

'Willow.' The metal object slipped a little in her palm so

240

that for a moment Laura saw it clearly. It was a cigarette lighter.

'She lives with me, you know. With us. She's my lodger. She, um,' Laura stumbled over the deceptive half-truth, 'talks about you.'

Finally, the fingers ceased their relentless movement and closed into a fist. Marianne opened her eyes and directed them straight at Laura. A misting seemed to clear.

'Ninepins,' she said.

'Yes, that's right.' Laura was eager, now, even while a warning tightness clutched her stomach. 'By the lode – by the water. You came there, remember? You've been there twice.'

'The brick house, up on the bank, with the water down below. The frozen water. Of course I remember. You were there with Willow. And a child – there was a child, a girl.'

'That was my Beth.' Laura's mouth felt dry.

'I met you, you were kind.'

Laura, who remembered no especial kindness, attempted to smile, but her lips were stiff and refused to stretch. And, anyway, Marianne wasn't smiling.

'So you're the new one. Like that Janey. And the man, Vince.'

'Oh, I'm not a foster carer or a social worker. I'm just . . . Willow just rents a room from me.'

But the green eyes had drifted down, and the mist was back, the moment of connection lost. 'Ninepins,' Marianne said again, her voice stripped of all inflection.

Nothing more appeared to be forthcoming, so Laura stood to take her leave, stealing a surreptitious glance at her watch, as the thought of her office pressed back into her mind.

'Well, goodbye, Marianne. I hope you didn't mind my coming here.' Though she saw now that it had been an irrational impulse, a fool's errand. She wouldn't come again.

The woman's head lifted. Laura wondered if lucidity had returned and she would say goodbye. Instead, she stared out wordlessly at a point beyond Laura, her brows drawn together as though in puzzlement or consternation. Then, all at once, her frown dissolved and she was smiling like a child.

'Skittles,' she said. 'Falling down like ninepins. All the pretty skittles come tumbling down like ninepins.'

Chapter 20

There was little immediate reaction to Laura's confession, that evening, of her trip to Stanforth House. Beth, it is true, had stared in disbelief and demanded baldly, 'Why?' but a minute later she was peering in the Rayburn and asking what they were having with the jacket potatoes. From Willow, too, there was a shrug and a rapid switch of subject. Laura waited until after supper when the girls were upstairs before she rang Vince, but if she'd feared his censure, she'd been worrying for nothing.

'I can see that. That you'd want to go and talk to her, after your encounters, to get more of a picture of her. And why not? Better that than to stay away and let it eat at you. She could always tell you to get lost. *Did* she tell you to get lost?'

'Not in so many words.' Laura grinned. 'She didn't have to. I think I worked it out for myself.'

'What did Willow say about it?'

'Not much.'

'Hmm,' he said. 'Give her time, maybe.'

But the subject of Marianne did not come up again for the rest of the week, and it seemed that the matter of Laura's visit was forgotten. Beth's, and thus Laura's, attention was diverted by a telephone call on Wednesday evening from Simon. It was not Beth's weekend to go over, but Jack, who was five on Saturday, had announced that his birthday celebrations would not be complete without the attendance of his big sister.

'If she can stand it,' said Simon, 'we'd be very grateful. Eleven little boys and Beth. Tell her to bring protective clothing – and ear defenders.'

The party was set for a two pm start, so Laura dropped Beth off. She chose to arrive a little early; Beth was useful in the kitchen and they might do with the extra pair of hands. When Simon let them in at one forty-five, however, the house was quiet and apparently deserted.

'Tessa's nipped out,' he explained, as he led them along the hall to the kitchen. 'Gone to fetch a new paddling pool. That is, she hopes she can borrow one, from Kathy down the road, but if not she's going to Homebase.'

'A paddling pool?' Beth's face lit up. 'Brilliant!'

But Laura eyed him sceptically. It was a cloudy April day and blowing a crisp easterly: ten or twelve degrees at best, without allowing for wind chill.

'Yeah. Jack was adamant he wanted a pool party. Alfie had one for his birthday, you remember, and everything Alfie does, Jack has to do, too.'

It seemed finicky to point out that Alfie's birthday was in August. Instead, she said, 'I thought you had a pool.'

'Mice. At least, we think that's what it must be. The pool's been in the shed since last summer, and when we brought it out this morning and started to fill it up, there it was all full of holes. Come and see.'

He led the way through to the dining room, where French windows opened on to the small back garden. In the middle of the lawn was the old paddling pool, semi-inflated and sagging slightly to one side; around it spread a broad quagmire, in which hopped and danced all three of Simon's offspring. As they watched, Jack grabbed Alfie by the knees and they both went tumbling to the ground in a squealing splash of muddy water.

'Tessa thought carrier bags might do the trick.' Simon had assumed the detached manner of the experimental physicist. 'Spread across the bottom of the pool, you see, to cover the worst of the holes. We thought the weight of the water would hold the bags in place, if the boys didn't kick them up too much. And it did work, too,' he added. 'For a while.'

244

'Should we fetch them in and get them changed?' wondered Laura. The boys were barefoot with their trousers rolled up, but the muddy spatters didn't stop at the knee.

'I could take them up and do it,' offered Beth, 'if you're busy with food and stuff.'

Simon's face was glum. 'They changed already. That's Jack's new party shirt.' And now that Laura looked more carefully, she saw the crisp white cotton beneath the smears of brown. 'Doesn't seem much point now, anyway. They'll only get wet again.'

Leaving the birthday boy and his brothers to their mud-bath, they returned to the kitchen, where plates of sandwiches and mini sausage rolls competed for table space with uno-pened packets of Jammie Dodgers, a laptop and a muddle of handwritten notes. Centre stage, on top of an industrial sized box of drinking straws, stood a large layered sponge cake, coated over approximately two-thirds of its surface with chocolate fudge icing.

'It ran out,' said Simon, catching the direction of Laura's gaze. 'I tried to spread it thinner but the cake began to crumble and lift away. I could have made another batch, but I've got this article to finish for Monday at nine, and it's barely started. I thought maybe I'd just stick some chocolate buttons on that side and they wouldn't notice.' He cocked an optimistic eye. 'There'll be candles.'

Beth moved to stand beside him. 'I'll do it. Where are the buttons?'

He flapped a hand vaguely. 'Somewhere around. I'm sure Tessa said she bought some.'

Just then, Alfie appeared in the kitchen doorway. 'Jack says, can Beth come out and play with us? We need someone to squirt the hosepipe.'

'In a minute,' said his father, 'when she's done the cake.'

Alfie took a sausage roll and began to munch. 'I had a cake, when I came home from hospital. George's mum says I could have died. She says anyone can die when they have an operation, even if it's just for their teeth. It's because of the anaesthetic.' He pronounced the word with reverent pride. 'Mum got my cake from Tesco's. It wasn't as big, but the icing was all over.'

Laura was wondering who was ensuring that Jack and Roly weren't drowning in the inch of water that hadn't escaped from the paddling pool, when the front doorbell rang.

'Aha.' Simon looked relieved. 'That'll be Tessa back with the new pool.'

But it wasn't. It was the first of the party guests, running into the hall ahead of a mother who carried a lumpy, gold-wrapped parcel.

'I'll leave this with you, shall I? Pick him up at five, I think you said? And he mustn't have dairy.'

'They're in the garden,' Simon told the child, who was already heading off. 'You know the way.'

'Great, then,' said the mother, and backed out rapidly.

Back in the kitchen, Beth had found the chocolate buttons and some jam from the fridge and was pebble dashing the cake. On her hip was a mud-drenched Roly, who was sobbing in short bursts between the chocolate drops that Beth was pressing into his mouth. 'Ja-a-ack,' he wailed. 'Pushed me o-o-ver.'

The doorbell rang again: two short, commanding blasts. 'Would you mind?' said Simon. 'You could get the door on your way out. Everything's under control here – you go.'

Gratefully, having shown in three more small boys, Laura went.

There was something perverse in Laura's attitude to the weekends – or in this case, just an afternoon – when Beth was over at Simon's. Beforehand, she looked forward to the peace and quiet, which should have been a chance to get some work done, clearing space in the week ahead to spend with her daughter. But when the time arrived and the house was silent, she could rarely settle to her desk. It wasn't exactly that she missed her. It was something less sentimental than that, something more atavistic, perhaps, like a dog that sleeps with both ears pricked for his master's return. Whatever the reason for it, Beth's absence was often more distracting than her presence would have been.

Today, after ten ineffectual minutes at her desk, Laura rose and drifted along the landing to her daughter's room. For some minutes she stood at the window. The lawn was long and lush and needed mowing; the pumphouse, with its gleaming exterior woodwork, lacked only a final coat of paint inside before the furniture could be moved back in – and with it, finally, Willow. Three weekends in a row, now, Laura had promised to get it finished, and Willow had said she'd help. But the emulsion still stood on its shelf in the shed.

At random, she turned and opened a drawer, then dropped to kneel in front of it, inspecting the contents. Beth's sweaters. She had the habit of wearing them for a week or so until they smelt lived-in and then putting them away again, and taking out another. By this means of rotation she apparently believed that knitwear somehow reached some kind of happy stasis in which it never needed washing. Unashamedly, Laura bent and inhaled, drinking in the aroma of her absent daughter. Then, on impulse, she lifted an armful of sweaters and pulled them out on to the floor, and then another and another. It was a fresh, breezy day and the morning's threatening clouds had dispersed; she would give Beth's jumpers a spring clean.

The hand washing of woollens was not her favourite domestic job. The soap flakes tickled her nose and, unable to work in rubber gloves, she always finished with her hands red raw. But the job needed doing, and she sensed it might be beneficial to her mood. She turned the hot tap on to full and poured in a handful of soap, agitating it beneath the blast. Then, scooping up a red sweater, she plunged it into the foaming water and began to rub.

Hard at her task, it was some time before she noticed that Willow had entered the kitchen, and was standing quietly by the table, holding an empty glass.

'Oh, sorry – I didn't see you there. Am I in the way? Did you want some water?' Turning the spout away from the bowl, she turned on the cold tap and let it play down the side into the sink, testing it with her fingers until it ran cool. 'Here, let me.'

Watching Willow drink gave her a thirst herself and she went to fetch a glass, filling it and drinking deeply, then filling it again. When she went back to her washing Willow seated herself at the table behind her. It was disconcerting: rinsing the red sweater, Laura couldn't rid herself of the feeling of being watched. After the red sweater came a navy blue one. Almost too small now, with anchor buttons at the neck, it had been a longstanding favourite. She saw that the wool was worn thin in places, when she held it, dripping, to the light. Then came the birthday jumper: the black Fair Isle with the snowflake pattern. She ran another bowl of water, tipped in another scoop of soap.

When Willow finally broke her silence, the words made Laura start.

'My mother never washed things.'

Laura's hands paused for a moment above the suds; then she re-submerged the jumper and continued her scrubbing. She neither spoke nor turned.

'Not like that, anyway, not by hand – at least, I don't remember it, if she did. We did go to the launderette some-times. Or one or two places, there was a machine.'

Still working at the wet wool, Laura said, 'Hand washing is one of those jobs, I suppose. I always put it off, too.'

'No.' Willow sounded impatient, almost angry. 'That's not what I mean. I mean she really didn't wash things. She hardly washed clothes at all. They weren't things you kept and looked after and had for years, until they wore out or got too small for you. Not like you do, with Beth's stuff, here.'

Laura was puzzled. 'What, then?'

There was a short pause, and Laura wished she dared turn round. Then Willow said, 'It was just baggage, and she hated baggage. Things weighed you down, she once said. I don't know what happened to it all, really. Given away, I suppose, or left behind when we moved on. She always just bought more stuff – jumble sales, charity shops – or else people gave us things. If she had money she spent it; she'd buy me new shoes, new dresses. But she never had money for long. And then we'd up and leave and the new shoes would be gone.'

It was hard to imagine that life, for a child. Laura pressed out the snowflake jumper on the draining board and tried to bridge the gulf of empathy; tried, and failed.

'Stupid loser.' Willow spoke with sudden venom: a bitterness that Laura had rarely heard in her voice. Once before: *useless bloody hippy.*

Of course then Laura had to stop what she was doing; wiping her soapy hands on a tea towel, she came and took a seat beside Willow at the table. But she couldn't think of anything to say.

After a moment, Willow asked, 'How was she when you went up there? What sort of state was she in?'

'Well . . .' Laura hesitated. 'We talked a bit, about this place, and you. But, you know, with the medication . . .' What was it Willow had said? *Flatter, hollow.* 'She's not herself, I suppose.'

'Useless junkie.'

The cold fury was almost shocking.

'Prescription drugs,' Laura reminded her gently. 'That hardly makes her a junkie.'

Willow, listless, stared at the table. 'Now, maybe. And what's the difference, anyway?'

'She needs the medication, you must see that. You know how she was before, without it. She wasn't exactly coping.'

'What – and now she is? Now her life's so great, is that it?'

Laura felt the weight of her impotence. *You shouldn't*

blame her, she wanted to say. *You shouldn't blame yourself. It's nobody's fault, the way she is.* But what did she know about Willow's life, or Willow's pain?

'She's sick.'

'Bloody right, she is.' But then the anger seemed to ebb away as quickly as it had come. Willow picked up her glass and took a sip of her water. 'Sick,' she said quietly. 'Yes.'

It appeared to signal the close of the conversation and, awkwardly, Laura stood up again, glancing back to the draining board and the bundled, wet sweaters. She should get the water wrung out properly, and hang them up outside on the line.

'Better get on,' she said. 'Unless . . . you don't have any jumpers you'd like washing, do you?'

A quarter of an hour later, Laura was back upstairs at her desk. She had booted up the computer and opened the file containing the half-finished draft on which she ought to be working. She scrolled to the end. *Rotational cutting*, she read, *has the effect of letting in varying levels of light to the understorey layer. This makes for a diversity of microhabitats, encouraging* – But what did it encourage? She found she had very little idea, nor the inclination to try to recall.

What must it have been like, growing up with Marianne? Washing, clean linen, the provision of meals: these might seem like trivial or mundane matters, but for her they represented a solid physical core, which lay at the heart of her notion of parenthood. If Willow at times seemed older than her years, this might be the reason. If the mother could not be a mother, how should the child be a child?

Rather than go back to her report, she clicked to open her e-mail inbox. A dozen new messages, most of them university or departmental circulars, but one was different and caught her attention. It was a Facebook alert – a novelty for her.

Punita Chand sent you a message on Facebook. To reply to this message, follow the link below. The message itself was just a quick hello, no doubt sent round to all and sundry, but it invited Laura to visit Punita's profile page and there to view her wedding photographs. This she did, and was entranced. The young woman who in Cambridge she had only ever seen in the student uniform of jeans and T shirt, appeared here resplendent in scarlet and gold, and garlanded with flowers. She looked like a princess from the *Thousand and One Nights*. Clicking back to Punita's message, she moved her mouse to the reply box. '*You both look so beautiful,*' she typed, '*and happy*' – then pressed 'send'.

After that, she idly selected her own home page, still with the anonymous white silhouette in place of a photograph and just two listed friends: Punita, and Beth. She clicked on Beth's page almost without thought. The profile picture her daughter had chosen brought a smile at once to Laura's lips; taken last summer on Laura's camera, it showed Beth in the garden, sitting astride her old spacehopper with a grin as wide as the one on the spacehopper's painted face. They had found it in the shed, beneath some old packing cases that Laura had been sorting for the tip, and Beth had insisted on fetching the car pump and restoring it to full size, before pounding up and down the lawn on it until she was breathless with exertion and laughter and Laura had had to warn her to be careful of her asthma.

The wall posts, when she scanned them, were innocuous enough; there was nothing here to raise alarm – except, perhaps, among grammarians. '*heeyy, im good n you? yeah i know :)*' read one, presumably in reply to some earlier post of Beth's. '*i's well bored lol but drama @ 2*' said another, beside a photo of a girl whom Laura didn't recognise. Scrolling down a page or so, she found what she was looking for: the glamour model image with the straight blonde hair. There were two messages from Rianna; one read '*hey there bethy babe you ok?*', the other simply '*hiiaaaa!!!!*'

In a side bar on the left, a box informed her that Beth had two hundred and eleven friends. Pictures of a handful were visible immediately; curious, she selected 'see all' to reveal the rest. The faces included few she recognised. Here was Alice, and Gemma, and her own anonymous silhouette. And boys, she noticed, as well as girls. Feeling suddenly conscious of intrusion, she thought of Vince: *like listening at keyholes*. She was about to close the page when her eye fell again on Rianna's photo, and on impulse she moved onto it and clicked the mouse.

She saw it straight away. Beneath the box for friends was one marked 'photos', and in the box was just one photograph. It was a casual snap, the quality less than pristine, doubtless taken on a mobile phone. In it, three girls were standing on a river bank, which Laura recognised as being the Cam, somewhere in one of the Cambridge parks, perhaps Jesus Green or Midsummer Common. The girls were leaning towards one another, arms linked and clutching shopping bags, the three laughing faces pressed close together. The one on the left was unfamiliar. A dark girl, but not Caitlin; this one was taller and more broad-faced. In the middle, unmistakable, was Rianna, daring the camera with a cool, unflinching eye. And on the right was Beth.

When had they been to Cambridge? The swathe of daffodils that flanked the river showed the picture to be recent; they'd come late this year, after all the frost. But it was weeks since Beth had been shopping in town without Laura. The last time must be when she went in on the bus with Alice – four, five Saturdays ago. She wouldn't, surely, go off with her friends while she was at Simon's for the weekend, would she? Or if she had, he would have mentioned it. But, anyway, at a weekend she would have been wearing jeans and not her black school trousers, the legs of which were clearly visible beneath her coat. In fact, when she looked closely, the three girls were all in their uniform trousers, though Rianna's were tucked into fake fur boots, and the dark girl wore a purple hoodie and matching purple beanie hat. This was clearly no class outing.

Round and round Laura turned the conundrum, while she stared at the photograph on the screen. There had to be an explanation. There had to be a reason why Beth should be in Cambridge, and recently, in her school uniform and without Laura's knowledge. There must be; there simply must. Otherwise . . .

Otherwise, Laura would have to face the truth, would have to accept the only obvious and rational explanation for the evidence that lay before her in the picture. Her daughter was playing truant.

At twenty to five, Laura shut down the computer and went downstairs. Her afternoon had yielded almost no productive work; for more than an hour she had stared at her file of text but seen only the photograph. It was almost a relief when the waiting was over and it was time to go and fetch Beth. The traffic in Cambridge was Saturday heavy and it was quarter past by the time she reached Simon's house. The party guests had all gone home, and Tessa invited her in for a coffee and to pick at the ruins of the birthday cake.

'I won't, thanks. I know you'll have all the clearing up to do and I don't want to be in the way. We'll get straight off, if that's all right.'

In the car, she drove to a soundtrack of Beth's oblivious chatter. 'The new paddling pool is massive. I swear you could actually swim in it. But it took forever to fill up even a tiny bit, and then Roly got excited and wee'd in it and no one wanted to go in after that so we mainly just played football. But the pool takes up nearly all the lawn so there wasn't much space and loads of the flowers got flattened . . .'

It would be so easy to forget about it, to forget the photograph and what it meant; to have her daughter here with her – her open, funny, affectionate daughter – and not embark on the inquest that would drive her away.

'. . . and the cake was totally gorgeous, except Dad had put the buttercream in the middle before it was cool and it had all

253

melted into the cake, but it just made it gooey and delicious. And I've brought a piece home for Willow in a paper napkin, because lots of them were taking a bit home for their brothers or sisters, and Tessa said it was OK . . .'

They could go home and have a comfortable, uncomplicated evening. Laura could make them beans on toast, because Beth was always still hungry after party food, and they could watch a DVD or play Scrabble and pretend that everything was just as normal, as it had been at lunchtime before Beth went out.

In fact, she waited until they were home and the car parked and Beth upstairs putting on clean jeans in place of her muddy ones. She gave her time to get changed and then knocked on the bedroom door.

'Hi, Mum. Where's Willow – in her room? What have you been up to this afternoon? Done loads of work, I bet. Honestly, you should have seen Jack with his pile of presents, he got them all in a heap on the floor and ripped off the paper in this total frenzy. And three people had given him the exact same Zoob robot kit.'

'Beth.' The best thing, she decided, was to sit down on the bed. But the signal for a conversation went unheeded; Beth was still on her party high.

'I wish I could have stayed and helped clear up. There was such a mess everywhere – seriously, it was a disaster area. At one point they were all chucking chocolate mini rolls at one another from behind the sofas in the sitting room. It was Alfie's idea. Some sort of battle thing, with spacemen on one side and aliens on the other – '

'Beth.'

This time, at last, she stopped and looked at Laura. 'What?'

'Sweetheart, I'm going to ask you something, and I need you to tell me the truth. All right?'

' 'Course.' Beth bristled. Stupid: the wrong start.

'I need you to tell me whether you have been into Cambridge without my knowing.'

254

'When?' The reply, and the slide of the eyes, were evasive. The effective admission of guilt, oddly, came almost as a relief. Laura's resolve hardened.

'Tell me,' she repeated, 'whether you have been to Cambridge when you were meant to be at school.' Was it for Beth's sake or her own that she avoided the unyielding phrase: *playing truant*?

Beth's eyes narrowed; clearly, she was not going to make this easy. 'How d'you know?'

'I saw a picture.' She swallowed. Complete honesty: it had to be the best course. 'A photograph of you with the other girls. On Rianna's Facebook page.'

There was a silence, while a variety of emotions battled for ascendancy in her daughter's face. The expression that won out looked very much like fury.

'Why were you looking? Why would you be looking at my friends' private space, poking through their photos? Spying on me, of course, that's why, like you always do.'

'Sweetheart, it wasn't like that. I didn't mean to pry.' How did she come so quickly to be on the back foot? She wished now that she hadn't sat down – or else she wished that Beth would sit down, too. She pulled herself up straight and took a breath. 'But I saw the photograph; I can't help that now. And we need to talk about it – about what you were doing there.'

There was a softening, then, or so she thought, if not a chastening; some of the tautness faded from Beth's face, and her shoulders dropped a quarter-inch, but she didn't speak.

'I think you need to tell me about it.' She indicated a space on the bed next to her, but Beth didn't move.

'Nothing to tell,' she muttered. 'We went into town, that's all.'

'When was this?'

'Last week. Friday.'

'What time on Friday?'

A shrug. 'Afternoon some time.'

Gently, Laura insisted. 'When in the afternoon?'

255

Beth's face was a scrunch of misery. 'During school. There – happy now?'

'I see,' said Laura, slowly; but Beth was in her stride now, out on the offensive and facing down the inevitable denunciation.

'It was after lunch. 'Bout half one, two o'clock. We only had PE and then Art. Total waste of time, anyway. Rianna needed to get some leggings and a pair of boots, and she wanted some help choosing.'

'Who was there?' Questions were, at least, neutral, and delayed the head-on confrontation.

'Rianna, Lacey and Amber. Amber's a Year 8. She took the photo on her iPhone.'

'No Caitlin?'

'I told you, she's fallen out with Rianna. She's gone off with this lot from Miss Chapman's class. They don't speak to us.'

'And is it the first time?'

'First time, what?' The innocent act was tissue thin, but Laura didn't challenge it. Better to play things straight.

'The first time you've skipped afternoon school.'

There was a pause, and then a grudging, 'Second.'

Whatever else, Laura was grateful she could trust her daughter's truthfulness. 'Well, look,' she began. 'You must know what I'm going to say.' Although she was far from sure of the detail, herself. 'I'm disappointed. I think that's the main thing: that I'm disappointed in you, Beth. You don't need telling how important school is, even if it's "only" PE and Art.'

There was more, much more, she might have said. About letting her teachers down, teachers who had faith in her and who'd shown that faith over that business with the chocolate bars and the matches; about being swayed by people undeserving of their influence into acting out of character, into being less than herself. She hoped very much not to have to say it. In spite of early bravado, past experience suggested that Beth, once faced with her mother's genuine displeasure, would soon capitulate into tearful apology, and loving conciliation.

This time, however, it was not to be.

'Willow skips class.'

The sidestep was so abrupt and unexpected as to rob Laura momentarily of words.

'She hasn't been into college for months. She's stopped bothering. She says it's boring.'

Still fumbling for purchase, Laura said, 'Willow's seventeen.'

'So?'

'So, she's left school. She's effectively an adult and can make her own decisions.'

'Whereas you still decide everything for me, like a little kid.'

Don't get drawn in, Laura warned herself. It was ridiculous, anyway. Beth couldn't seriously be arguing for being allowed to choose not to go to school. Instead, she moved back a step.

'Besides, things are different for Willow. Very different. She's not had things easy, you know she hasn't. Maybe she's not ready for more education just at present. Maybe she needs a little freedom.'

'Well, maybe I do, too. D'you ever think of that? That I might want some freedom, sometimes, instead of being treated like a baby all the time, and never allowed to do anything or go anywhere?'

'But Willow isn't – '

'Oh, can't you *shut up* about Willow for a minute! If you're so bloody keen on her, why don't you adopt her or something?' There was a turbulence in her voice and in her eyes, a wildness that Laura hadn't seen since Beth was three, and given to toddler tantrums. 'I'll go and live with Dad. I'd much rather. Dad lets me do things, he doesn't nag me all the time. Dad's *fun*. And you're just a miserable, controlling old cow.'

With that, she bolted from the bedroom, slamming the door behind her.

Along the landing in the spare room, Willow lay on her bed with the box of matches.

Did they imagine she couldn't hear them when they had their rows? Like that other time, with the hair straighteners: Laura dragging Beth off to her room to tell her off, with that stupid excuse about helping her with the bed, as if that would mean she couldn't hear them arguing in there just the same. It was only a few yards away, after all, and she wasn't deaf.

She pushed open the cardboard drawer and picked out a matchstick. They were the kind they sell for kitchens, longer than normal, and chunkier between her finger and thumb. The head was plump and pink and smelt faintly sulphurous.

It was Beth's voice she heard most when they argued. Not so much Laura: she always kept her voice quiet and controlled. Maybe it occurred to her that Willow might be listening, or maybe it was for Beth's benefit, because she imagined that mothers didn't shout. She was always the one to appease and ingratiate; Willow has seen it over and over. It was pathetic, really, creeping round her kid, trying to please her all the time, as if Beth were the mother and Laura the child.

Gripping the match in one hand and the box in the other, she struck firmly away from her. It was a fresh box, the abrasive strip unworn, and the friction was highly satisfactory; the match lit first time. She held it steady for a moment in an upright position to allow the flame to stabilise, before tilting it to the horizontal. If she didn't breathe, the flame remained perfectly smooth in front of her face, even while it crept slowly downwards. Immediately above the head of the match was a thin halo which appeared black; or perhaps it was merely transparent, colourless. Beyond and above the halo were gradations of orange, containing at their centre an incandescence that was almost white; she had the impression

258

that if she stared at it too long her eyes would begin to smart, as if they, too, were burning.

A lighter would be better – a lighter like her mother's. With a lighter, you could strike a flame and hold it there for as long as you chose. She had seen people on the television, in crowds at concerts or on prison gate vigils, holding aloft for minutes on end the same, single, undiverting flame.

Laura might be careful, but Beth always lost it a bit – like tonight, with her voice rising in pitch to an injured whine, and then running out of her bedroom and along the landing, sniffling and sobbing, heading for the stairs. Whining, crying – as if she had anything to complain about. Princess Beth with her perfect life, who had everything and took it all for granted; stupid, thoughtless Beth who had it all but was determined to wreck it, to chuck it all away. She would ruin everything, and not only for herself.

The flame had reached her fingers; she felt first warmth, then heat, and finally, fleetingly, a liquid burn which seemed more cold than hot, more ice than fire. She snuffed the match, which died at once, leaving only a question mark of smoke and the sour tang of phosphorus.

Chapter 21

'Laura, I need you on Saturday night.'

She smiled: Vince. It was a pleasing distraction to answer the phone and hear his voice. The atmosphere in the house had been fraught since the weekend. Beth had appeared contrite at breakfast on Sunday morning, offering an unspecific apology, and Laura had left it at that, too afraid of further confrontation to risk a stirring of the waters; an uneasy truce had settled, but the air remained perceptibly uncleared. Willow must have sensed the tension, for she had been quiet too, avoiding family meals and keeping largely to her room.

'I need your company,' he said. 'For the simple delight of it, obviously – but also as cover.'

'Oh, yes?'

'Cover, or camouflage, or safety in numbers – call it what you like. I have to go and hear an anarchist garage band play in a pub, and I don't want to be the only person present who's over the age of twenty-five.'

Now she was laughing. 'You mean you just want me along to make you look younger.'

'Not in the least – I thought we could be overage together. Willow's young, she can come along as our entrée. We'll hide behind her on the way in. And Beth's young, too, of course, though maybe a little bit too young to pass as an anarcho-garage fan.'

'Ah. Well, I expect Willow might come, but it's Beth's weekend to be at her father's.'

It would be a relief to both of them, she suspected, to

be spending the weekend apart, gaining a little breathing space.

'Pity. Just you and Willow, then.'

'So, what is an anarchist garage band, anyway – or would I be better not to ask?'

'Can't say I'm terribly sure. It's an ex-client of mine, Raf, he's been badgering me for ages to go and see him play, and I'm running out of excuses. He copied me their demo tape – or demo CD, I should say – and I've listened to bits of it, as much as my eardrums would take. It's pretty shouty. What you and I, in our day, might have called punk.'

'It sounds delightful. I can hardly wait.'

As events turned out, Willow arose on Saturday morning with glands in her throat the size of golf balls, and returned to bed soon afterwards, complaining of a thumping headache. Laura was glad to be bundling Beth away from contagion and out to Simon's house. She felt guilty, when the evening came, to be leaving Willow alone. But she'd filled a flask with hot, sweet tea and left it by the bed, along with aspirin and her old portable radio; even then, she might have rung Vince and cancelled, had Willow not been fast asleep.

The band was loud and, as Vince had accurately billed them, shouty, but it was over with merciful speed. There were three band members: the consumptive-looking Raf, on bass, and two equally sallow colleagues, wearing black vests and jeans and metal-studded wrist bands. The electric guitar looked too heavy for the one in the middle. Vince made sure to catch Raf's eye and raise his glass, which, soon afterwards, he rapidly emptied. Laura followed his example, and within twenty minutes of their arrival they were back out on the pavement, gulping the quiet air.

'Noise Coercion?' said Laura – her first opportunity, since conversation had been impossible inside the pub unless by expert lip-readers. 'What kind of a name is that? It sounds like something you'd have done to you following extraordinary rendition.'

'It's an homage, I understand,' said Vince. 'There's a Swedish anarcho-garage band called the International Noise Conspiracy.'

'Really?'

'Really. So – what now? It's not even nine o'clock. Shall we find a pub more suited to the elderly, or go back to mine for a nice mug of Ovaltine?'

It was a fine evening, and not far to his flat. 'How long has Raf had the band, then?' enquired Laura as they walked along.

'About a year, I think, but they've only really started picking up bookings since Christmas. He always played, though, when he could lay his hands on a guitar. Then next thing he'd sell it again, when he needed money for drugs.'

'Oh, dear.' It didn't seem quite the right response, but it was all she could come up with. 'And is he really an anarchist? Or is that just an image, for the stage?'

'I think he used to be one, yes. But if he still is now, it's only weekends and evenings. He's got a job in Specsavers.'

She giggled. 'Working for the overthrow of the system from within.'

He opened the front door to the block of flats and led the way upstairs. At the landing with the sad plant, Laura paused. 'Doesn't anybody ever water this poor thing?' she wanted to know.

Vince stared at it with curiosity, as if he'd never seen it before. 'I couldn't say. Maybe Mick, the caretaker. He comes once a week to tidy the garden out the front there, and vacuum the stairways.'

Once inside Vince's flat, he showed her to the kitchen. 'Coffee, or something stronger?' he asked. 'I was lying about the Ovaltine.'

'Wine would be lovely, if you have some.' For once, she had come on the bus.

'Certainly. But I'm afraid it won't be sparkling.'

He opened a bottle of red and they sat up on the stools at his breakfast bar, companionably side by side.

'Have you worked with Raf for long?' she asked.

'Since he came into care, when he was eleven. So, yes, I suppose so. More than ten years.'

'He's over eighteen, then?'

Vince laughed. 'Twenty-three. I know – he doesn't look it. There seems to be almost nothing he's prepared to eat.'

'But I mean, you're still supporting him?'

'If turning up to have my senses deadened by his infernal band counts as providing support, then yes.'

'I should jolly well think it does,' she said. 'Quite beyond the call of duty.' She was smiling, but the questions she wanted to ask she knew would be off-limits. Where was Raf from? Who were his parents? *Tell me his story.*

It was her sense of this barrier which always seemed to come down between them that made her kick against it, that fired her urge to confide – and to talk about her daughter, though she had vowed to forget about that subject for tonight.

'I had a fight with Beth last week.'

'It happens.' He took a sip of wine. 'Bad one?'

'Horrible.' The admission felt good, like tearing off a scab. 'She said some things, you know, in the heat of it. She was . . . well, she seemed furious with anger at me, almost out of control. I haven't seen her so worked up, not for years. It made me think of when she was young. Really young, I mean – like a three-year-old.'

'Maybe not angry with you,' he said gently. 'Or not specifically, not because of anything you've done or haven't done. Maybe just angry, full-stop.'

She studied him doubtfully. It had certainly felt very much directed at her.

'And the three-year-old comparison is spot on, I'd say. Teenage rage and toddler rage have a great deal in common. An emerging sense of self and with it of limitations, a powerlessness, a striking out against the stays.'

'I suppose so.' When he talked this way, straight from the textbook on child development, it was hard not to feel distanced, pushed away. But after twenty years in social work, she supposed, some things must be internalised. This, she told herself, was Vince being Vince.

'Hormones,' he said. 'Human sex hormones are to blame for half of the evils in the world. And I expect Beth's are all over the place at the moment.'

Perhaps. Laura was not about to enlighten Vince on the matter, but Beth had begun to menstruate early, in Year 6 when she was ten. She had taken it completely in her stride; there had been no apparent mood swings then, so was it likely that her hormones should suddenly be playing havoc with her emotions now?

'What is it?'

Glancing up, she found Vince surveying her face. 'Oh, nothing.' Did the heat show in her cheeks? She hoped not. 'Just, you know . . . Beth.'

She swallowed a quantity of her wine, which was very good.

'What was it about, anyway? This fight the two of you had.'

'Well, actually, I found out she's been playing truant.'

'She has?' He put down his glass and touched her hand, a brief pressure, but hearteningly human. She wondered if he was going to tell her not to worry, that everyone bunks off school or that his friend who'd once skipped double geography was now the chairman of Oxfam. But he didn't. He simply said, 'I'm sorry.'

'Only twice, and only very recently – well, once since Easter and once just before, I gather. And she didn't deny it. It's good that she was honest about it, isn't it?'

'Very good.' If he thought her need for reassurance pitiable, he was making sure not to show it.

'But then she blew up and was angry about it, so I can't tell if she's really sorry or not. She did apologise later, in the morning. But she hasn't said she won't do it again.'

He said nothing for a short time, so she drank some more of her wine and wondered if she was being spineless, whether she ought to have it out with Beth again.

At length, Vince asked, 'When does Beth get angry?'

She stared into her wine and gave the question thought. 'When she's upset,' she said.

'And when does she get most upset?'

'When people are mean to her, I suppose. And about cruelty and unfairness generally – incidents at school when someone's been picked on, even stories on the news, people hurting animals, people being hurt.' And Dougie, of course: when Dougie died.

'So, she's angry and upset when people have hurt her, or have hurt one another. And is that all?'

She looked at him in puzzlement for a second before she understood: he was right, he was absolutely right.

'And when she's hurt someone herself.'

'Exactly.' He grinned. 'Being in the wrong. It's often the most painful of all.'

If this was the case, then Beth might have been longing all week for the chance to put things right, but too proud to bring it up, and all Laura's avoidance and pussyfooting had been quite misjudged, completely the wrong way to handle things. Oh, why did it have to be so bloody difficult?

His fingers skimmed her wrist again. 'What are you thinking?'

She raised a smile. 'I was just having a self-pitying wallow, if you must know. All the usual crap about how hard it is raising Beth on my own and how I always seem to mess it up.'

That made him laugh out loud. 'I shan't dignify your appalling self-flagellation by telling you that you're very far from messing things up. You know that. But as to the other thing, maybe you're not completely on your own.' His voice was soft and serious, causing Laura's heart to lift, so that she was knocked off balance when he said, 'What about Simon?'

'Simon?' she repeated, stupidly.

'Have you told him about it? About Beth skipping school?'

'N-no. He has enough on his plate with his own three. I don't want to load this on him, too.'

'His own three.' Vince turned her words over carefully. 'And isn't Beth his own as well?'

'Oh, you know what I mean. His new family. Three little ones are such a handful. It's right they should be his priority at the moment – isn't it?'

When he said nothing, she focussed back on her wine glass, took a sip, and then another. She wished he would stop looking at her like that.

'The thing is,' she said, 'Beth worships Simon. And he thinks the world of her, too. I don't want to trample on that. She would be so distraught to lose his good opinion.'

'*Would* she lose it?'

Bloody counselling training. He was too good at this game: at feeding her own words back to her for re-examination, exposing the flaws. 'No. Of course not. But she'd feel she had lost it, and she'd hate that.' And hate me, she added silently, for being the one to tell him.

He nodded slowly. 'And Simon,' he said. 'If you were in his place, would you want to be told your daughter was playing truant?'

Running round in circles after three young boys, a house in chaos, financial uncertainty . . . But – 'Yes. You know I would. And I suppose you're going to tell me he has the right to know, as well?'

He shrugged this off, although without denial. 'Perhaps Beth, too. She might not think so now, but perhaps in the end she'd actually prefer him to know what's going on in her life.'

Was it the wine going to her head, or the warmth of the kitchen, or was it Vince and his seductive confidence that were inducing this dizzy, sliding sensation of letting things go? His rightness ought to irritate her – his smug, all-knowing rightness – the way she remembered it sometimes did, but when she reached inside for the feeling, she couldn't locate it.

Instead, she felt lulled and cosseted – and more than that, absolved; it felt good to be told these truths about her life, to be allowed the illusion of shifting off the responsibility for a moment, for an hour, a night.

When he filled her glass again she didn't move to stop him, but glanced at her watch and said something vague about its getting late.

'I ought to go home and look in on Willow, see how she is.' She might be awake now and in need of more hot tea, or a change of bedclothes if she'd sweated out the fever.

'Let it go,' he murmured, with a quaver of amusement. 'Willow's a big girl. I'm certain she'll be fine.'

She laughed at that. 'Oh, well. After this glass, then.'

There was the fraction of a pause. 'Or you could stay here,' he said.

Something in his voice made her want to turn and interrogate his face, but he was too near, much too near, and she didn't dare. Then, as she struggled to adjust her thoughts, his lips were in her hair, somewhere above and behind her left temple, and he was repeating, 'Stay.'

Laura's mouth was dry. Where had all her saliva gone? Why, of all things, were her feet trembling, on the rung of the bar stool? Then, *he's going to kiss me*, she thought, but distantly, as if she were telling herself a story. *Vince is going to kiss me, and I'm going to let him.*

Even so, his mouth was a shock: the cool otherness of this mouth that she'd been watching and talking to all evening, the taste of the wine which was different in his mouth from the way it had been in hers. He wasn't insistent, as she'd have thought he might be, more gently coaxing, and at the same time completely affirmative. His certainty infected her with a rush of boldness and she tilted her face and raised one hand to the back of his neck, and he grunted his appreciation and for a second it was simple and sweet and right. And then she remembered, and broke away.

'I can't. We can't.'

267

Beth.

She swallowed and stared down at her hands, now clasped together on the breakfast bar; her mouth, from being dry, now seemed awash with too much saliva. They were both breathing raggedly in the silence, making it difficult for her to recover her equilibrium.

'Beth would know. Willow's at home, so she'll know, and she'll tell Beth.'

It was all nonsense. Of course she would have to tell Beth herself. She would have to talk to her first, and tell her, before she could . . . before anything . . .

Vince hadn't moved from the position in which she'd left him; he'd said nothing. But still she felt the weight of his silent persuasion.

'No,' she said, as firmly as she could manage. 'It's no good, we can't. It wouldn't be fair on Beth, not now, not as things are at the moment. She needs more time. She needs . . . It just wouldn't be fair to her, that's all.'

After a moment, very quietly, he spoke. 'And what about you, Laura?'

Brushing this aside, she returned to her theme. 'Things have been tough for Beth recently. At school, with friendships, and getting into trouble. And at home, too. Dougie, and other things as well. If I . . . if we . . . well, what good would it do? It can only make things worse.'

'What *good*?' His voice had risen in pitch, not by much, but enough to register some quickening of emotion – anger, was it, or frustration? But when she braved for a second his brown eyes, she saw only amused affection. Could it be that he was laughing?

He muttered something indistinct, which she heard as, 'Might do us both some good.' Then he laid his hands over her clasped ones on the table top and sought her eye.

'Not everything has to be for the good it does. For Beth, for other people. There's you as well, you know, Laura. What do you want?'

268

What did she want? Incongruously, it was Willow's words that flashed through her mind. *A proper family.*

'I don't know, Vince. I'm sorry, I – ' Floundering, she'd lifted her hands, not to shake off his, which she had forgotten were there, but in a gesture of pure helplessness. In doing so, she caught the stem of her glass and it tipped and fell, sending red wine spreading wide across the laminated surface.

'Damn it. Sorry.'

As he rose to fetch kitchen towels to mop up the spill, she was grateful for the small distance it placed between them, breaking the tension; she wondered if he might grateful, too. Certainly he kept his eyes on his wiping as he said, 'Perhaps I should call you a taxi.'

'Thank you.'

While they waited for it to arrive, he poured her the last dribble of wine from the bottle. Neither of them spoke much, and she wasn't sorry when the entryphone sounded before she'd emptied her glass.

'Let me come down with you,' he said.

'Really, you don't need – '

'I'll see you into the taxi. Let me do that, at least.' There was no reproach, but he sounded stiff and wretched, and she hated herself for being the cause.

Then he caught her expression, and shrugged, and grinned. 'Come on. I'll bring a jug of water with me. Then on my way back up I can give a drink to that benighted plant of yours.'

Chapter 22

The rain that had threatened but held off on the day of Jack's birthday party was the last to be seen for a long time. April and May were often showery, unsettled months in the East Anglian fens, but this year the succeeding days were first clear and cool, then clear and warm and finally clear and hot, as temperatures by the middle of May soared to an unseasonably early high. The vast, open skies stretched in unbroken blue from dawn until dark, shifting through palest aquamarine to rich cobalt and back to pale again with the slow arc of the sun. Every day from mid-morning a shimmer of heat hazed the fields around Ninepins, their surface never dappled by the shadow of a cloud.

The flow in Elswell Lode was reduced to a meander, the level as low by Whitsun as it often was in August; the swallows darted and dived over trickles which grew slenderer by the day, and the heron took flight in search of some more reliable watercourse. Only the skylarks appeared to embrace the heat. They filled the air above the fens with a constant dizzy twittering; when she was out of doors, Laura's ears filtered out their noise as her lidded eyes shaded out the sun.

The earth of the dykes and the garden and fields baked hard and began to split and crack. Instead of the water rising up to reclaim the land as it had in the autumn, now the artificial land seemed to shrink and recede, back towards the mire from which it had come.

Laura examined the rear wall of the house with some anxiety. A long, jagged crack ran down between the bricks from just below the eaves to around the height of her own head. It had been visible last summer, but seemed to close up again with the autumn's damp; now, as the drought continued, it gaped worse than before. She could almost imagine it widening as she watched.

Alan Cowling of Cowling and Son suggested a chartered surveyor, who in turn recommended a structural engineer, who came in a suit with spirit level and measuring rods, took a good look and blew out his cheeks.

'Always a risk of subsidence with these waterside properties,' he informed her, with gloomy satisfaction. 'Built up on a bank, as well – asking for trouble. I don't like the look of this at all.'

He extended rules and read gauges and poked and peered, and then he stood back again, looking no less glum.

'Blame it on Vermuyden,' he said. 'Him and his Dutch engineer friends. What did they expect? To drain three hundred thousand acres of evaporating peat and then to build on it? It's all sinking, you know. The fens are sinking at the rate of a centimetre a year.'

There was further alarming talk of heave and landslip, of diagonal shift and tensile strain, and finally of underpinning.

All the pretty skittles, thought Laura with a flutter.

'Should I be getting some estimates, then?' she asked. 'And contacting my insurance company?'

'Oh, well, I shouldn't worry just yet. I should leave it for a while, if I were you, and see how it develops. Keep a watching brief, so to speak. You never can predict how it will go, with this fen soil.'

On Beth's return from her father's on the weekend of the Noise Coercion gig, Laura had followed Vince's advice and raised again the matter of her truancy. Beth had cried and sworn remorse and promised to be good, and when, a few days later, Willow's throat infection had transferred to Beth and gone to her chest, Laura had sat up late and read aloud old favourite books, to the accompaniment of a musical wheeze.

At school, things were quiet. She seemed still to be friends with Rianna; at least, her name was mentioned from time to time, and Alice's and Gemma's, never. Nobody came to the house for supper, or round on their bikes, or to watch TV. If Laura occasionally suggested an invitation to a friend, she was met with an apathetic shrug. Beth spent less time on Facebook and more outside, alone or with Willow. The hot weather seemed to draw the two of them out into the garden and along the lode to roam like feral things; they went on long bicycle rides – with Willow's knees knocking the handlebars of Beth's old bike – or sat together in the tree house for hours on end.

Laura was disposed almost to be grateful when, the week after half term, Beth came home from school and asked to go to Rianna's house.

'On Friday. She says, can I go there after school and have supper and sleep over? Her Mum's out and we're going to watch DVDs.'

'Her Mum will be out?' said Laura doubtfully.

'Yes, but it's OK, 'cos Rianna says Liam will probably be there, and he's nineteen. He might have some friends over, too.'

Quite how this made it 'OK' was lost on Laura. Older boys, on a Friday night and probably drinking. But nineteen, she told herself. Don't be silly, Beth's just a child.

'Rianna says they always have chips on a Friday when her mum's out. Not oven chips – proper ones from the chip shop. Liam fetches them in the van. Why don't we ever have proper chips?'

'What DVDs was she thinking, do you know?' It might be the wrong thing to be worrying about, but you could bet it wouldn't be Wallace and Gromit.

'Oh, I don't know. She says Liam sometimes gets films before they're out. But I don't think she's into horror or scary stuff or anything, if that's what you mean.'

'All right. Well, I suppose I don't mind 15s, but you

definitely shouldn't be watching anything that's an 18. You're only twelve, remember.'

On the Wednesday, two days before the projected sleepover, Laura came home from work early. Her office faced due west over a busy, narrow street; the afternoon sun struck the glass behind her desk, which amplified it to an insupportable intensity, but if she raised the sash the noise and fumes of buses and cars were equally unbearable. A small electric fan, clipped to the edge of her bookshelf, did nothing but slowly rotate the same clogged air. She craved the wide spaces of Ninepins.

Thus, with a back seat piled with books and papers, she drew up on to the dyke beside the house at barely ten past four. There was nothing unusual in seeing two bicycles lie sprawled by the front door; the surprise came as she climbed from the car and approached, with books and key in hand. Both bikes were full sized, and only one was familiar: Beth's birthday bicycle and a battered red mountain bike that Laura didn't recognise.

'Hello there.'

When there was no reply she guessed they were on the computer, Beth and the owner of the foreign bike. But the sitting room was as deserted as the kitchen. The kettle was cold. Perhaps they had gone out for a walk, or to the tree house. It was too hot an afternoon, surely, for them to be closeted in Beth's stuffy bedroom; besides, from up there Beth would have heard her greeting, and shouted back or wandered out in search of tea. Laying down her books, Laura stood still for a moment to enjoy the empty calm of her kitchen, which always stayed cool in the summer.

That was when she heard it: the sound of strangled sobbing. Even through a floor, two walls and possibly a pillow there was no mistaking Beth. There could be no number to the times she had heard her daughter cry: from the first small Moses basket next to the bed, when one snuffle would have her wide awake and watchful, through grazed knees and

273

bumped heads to the larger losses and disappointments that no mother could keep away. And still, every time when she heard the sound, it tugged at the same place beneath her ribs where the invisible line connected. She moved for the stairs.

The crying was coming from Beth's bedroom, of which the door stood slightly ajar.

'Love?' called Laura softly as she grasped the handle.

Her mind had emptied of everything but Beth, so she was startled to come face to face with another girl. Dark-haired, slim, with a narrow nose and sharp cheekbones: it was the other one, Rianna's sidekick, Caitlin. *What have you done to my Beth? How have you upset her?*

'I brought her home, Mrs Blackwood. I thought I'd better.' Laura couldn't recall hearing her voice before – or else it was not how she'd remembered. 'She was in a terrible state at the end of school. I didn't like to leave her to get home on her own. You know, on her bike and everything.'

'Oh. Right. Er, thank you.'

Caitlin stepped meekly aside to let Laura to the bed, where her daughter lay doubled round a folded pillow, which she clutched like a life preserver. Her face was invisible, pressed down between her arms. Her back was tense but no longer shaking; the noise had ceased.

'Love,' she said again, and placed a hand lightly on the nearest of Beth's shoulders. 'What is it, sweetheart?'

A muffled moan was the only response, so she sat down on the bed and fretted gently at Beth's shoulder and neck, murmuring the usual nothings. 'Never mind . . . later . . . doesn't matter . . . baby girl.'

From by the door, Caitlin, forgotten again, gave a cough. 'Perhaps I'll go, then. Now that you're here.'

Laura looked up. 'Oh, well, if you need to be off, then of course. Thank you so much for bringing Beth home and looking after her. It's terribly kind of you. But you know, you're very welcome to stay a bit, if you like. Stay and have supper with us.'

The girl shifted on to one foot. 'Well . . .'

'Go if you like. Or stay. We're grateful either way.'

'It was Rianna.' Caitlin said the words quickly, and with her eyes downturned; they seemed to have cost her some effort of will.

'Rianna?'

She nodded. 'That made her cry, yes. It was at the end of last lesson, in the cloakroom, but I don't know what it was about. Just that they'd been talking and Rianna said something and Beth was really upset.' Then, with a surge of vehemence, she added, 'Rianna's a cow.'

'I see. Well, thank you for telling me.'

Rianna – again. So much for the sleepover and the DVDs, the chip shop chips.

'Um, do you think . . .?' Caitlin sidled closer to the door. 'Maybe Beth'd like a cup of tea or something?'

Laura smiled. 'I'm sure she would. Maybe we could all have one? I'm sure you'll find the things. Thank you, Caitlin, you're a good girl. I expect we'll be down soon.'

Caitlin escaped for the kitchen, leaving them alone. Laura bent forward and snaked her arms round Beth, who shifted and rolled until she was cradled in her mother's lap. There was no need to say anything more, not for now; it was enough to hold her close and slowly, slowly, rock her to and fro.

It might have been two minutes, or five, or ten, before finally Beth stirred and made a throaty sound.

'Thrrrghk.' Then, more distinctly, 'Thanks.'

'Feeling a bit better? Shall we go down in a minute?'

'Uh-huh.'

'I bought some Jaffa cakes. A cup of tea and a Jaffa cake.'

'Mm.'

'And macaroni cheese for supper?'

'Mm. Mum?' Beth raised a blotched and tear-blurred face.

'What, love?'

'Tell me you didn't just call Caitlin a good girl.'

Downstairs, Caitlin had found the kettle and mugs and

milk but not the tea bags; instead, the china tea pot, which had come from Laura's aunt and not been used in years, stood steaming in the middle of the kitchen table, next to a battered packet of leaf Darjeeling.

'Where's Willow, I wonder?' said Laura, as she searched through her bag for the Jaffa cakes.

'In the pumphouse, I should think.' Beth had rinsed her face in the bathroom before they came down, but her face was still mottled and her voice clotted thick. 'She's always down there now.'

The sunny weather had finally shamed Laura into finishing the decorating, and Willow had been moving back in by slow degrees. The spare room was still very much hers, but bits and pieces of books and clothes had found their way down to the pumphouse, which she now used as a daytime bolthole and, just recently, an occasional place to spend the night.

'Perhaps I won't call her, then, just at the moment. We'll see if she wants to come in and join us for supper, later on.'

The present arrangements seemed a good idea to Laura: let Willow acclimatise, move back out of the house at her own pace.

'Can me and Caitlin take her down a Jaffa cake, though? After we've drunk our tea?'

'Of course, love.'

'Is Willow your sister?' asked Caitlin. Laura was curious. Had they really never met? Did Beth not talk about Willow to her school friends?

'Lodger,' muttered Beth through a mouthful of orangey crumbs.

Caitlin put her mug down on the table. 'My nan had a lodger,' she said. 'He drank all her sherry and filled the bottle up with water. Then he took the electric drill out of the garage and left without paying the rent.'

'Wow. Did she call the police and everything?'

'Yes, but they never caught him. He said he was called Walter but the police said it might not be his real name. I hated him. He used to babysit for me sometimes and he stank.'

Beth stared at her. 'Well, Willow's not like that. Willow's OK.'

The tea drunk, Beth stood up and reached for the packet of Jaffa cakes. 'OK if we take them down there, then, Mum?'

'Yes, you go.' Laura turned to Caitlin, who had also risen from her chair. 'So, does that mean you're going to stay for supper?'

She smiled shyly. 'If you're sure that's all right? Thank you very much, Mrs. Blackwood.'

The confounding of expectation, decided Laura as she sat alone at the kitchen table much later, could sometimes be a pleasurable thing. But if Caitlin, at least, was not the demon of her imaginings, that still left Rianna, and what she could have had said to cause so much distress to Beth.

It was after eleven thirty and she ought to be heading up to bed. But the kitchen was cool, the tiles fresh and smooth beneath her bare feet. Upstairs, beneath the eaves, the heat seemed to gather and coalesce to a warm syrup, clogging her lungs. Even with the window wide open since she first came home, her bedroom, she knew, would be stifling. Sleep would be impossible.

Willow might have the best idea. She was sleeping in the pumphouse again tonight, claiming it was cooler down there. Perhaps the damp soil at the base of the dyke, which for most of the year waged a siege to be resisted, was now to be counted a blessing. Yet it must be an airless spot; Laura was thankful for the house's elevation, giving it surrounding space.

Sitting here at the table, in any event, was hardly a solution, and she was too hot and tired to read. Perhaps she should go out for a stroll along the lode, take a look at the stars. But she feared to find the outside air as thick as that indoors, and to come back more oppressed than ever. Instead, she might go up and have a cool bath, or at least clean her teeth and splash cold water on her face.

As she stood, eyes screwed and dripping, at the basin and turned off the tap, she heard a stirring in her daughter's room. Evidently Beth could not sleep, either. Still with towel in hand, she walked along the landing and tapped at the door.

'Beth,' she said quietly, 'are you awake?'

A groan supplied her answer; she pushed the door open and stepped inside.

'Urggh. Why's it so freaking hot?'

Beth was in the bed, or rather on it, but she wasn't lying down. The top sheet that Laura had given her as an alternative to the duvet when temperatures first began to spiral lay on the carpet in a tangled heap, while Beth sat sideways across the bed with her back to the wall and legs spread forward and wide, clad in knickers and a vest top. She tilted back her head and blew upwards, sending her fringe into a dance.

'Too ho-o-ot.'

'I know, love. I've had enough of it, too. It's hopeless for trying to get to sleep.'

'Tell me about it.'

Laura picked up the discarded sheet and shook out the sticky creases, lifting it high and letting it billow. The movement caused the stilted air to shift a little.

'Oh, yes, please. Do that again, Mum.'

Laughing softly, she began to rotate on the spot, flapping the sheet like a mainsail cut loose from its rig. Soon Beth was off the bed and grabbing for the bottom corners, lifting them up to join in the game. By the time they collapsed together on the bed with the sheet on top they were giggling like a pair of eight-year-olds but, if anything, even hotter than before.

Beth lay and panted, tongue out, until gradually her breaths returned to normal. When all was still again, she spoke. 'I trusted her, Mum.'

Without turning to face her, or even raising herself from where she lay half-prone, Laura said, 'Rianna?'

A short nod. Another pause, and then, 'Stupid. So totally stupid of me, but I talked to her. I thought I could trust her. Why on earth did I ever tell her anything?'

The best thing was usually to bide her time and wait, but Laura's impatience overcame her. 'What did you tell her, sweetheart?'

Beth pulled herself upright, and slightly away from her mother, face averted. Laura sat up awkwardly and cursed herself for a clumsy fool; she had pushed too hard. But after some moments' silence, Beth spoke again.

'Dougie.' It was a croak, not much more than a whisper. But then she added, more strongly, 'I told her about Dougie.'

'*Oh, Beth.*'

Inadequately, she reached over and laid a hand on her daughter's knee. The skin was clammy with sweat.

'I told her . . .' Her voice choked; the tears were back again, welling to the surface beneath which they had lain only shallowly buried. 'I told her, and she . . . and she . . .'

It was too hot to venture a hug; she was scared that Beth would find it uncomfortable, irksome, and shake her off – or, worse, might wish that she could. She made do with fishing a clean tissue from her pocket and passing it across. Beth blew her nose wetly and swallowed with a glug.

Through the open window, Laura thought she felt the first sigh of a slight breeze. It raised – or something else did – the fine hairs on the backs of her forearms. Somewhere off in the night, an unknown bird cried out its alarm. Laura, without intending to, strained her ears to listen. In the far distance, a car engine flared, then fell away; Beth's bedside clock ticked off the seconds. Otherwise, the silence was complete. Now at last, in the enveloping quiet, sleep seemed almost a possibility. Its lure settled over her; perhaps they might both sleep here, together, in the silence of her daughter's room.

'She laughed.' Beth's words, hard and shocking, roused

Laura from her reverie. 'Rianna. She laughed about it. *Dougie the doggie*, she kept saying, and laughing like it was something funny.' Beth's voice ratcheted upwards through mimicking singsong until she was close to hysterical, caught between tears and a terrible, mirthless laughter. '*Dougie the doggie, Dougie the dead doggie, Dougie the dead doggie.*'

Laura stayed with Beth until she was calm; then she covered her over with the sheet and knelt by the bedside, stroking her hair until she fell asleep. By the time the slow, even breathing told her she was safe to leave, it was after one am by the bedside clock. The heat was not perceptibly less.

Taking a drink of cold water from her cupped hands at the bathroom tap, she noticed a pair of earrings, narrow twists of gold wire threaded with turquoise beads, which she recognised as Willow's. She must have taken them off to wash and then forgotten and left them on the tiled rim of the hand basin. They were so small, they looked as if they might quite easily fall down the plughole and be lost. Picking them up, Laura wandered back along the landing to the spare room.

Already, denuded of even half of Willow's things – the dressing gown from the back of the door, the trainers from next to the wardrobe – the room felt subtly more her own again, more how it had been when her parents had slept here. The duvet, in the black and grey geometric cover she had bought for Willow after the autumn's flood, was down with her in the pumphouse; its absence left the mattress looking tired and bare. The old bedspread that used to cover it, the rose pattern one that had been her mother's, was still in the linen chest. Lifting the lid, she took it out, shook it open and laid it across the bed, smoothing it out from centre to edges. Willow had left the window only slightly ajar, but now Laura threw it wide to the night air.

She had put the earrings down on the night stand, but now it occurred to her they were hardly safer there than in the bathroom. They really were so delicate; Willow might fail to notice them, and knock them off. Turning to the dressing table, she looked for a suitable receptacle. Beth had always had a magpie eye for trinkets; a hoarder of tiny pots and pretty boxes, she filled them up with beads and bangles, and buttons and hair clips, and pretty pebbles from the garden. Not so Willow. Apart from a jar of moisturising hand cream, the surface was almost empty. There was nothing else but the old blue shoebox, wrinkled and misshapen from its immersion in the flood. The only thing was to put the earrings in there.

Feeling slightly guilty as she did so, Laura took hold of the cardboard lid. It was wedged tight due to the distortion of the box, and came off only with some prising. The inside of the box was crammed with paper: private letters, no doubt, and photographs, at which Laura took care not to glance. On the top, however, where she dropped the earrings, lay something which unavoidably caught her eye. She couldn't help it; it was right there. It was a cigarette lighter. Slim and silver, smooth-cornered, slightly lozenge-shaped, it looked very much like the one she had last seen in Marianne's hand at the psychiatric hospital. Now that she saw it properly, she noticed the engraving. With all the swirls and curlicues it was difficult, at first, to make out anything figurative at all. But from among the flourishes, as she examined it more closely, there emerged the two looping, intertwined letters, each the mirror of the other. M and W.

Laura replaced the box lid carefully and drifted to her own bedroom. It wasn't so bad. The air temperature must have come down a good way since nightfall, logic, though not her senses, told her; at least her sheet, when she touched it with her hand, felt almost cool. She should undress and lie down, and soon she would sleep.

The pumphouse wasn't visible from her bedroom window, which faced east towards the gate and the cinder turning space, where the drove led away to the road. Was Willow

281

asleep, down there in the darkness? Did she sleep curled tight the way Beth sometimes did, her knees hugged high beneath her chin, or straight out on her back with arms and legs flung wide? Restlessly, with much turning, or calm and still all night?

Suddenly, with a sharpness that surprised her, she wished that Vince were here. Vince would have the answers to her questions; Vince always knew. He hadn't called her since they parted company on the pavement outside his flat, when he leant to swing shut the taxi door. He hadn't called her, and she hadn't called him.

Dangerous, or vulnerable – which one was Willow? He would know. What would he tell her now, if she could ask him? As she stared out at the garden in its pool of black and the starlit fields beyond, she knew his answer with perfect clarity; she knew exactly what he would say. That the two were inseparable, that they were two faces of the same coin; that in Willow's case, at least, they were simply two ways of saying the same thing.

Chapter 23

It was at supper on Friday – the night when Beth had been due to go to Rianna's – that Willow issued her invitation.

'Why don't we have a sleepover here? Just you and me, in the pumphouse.'

'Really?' Beth's eyes lit up at once.

'Why not? It might be fun – and besides, it's cooler down there than in the house. When I leave the door open, it's nearly like being outside.'

'Like camping? Oh, Mum, please, can I?'

Laura smiled, glad to see her daughter enthused again. Since her run-in with Rianna, she'd been looking dull and exhausted; Laura would bet she hadn't been sleeping much.

'What'll I use for a bed?'

'How about taking the cushions off the settee and pushing them together on the floor? Take your own pillows. And you can use my old sleeping bag, if you like, so you don't need to bother with sheets.'

'Can we have some biscuits or chocolate or something, if there is any? In case we get hungry.'

'I'll see what I can find. And don't forget to take your inhaler with you.'

They headed off straight after supper, leaving Laura to wash up. Before they left, she found the sleeping bag at the back of the airing cupboard, and a Battenburg cake and a bag of Maltesers. Willow took them from her with a grin; seventeen was apparently not too old for midnight feasts. The settee cushions looked enormous piled up in Beth's arms.

'Can you manage those all right? Would you like me to come down and carry some things?'

'No thanks, we'll be fine.'

When they were gone, the house jangled with silence. Laura banged on the radio for company while she gathered together the dirty dishes. Jonathan Dimbleby's voice was soothing to the mind, as he marshalled his feuding panellists with aplomb. *Any Questions?* Plenty, thought Laura as she ran the hot water into the bowl, but none that wouldn't keep.

When the kitchen was clear, she took the newspaper through to the sitting room and read for a while, but her thoughts kept scattering off at tangents. In spite of the continuing heat – tonight, if anything, seemed hotter than ever – she decided to go to bed early. She ran a tepid bath, barely warm enough to melt the lavender salts she swilled in, and soaked herself until the water was cold. With a shiver, she pulled herself out and rubbed quickly dry, before enjoying the rare luxury of walking naked to her bedroom.

Sleep claimed her almost at once. She surfaced at around midnight for long enough to glance at her watch and be surprised to have slept so well and so quickly, since when Beth was away she was often restless, and what with the heat as well. She was dimly aware of having been dreaming, and disturbingly so, but without knowing of what. The bottom sheet was rucked, and damp with her sweat. She rolled to the other side of the bed where the bedding was smooth and cool – the side where she never slept because it had been Simon's.

This time, as she drifted again beneath the layers of her consciousness, the dream came vividly alive. She was out of doors, walking naked across the fields behind Ninepins, which were not the wilted green of a hot early June but grown high with dry, ripe stalks of corn. Too high, in fact, for the ears reached almost to her waist, impeding her progress. Perhaps it was not the wheat that was taller but she herself who was shorter, perhaps a child. Sharp stones and ends of stalk jarred and jabbed at her bare feet. There was a strange

284

light in the dream, which felt like neither night nor day, and the heat was harsh and hard-edged, as much a physical barrier as the impenetrable corn. It scorched her soles, it battered her head and shoulders, and beat upon her face with such intensity that she had to raise her hands to shield her eyes from the glare.

After a time, it occurred to her that something was wrong. The heat, the light, came not from overhead where the sun should have been, but from the ground, and all around her. The cornfield was on fire. As soon as her dreaming mind had grasped this fact, the smoke closed round her, too; or perhaps it had been there all along, accounting for the weird half-light, but now it choked her nose and throat and stung her eyes, which were soon awash with tears. Through the blur and the fumes she made out walls of flame, surging from every direction towards the sky, and, as she saw, she understood the truth: that the whole of the fens was ablaze.

She was coughing as she jerked awake. The scent of smoke still lingered in her nostrils; she rose and went to the window to drink in the night and dispel it, but it would not seem to shift. Her watch said five to three.

Without any conscious decision, she walked out on to the landing and along to Beth's room. The door was still wide open as Beth had left it. The bed was unmade from the previous night's occupation; now, without Beth and stripped of its pillows, it looked very empty. The curtains were not drawn across but open to the blackness beyond, which, however, was not as black as she would have supposed, but flickering with light, and the window was wide open, so that now, borne to her on rising air, the smell was unmistakable – as was the sound, the low, hissing, sputtering sound, the same as in her dream.

The pumphouse. The girls. *Beth*.

She didn't take the time to cross to the window and look out, but turned at once and ran for the stairs. She hardly knew how she made it down them, tumbling, two, three at a time;

285

she was even half way to the door before she remembered she had nothing on, and grabbed her longest raincoat from the peg to wrap around herself. Shoes took too long, so she went without.

The heat of the fire hit her with a smack the moment she rounded the corner of the house. There were no flames immediately visible, but a dense, rolling pall of blue-black smoke engulfed the upper structure of the pumphouse, obscuring the chimney and half of the walls, and issuing in billows from the one exposed window. Even here, at the top of the dyke, the air was red hot and laden with soot and ash, smearing greasy where it touched her skin; her eyes blinked against the acrid smart.

As she descended the concrete steps, the heat, though it seemed impossible, grew greater. Raising one arm, she held it across her eyes and brow in an attempt to protect herself as she edged down the final few steps. She should have brought a scarf soaked in water – isn't that what you were supposed to have? And what use would she be without shoes? But it was no use, in any case. The fire was too well entrenched. The smoke was all round and inside her, congesting and clogging and burning; it poured in through her mouth and nose and seemed to soak even through the pores of her skin, until she felt so full of it that her chest might burst.

She should retreat. She should go back up the steps, go back in the house and phone for help. It was the best she could do. The only thing to do.

Too late, drummed a distant voice in her head. *Too late, too late, too late.*

That was when she saw it. It was away to the right; not towards the pumphouse but the other way, off in the middle of the dark lawn, through the miasma she made out a darker shape, slumped on the grass. She ran towards it, dropped down beside it, leaned over it, dragged it up against her heart.

'Baby. My baby.'

Beth was breathing, but with difficulty. Rapidly, Laura

released her from her arms to give her space and air, man-oeuvred her into a more conducive position for the single action by which she clung to life: the painful, scanty, all-consuming task of drawing in oxygen.

She was hovering somewhere between conscious and unconscious. Her face, in the starlight, was wholly without colour; her eyes were closed and underscored with darkening patches. Each breath was a struggle, racking her chest and arching her back, but, for all the effort, finally shallow and unsatisfactory. Not enough, Laura saw, with a shot of panic. Not nearly enough.

Beth's inhaler would be in the blazing pumphouse, but they kept a spare in the kitchen drawer.

'Hang on for me, sweetheart.'

It was the hardest thing that Laura had ever had to do: to stand up and move away, to leave her daughter gasping on the grass and run to the house to fetch it, scrambling straight up the dyke to avoid the choking smoke by the steps. She was back in two minutes at most, clutching the inhaler in one hand and her mobile phone in the other. She knelt down and raised Beth up again, cradling her across her knees; her breathing seemed jerkier, less effective than ever, and she was barely aware. Laura pulled the cap from the mouthpiece, shook the inhaler and laid it between her daughter's lips, pressing down firmly on the button. Breathe, she beseeched her silently; please breathe. But Beth's lips lay slack around the mouthpiece. There was no improvement in her laboured breathing. It wasn't getting through.

Flicking open the phone, Laura found the nine and thumbed it three times in quick succession, then pressed the green button.

'Emergency. Which service do you require?' The words were disembodied in the darkness, as from another reality.

Then came her own voice, sounding high-pitched and over-loud. 'Ambulance. Please hurry.'

Come now. Be here now. It seemed inconceivable that she

should have to wait, when everything, the whole world of time and space, was concentrated in the shape of the limp body in her lap.

A click, followed by another voice, equally unreal, saying, 'Emergency ambulance. Please give your location.'

'Yes. Please. It's Ninepins, Elswell. Four miles past the village on the Stretham road, then left into Ninepins Drove. We're outside in the garden and I can't move her. It's Beth – my little girl. She can't breathe, can't use her inhaler, she's only half conscious. She's asthmatic, you see, and with the smoke – '

Smoke! How impossible, almost ludicrous, that she could have forgotten the smoke, and the scorching heat at her back. The pumphouse – and Willow. *Oh, God, Willow.*

'A fire. There's a fire, too – we need the fire brigade. And there was another girl in there, a teenager . . .'

Some other distant self relayed the details of names and postcode, of medical history. Then everything else receded until there was only Beth and the scourging battle for air. With a fierce, tight focus of will, Laura drew in each breath along with her daughter. Breathe, Beth. Breathe, my sweetheart. *Please breathe, please breathe, please breathe.*

Chapter 24

The events of the rest of the night were indistinct, or rather, consisted of a series of discrete and vivid episodes, spliced apparently at random into an unfamiliar version of time. The ambulance arrived before the two fire engines, which came only as Beth was being lifted onto the stretcher. A minute, ten minutes, half an hour: Laura could no longer judge things in the intervals of normal existence.

The paramedics were kind, but as they swung into their practised routine they distanced Beth from her, relegating Laura to a bit part player, a redundant bystander. The oxygen mask was bulky, swamping Beth's pale, pinched face and taking her further away, and in the ambulance the cylinders to which they connected her were tall, metallic and torpedo-like, making Laura feel she might be inside a military aircraft. She was obliged to sit in a bucket seat and wear a belt, which meant she couldn't reach to hold her daughter's hand. Instead, she kept up a constant, quiet stream of reassurance, which she had no idea if Beth could hear.

In A&E, they took her away completely for a time, bowling her off on a trolley through doors that swung shut behind her. Her mobile, Laura realised, was still in her hand. Vince. She badly wanted to call Vince, she wanted him to be here, but of course it was quite impossible. Instead, although her watch told her it was barely five am, she rang Simon.

'Hi. Look, sorry, I know it's stupidly early – '

'Laura – are you OK? Is it Beth? What's happened?'

'A fire. But it's all right, Beth's all right . . .'

A nurse found her some clothes to put on under her

raincoat: disposable knickers, an unaccustomed summer dress and a pair of hospital slippers. She struggled into them in a narrow toilet cubicle, and on her way out she glimpsed in the mirror a haggard stranger who could not possibly be her. No wonder the nurse had been tight-lipped; she looked like a drunk or a madwoman.

Some time later, she was allowed into a room where Beth was trussed up in a metal-framed bed, with smaller torpedoes at her side, and a heart monitor straight off the television. Laura found a plastic chair and sat down to watch and wait. Her daughter, she saw, had been undressed and dressed again in a white hospital gown. Her vest top and pyjama bottoms were folded neatly on a shelf at the foot of the bed; on the top, on its plaited string, lay the mirrored sun of Willow's good luck charm.

Just once, Beth surfaced from the place where she was trapped, a place where all there was was breathing. She opened eyes, above the mask, that were clouded with fear; they met Laura's, registered some slight alleviation, and flickered closed again.

After what could have been days or only minutes, a plain-clothed fire officer came in, together with a woman, not in uniform either, who identified herself as 'police liaison'. Willow was not inside. Laura asked them to repeat the intelligence three or four times, in her trembling anxiety to believe it true. Willow was not in the pumphouse; it was empty, completely empty, as it had been on the night of the flood. *Thank God.* But the faces of the officers were grave and their manner still noticeably reticent.

'What is it? There's something else, isn't there? Tell me.'

'You will receive a full report in due course,' said the man from the fire service, 'once our investigations are complete. But I think you should know that there are suspicious circumstances.'

'I'm sorry, Mrs Blackwood,' said the woman. 'I'm afraid we are treating it as a possible case of arson.'

Laura heard them as though from inside a bubble, as if it were she and not Beth who lay drifting behind the oxygen mask. A petrol can was mentioned, found empty by the pumphouse window. Did she keep one in her shed, perhaps? Fuel for her lawnmower? Really, she should have a lock on the shed door. A search of house and garden and the area surrounding had revealed, to date, no trace of Willow.

When they were gone, she switched back all her attention to her daughter in the bed. Anything but Beth was a distraction for the moment, an irritation, an irrelevance, and far too burdensome for her exhausted brain.

Nurses came and went with charts and checked readings and tweaked tubes but Laura was too numb and tired even to smile at them. Presently, morning noises began to filter in from the corridor outside the room: voices, and doors banging, and the clank of metal trays and trolleys. Thirst, hitherto unnoticed, seared her throat; when she swallowed, she tasted ash.

It was just before six when Simon came.

'Hello, sorry it's taken me so long to – '

'Shh!' Rising slightly from her chair to greet him, she cocked a thumb towards their daughter in the bed. Beth still wore the mask, was still wired up to all the monitors, but her state of inward concentration had relaxed and her breathing had slowed to an easier rhythm which Laura, the experienced watcher, could recognise as sleep. 'Don't wake her,' she whispered.

'Sorry,' he said again, now *sotto voce*, and approached the bed. 'How is she? What have they said?'

'Not much. You know how it is in hospitals. But they say there's no cause for alarm.'

'But the mask?'

'A precaution, I gather. They're going to run some tests, they say, and keep her under observation for a while.'

'Tests?' His voice had risen again, and she flicked her eyes warningly towards the bed.

291

'Because of the smoke – to see what she's inhaled. In case there were toxins or something, I suppose.'

'Toxins?' he repeated, and she thought, in her weariness, what a child he still was, sometimes – and then, more charitably, how very much he loved his daughter.

Simon stayed for as long as he could. There were frequent texts, no doubt from Tessa, which he was trying to ignore.

'Look,' said Laura finally, 'there's nothing you can do here. You're needed at home. Go.'

Uncertainly, and with repeated promises to call and check on progress, he did as he was told. When he had gone, Laura subsided in her chair. She pushed it back against the wall next to the bed and let her head rest there on the cold plasterwork, closing her eyes. The wall was hard and the chair uncomfortable but she was dog tired, and it wasn't long before consciousness began to loose its hold.

Suspicious circumstances. A petrol can.

When she woke with a start, somebody else was in the room.

'Did I wake you?' The voice, from close beside her, was gentle and familiar.

'Vince.'

He was standing between Laura and the bed, where Beth was still asleep behind her mask. 'How is she?'

'She'll be OK.'

He studied Beth closely. 'She looks pale,' he said. 'But peaceful.' Then he turned to Laura. 'You look pale, too. Maybe it's the light in here.'

He hunkered down at her side and took hold of her hand, and she couldn't remember why it was she'd imagined she shouldn't ring him. It was so right that he should be here. But confusing, too, now that her thoughts began to clear.

'How did you know . . .?'

His laugh was low, no more than a rumble in his throat. 'Cambridge is a small place. I heard it on the radio: a fire in a historic pumping station, converted to residential use; a village to the north of the city. How many places could it be?'

She nodded dazedly.

'I was terrified.' His simple admission touched her with surprising force.

'I drove straight out to Ninepins. The fire brigade are still there. They said to try the hospital.' Then, more softly, he added, 'What a mess.'

Her throat clenched as she wondered what he meant. 'The pumphouse?'

He grimaced. 'That, certainly. It was still smoking when I was there. The roof has gone, and everything's blackened to buggery – not to mention the two tankerfuls of water they've dumped inside.' His other hand was on top of hers now, tracing patterns on the back of her knuckles. 'But that's not the only mess.'

'Willow?'

It was his turn to nod.

She licked her dry lips. 'What do you know? Who told you?' Surely the firemen didn't talk to every passer-by who called to take a look?

'Here.' Without releasing her hand, he reached to his jacket and a produced a bottle of water. 'Drink?'

To take off the lid required both hands, and she drank deep and gratefully, but when she set the bottle down, he captured her fingers again.

'How do you know about Willow?' she asked again.

'I had a call from the duty social worker. She'd had the police on to her. Wanted to know if I knew where she might be.'

Laura felt foolish then. How could she have forgotten that he was Willow's social worker?

'And do you? Know where she might be, that is?'

'No.'

She examined his face. 'You would tell me, if you did?'

The brown eyes met hers seriously. 'Yes.'

Just then, there was a slight stirring from the bed by their

293

side. They rose as one and bent over Beth. Her eyes opened, mistily at first, but then they cleared, and moved slowly from Laura to Vince and back again.

'Hello, love,' murmured Laura. 'You're all right, we're here. Don't try to talk.'

Vince nodded at the oxygen mask with its tapes and tubes, the white plastic reservoir bag which trailed beneath her chin, rising and falling with her breaths. 'Nice beard, Santa.'

A grin was visible beneath the mask; one finger lifted from its place on the blanket and wiggled in his direction.

'You need to rest,' Laura told her daughter gently, but Beth's eyes had already closed again.

Conscious all at once of her own tiredness, Laura sat back down on the chair and shut her eyes, while Vince slid to sit on the floor at her feet.

'And as for your footwear,' he said, 'it's quite the fashion statement. What's with the dress, by the way?'

She opened one eye, narrowly. 'I-I came out without much.'

There was mockery coming, she knew there was, she could see it in his face. But, 'You look great,' was all he said.

Neither of them spoke for some time, and Laura's mind might have drifted towards sleep, had it not kept returning to the same stubborn, knotted thought.

'I know it's stupid. I know it makes no sense at all. But I can't help feeling I want us to find her, get to her, before the police do.'

Vince squeezed her hand. 'Yes, I know. Me, too.'

'What time did you leave your flat?'

'Not until almost seven. She hadn't rung there, and her phone's off. I've texted her, but she hasn't replied.'

She had their mobile numbers, Laura's and Beth's as well as Vince's. If she'd wanted to be in touch with them, she would have rung. Even without her own mobile, even if it was lost or burned, she could surely find a call box, borrow a phone . . .

'I tried the hospital – the other hospital, I mean. I had some idea she might have gone there, to Marianne. But they couldn't help. I spoke to a nurse on early duty, she said they hadn't seen Willow since Monday. And in fact, she's gone AWOL, too. Marianne – she seems to have done a bunk again.'

Oh, God. What a mess, as he had rightly said.

'Where can she be, Vince? Do you think she's all right? Oh, where in God's name can Willow be?'

Her voice must have risen rather more than she'd intended. In the bed, Beth stirred again, shifting her legs beneath the blanket.

'Are you OK, sweetheart? Do you need anything? Are the blankets too tight? Here, let me loosen them a bit.'

Beth shook her head impatiently, twisting it from side to side on the pillow as far as the network of tubes would allow. Behind the cone of perspex, she was mumbling something.

'Don't worry, love,' said Laura. 'Just keep calm, don't try to speak.'

But Vince moved up to her head and loosened the tape at the side of her mask; it was only lightly connected, and with the tape undone it lifted away by a few inches with very little incumbrance.

'What is it?' he asked her quietly. 'What did you want to say?'

Without the oxygen feed, her breathing was slightly more arduous, though the rhythm remained regular enough. She fixed Vince intently in her gaze, and a slight frown indented her brow.

'Maybe,' she said, and took a gulp of unenhanced hospital air.

'Maybe?' Laura drew closer, too, bending to survey her daughter's face.

'Maybe.' Breathe. 'The houseboats.'

'Houseboats?' For a second, Laura wondered if she had

misheard – before she remembered, just as Beth gasped out the next two words.

'Wicken.' Breathe. 'Fen.'

Vince slipped the mask back over Beth's mouth and nose, and secured it in place with the tape. 'Good girl,' he said. 'Just breathe now. Just try to relax, and breathe.'

Chapter 25

It was the glass in Willow's wristwatch they had to thank for saving both their lives. It ought, by rights, to have been the smoke alarm, which Laura had screwed back into place, high on the pumphouse wall above the microwave, toaster and kettle, after they'd finished the decorating. But it was annoying there; the toaster was prone to jamming, and whenever it did, black smoke rose up and sent the alarm, at very first sniff, into its high, complaining wail. So Willow had climbed on a chair and lifted it down from its brackets, and stowed it in the wardrobe beneath a pile of magazines.

She wasn't wearing the watch, which chafed her wrist in hot weather if she kept it on it at night; that fact also may have kept them both alive. She had placed it on the carpet, beside the book she'd been reading before she turned out the light.

Beth, in the end, had slept in the bed. She couldn't get comfortable on the settee cushions, which shifted apart, she said, and left a gap whenever she tried to turn over. Willow offered to swap, and took the cushions herself. Once in the bed under Willow's duvet, Beth was asleep in minutes. Willow took longer, not because she found the floor uncomfortable, nor due to the close-wrapped heat, but because she always liked to lie awake in the darkness for a while and listen to the noises of the night.

The sound which wakened her two hours later was not the familiar creak of cooling timber, nor the cry of a nocturnal bird, nor even the gurgle of the lode behind its bank, which could sometimes be heard through the pipework of the old pump. It was only a small noise, but she knew it at once for something unusual, something urgent. Though she didn't recognise it, it was the snap of glass cracking in the face of her watch.

If she had not taken off the wristwatch; if she and Beth hadn't swapped beds; if she hadn't been on the floor, with her watch lying by her book, close to the pumphouse window, where the tossed match landed in the pool of spilled petrol. . . . But all these things did happen, and Willow woke up.

How strange it was, too, that fire itself should be so silent; that there was no audible whoosh as the flames swept across the sheet of lawnmower fuel and lit the carpet, no crackling as it embraced the slowly curling pages of her discarded paperback. How strange that the first sound she heard was the quiet crack of a small circle of glass.

As soon as she was half awake she felt the heat, and knew that this was not the warmth of a June heatwave but something hostile, to be flown from. Following first, unconscious instinct, she scrambled towards the door and the outside air and safety. Only when she lay panting on the cool grass did she remember where she was, and that she had not been alone in there.

There was no deliberate decision, no application of her surface mind at all. She simply stood up and walked back towards the pumphouse door.

The flames were clearly visible now through the open doorway, but they were centred over to the right, beneath the window, and not around the door itself, nor the bed, to the left. But the heat, as she came within a metre or so of the entrance was so intense that it almost beat her back; it felt like a solid thing, a wall of bruising, scouring brick through which she must somehow try to force a passage. She had on only shorts and a T shirt; the exposed skin of her arms and legs and face seemed to draw and lap the heat until it seared and smouldered from the inside.

But the smoke, the insidious, lethal smoke that wreathes around and penetrates and kills the sleeper before she wakes: for her that was the easy part. She'd practised so long and so

298

often that it came as second nature. She emptied her lungs completely, so that she imagined them pressed out flat as burst balloons within her chest; then, with shoulders drawn back and throat thrown wide, she drew in as much as she could hold of the clean, cold, outdoor air.

One, two, three . . .

With lungs stopped tight and thought suppressed, Willow shut her eyes and stepped forward into the fire.

She'd smelt the petrol, even before she saw the empty can. Right from the first, on the floor of the pumphouse, before she was properly awake, before awareness of where she was or what was happening had imprinted itself on her brain, she'd caught the odour and known what it must mean. There was only one thing it could be, one person.

Petrol had a different smell from lighter fluid. It was heavier, more permeating, less pure and clean. But its effect was just as sure.

Her chest was close to bursting as she dragged Beth clear of the pumphouse door, and laid her on the lawn. She released her breath on three hundred and fifty-four. Beth had a pulse, and she was breathing, and Willow herself did little else for more than a minute. But then she was up on her feet, and looking around her, alert for a sign, a mark, a scent, that would set her on the trail.

Her mother.

She was out here through the smoke, somewhere in the scorched June night, and Willow had to find her.

At dawn's light, when the reality of failure showed up stark and grey, she found herself on the road, where she flagged down an early farm truck, headed for Littleport laden with carrots. She didn't know what to do, or where to go. All she knew was, she couldn't go back. She couldn't face Laura, and Beth, and Vince, with the enormity of what had happened, and of what she'd brought upon them.

So when the driver, whose name was Mick if his baseball cap could be believed, pulled over to let her in, she had no plan in her mind. She opened her mouth, said 'Wicken', and climbed up beside him.

She saw him looking at her bare feet, but he said nothing; on her side, she kept up a silence as off-putting as she dared, and hoped it was too early in the morning for sexual molestation. When he put her down in a layby on the edge of Wicken village, he gave her some gum and a can of Red Bull, and she felt a pang of guilt. She watched the truck go, and wished she could call it back.

She had only been here once, the day they didn't go skating. But she remembered the sign, and the turning, and the lane that led down to the fen. The gravel hurt her feet, so she walked at the side on the narrow strip of grass verge, and braved the nettles instead. Where the metalled road ended, the going was easier. Here the track was soft, black dust, with ruts that still held slime, in spite of the weeks of drought. When she trod in the mud, it squeezed up in worms between her toes.

The two houseboats were still there, and still deserted. She chose the taller, stumpier boat, the one that was metal and going rusty. It was a haul to get herself up on the deck; she reached up and grabbed the edge, dragging herself up by her arms while she scrabbled for toeholds on the flaking hull. The door to the cabin was locked, but the hinges had disintegrated and it swung loose at the second good, strong tug. Inside it was dank and musty, calm and secret. For the first time she noticed the cold and wished she had a blanket.

Even without it, she curled up on the floor and was very soon asleep.

Stupid, was her first thought when she awoke. Without a watch she could only guess the time from the sun which streaked through the green and grime of the windows, discoloured, like swimming pool light, staining her flesh a pale turquoise. It must be around mid-morning.

300

Stupid, stupid, stupid, stupid. She should never have left. She should never have run off in the night on a stupid chase to nowhere and nothing. Marianne was her mother, but she was also Marianne, and there was nothing Willow could do about it. She should have stayed; she shouldn't have left Beth. She was only a kid, and she should have stayed with her. Stupid stupid stupid.

If only she had her phone. She would ring Vince, or Laura, and they would come and get her, take her home. She wanted them here, she wanted the three of them: Vince and Laura and Beth. She wanted Ninepins. She wanted to go home.

Clambering stiffly to her feet, she moved to the cabin window and, pulling down the sleeve of her T shirt to cover her elbow, wiped a swathe through the dirt and condensation. The morning sun was bright, winking and fragmenting in the smear of moisture that remained, so that at first she couldn't be certain of what she saw. Two figures, close together, dark against the dazzle of the day. But as they drew nearer, her heart jumped and she knew that there was no mistake. It was Laura and Vince, walking side by side along the river bank towards her.

Chapter 26

On Sunday evening Laura made pizza for supper again. She did it the cheat's way, slitting baguettes in half lengthways and topping them with the tomato and cheese. The mozzarella, this time, was the vacuum-packed supermarket variety, and well within its sell-by date.

Beth and Willow were supposed to be helping, but mostly they were sitting at the kitchen table and feeding themselves by the handful on the olives and peppers and sliced salami that Laura had laid out in bowls.

'Hey, you two. There'll be nothing left to put on the pizzas.'

'Never mind,' said Beth, giggling. 'Make mine a Margherita.'

'And what about Vince? At this rate, it'll be all gone before he even gets here.'

' 'S'OK.' Willow grinned. 'He likes Margheritas, too.'

'Here, Mum. Have an olive and shut up.'

It was their first evening back together. Willow had come home with Laura and Vince on the Saturday, though she'd had to go out again in the afternoon, when Vince drove her to Cambridge to make a statement at the police station. When they had gone, and before she herself drove back to the hospital, Laura went up to the spare bedroom and opened the window wide to let in some fresh air. Still on the night stand, untouched and unharmed, sat the old, blue shoebox. She folded up the rose pattern bedspread and laid it back in the linen chest, closing the lid with a smile. Willow could have her own spare duvet for now, and on Monday they'd go shopping and buy her a new one. Plus maybe some cushions, perhaps, if she wanted them, and posters for the walls; it was rather plain in here.

Beth, to her immense chagrin, had been kept in a second night for observation. Her fever to be out of the bed and back home to Ninepins was a testament to her recovery, which was rapid and robust. She could patter out long sentences now and hardly seem to draw breath, though a hospital pallor still lingered in her cheeks, and every so often she gave a dry, rasping cough.

Vince, when he came, brought wine as usual, and a pack of Diet Cokes.

'I've noticed,' he said to Willow, 'that Laura keeps a rather too virtuous fridge. We may need to work on that.'

They shared out what was left of the toppings between the eight halved baguettes and ate them in their fingers, scalding from the grill. There was salad, ready-washed from a bag, and Laura let them eat that with their hands as well.

'Things taste better in your fingers,' Vince informed them. 'It's a scientific fact.' And Laura, pulling a slice of salami off her pizza and rolling it up to push in her mouth, decided the scientists might be right.

There were fresh cherries for pudding, and cream meringues.

'Can me and Willow take ours to the tree house and have it there? We want to watch when it starts to rain.'

'All right – go on, then.'

From early in the morning, clouds had been gathering in the western sky, the first they had seen in what felt like forever. They had stacked and swelled until by lunchtime the whole sky was overcast, but there had been no sign yet of the rain, which must surely come before nightfall.

When they were gone, Vince refilled their wine glasses; she handed him a plate with a meringue, and pushed the open bag of cherries in his direction.

'She's different, you know, since she's been here with you.' He twisted off a cherry stalk. 'Willow – she's a different person.'

303

'She's seventeen, eighteen very soon. She's growing up.'

'No.' He put the cherry down on his plate. 'I don't just mean that. She's changing, really changing. She's more . . . open. Open to things, and to people. It's as if she's finally learning to breathe freely.'

They both sipped their wine, thinking their own thoughts. Presently, Laura asked, 'What did they say at the police station?' She hesitated, before adding, 'If it's not confidential.'

'Oh, it is, almost certainly.' Then he grinned. 'But confidentially, I don't care.'

She offered a grin back. 'So, what happened?'

'Willow gave her statement, and they put it on file. They picked up Marianne last night, along the lode towards Wicken. She was down near the sluice, they said, standing in the water, ankle deep. She didn't deny what had happened; her hair was soaked in petrol. They'll be thinking about charges, of course.'

There lurked, underneath, the gnawing question. 'Why, Vince? Why do you think she did it?'

Looking sad, he shook his head. 'I don't know. I don't suppose we'll ever know. She may not know the reason why herself – or even really be aware of what she's done. Could be jealousy, maybe? Of Willow, of you, of us? But she hears things, remember; she hears voices. Her reality is not the same as other people's.'

Stories, remembered Laura, out of nowhere; *she told amazing stories*.

'The case will go to the CPS,' he continued. 'But the officer I spoke to didn't seem to think it will come to court. She's already in hospital, already on a section. There's nowhere better for her than where she is now.'

She nodded, frowning. It didn't seem much of a solution. But maybe solutions were too much to hope for, in Marianne's case.

'Tough on Willow, whatever happens.'

'Bloody tough,' he agreed.

He tucked into his meringue, then, so she attacked hers, too, and conversation was rendered impossible for a time by collapsing mouthfuls of icing sugar and whipped cream. They both resurfaced approximately together, and began to speak at the same time.

'Vince – '

'Laura – '

'No, you go,' she said, smiling.

He looked a little awkward – something she was unaccustomed to seeing in him – and he sounded deadly earnest. 'I was going to say, that I hope you'll forgive me if I haven't always told you everything there was to know about Willow. But also, I hope you'll believe me when I say there were things I didn't always know.'

These seemed to be important matters, important to him, as they would have been important once to her. She took the time to ponder what he'd said. But she found she wanted to tell him that it didn't matter any more; that nothing did, nothing that was done and gone. *We're here now, we're here together, and that's all that counts.* But she could never say it, or make him understand it if she did, so instead she caught his hand and held it.

'And you?' he prompted, after a moment. 'What were you going to say?'

'Actually, I was going to ask you something about Willow.' How strange, the closeness of the tracks on which their thoughts had been running.

'Ask.'

'It's the thing that has always bothered me about her, I suppose. The arson. When she was thirteen, and set that garage on fire. It doesn't seem – I don't know, I guess I've just never been able to understand why she should have done it. Willow is so . . . controlled. She's never seemed to me to have that wildness in her.'

He nodded slowly. 'No.'

'What I've been wondering – especially since, you know,

305

Friday night . . .' She took a breath, let it out again. 'I've been wondering if maybe it wasn't her – if it wasn't really Willow who set fire to the garage, but Marianne. I thought maybe Willow might have known about it and taken the blame for it to protect her mother. Crazy, I know. But she knew Marianne was fragile. She'd probably always protected her, in her own way – in whatever way she could. And kids can do crazy things in defence of a parent, can't they? Stupid things.' What was it Vince had said? *Never underestimate the resource of a mother in shielding her child.* So why not the other way round? 'Might it have happened that way?'

Vince did not reply. She slid her hand more closely into his. 'What do you think? What do you believe really happened?

With his free hand he was playing with his wine glass, twisting it round on the edge of the base, and she wondered whether there would be a withdrawal, even now.

But at last he said simply, 'I don't know. I've never known. She's never talked about that day. She's told me many things about her past, but never that.'

So that was it? A dead end. She had finally asked him, and he was ready to tell her, and there was nothing to tell?

'But – ' he began, and stopped.

She squeezed his fingers. 'Go on.'

'Well,' he said slowly, 'she's never told me herself, not explicitly, but I think I know. Just recently, these past few months, I think I've worked it out. The thing is, it can't have been easy, living with a severely bipolar mother.'

Laura, who knew this already, nodded and tried not to let her impatience show.

'She didn't get a lot of looking after, as a kid – or if she did it was patchy, inconsistent. The last few years, when she was eleven, twelve, she was the one doing most of the looking after.'

Beth's age, thought Laura.

'It must have crossed her mind, as she grew older, that some kids got taken away. That parents had their kids removed, and placed in foster care. Marianne was undiagnosed, as I mentioned before. They were always on the move. But it wouldn't have been hard for Willow to say something to somebody. To raise the alarm and ask for help.'

'But she didn't,' said Laura slowly, beginning to see where he was heading. 'She never spoke to anyone about Marianne.'

'Right. I think this was her way out. I think setting fire to an empty garage was a way of getting herself taken into care without its being her mother's fault.'

She nodded again, eager now. 'It's admirable, when you think about it – admirable in a crazy, cockeyed way – the same cockeyed, admirable craziness as in my version. A child's muddle-headed plan for taking the guilt upon herself, to avoid betraying a parent.'

'Or perhaps,' he said, 'for taking on one kind of guilt in order to escape another.'

Outside the window, the sky had darkened, casting the table between them in a softer, muted light. They both looked up at the world outside as if they had forgotten it was there.

'Looks as if the weather's going to break,' said Vince. 'Come on.'

He led her by the hand, through the hall and out on to the top of the dyke. A breeze, the first of any consequence for days, was skimming in across the fields, lifting the tired grasses and snatching at Laura's hair. The skylarks, whose babble had been a ceaseless soundtrack to the heat, seemed to sense the change and fell silent. Then, as fast as it had risen, the breeze fell away, and the entire flat, earthbound world seemed to hold its breath in anticipation. Laura waited for the rumble of thunder, for the first wide-spaced, fat, fizzing drops that would herald the expected torrential downpour. But when it came the rain crept in by stealth, and it was fine and gentle, misting the air and hazing the bare skin of their arms and necks and faces. It dappled the mud and low water of the lode in soft recurring patterns and, behind them in the garden, it shed its soothing balm on the four blackened walls of the pumphouse, and the smoking wound between.

From up the concrete steps came the sound of voices, Beth's and Willow's, then running footsteps, and the girls appeared, linked arm in arm, laughing and streaked with rain. The four of them turned together and walked back into the house. And when they had gone, there were only the swallows, swooping to trap the evening's insects over the slow procession of the lode.